PARADISE DESCENT
A WELSH MAFIA ROMANCE

RAYA MORRIS EDWARDS

This book is for all the ladies who just want a soft mafia daddy who would burn the world down for them.

AUTHOR'S NOTE

This book contains a fictionalized depiction of adult ADHD and OCD. This is based purely off my personal experience living with these diagnoses. It may or may not reflect the personal experiences of others and should not be used to diagnose or determine any opinion regarding ADHD or OCD. If you think you may need help, always reach out to licensed professionals. Additionally, this book has undergone representation review for these and all diverse depictions included therein.

TRIGGER WARNINGS

OCD and ADHD symptoms including food aversions and obsessive behaviors
Flashbacks and discussions of childhood neglect/threat against a minor with a weapon
Parental death/abandonment
Discussion of past violent murder in a combat situation
Depiction of violent murder
Depiction of domestic violence and aftermath
Age gap related content
Brief discussion of PTSD

SEXUAL CONTENT

Frequent and explicit depictions of oral and vaginal intercourse
Daddy kink
Restraints
Virginity loss/light blood
Explicit dirty talk

CHAPTER ONE

MERRICK

I'd always lived alone until Clara came along.

The morning after Edwin passed, his estate manager met me in my office in downtown Providence to go over his last wishes. He'd died unexpectedly, but his will was already made up. It was very clear.

His eighteen-year-old daughter was now my financial ward.

In the Welsh mafia organization, every woman had a male guardian for the purposes of financial support and protection. We'd carried that tradition on for hundreds of years.

Edwin had been my closest friend and my right hand for fifteen years. But it still took me by surprise that I was now responsible for his only child.

Me—I was in charge of a person.

I'd run the Welsh organization, an underground mafia along the eastern coast for twenty-six years. I could threaten, coerce, negotiate, charm, and manipulate my way in and out of everything. I'd trained and commanded hundreds of skilled men over the last year alone.

But I'd never taken care of a woman before. That was a bigger challenge than anything I'd faced.

She didn't have any money of her own, many of our women didn't by choice. But I still thought it was a shitty move on Edwin's part to leave her without an inheritance. Everything he owned was left to the organization.

His only child was completely dependent on my generosity.

My organization's men took a lot of pride in this type of guardianship. How well our women were treated was a mark of honor.

I was the king and I felt the weight of this new responsibility. I felt the eyes of my men on me.

It was my duty to set the standard.

I fixed up the only bedroom on the first floor that night. I wasn't sure what to put in it, so I looked it up online, which only got me more confused. Finally, I settled on some simple, but feminine, pieces of furniture. Then I put in an order for groceries that I thought she would like. It didn't occur to me that stocking the fridge with coffee, chocolate, and ice cream was...well, maybe it was stereotyping a bit.

I facilitated Edwin's funeral, it was my duty as *Brenin*—the Welsh King. Clara sat at the end of the row, nearest to the coffin. The sky roiled overhead as we lowered Edwin into the ground.

Inside, I was raw. Edwin was my closest friend. We'd spent every day for the last fifteen years together. We'd conquered the coast below Boston, we'd mobilized our soldiers into a real standing army, we'd made this organization into the most powerful in the United States.

But here I was, unable to show a shred of emotion while I read out his eulogy. It wasn't my place. Later on, I could get a little drunk in my therapist's office and she'd listen while I poured everything out.

Everyone tossed a handful of dirt and a myrtle leaf onto the coffin. Clara didn't.

She just stood there in her black wool coat with her hands shoved deep in the pockets. Her sheet of dark hair hung over her face. I hadn't actually gotten a chance to see her yet—Edwin never talked about his private life or allowed anyone into it.

Today, at his funeral, was my first time meeting Clara.

People began dispersing, some stopping to speak with her although she barely responded. Others just walked away, unsure how to deal with the stiff, little figure standing at the graveside.

I tucked my eulogy notes into the inner pocket of my jacket and crossed the damp grass. She didn't move until I gently put my hand on her back. Then she lifted her head in a quick, wary movement. Like she didn't trust me, which made sense. We didn't know each other.

She was lovely, but unusually pale. Like she never went outside. Her eyes were a mottled blue-gray, like the ocean in a storm, lined with thick lashes. Her nose was small, her face round, and her mouth full, painted a deep berry pink. Her brows and her hair were almost black and stark against her complexion.

She didn't look very much like Edwin, but she did look Welsh.

"Clara," I said, extending my hand.

She stared at my palm before shaking it and releasing me quickly.

"I'm sorry for your loss," I said.

Her brow arced.

"You must be upset and ready to get back home," I said, gesturing toward the Audi parked on the gravel drive. "Let me take you back. I had someone pick up your things so you can get settled in today."

She cleared her throat, not moving.

"You were my father's friend," she said, her voice hoarse.

I nodded.

"Did you like him?"

"We were very close and I had a lot of respect for him," I said carefully, unwilling to unload the last decade of the closest friendship of my life onto his daughter.

She tilted her chin, squinting across the cemetery.

"I'm glad you had a good experience with him," she said. "I didn't. I'm not happy he's dead, but I'm not sad. Does that bother you?"

I fumbled for words, unused to such honesty.

"No...anything you feel is valid," I said.

"Good," she said. "I just wanted to get that out of the way. I didn't like him very much, I'm not really sad, and I'm ready to move on. Okay?"

I nodded, speechless. My grief had made me a shadow of myself for the last week. Sitting alone late at night with a whiskey in my hand. Staring up at Edwin's portrait on my office wall. Eyes dry and mind reeling.

She lifted her hand, palm up, and I stared down at it, unsure what she wanted me to do with it. She gave a little sigh of exasperation and grabbed my hand, threading her fingers through mine.

I stared down at it and a slow, pleasant warmth moved up my wrist to my forearm and ended up somewhere near my heart.

"I want to have lunch," she said.

She told me later that was the first time she'd ever held anyone's hand, except her best friend Candice's. I wondered, as I led her across the grass to my car, why she was so eager to trust me.

It made more sense as time went on.

She'd lived her life without the sun. Her father's death had ripped the curtain from the window.

We were both silent as I drove back to my house outside Providence. It was a huge, East Coast mansion surrounded by an iron fence and locked with a gate and a guardhouse.

I guided the Audi down the winding driveway, around the loop, and pulled up before the front door. She kept her face glued to the window, staring around with big eyes. Taking in the neatly trimmed garden and the pool, covered for the winter.

I got out and went to circle the car to let her out, but she was already on her feet, crunching across the gravel. Turning in slow circles with her big, ocean eyes drinking everything in.

She stopped at the bottom of the steps, spinning to face me.

"Do you live alone?"

"Not anymore," I said.

Her face broke into a slow smile. "This is the most beautiful place I've ever seen."

I'd spent a lot of time and money to make my house exactly the way I liked it. It was a quiet estate and the house was decorated with only the finest materials. Dark oak, hardwood, marble counters, brass doorknobs.

It meant a lot to me that she liked it.

Inside, I led her down the hall to her bedroom and pushed open the door. My assistant had purchased a cherry wood frame and white, fluffy blankets for the bed. The floor was garnished with a soft creamy rug and the heavy drapes matched.

It was elegant and feminine, what I assumed young women wanted.

She turned in a slow circle and sat on the end of the bed. Her fingers curled, nails skimming over the bedspread.

"It's really, really nice," she said.

"You are free to renovate it how you please," I said. "I'm going to get you a credit card with both our names on it. You get the things you need and all the bills will be sent to me directly."

Her brows shot up.

"Really?"

"Of course, I'm here to make sure you're taken care of. I stocked the fridge, but you can make a list of things you want if I missed anything and I'll give it to my assistant."

She nodded slowly, clearly struggling to process everything. I stood in the doorway and watched as she pulled her shoes off and tossed them aside. I winced as her coat hit the floor.

She was clearly a little messy.

I picked it up, folded it, and laid it over the chair. She'd gone to the window and she stood, holding the curtain back, staring out over the hills.

"Do you actually like the room?" I asked.

She spun, a surge of energy in her step. "It's really nice for now. But I like things to be a little more glittery and bright."

Glittery and bright sounded like hell. I swallowed my words and nodded, reaching into my back pocket for my wallet. I didn't have any cash on me, but I did have my secondary credit card.

I held it out. Her eyes dropped and her fingers clenched together. Twisting into a little knot over her stomach.

"Go ahead and go shopping now," I said. "I have to work this afternoon, but I'll see you later tonight."

She took the credit card tentatively, like she'd never seen anything so precious. Then her lips curved and her eyes lit up. When they fixed on mine, I noticed her lashes were wet.

"Thank you," she said.

"I know we don't really know each other, but I'm here for you, Clara. I want to make sure you have a comfortable home, that you get to go to a good school. And when you graduate, I'll arrange a good marriage for you."

She nodded once, staring up at me like I was the sun, the moon, and all the stars in the sky. I'd never had anyone look at me like that before and...well, it felt really fucking good on my ego. In fact, I liked it enough to jump through some hoops just to see it again.

"I thought you were going to be mean," she said.

I frowned. "I'm not mean."

"I mean, clearly not. Where do you sleep?"

I pointed at the ceiling. "My bedroom is upstairs. I felt it was best to have our rooms separated by a level, as you are an adult woman living with me and I'm not your blood relative. It's only proper."

"I understand." She nodded vigorously.

She needed time alone to unpack. I left the house and went to the office. My chest ached less and the grief in the pit of my stomach felt more distant. There was something about Clara that lit up the entire house.

For the last decade, I'd lived my life in a safe cage of strict routine. But looking at Clara...maybe I was ready for something different.

It was almost eight when I got home that night to find her in the kitchen. She was making coffee and playing soft music from her laptop. When I walked in, she froze and her eyes widened.

"Sorry, is this okay?"

"You live here now," I said. "What's mine is yours. Just don't bother my bedroom or office."

7

She grinned and I noticed she'd changed her clothes completely. Instead of the black dress and short boots, she wore a pair of berry pink shorts and a fluffy oversized black hoodie. Her hair was piled on her head and secured with a glittery pink clip.

I dragged my eyes over the counter. Over the spilled coffee grounds, the ring of cream, the dirty spoons.

This was going to take some getting used to.

I took off my jacket and rolled my sleeves to the elbow and began loading the dishwasher. She watched me in silence, sipping her coffee.

"Did you eat yet?" I asked.

She shook her head.

"Would you like to go out to dinner with me?"

She hesitated and that brilliant smile broke over her face again.

"I would love to."

I wiped the countertop and washed my hands carefully. "Do you have any food allergies? Any preferences what you'd like to eat?"

"No. What's your favorite restaurant?"

"There's a steakhouse on the east side I like."

"Okay, let's go there," she said, standing and setting her empty cup aside. "Do you want to come and see what I bought for the room?"

I nodded and snagged her cup, washing it out and putting it in the dishwasher. She lingered in the doorway, watching as I scrubbed my hands and dried them on a paper towel.

"You're really clean," she said.

I shrugged. "You're a little messy."

"I am not."

"Oh, yes, you definitely are."

I made sure to smile so she would know I wasn't annoyed and she lit up, ducking into the hall and leading the way to her room. She pushed open the door and I stepped inside, half expecting to cringe.

It actually looked alright.

Granted, it was not my taste, but she'd picked out some nice pieces. The bed was a soft pink now, and somehow she'd managed to

8

order a new frame and have it delivered while I was at work. This one had a plushy headboard attached, each section pinned with a tiny crystal.

The curtains were white with little pink dots and the carpet was fluffy pink to match. Everything felt sugary sweet, almost saccharine, but it wasn't over the line. She'd kept it tasteful and grown up.

"It's nice," I said.

"You hate it," she said, narrowing her eyes.

"It's not my style, but it's not my room."

She spun and sat on the edge of the bed, her face going sober.

"My father was really rigid. He never let me have anything nice in my room or my closet. I kind of went a bit wild this afternoon. Sorry."

"If this is what you need to adjust to your new life, Clara, then this is what you should do."

She smiled again, her mouth trembling. "Thank you."

There was a short silence and I stepped back into the hall. For some reason, it felt a bit inappropriate to be standing in her bedroom. It was also suffocating me with all the glitter and gauze and pink.

"How fancy is this place we're going for dinner?" she called.

"It's very nice. Wear a cocktail dress."

The bathroom door slammed and I heard the shower turn on. I went upstairs and put on a dark blue suit and tie.

I'd known Edwin was a rigid, disciplined man, but I hadn't realized it had extended so deeply into his life. Poor Clara, a girl without a mother, growing up in her father's austere house.

It made my chest ache a little.

As I walked through my office, I glanced up at the portrait of Edwin on the wall. I paused, gazing up at him, conflicted.

Then, I decided, as long as Clara was living here, I would put a curtain up to cover it.

CHAPTER TWO

MERRICK

She was late, but I wasn't worried. No one canceled reservations on me no matter how late I was—one of the perks of being the Welsh *Brenin*.

The door slammed and she appeared on the porch, wearing that same shade of berry pink. Her dress was a little short and maybe a little tight, but there was no way in hell I was criticizing it. She'd probably crumple up and start crying in my passenger seat if I did.

And it wasn't my place anyway. She was a grown woman, she had the right to wear whatever she chose.

I'd asked her to lock the door and she did. I swiped my phone and brought the security app up, checking it three times to make sure it showed every door as being secured. Then I got out and circled the car, pulling her door open and holding out my palm.

She hesitated and then, slowly, she put her hand in mine and I helped her into the seat. Her fingers were slender and soft, her nails manicured. She must have stopped at the salon while she was out.

There was a little smile on her face as I got into the seat beside her and turned on the engine. Her eyes stayed glued to me as I pulled out onto the road and settled back, letting my hand rest on the top of the wheel.

"What's so funny?" I asked.

She shook her head, chewing the inside of her mouth.

"I've just never been around a man other than Candice's father who didn't just treat me like an annoyance," she said. "And...I guess I can be kind of annoying."

It took me a moment to gather my thoughts. She chewed harder on her mouth.

"I mean, I know I'm annoying," she said, her mood taking a quick nosedive. "And I'm really grateful to you for taking me in and being so kind to me. I know it's a big burden."

That hit me where it hurt most. My parents had passed away in a car accident when I was six months old and my mother's sister, Ophelia, and her wife had raised me. I knew what it felt like to wonder if I was inconveniencing someone else's life.

"You're not annoying," I said firmly. "And you're not a burden on anyone."

She chewed harder, looking out the dark window.

"Clara." My voice was more forceful than I'd intended.

"I understand," she said quickly.

"I'm not angry, I just want you to understand that you are a talented young woman and your presence is a privilege," I said. "I'm sorry if you ever felt like that wasn't true, but from now on, I'll make sure you understand it. And I will show you how you deserve to be treated."

She cleared her throat. Her mouth turned up in a small smile again.

"Thank you, Merrick. You're very...."

"What?" I said. "You can say it, I can take it."

"No, it's not bad. You're just a gentleman and...well, I wasn't expecting that."

I glanced at her and her eyes caught mine.

"Even the devil is a gentleman, Clara," I said. "You're very sweet."

Her jaw worked and I could tell she was chewing the inside of her mouth.

"You're different," she said.

11

"How much experience do you have with men outside your family?"

"None," she whispered.

I caught the look in her eyes and I regretted bringing the subject up. Her openness had caught me off guard and, if I was honest, it scared me a little. It was my duty to protect her, but if she was going to treat all men the way she was treating me, I was going to be busy.

"Don't worry about it," I said.

"I'm not stupid," she said, her voice a little stiff. "I'm not just going around getting in cars with strange men."

Something odd surged in my chest, something that felt a bit like...anger. The image of her with a faceless man who could hurt her roused an ugliness in me I'd never felt before, a bit like my control had slipped.

"Good," I said. "Because I'd rather not have to kill anyone."

She laughed and then her smile faltered.

"Are you joking...I can't tell if you're joking," she said.

"Don't worry about it, *cariad*," I said.

I wasn't sure where that word had come from. It was an innocent term of endearment in Welsh and it fit her perfectly. If she knew what it meant, she didn't show it. She just released a sigh and nestled back into the seat, her fingers tight around her purse.

We were both quiet as we crossed the bridge and I pulled up to the upscale steakhouse. It was a little colder by the water and I offered her my jacket.

"I'm okay," she said.

"I'm not cold, Clara, you wear it until we get in."

She looked up at me in the dark, still chewing lightly on her mouth.

"It won't look good with my outfit."

I was about to drape it over her bare shoulders anyway, but when she spoke, a little bit of blood slipped from the corner of her mouth. I reached out and took hold of her face without thinking, turning it up.

"You're bleeding."

She wriggled away, bending her head. Her manicured fingers swiped over her lips, coming away with a little crimson smear.

"Sorry, it's fine," she said. "I just have this nervous habit of chewing a spot in my mouth. I bit it by accident, it's fine though."

I got a tissue from the car and made her sit still while I wiped the blood. She wouldn't meet my eyes.

"Open your mouth."

She obeyed hesitantly, revealing a tongue streaked with blood.

"Jesus," I muttered.

"It's fine, it always stops bleeding really fast."

"Do you—"

"Merrick," she said firmly, pulling back. "This is really fine, I don't want you to make this a big deal. Please just let me handle it and let's go in and have dinner. I'm starving."

I'd spent a lot of time in therapy and I knew what deflection looked like, but I decided to let it go for tonight. She didn't protest as I draped my jacket over her shoulders and guided her into the restaurant with a hand on the small of her back.

We sat by the window so she could watch the river glitter in the moonlight. I ordered her a glass of wine. She'd never had it before so I got the most expensive red blend they had.

She loved it.

I had a lean cut of steak and steamed vegetables. She had lasagna, two more glasses of red wine, and a piece of chocolate cake the size of my fist. I watched her eat, impressed.

"Have you eaten today?" I said.

She shook her head. "I forgot to have breakfast and I got caught up with everything else and didn't eat lunch."

I sat back, crossing one leg over the other. "I have a late morning tomorrow. I'll take you to my favorite bakery in the city before I leave."

There was a lot I needed to get done tomorrow, but making sure she was comfortable took priority. My two right hand men, Yale and Caden, could handle things for me until noon. Her eyes lit up again and a glow of pride swelled in my chest.

13

It turned out, I liked being the reason her eyes lit up.

"I'd like that," she said, a little shyly.

I was late for work the next day, but I didn't regret it. Clara was unlike anyone I'd ever met and she had turned my entire worldview on its head in a day.

She didn't want a career, but she was bright and witty and knew what she liked and what she didn't. I'd never known anyone who had so much energy for life, for just enjoying themselves without guilt.

I told her she needed to pick what degree she wanted to pursue in the fall and she chose folklore, which confused me because she didn't read very much. Or seem to care about the traditions and stories of our people.

She was standing in the kitchen with her iced coffee gripped in her glittery, manicured hand. It was the middle of the summer and she wore a pink t-shirt and shorts that were definitely not long enough.

Again—that was not my business. If anyone bothered her, I would deal with them.

"Why folklore?" I pressed.

"I just like fairies," she said, shrugging.

"What...fairies?"

"Tinkerbell," she said. "Duh."

My eyes watered. "Jesus Christ," I said under my breath.

"I'll do a double major," she mused, spinning and heading to her room. "Maybe like...astronomy."

"It's not like astrology, Clara," I called down the hall.

She put her head back around the corner. "Oh, I'm pretty sure it is."

I decided not to intervene further. She packed up her things in September and went to North Carolina for her first semester of college. I'd honestly expected her to be back within a month, but she returned for Christmas with the highest grades in every single class.

I was shocked, seeing as I'd never witnessed her crack open a book.

"How did you manage this?"

She looked up from her laptop where I knew she was racking up another bill on her credit card. Her brow arced and her lips curved in a smirk.

"Maybe you should try not being so judgemental," she said, clearly savoring my confusion.

"Do you...study?"

She shrugged. "Not really."

Jesus, this girl was a menace. I cornered her best friend Candice, a blonde with a sharp tongue, one day and asked her what the hell was going on. She sighed deeply and snapped her textbook shut, giving me her full attention.

"Clara is just finally getting to be who she wants to be," Candice said. "She was never allowed to do anything but school growing up. She wasn't allowed to wear anything but horrible clothes. Please, don't take this away from her, Merrick. She's actually studying really hard."

I was taken aback and grateful I hadn't said anything.

"Of course not," I said. "I was just confused. I want her to be happy."

Candice leaned in, regarding me with a critical gaze.

"She's the most happy she's ever been since she came to live with you."

That comment burrowed its way into my brain and came to define my entire relationship with Clara.

I'd fucked up a lot in my life and I had an endless list of regrets. My job as the Welsh *Brenin* was exhausting and sometimes when I got home I had to scrub literal and metaphorical blood from under my fingernails. It was brutal and thankless work that haunted me sometimes.

But when I walked through the front door now, there was Clara.

Bright, full of energy, ready to chatter about her day or beg me to take her out to dinner.

My romantic life waned. I no longer felt comfortable bringing women home while she was living there, even when she was gone at

15

college. It was hard to explain why there was a woman who wasn't related to me living in my house.

People usually assumed I was cheating no matter what I said.

I found I didn't mind.

Life with Clara was more interesting and exciting than filling my days with endless work and my nights with strangers.

When people asked what we were, I said I was her guardian and she was my financial ward because that was true. We were platonic friends, but the kind where I doted on her, bought her everything she wanted, and she brought a lightness to my life I'd never experienced.

It was hard to explain because it was so simple and complicated all at once.

CHAPTER THREE

CLARA

SIX YEARS LATER

My heart thumped and my head spun. Sweat dripped down my neck. Body glitter melted on my naked shoulders and down my spine, disappearing beneath my dress. The gold jewelry on my wrists and neck was slick and stung my skin.

It was Saturday night and the dance floor was packed with bodies. Moving, twisting, grinding. Caught up in a whirlwind of liquor and probably a few pills. The music was so loud it was making the speakers crackle with static.

I felt so fucking good. I was in the prime of my twenties, about to be twenty-four next Sunday. And I knew I was beautiful.

My dress barely covered me, glued to my skin to keep from flashing everyone. The music had shifted to "Poker Face" and the half dozen shots of vodka I'd just taken were hitting my brain.

Candice danced behind me, much drunker. We probably had about thirty more minutes on the dance floor before she made a dash for the bathroom to empty her stomach.

It was the end of summer and I was done with college for good and back from a summer in Europe. I was tanned, feeling amazing, and ready for the next part of my life to start.

After I got so completely drunk I forgot my own name.

I knew I would regret this in the morning and I did.

Twelve hours later, I woke abruptly with my eyes burning and my stomach roiling. Peeling myself up on my elbows, I blinked around the room. My slinky dress and heels lay on the floor beside Candice's yellow dress. Was she still wearing her shoes?

I turned, my arm hitting on something hard. Candice's heels. I dug under the covers and pulled out her shoes and threw them over the edge of the bed.

She slept beside me, completely covered with just a tuft of blond hair on the pillow. Candice always slept fully swathed in thick blankets, right on the verge of suffocation.

I pushed myself up with difficulty and stumbled to the bathroom just in time to throw up into the toilet. It took me a moment to recover and rinse my mouth out, but I felt a lot better when I finally got back to my feet.

A puffy face greeted me in the mirror. I looked like death. I still wore my lace bra and thong, but it was stained with sweat and body glitter. My hair was tangled, matted into a knot around a pink scrunchie.

I flipped on the shower and dropped a jasmine shower melt into the drain.

As the steaming water rained down and the soothing flowery scent wafted up, I attempted to gather my head. It was Sunday, which meant Merrick would be home all day. He might have a business dinner later, but usually we spent most of the weekends at home.

He could cook really well. I could make a couple of things, mainly just instant rice and boiled eggs. So he usually made Sunday dinner while I sat on the counter and had a glass of wine and watched.

My fingers running over my scalp felt heavenly and I considered scheduling a massage tomorrow. The only problem with that was I'd maxed out my credit card and I needed to ask him to pay it off early.

He always did without reprimanding me once. He spoiled and protected me, never once casting judgement on anything I did.

He was everything my ice cold father never was, and in the last six years of being my guardian, he'd created a monster.

And that spoiled monster was me.

But, I mentally argued, I wasn't the mean kind. I was the nice, pretty monster who made his day better, despite draining his wallet.

Candice was still sleeping when I pulled on a berry pink sweatsuit and braided my wet hair and slipped from the room.

Merrick had a restored estate house, with airy white walls and dark wood furnishings. Everything in it was worth something, shipped from somewhere expensive, at the behest of a handsomely compensated interior designer.

I padded into the huge kitchen. As usual, Merrick sat at the long, rectangular table with his silver laptop open before him. He was gazing at his screen with his lips moving, totally absorbed in his work.

He was handsome and he drew people like a moth to his flame. Those cobalt blue eyes burned with energy, occasionally frightening, but almost always kind when they fixed on me. Surrounding them were dark, thick lashes.

His jaw was broad, his face tall, and his nose was prominent, but slender bridged. He was the kind of handsome that made me feel safe, that let me admire him without wanting him.

His hair was dark and usually slicked loosely over his head. Occasionally, when he was tired after a long day, the waves would start to spring free on top and fall over his forehead. Giving him a kind of casually sexy look. His skin was a light beige and he always had a permanent shadow across his jaw, even after he'd shaved.

I paused in the doorway to stare at him for a moment.

From that first moment in the graveyard, one thing had baffled me.

Why had Merrick Llwyd been such good friends with my ice cold, distant, asshole of a father?

Because Merrick was anything but those things.

He was a warm, magnetic presence everywhere he went. His rich laugh lit up a room and when he spoke Welsh—which I hadn't admitted to not understanding a word of yet—it sounded like deep, resonant music.

He was funny, he could banter a mile a minute. But he could also be serious and hold his own in any conversation. He charmed everyone and everyone either wanted to be him or be with him.

If I had been older and not his ward, I was sure I'd be head over heels for him. He was that type. Tall, dark haired, and smooth as a fine red wine.

Not that I was looking. Merrick and I weren't like that.

He was also incredibly anal, in his own words. In our shared spaces like the kitchen, there was a right way and a wrong way to do things and Merrick's was the right way. I learned that quickly.

He was always kind and patient about it, but incredibly firm.

"Load the dishwasher only after everything is rinsed, *cariad*."

"Don't use the dish soap in the washing machine."

"I'll renovate your closet and make it twice as big if you'll just stop leaving your shoes in the hall."

I was pretty sure in Merrick's mind, everything was teeming with germs and the world would collapse if the dish towel wasn't hung up to dry properly. It was a bit weird for someone who was rumored to have killed twelve men in an arena with his bare hands to win his place as *Brenin*.

But that was just a rumor.

I padded into the kitchen and he glanced up, closing his laptop with a snap. The arms of his shirt were rolled up to his elbows, revealing his muscular forearms. There was a tattoo a few inches above his wrist, a single Welsh word. It occurred to me as I walked into the kitchen that I'd never bothered to ask him what it meant.

"Burning the birthday candle at both ends so early?" he remarked.

"What?"

"I was at the club briefly last night and I saw you and Candice."

"Don't spy on me, Merrick." I rolled my eyes, opening the fridge.

"It's my club and I was working."

He took my elbow and moved me out of the way, steering me to sit down in his seat. I pretended to huff a little, but honestly, I liked it when he waited on me.

"Let me make the coffee," he said.

He cleared away his laptop and took down the pour-over and the kettle. It felt so comforting to watch him move about the kitchen. Like finally being home.

I'd toured Italy, England, Ireland, and Wales for the final week and enjoyed it, but there was something about being home that made me feel so at peace. I loved Providence, Rhode Island and I loved sharing Merrick's beautiful house with him.

Just existing alongside him was a pleasure. Eating out along the coast, scrolling my phone in the living room while he worked in his chair, or sitting on the kitchen counter while he cooked.

Merrick turned and crossed his arms over his chest. Behind him, the coffee leaked slowly through the pour-over and filled the bottom with rich, dark brew. In the corner of the kitchen, the radio was playing softly, barely audible.

"What are your plans for the day?" he asked.

"It's Sunday," I said, resting my chin on my hand. "I assumed we'd just hang out and have dinner together. Candice said she has to get home because her grandparents are coming over later."

"I actually have to work today."

"Oh," I said, unable to conceal my disappointment. "On Sunday? You never work on Sunday."

"Actually, I usually do when you're at school. I have some things that need wrapped up."

I arced my brow as he poured my coffee and swirled it with my favorite peppermint creamer. Merrick hated it, he said it tasted like toothpaste, but he knew it was my favorite so he always made sure the fridge was stocked with it.

"Thanks," I said, accepting the warm cup.

"We should probably sit down and talk about what happens next."

I blinked up at him. He poured the rest of the black coffee and turned to face me. Arms crossed and mouth pressed in a firm line.

21

"Uh oh," I said.

"Change isn't always bad, Clara."

"Says the man who hasn't changed a thing in ten years."

"Fair."

"Okay, what were you going to say?"

He cleared his throat and a flicker of something I didn't recognize crossed his face.

"You said you wanted me to go ahead and arrange your marriage when you graduated," he said, his voice oddly controlled. "So I took the liberty of having a few meetings and setting it up."

My whole body seized as I stared up at him. Yes, I had told him that, and yes, I still wanted to get married.

I wanted to be comfortable, to have beautiful things, to be one of the trophy wives that decorated the arms of the organization's important men.

At least, that's what I wanted when I was eighteen. Fresh-faced and about to enter my first year of college. When graduation felt like it was decades away.

But the time had flown by in a blur and now I had to face change head-on. I was turning twenty-four in a week and I hadn't given a second thought to my impending arranged marriage.

"Okay," I said, forcing my voice to stay casual. "That's good with me. Who is it?"

"Osian Cardiff."

"Hmm...I'm not familiar with the Cardiff family," I admitted.

He took a slow sip of coffee and his jaw worked, his cobalt eyes simmering with that unfamiliar emotion. I saw his chest expand as he took a quick breath.

"They're very wealthy. Rhys Cardiff, his father, is organization adjacent and he married one of our women a long time ago. Their family owns a huge chain of hotels and I'm negotiating a business deal to invest in them as they expand further up the coast into Canada. It'll be incredibly lucrative."

"Is that why you picked him?"

"That was just icing on the cake," he said, and I could tell he wasn't being completely truthful. "No, Osian Cardiff seems harmless and he'll provide you everything you want. He's handsome enough and he's got decent business sense."

"How old is he?"

"Around thirty, I think."

"Is he rich now?"

"He works for his father and brings in a sizable salary, but Rhys is making plans to retire over the next decade so Osian will step into his place in just a few years."

I thought it over and decided it didn't sound all that bad. I'd have enough money I could be anything I wanted and if Osian was organization adjacent, he would treat me well out of fear of Merrick's retaliation.

"When will I meet him?"

Merrick flicked his wrist, checking his custom watch. Everything he wore was custom, from his suits to his shoes to his watches.

"I was hoping we could all go to dinner tonight actually. Sooner rather than later. The organization has a lengthy engagement process so we should get started soon if you want to be married by next summer."

"How long does it take?" I asked.

"A while," he said. "It also depends on how long I want to drag it out."

"Will I get a ring?"

"You'll get a whole set of jewelry," he said. "Bought by Osian and approved by me."

"That sounds fine," I said, stretching slowly and letting out a little moan. The sore muscles in my back twinged. My whole body ached from dancing.

His eyes flicked away as he drained his cup and set it aside. There was a short silence and the song on the radio changed. Strains of "Graceland" by Paul Simon filled the kitchen.

He crossed the room and picked up his wallet and keys from the table. Then I felt his heat brush over my side as he leaned in. His lips touched the top of my head for a brief moment, his big, lean hand skimming over my upper back.

Warmth swelled in my chest.

"It's good to have you back, Clara," he said. "I'm sorry I can't be with you today, but I promise to make it up to you this weekend."

"This weekend?"

He cocked his head, a line appearing between his brows.

"Your birthday. Did you think I wouldn't go all out for your birthday?"

"Oh, duh, sorry," I said, getting to my feet. "So what are we doing?"

A flicker of excitement moved over his face and he bounced slightly on his heels, looking like a child on Christmas.

"What's your favorite movie of all time?"

"*Casino Royale*," I said.

"We're doing a themed party at the Bach's mansion," he said. "So make sure to get your best Bond girl outfit before Saturday."

He loved James Bond. I just liked watching movies with sexy older men in them, but I'd never had the heart to inform him I'd told him it was my favorite only because he liked it so much. And I was glad right now that I hadn't. He looked so pleased with himself.

"That sounds amazing," I said.

There was a scuffle behind him and Candice appeared, wrapped in a blanket. Her blonde hair was wild, her messy bun falling out, and her eyes were puffy. She stared up at Merrick for a long moment, seemingly stunned by having to reenter the world.

"Can I have coffee?" she rasped.

"I can make it," I volunteered.

She blinked around the room. "Merrick's coffee is better, no offense."

I rolled my eyes, pulling out a stool. Merrick graciously set his keys and wallet back down and made her a cup of coffee. It only took a few sips for her to start looking less pale.

"Thanks," she sighed. "I really need to drag my ass back to my parents soon. They're going to be pissed I'm hungover."

"I already texted Yale to come pick you up and take you home," Merrick said.

She bristled at the mere mention of his name. "I'd rather walk."

"Your father would have my head if I let you walk home, still drunk from last night. Yale will take you home. Understood?"

Merrick sent her that stern look that always shut me up, his mouth pressed together and his right brow lifted. She pushed out her lower lip and scowled.

"You're being misogynistic," she muttered.

"No, I'm being responsible."

She snorted.

"I am all for the liberation of women," said Merrick. "But not for the liberation of Candice Roberts. The world did nothing to deserve that."

The front door buzzed and I heard heavy boots on the polished floors. They moved down the center hallway and Yale appeared in the kitchen doorway. His crystal blue eyes lit up as they fell on Candice and a grin flashed up his square jaw.

"Look at you, Miss Roberts," he drawled. "Gift wrapped and everything."

She lifted her middle finger and flounced past him and down the hall toward my bedroom, leaving Yale laughing in her wake. Merrick shook his head and picked up his keys and wallet again.

"I'm headed out," he said. "See you tonight, Clara."

"Alright," I said. "Have a good day."

Yale followed him up the hall to the foyer and I took the other way back to my bedroom. Candice was furiously searching for the tiny, yellow dress she'd worn out to the club last night to no avail. I shut the door and went to the bathroom to turn the shower on for her.

There was a frustrated groan and Candice burst into the bathroom, unfastening her shirt and pulling it off.

"You already showered?"

"Yeah, my hair is still wet."

We were incredibly close, maybe in a co-dependent way sometimes, and we did everything together. Ate, slept, dressed, showered, and shared our darkest, dirtiest secrets. There was nothing Candice didn't know about me,

"There's body wash in there," I said. "But I'm almost out of shampoo."

"That's fine," she said, tying up her blonde waves. "I just washed my hair yesterday and my curls are still good for a day."

She stepped behind the glass door and stood, her arms wrapped around her body and let the water run down her shoulders.

"You shouldn't be so mean to Yale," I said. "He likes you."

She snorted, scrubbing herself wrathfully with my jasmine body wash.

"He does like you," I insisted. "He's smitten."

Candice pressed her lips together.

"He wants to sleep with me."

I sobered, thinking about it. "Would that be so bad? I'll bet he's pretty good in bed."

"I'll bet he's awful."

I cocked my head, raising an eyebrow. "Be serious. You know that's not true."

Her lips got even thinner. I could see the vengeful gears in her head turning.

"Have you thought about him like that?" I pressed.

She jumped out of the shower and slid the glass door shut, grabbing a towel. "I have to go, Clara, I just really don't have time to discuss Yale."

I bit back my words and wandered back into the bedroom as she dried off and pulled on one of my sweat suits. Candice slept over so often she'd probably stolen half my wardrobe at this point.

"Okay, I have to go," she said, appearing at my side and hugging me briefly. "And I'm literally never drinking again. I feel like shit."

"Yeah, okay," I said, watching her disappear into the hall. "Like that's going to happen."

CHAPTER FOUR

MERRICK

I'd promised Caden I'd run the training class for the early trainees but I'd have done anything to stay home with Clara. The disappointed slump of her shoulders made me feel even worse.

I'd always fucking hated letting her down.

To her, I knew, I was a different person.

But to the rest of the organization, to the powers that be, I was a man with a fuckload of responsibilities I couldn't just shirk to have lunch with my ward.

So I did what I'd always done and detached from what I really wanted and forced myself to do what needed done. Sometimes that was easy, but this morning I found myself having to set a timer on my phone just to get anything done.

Shower—ten minutes.

Put on clothes—ten minutes.

Drive to the warehouse—fifteen minutes.

Warm up—twenty minutes.

The warehouse was a huge building we used for training soldiers. The dirty little secret in Providence was that it was a training ground for some of the best soldiers and agents for hire in the United States. Powerful people paid a lot of money to hire my men for whatever discreet task they needed done, be it a simple delivery overseas or a full blown hit.

That, and a side of blackmail, was how I'd kept such a tight grip on the Eastern Seaboard.

It had been my idea, but Edwin had been instrumental in carrying it out.

Now that he was gone, I ran the whole operation with my two closest men, Yale and Caden.

Speak of the devil. I sank into a seat in the corner of the boxing ring and began unwrapping my hands. Yale appeared, wearing his training clothes. He was already bathed in sweat so he must have gotten to the warehouse early.

"Where's Caden?" I asked.

Yale paused, swiveling his broad body, scanning the room. He was a handsome man of a little over thirty with a bulky frame and medium brown hair. People liked him, they felt comfortable around him. They liked his Hollywood smile, his almost dazzlingly handsome face, and the glitter of mischief always in his eyes.

"Might be having a smoke."

I decided to let it rest instead of criticizing Caden for it when he finally showed up. My soldiers needed to keep healthy. Having an occasional smoke was one thing, but I was adamant we didn't tolerate addiction.

Yale sank down beside me, running a hand over his slick face.

"What's on the agenda?"

He was my brawn and I had him run most of the physical training. Keeping the men in shape. Caden was my brains and my weapons expert. He was the one I sent in when someone needed an operation done cleanly and quietly.

Yale was effective, but wasn't very good at being subtle.

The door behind us banged open and Caden strode through. If Yale was the human equivalent of a Golden Retriever, Caden was a black cat with razor sharp claws.

He was well muscled, but slender, and about the same height as me. His skin was pale beige and tattooed down one arm and up his throat to his jaw. His jet black hair was slicked over his head and his eyes were heavy lidded and an oddly bright blue.

Yale was pleasant and conversational.

Caden was a massive asshole with a chip on his shoulder about anything and everything.

But they were both incredibly talented and together they made an unbeatable team.

"You're late," I said, rising.

His brow arced. "I was on the phone with Trystan."

I pulled open the door that led to the shooting range. "What's the progress report?"

Caden followed me into the hall, Yale tagging along behind him. He was scrolling his phone, likely not even listening. I wondered for a moment just how involved with Candice he was and if this was something I needed to monitor in case it blew up and soured my inner circle.

The corner of his mouth jerked. Yeah, he was definitely texting her.

"Seems to be going well," Caden said.

Trystan was my third in command, after Yale and Caden, and right now he was out west in Wyoming. Spending his time supervising a new venture we were planning.

Out in the middle of nowhere, I'd purchased several thousand acres and closed it off completely to anyone on the outside. In the center, with the help of some powerful, unnamed people, I was building a training base for hundreds of new soldiers.

It was a labor of love, one that I hoped would pay off.

With that many soldiers, we'd be unstoppable. We could expand up and take Boston, we could move into New York and give the Italians something to worry about. We could become a training ground for private security and put our soldiers into the office of every person in the United States who mattered.

It was a lot to handle.

Maybe that was why I was always so eager to be at home with Clara. I loved listening to her problems and I loved fixing them. It was so much more satisfying.

Figure out how to transport several tons of military-grade equipment thousands of miles? That was a giant fucking knot to untangle.

Figure out what kind of sushi I should order to fix Clara's bad mood? That was easy and it came with the sweetest smile as a reward.

Caden was talking and I was thinking about Clara again. I shook my head slightly as we strode down a set of stairs and entered the range. An entire class of young men in their late teens were lined up along the opposite wall, waiting.

I ducked into the changing room and pulled on my fatigues and a t-shirt. In the safe, I selected my favorite pistol and an extra magazine.

Caden leaned in the doorway, arms crossed.

"Trystan had a private conversation with me," he said.

I paused, turning slowly. Thinking through my words carefully.

"About Delaney?"

Caden's head dipped. "Yale is pissed over it, he won't speak to Trystan, which I get. It's his little sister, he's been her male guardian for eight years."

"I know he doesn't want me arranging that marriage," I sighed. "But I need to make sure I keep a tight grip on the Wyoming base. Having Delaney there as his wife would strengthen ties and make me feel much more comfortable."

"I get it," Caden said. "Arranging marriages isn't your favorite thing."

"It feels so fucking dirty."

"It's just business."

"Business with the bodies of our women," I said, hating the words coming from my mouth.

"You've never once pushed anyone into a marriage they didn't fully consent to," Caden said, his voice low.

An ache moved through me as I remembered the hesitation on Clara's face this morning. Years ago, she'd seemed perfectly happy to agree to me arranging her marriage, she'd even asked for it. Now I was wondering if her feelings had changed.

I wasn't stupid. I saw her chew that spot in her mouth.

"I heard you were setting Clara up with Osian Cardiff," Caden said. His heavy eyes raked over me, unreadable as always.

I ran my hand over my face, slicking back my hair. Stalling as I tried to understand why I felt so strange about the prospect of Clara's marriage. I'd known this was coming the whole time.

"You okay?" Caden said quietly.

I nodded once, blinking. Snapping myself out of my reverie. "Yes, I'm fine. The Cardiffs will be powerful allies and the business deal Rhys is offering is a fucking good one. It's basically my net worth and it'll pay for the base in Wyoming."

"Shit," Caden drawled. "Better make sure he nails her down then."

I slid the magazine into the gun and strode past him.

"I intend to."

CHAPTER FIVE

CLARA

In the empty house, I worked on unpacking my suitcase from school. It felt strange, after four years of constant studying, to throw out all my old notes and scribbles. I carried the textbooks upstairs to the enormous library and stacked them on the table. I didn't dare shelve them and mess up Merrick's carefully coded system of organization.

When I got back to my room, Candice had texted me.

Want to come over when I'm done with dinner?

For a second, I was tempted to invite her tonight, but I knew I'd be stepping all over Merrick's plans.

Can't. Sorry, Merrick is taking me out to meet the guy he picked out for me.

Wait...what?

Merrick finally picked someone for me and I'm meeting him tonight to see what I think of him.

Oh my God. Who is he?

Osian Cardiff.

There was a long pause and then:

Ew.

I called her, tapping the speaker button. "Why did you say that? Do you know something about him?"

"No, not really," she said, yawning. "He's hot, but he's kind of a player."

"Are you shaming him?"

"No, I don't mean a player like that," she said. "I mean, he runs through women and just dumps them. Uses them for sex."

The pit of my stomach tightened and I met my gaze in the mirror. My mouth twisted as I chewed on the inside of my lower lip. About three years ago, Candice had lost her virginity to a man like that and I'd held her while she cried.

"He kind of made me feel like a human fleshlight," Candice had told me. "Just pumped and dumped even though he knew it was my first time."

She'd sworn off men after that, deciding to throw herself into her academic pursuits instead. I hadn't told her, but her experience had made an enormous impression on me.

So big that I'd refused to date anyone during college. I knew what it felt like to be treated well, Merrick had made sure of that. The idea of being used, of being put through unnecessary pain, didn't sound inviting.

I wasn't in a hurry to lose my virginity. In my mind, I had a little pink card with a glittery gold V on it. It was kept in my buttoned wallet and zipped into my purse.

Safe and unswiped.

"Okay, that makes me feel like shit about tonight," I said, throat tight and stomach fluttering.

"Merrick will be there," she said. "It's not like he'd ever do anything while Merrick's with you."

I swallowed. "Merrick won't always be with me."

She cleared her throat and I knew she was remembering her experience.

"Okay, we'll talk about it over coffee this week or something," she said. "I don't know, maybe I'm just being paranoid. He just makes me feel...on edge. You know that kind of guy?"

I did know, every woman knew that kind of man. The kind who didn't show any obvious red flags, but exuded a nagging, unsettling feeling. It was probably some kind of evolutionary protective system we still had from millions of years ago.

Or maybe I was just being paranoid. I shook my head once and took a quick breath, releasing it slowly.

"Okay, I'm going to get ready," I said. "I'll text you how it's going if I get a chance."

I showered, shaved, moisturized, and applied a light dusting of highlighter on my collarbones, shoulders and forearms. I could hear Merrick had returned. He was walking around lightly in his room upstairs, pacing the way he did when he was on a phone call.

I felt better just hearing him.

I pulled my hair back in a low bun at the nape of my neck and tugged some waves free by my ears. Then I slipped on my tight, ruched cocktail dress and matching blue heels.

It was strapless, but it had little puffy sleeves that sat just above my elbows. The skirt was tight until it hit the middle of my thigh and then it flared out in a high-low style with a little bow on my left leg.

I felt like a blue cupcake and I loved it.

I put my hands on my hips and pivoted, bending slightly to look at my ass. Hmm, it was a little bit revealing. Should I change? I took a deep breath and bent over the sink to put my berry red lipstick on.

No, I was fine. Merrick was there. There was no need to be nervous tonight.

Gathering up my handbag, I left my room and clicked down the stairs to the front hall. Merrick was still in his room, but I wasn't worried. He'd never been late to anything in his life.

Five minutes later, he descended the stairs and stopped short, his eyes flicking over me. He looked amazing in a tailored black suit with a burgundy shirt underneath, open at the collar. His wavy hair was tamed, slicked back over his head.

"You look beautiful, Clara," he said in that respectful tone he used when he gave me compliments. "Osian is a very lucky man. And he'd better understand that."

"Don't threaten him before he's done anything," I scolded.

He picked up his keys from the hall table and flipped them once, catching them in his palm. "Are you ready?"

I nodded, pulling the door open. "I'm as ready as I'll ever be."

"Aren't you going to bring a coat?"

I paused, shaking my head. "It's warm out and I don't want to ruin my outfit."

"Ah well, you can just steal mine later," he said.

I stepped out onto the porch. "I promise I won't, okay. Come on, we're going to be late."

He locked the doors, checking them twice, and moved down the steps on his long legs. I followed him out to where he'd parked the Audi and he opened the door for me, helping me in with a light hand on my elbow.

I watched him circle the car. Maybe part of the reason I trusted him to protect me was in the way he walked. He had a tall, lean body, dressed to kill in those custom suits, and he moved like he knew exactly what was up ahead.

Like he'd already conquered the world.

Like he had nothing to fear.

He didn't, I mused as he pulled up the long driveway to the road. He was Edwin Merrick Llwyd, the Welsh King. He'd fought his way to the top—some people claimed with his bare hands—and now he had the world on a string.

That was part of the reason I trusted him so completely. I'd never felt safe, ever, growing up.

With Merrick, I was always protected.

A few miles down the road was the country club Merrick owned. It was a huge white house that sat at the top of a hill like a beacon. As the gates buzzed and opened and Merrick guided the Audi up the curvy driveway, a sense of calmness settled over me.

"I liked being in North Carolina for school, but I love Providence so much," I said aloud. "I hope I never have to leave."

"You never will," he said.

The valet took the car and Merrick held out his elbow and I took it. We climbed the porch and entered the front room of the club. Inside, the club reminded me a bit of an upscale lodge with low ceilings and fake fireplaces. There were a crowd of people waiting to be seated, filling the dining room just beyond.

"Merrick Llwyd."

I turned to find Lowri Bach, a stylish, willowy woman of about fifty standing beside her stoic husband, Louis. They were both prominent members of the organization, Louis having just retired from service in Merrick's ranks. Lowri's eyes fell on me and she offered me a warm smile, hugging me awkwardly. I hadn't seen her in a few years.

"Clara, you look so grown up," she said. "A real knockout."

"Takes one to know one, Lowri," said Merrick, offering her his infectious grin.

I always forgot what a shameless flirt he was because it was so smooth he just slipped it in there and no one was ever the wiser.

"Oh, hush," she said, waving a hand.

"It's wonderful to see you again, Clara," Louis said, stepping up behind his wife.

"Thank you, sir," I said. "It's very good to be back in Providence."

Lowri waved her ring covered hand again, letting it rest on her collarbone. "Are you so excited for this weekend? The party?"

I nodded shyly, a little overwhelmed by the attention. Merrick cut in, assuring her I couldn't wait and we were so grateful to them for hosting my birthday.

They exchanged a few more words and then we parted ways. Merrick slid a hand around my waist to navigate me through the people to a round table at the far side of the room. We didn't have time to debrief from the first conversation because suddenly my heart was thumping in my chest.

My future husband sat there, sprawled out in his chair. Knees apart and arm resting lazily on the table.

Our eyes connected and I shrank back, cowed by his unabashed stare and his casually opulent clothes. His parents sat on the other side of the table, both dressed to the nines. His mother intimidated me right away with her rail thin figure and perfect hair.

36

In my frilly, little dress, I felt very young.

Osian had the same complexion and hair color as Merrick, but they looked nothing alike. He was handsome in a rich boy way, his eyes bored beneath the curls hanging over one eyebrow. The other brow had a scar running through it and he had another small nick on his lower lip.

Okay, so at least that was a little sexy.

"Nia and Rhys," said Merrick, leaning over to shake their hands. "And Osian. Pleasure to see you all."

I kept my eyes on the floor while Merrick exchanged quick pleasantries with them. I stayed back, cheeks flushed, my fingers clasped around my handbag.

Merrick turned after what felt like an eternity. My heart pumped hard, but I forced myself to step forward, offering a shaky smile. Nia Cardiff's eyes raked over me, assessing me and my tiny dress and towering heels. It was easy to tell she didn't approve.

"Hi," I whispered, my voice raspy.

She bent and shook my hand. "How are you, Clara?"

Her voice was a little chilly, like frost and pure judgement.

"Very good, thank you," I said.

At least, I tried to say that, but all that came out was a little cough. Shocked, I took a second to clear my throat and this time the words came out. My cheeks flushed and I saw Osian smirk in the corner.

I felt Merrick's hand rest on the middle of my back. Stabilizing me.

"Osian Cardiff," he said. "May I present, Clara Prothero."

Osian stood abruptly and circled the table. He approached, one hand in his pocket, and loomed over me. He was an inch or two shorter than Merrick and his lanky body didn't have the broadness of a mature man.

His presence was suffocating, but he did smell nice. Like spicy cologne.

I couldn't stop myself from chewing that tender spot in my mouth. He offered his palm and I laid my fingers in it. To my surprise, he lifted my hand and kissed the back lightly. When he looked at me from below his thick brows, there was a hint of amusement in his eyes.

"Pleasure to meet you, Clara," he said.

He had a nice voice, but it had a tinge of something that didn't sit well with me. Almost a hint of contempt, like he didn't think I was good enough for him.

He could probably tear me apart in an argument with a voice like that.

I felt Merrick's attentive gaze as Osian led me around the table and pulled out the chair beside his, pushing it in for me. Merrick sat beside Nia, directly across from me, and I found myself wishing he was closer. I wasn't good at meeting new people.

The waiter brought out ice water and a bottle of wine. Osian poured my glass like a perfect gentleman and I accepted it, trading it for a small smile. His mouth twitched and the corner jerked up in a jaunty smirk.

Did this man know how to do anything else but smirk?

"You're a little shy," he said quietly.

The odd thing was, I wasn't normally this uncomfortable. Meeting my future husband and in-laws was just...intimidating.

"Sorry," I said, giving him puppy eyes. That always worked on Merrick.

His mouth jerked. "I like it," he drawled. "It's sweet."

Sweet? Did I want him to think I was sweet? I dropped my lashes and reached for my drink. The wine was crisp and cool, helping tame the flush in my cheeks. Merrick was already deep in conversation with Osian's parents, speaking Welsh quietly in the corner.

"So, you just graduated then?" Osian asked.

I turned in my chair to face him. His gaze traveled down, assessing me for the first time. Taking his painstaking time looking at my mouth, then my throat, and finally my breasts.

He was thinking about me naked. It was so obvious and he wasn't even attempting to hide it. Heat flared in my belly and I looked away, embarrassed and shocked that he would be so blatant about checking me out.

"Yes," I said, remembering he'd just asked me a question.

He dragged his eyes back up. "What are your plans now?"

"I guess, get married," I said.

Was that the answer he was hoping for?

"No plans to use your degree?"

I shook my head. "I went to school for fun."

He sat back, letting his arm rest on the back of my chair. "That's a good girl."

I felt my jaw drop, but I hurried to cover up my shock. Candice would absolutely loathe this man.

"Um...where did you go to school?"

"Duke for my undergrad," he said. "I have an MBA."

"Oh, I went to school in North Carolina too."

"Really? Where?"

"Chapel Hill."

"Really?" he said, his scarred brow lifting. "I'd have thought Merrick Llwyd could afford to send you to an Ivy League."

"I got into one, but I wanted to go to Chapel Hill because I liked the setting better," I explained. "I figured I could go wherever I wanted if I wasn't planning on using the degree."

He shrugged. "Makes sense."

There was a short silence where I felt his gaze once more move over me at a snail's pace. Fixating on the tendril of hair by my ear. I knew I looked good in my dress, but I hadn't expected such shameless attention. It was throwing me off, making me feel naked.

Not in a sexy way either. My body just felt so small under his gaze, like he had me laid out on the table ready to carve me to pieces.

I shifted awkwardly and my eyes fell on Merrick across the table. He had taken his jacket off and rolled up his sleeves to the elbow. It was hot in the corner of the room and the base of his throat was flushed.

His eyes fixed on Osian. Observing him closely as my future fiancé made his slow, bold perusal of my body. I'd never seen Merrick look like that.

Like there was something dark and dangerous bubbling just beneath the surface.

I shivered.

"You cold?" Osian asked.

"No, I'm good," I said, offering a quick smile.

Osian stood, shrugging out of his jacket, and draped it over my shoulders. It smelled good, like him, but it didn't help my anxiety. My heart pumped so loudly I could feel it all over my body. Osian sat and pushed his chair in, leaning close so his mouth was an inch from my ear.

"Does Merrick hate me?"

We both glanced at Merrick, but he'd turned away. He had his elbows on the table, which was odd for him, and his hands clasped.

He was back to talking easily with the Cardiffs as though nothing had happened.

"No, he spoke highly of you," I said.

"He's been looking at me like he wants to break my neck."

"Merrick can be very protective," I explained. "It's nothing personal."

The rest of the meal went much better. My heart slowed and I wasn't so hot and cold anymore. I made small talk with Osian while we ate and I found myself relaxing more and more around him.

He was smart and he could hold a conversation well. We talked about college some more and he told me about his future plans as the heir to his father's empire. They ran thousands of luxury hotels and resorts and he'd been groomed from a young age to take over the business.

It sounded very glamorous.

Exactly how I'd imagined my future.

After the meal was over, Merrick and the Cardiffs split from us so we could have time alone at the bar. Osian took my hand, leading me behind him as he crossed the room. I glanced behind me, making sure I could see Merrick out on the porch through the glass doors.

He was deep in conversation, but the minute I looked for him, he turned and sent me a quick glance of reassurance.

Osian helped me onto a stool and turned his seat so he could face me. "What are you drinking?"

"A Cosmo," I said.

He ordered for both of us, shifting his seat closer to mine. His knee was between mine and I felt the contact in my whole body. But nothing prepared me for his palm settling on my bare thigh.

Hot and a little overwhelming.

"As is tradition in the organization, I'll bring you a piece of jewelry in the next few weeks," he said. "If you accept, and Merrick approves, then I'll buy you more and we'll be engaged when you accept the last piece."

"So we won't be engaged for a while?" I asked. "I don't know a lot about the formal engagement process."

He shook his head. "We won't actually get engaged or be exclusive until you've accepted all the gifts. Usually happens several months after the first piece of jewelry. It's a whole silly process, but it's tradition."

I sipped my Cosmo, glad for the liquid courage.

"So what kind of jewelry?" I asked, just trying to make conversation.

He leaned back, taking his distracting palm from my thigh. "Usually a full set of jewelry. Diamonds."

"And it ends with an engagement ring?"

He shook his head, smirking again. His bored eyes were gleeful for a second as he sipped his drink lazily.

"Not usually. That's reserved for more intimate things," he drawled.

I stared at him, unsure where he was going with the conversation.

"Okay, maybe I...don't want to know," I whispered.

He shrugged. "We're both adults. If you accept all of the gifts, and they are approved through Merrick, then I get to lay intimate claim to you. That's when we'd become exclusive."

"How?" My voice sounded raspy.

He leaned in and my stomach flipped. He was very close and I could see the little scar on his eyebrow and lip in high definition. His

41

eyes were a mottled blue-gray and they bored into me until I felt like I was burning up inside.

"A clit piercing."

My thighs clenched. Beneath my panties, my clit throbbed painfully at the idea.

His mouth jerked up, giving me that arrogant smirk again. I had never been more mortified in my life. My ears roared and my jaw went slack. My heart began pumping again, hard and fast like a rabbit's.

He glanced down at my thighs, clenched together, and laughed softly.

"Are you joking?" I whispered.

He shook his head. "It's been the tradition in the organization for a while."

I stared. Candice really would hate him.

"What if I don't want it pierced?" I said.

He shrugged. "You don't have to if you're uncomfortable with it," he said, his voice going silky smooth. "But...I'd like you to get it pierced so I can put my diamond on it. You probably have a lovely pussy."

My throat tightened and heat seeped through my hips. I'd never had a man talk to me like this and it was both alluring and mortifying. He reached up and brushed the hair hanging by my cheek back, tucking it behind my ear.

I swallowed.

"You're fucking beautiful," he said. "I wasn't sure what to expect, but you've got a tight, little body and a beautiful face."

I internally gagged at his description of my body, but decided to let it go.

"I'll think about it," I said.

"About what?"

I took a sip of Cosmo to fortify myself. "About getting my clitoris pierced."

He shrugged, staring at me lazily. "You know we're not exclusive until you accept the piercing and we get engaged. I'm not planning on abstaining from sex with other people until then."

Taken aback, I scrambled for words. It was my understanding that was pretty normal for our world, but I hadn't expected him to be so forthright about it. Maybe that was for the best.

"Um...yeah, I mean, that's fine with me," I said.

"Are you fucking anyone?"

His gaze raked over me, less relaxed than when he was speaking about his sex life. There was a hint of darkness in that stare and it sent a shiver up my spine. I considered trying to make it seem like I also thought sex was no big deal.

But I couldn't find it in me to lie.

"I'm not," I said, my voice low. "I actually haven't...done that yet."

His brows rose and his head cocked. Then he leaned back and crossed his legs, the way Merrick always did. One over the other, all stretched out and loose.

I swore I saw a rise under the zipper of his pants as he did.

My stomach flipped and I took a large gulp of my drink.

"Is that a problem?" I whispered.

The corner of his mouth jerked up and he shook his head once. "Nah, I like it...it's sexy and kind of sweet. Are you planning on saving yourself for our wedding night?"

I shrugged. "I'd...assumed you would want to sleep with me before then."

"I would," he said, sending that gaze raking over my body again.

I cleared my throat awkwardly. "Well, I guess it's all yours then," I said lightly.

That smirk deepened. "You're a good girl, Clara."

I really had nothing to say to that. Merrick had called me a good girl a few times before, but it had always felt affectionate and loving. Coming from Osian's mouth, it made my skin itch with discomfort.

I barely remembered the rest of our conversation. He flirted with me, even going so far as to kiss my cheek briefly when we parted. Merrick was sober as we watched Osian's car drive off into the dark.

"What did you think of him?" Merrick asked lightly.

"Honestly...he has some rough edges, but he was nice," I said.

"I'm glad you liked him."

The valet fetched the Audi. We were both quiet as he drove down the hill and pulled back onto the road. I was still reeling from my conversation and wishing that Merrick had given me a more detailed answer when I'd asked him about the engagement jewelry.

But then, he never talked about sex. At least not with me.

"Merrick," I said.

"Yes?' He glanced at me through the dark, lit only by a red light on the dashboard.

"Osian said he would give me gifts," I whispered. "Like you said he would."

"That's the tradition," he said. "Has been for a while. You don't have to, but people might find it strange if you don't."

I swallowed. "You never told me what the jewelry was."

His jaw worked. "Did he tell you?"

"It came up, yes."

He kept his eyes on the road as he pulled up to the gate outside his house. There was a quiet hiss and they parted, letting us through. He cleared his throat and shifted in his seat.

"It's generally an intimate piercing."

I kept my gaze on the dark window, burning up with embarrassment.

"Osian said it was a clit piercing."

He parked the car and shifted to look at me. "What do you want to know? I assumed you were somewhat aware of this."

I shook my head. "I've been kind of checked out with school and everything."

He released a sigh. "Well, alright, I can explain in simple terms. It's not a clit piercing, it's a VCH, a vertical *hood* piercing, so it only runs through the hood of your clit."

My stomach fluttered and I opened my palms, looking down at the damp skin. Listening to him casually talk about my clitoris was a bizarre experience.

"Does it hurt?"

"Well, I don't have a clitoris, so I couldn't tell you exactly what it feels like," he said. "But I've heard it's one of the least painful genital piercings. It's generally a little bar with a bulb or diamond that rests directly over the clit."

"What...what is the point of that?"

"Pleasure," he said.

There was a long silence. "So I'm expected to get pierced," I said slowly.

He lifted a shoulder in a shrug. "It's between you two. If you're very much against it, some women opt to get their nipples pierced instead."

I sat there, burning up. "You know what I think?"

"What?"

"I think this is just another way for men to own us." I got out of the car and began striding up the porch steps.

Merrick locked up the car and moved past me to open the front door. "You didn't believe the part about pleasure, did you?"

I shook back my hair, flouncing past him into the house. "Why don't I just let Osian brand my ass with his family crest? It's the same thing, just in a different font."

Merrick laughed, the rich sound echoing through the hall.

"He'd probably like that, judging from the way that fucker was looking at you tonight."

He was joking, but I felt the veiled threat in his voice. I chewed the inside of my mouth and watched him as he took off his coat. That spot was raw and little bloody, staining my mouth with metal.

"Isn't it good that he wants me?" I asked quietly.

Merrick's eyes softened. "As long as he respects you, it's fine."

He went into his office and I went to shower off my makeup. My body was a tangle of mixed emotions.

Did I like the way Osian had looked at me? Like he wanted to use me, to devour me until I was just bare bones?

And why did my whole body ache after that conversation with Merrick?

45

Feeling a little ashamed, I slid my fingers down between my legs. I didn't touch myself very often because it only worked about half the time. Usually I just built and built until I was overstimulated and annoyed, but never went over the edge.

This was one of those times. My hips were tight and there was a pressure I needed to fix between my thighs. I got out and toweled off and crawled into my bed, fixing my eyes on the ceiling.

Closing my eyes, I tried to picture Osian as I circled my finger, but it was having the opposite effect. Any desire I had to come had waned and disappeared. Frustrated, I flipped onto my stomach and closed my eyes.

Maybe getting the piercing would be a good thing. Maybe it would make me more sensitive and I could finally orgasm consistently. Otherwise, Osian was going to be in for a disappointment when he finally got me into bed.

CHAPTER SIX

CLARA

A childish thrill of excitement woke me on my birthday. I bolted upright and crossed the room, reaching out to pull the door open. My hand froze. I was wearing a worn out t-shirt I'd taken from Merrick a few years ago. It was a comfort shirt, like a security blanket, and I always wore it when I couldn't get to sleep.

For some reason, it didn't feel right wearing it around him this morning.

I chewed the inside of my lip. God, it was getting raw in that spot. A tingle of metal spread over my tongue.

Why did it suddenly feel strange to wear Merrick's shirt?

I lifted the neckline and pulled it over my nose. Clean. Masculine. Comforting.

My hand hovered over the doorknob. Goddamn it, I was just going to change.

I seethed a little at myself as I pulled on leggings and a bralette. What had changed in the last week?

Nothing. Nothing had changed, I was being stupid.

Merrick was still Merrick. Even after our awkward conversation in the car after he'd introduced me to Osian, he'd remained the same. Nothing bothered Merrick or threw him off his game. He was still his protective, affectionate self.

Out of nowhere, I was painfully aware of him this morning.

But why?

I shook my head in frustration and went to open the door, but caught sight of myself in the mirror. My nipples were hard and poking through the thin bralette. I pushed my thighs together and the faint crease of my pussy showed.

Had that always happened? I'd worn this outfit before and never noticed that.

I pivoted again and put on a sweatshirt that went to my knees.

The house was silent, but it was early so that made sense. It was still warm out and the windows were open in the front room. The soft scent of honeysuckle filled the air.

It was going to be a perfect day. And night.

I entered the kitchen to find Merrick standing where he usually sat with his laptop. He wore a pair of casual Chinos and a button down, rolled to the elbows. There was a bowl of fresh apples from the local orchard before him.

When I entered, he looked up and his face broke into a smile.

"Happy birthday, Clara," he said, holding out his arm.

My chest filled with warmth. My father had never celebrated birthdays so I hadn't had one until I was eighteen. But after that, Merrick spoiled me like a princess every single year.

I went to him, letting him pull me in for a brief hug.

Heat, a firm chest, the scent of oak.

Then he drew back and wiped his hands. "I'm making your favorite."

"*Pwdin eva?*"

It was a Welsh classic, rich and crumbly like cobbler. Best served hot with a generous scoop of vanilla ice cream.

"The very one."

"You're amazing," I breathed, ducking past him to take the pour-over from the upper shelf.

It was out of my reach. I gripped the countertop and hoisted a knee up, straining to reach the glass funnel.

"You can ask for help, Clara," said Merrick, amused.

I slid back down, my feet hitting the floor. He appeared at my side, his hand brushing my back, and retrieved the funnel. I gripped it, feeling suddenly on edge as he searched for the strainer.

My eyes fell down his lean body to the place where his shirt met his pants. Or rather, where it was supposed to. Instead, there was a strip of skin visible.

Tanned, smooth.

A sharp V disappearing below his belt.

A trail of short, dark hair going up to his navel.

He shifted and the V flexed and his shirt slid down to cover it. My stomach twisted and I tore my eyes away. It was good I'd worn the sweatshirt because for some reason, my nipples were rubbing against my bralette.

Hard and oddly sensitive.

I swallowed past the dryness in my throat and spun on my heel. Clutching the funnel in one had, I searched for a paper towel to wipe it with even though it was clean.

Feeling like a newborn colt on wobbly legs, I attempted to pull myself together. Maybe I was just ovulating and that was why his presence felt like someone had poured hot water down my pants. Mentally, I calculated my cycle.

No, I was about to start my period in a week.

So it wasn't that.

"Alright," he said cheerfully. "I'll finish breakfast and you make the coffee. Think you can handle that?"

"Yes," I said quickly.

He handed me the strainer and frowned, studying me with those cobalt eyes. I tensed as his hand came up and the backs of his fingers brushed over my forehead.

"Are you okay?" he asked. "You look sort of…off. But you don't feel warm."

Alright, it was time for me to pull it together. Or try to, at least.

"I'm just excited for tonight." I shook back my hair and busied myself with making the coffee.

"Nervous?"

49

I glanced at him over my shoulder. "No, it'll be fine."

There was a knock on the door and he looked up, his eyes glittering.

"Better go get that, Clara," he said.

I knew it was for me, Merrick always sent me flowers on my birthday. And every other Tuesday. Childish excitement rising in my chest, I set the coffee funnel aside and skipped out into the hall.

I had to type in the security code twice and then I had to scan my thumb, but finally the locks eased. Pulling the door open, I squinted out into the morning sun and gasped.

There was a topless, white car with berry pink accents parked in the driveway. Every sleek inch of it gleamed, including the creamy leather seats. On the passenger seat was a round box of jet black roses tied with a pink ribbon.

All of my favorite colors.

My fists clenched and my throat tightened. Part of me wanted to run out and inspect every inch of it, part of me wanted to hug Merrick. But the part of me that decided to ugly cry in the hallway won out.

"*Cariad*," Merrick said, appearing at my side. "What's wrong?"

I pushed my face against his chest, breathing in his scent. "Nothing," I said, my voice muffled. "You're just too nice to me, Merrick. No one is ever going to measure up."

He stroked my hair. "That's the point, now you know what you deserve. I hope Osian is taking notes."

I laughed weakly. "I thought you didn't want me to drive."

"No, I said I wasn't comfortable with it outside Providence," he corrected. "Feel free to go where you please in town."

He handed me his handkerchief that smelled like him, that rich, dark oak scent, and I wiped my face. I handed it back to him and he took it gingerly, disassociating for a moment as he pushed it back into his pocket.

I felt his eyes on me as I ran out to the driveway and climbed into the front seat. The keys hung from the dash. There was a little round leather tag embossed with my monogram.

I pulled the keys out, gathered up my flowers, and carried them back up the stairs. He had a faint smile on his face and a strange expression in his eyes. It looked almost like wistfulness.

"Are you alright?" I asked.

He cleared his throat. "It just occurred to me that after you marry Osian, you'll be with him for your birthday. This is our last year together."

Well, that poured a bucket of ice cold water on my mood. And it also reminded me that Osian hadn't sent me anything. I shook back my hair and stood on my toes, kissing his jaw. The stubble tickled my lips and made me want to rub my nose.

"Let's not think about that now," I said. "Can I drive the car over to Candice's house after breakfast? I was going to hang out with her while you were at work."

"Sure," he said. "Do you need me to bring you to the Bach's tonight?"

"Yes, please," I said. "But I have to go shopping first."

"I paid off your credit card," he said, crooking a brow.

I cringed. "Sorry, I needed a lot of retail therapy during finals week."

"Just let me know before you hit the ceiling next time," he said. "They sent me a notice and there's no reason for that."

"I'm sorry," I whispered.

"It's alright, Clara," he said softly, sending me a look that made me feel like it really was alright.

We had breakfast together in the front room, although I could tell Merrick was distracted. His phone kept pinging and every time he'd look at it, his lips would move slightly. There was a slight frown on his face when he left the house an hour later to take the Audi into work.

I didn't ask him about it.

Instead, I spent the afternoon with Candice, wondering why Osian hadn't sent me anything for my birthday. Surely he knew what day it was and that he was expected to at least acknowledge it. But he hadn't even texted, which I found annoying.

And a little hurtful.

I mentioned it to Candice as we were getting ready for the party later that afternoon. She was bent over the sink applying her lipstick. I was Vesper Lynd from *Casino Royale* and she was Madeleine Swann from *Spectre*. The silver, silk dress looked amazing with her blonde hair, gathered at the nape of her neck.

"Maybe he's planning something for later," she mused.

I shrugged.

"Or maybe he's just stupid."

"Candice!"

"What?" She whirled.. "He has to know this isn't just about getting you a gift."

"What do you mean?"

"I mean, he has to know Merrick's breathing down his neck waiting for him to fuck up. This is his trial by fire and if he blows it, Merrick won't accept him when he finally does give you a gift."

I hadn't thought about it like that, but she was right. That made Osian's silence all the more strange.

I obsessed over it as I did my makeup with a perfect smoky eye and slipped on the deep purple gown I'd picked out from my closet. It was a designer dress I'd had altered last year and never worn, but it was perfect for tonight.

The bodice was a deep V and it tied in a halter around my neck, leaving my back completely bare down to my waist. Crystals ran down between my breasts, matching the diamond set I wore on my ears, around my wrists, and at my throat.

"Is this too fancy?" I asked.

Candice shook her head. "It's your birthday. You can literally wear whatever you want. And it's not fancy, it's elegant, and you look amazing."

I shook my hair back and fluffed the waves falling over my shoulders. Then I slipped on my heels and turned in a slow circle. I looked grown up and, Candice was right, elegant.

Usually I felt cute or pretty, but this was the first time I'd felt elegant.

Like a woman.

Swallowing back the nostalgia, I reached for my berry pink lipstick.

Yale showed up to drive Candice to the Bach's house, which made her fighting mad although she didn't have a good explanation as to why she was so offended. As soon as his sports car revved up the drive, her brows went down and her glare followed him as he pulled up to the porch steps.

He pushed down his sunglasses and raked his eyes over her body.

"Looking good, Roberts," he drawled.

She rolled her eyes. "Don't even start with me tonight."

His face split into a grin and, quick as a flash, he made a V with his fingers over his mouth and flicked his tongue through.

Her jaw dropped and there was a shocked silence. I hung back, unsure exactly what that gesture meant. Clearly it hit Candice exactly where Yale wanted because a flush burned up her neck and she stomped down and got into the passenger seat.

The door slammed so hard I was afraid the glass would shatter. Yale peeled out of the drive. They passed Merrick's Audi as it turned the corner and I saw his frown as he stepped out and observed the faint tire tracks.

"If Yale wasn't such a good soldier, I would beat his ass into the dirt just for being a dick," he said casually.

I barely heard him. I'd never seen Merrick in a tux—and honestly I didn't really like tuxedos—but he looked drop dead gorgeous. The aviator sunglasses were just the cherry on top.

He paused at the bottom of the stairs. "You're beautiful, Clara."

"Thank you." I accepted his hand as he helped me down and into the front seat of the Audi.

He got in and made the engine purr as he drove out onto the main road. I settled back, locking my ankles awkwardly to keep my legs together. The dress was beautiful, but not the most comfortable.

"So who are you?"

He frowned, glancing over. "What?"

"Who are you supposed to be?" I asked. "I'm Vesper Lynd."

"I mean...I'm supposed to be James Bond," he said, clearly confused.

"I was setting you up to say the line."

"Oh, sorry, I'm a bit tired," he said, running a hand over his hair. He patted my knee briefly and for some reason, a shock of heat moved up my thigh.

"Are you too tired to go out?"

"No, no," he said firmly. "I'll be good when I get a drink and something to eat. It was just a long day at work."

I knew he actually did want to go out for my birthday, but I still felt guilty. Merrick worked extremely hard, sometimes putting in fifteen hour days, sometimes waking up at odd hours to deal with some mysterious emergency.

I glanced at myself in the mirror, the diamonds on my neck glittering.

He'd paid for those, with his time and energy. Even though Merrick never made me feel guilty about it, I still felt a little ashamed of myself.

That sort of meant that everything I wore belonged to him at the end of the day. I spread my fingers to look down at my manicure, simple French tips, and the white gold rings.

A sudden and intrusive thought popped into my head.

Heat curled in my stomach.

Underneath this dress, I wore my most expensive pair of panties. They were from a boutique in Italy and the delicate lace was worth a few hundred dollars. The little diamonds on each hip were worth more.

Unknowingly, Merrick had paid for those too.

Why did that realization make me feel so strange? Subtly, I slid my hand down my inner arm and found my pulse.

It was going a little faster than normal.

I glanced at him, but he was completely oblivious. Gazing ahead with his hand resting on the top of the steering wheel.

What was wrong with me today?

CHAPTER SEVEN

MERRICK

The Bach's house was lit up and already filled with people. They lived on the western side of the city in a huge house surrounded by an estate. It fit in well with the theme and I could tell Clara was in awe as I helped her from the car.

She was stunning tonight, although I secretly wished she was a little more covered. Osian would be here tonight and I'd noticed during their first meeting that he had a wandering gaze.

Probably wandering hands too.

I took a beat and checked myself. He was going to be her fiancé and, if she was fine with it, he had every right to admire her. I was just being overprotective, afraid of seeing her get hurt.

Inside, I glanced over the packed front room and spotted Osian at the bar with a handful of his friends. They were all Ivy League grads with bored expressions, faces already red from drinking. Beside them, Rhys Cardiff leaned on the bar talking to a blonde woman who was definitely not his wife.

I wasn't surprised. I knew his type.

Candice appeared on my other side and seized Clara's elbow and dragged her into the crowd. I saw them huddle by the bar, sending glances over to where Yale stood with Caden by his side.

They were both dressed identically to me, not on purpose. The women had done a good job coming up with creative ways to stay on theme, but every single man had gone with the basic fitted black tux.

Yale was smirking and practically eye-fucking Candice, who kept shooting him dirty looks over her shoulder. Caden lounged over the bar beside him, ice cold and checked out as usual. He never had to put in effort to get laid, he just zeroed in on his prey and pulled one of his low effort party tricks out. Nine times out of ten, it worked.

But I was here for Clara, not to get laid.

Until she moved out that wasn't an option.

Drawing up beside Rhys Cardiff, I jerked my head at the blonde woman and she disappeared. Rhys scowled.

"Where's your wife?" I asked lightly.

"Too tired to come," he said.

I tapped the counter and the bartender leaned across. "I'll have the ten-year bourbon."

He passed me a glass and refilled Rhys's martini and disappeared. I turned so I could keep the room in my field of vision.

"I'm not impressed with how your son is handling Clara's birthday," I said in a low voice.

"How's that?"

"He hasn't sent her anything. And, last I checked, he hasn't texted or called her. Do we have a problem?"

Rhys frowned. "He bought a gift, I know that."

"Well, at this point, it better be fucking diamonds."

We both watched as Osian broke away from his friends and made his way slowly across the room to where Clara stood. He put his hand on her lower back and she jumped, turning. Her cheeks went a little pink as he leaned in and whispered something into her neck.

"They seem like they're getting along," Rhys said.

Osian bent in closer and his lips brushed her cheekbone. This time Clara blushed up to her hairline and accepted his hand, letting him lead her to the far side of the room. They paused in the corner, half hidden by the crowd, and I saw Osian reach into his pocket.

I noticed he was wearing almost the same watch as me, which I found vaguely annoying. I knew I should have gone with a custom instead of my Rolex.

Something ugly simmered deep in my chest.

"I'm...got to go," Rhys said, his eyes fixing on another woman at the other side of the bar.

"Good to see you," I said crisply. "Tell your wife I said hello."

He nodded curtly and disappeared. Before I could move I felt a hand on my lower back and I turned to find my therapist, Gretchen Hughes. She was a slender, blonde woman of about fifty-five with a feline face and silvery gray eyes.

"Gretchen," I said, leaning in to kiss her cheek. "I didn't think you'd come."

"I'm actually here as someone's date, but thank you for the invite."

Her voice was soft and cultured. For other people, this situation might have been strange, but Gretchen wasn't just my therapist, she was my friend as well as part of my social circle.

We both knew many of the same powerful men. I made business deals with them in boardrooms by day and she made them beg in bedrooms by night. It was a comfortable arrangement where we traded clients back and forth.

Both making a tidy stream of income from it.

Caden appeared on my other side and zeroed in on Gretchen, his eyes narrowing. He was at least sixteen years her junior, but that wasn't going to stop him.

"Who's this?" he drawled.

Her eyes flicked over him. "Nice neck tattoos."

"Thanks, I've got one on my dick if you want to see that too."

Stuck between them, I was feeling annoyed.

"Back off, Caden," I warned. "She's not your type."

That was a lie. Caden loved fucking women twice his age and he had no qualms about letting it be known he had raging mommy issues.

"What type is she?" he asked.

Gretchen rolled her eyes and tapped the bar for another glass of champagne. "I'm a therapist, but I don't practice anymore technically. As of right now, I am a dominatrix for my own amusement. I am however very expensive and there's a wait list, darling."

Caden's brow lifted slowly and he cocked his head, leaning in. "I'm open to trying anything once, sweetheart."

"Caden," I snapped. "Do not try to fuck my friends. Go torment someone else."

He disappeared, leaving Gretchen with her mouth hanging open.

"Sweetheart?" she whispered.

"I'm sorry about him, he's not been domesticated yet."

Her eyes flickered with irritation. "Maybe I should offer him a space on my list, teach him a thing or two about respect."

I gazed after Caden, incredibly uncomfortable with the idea. "No use, I've had him for ten years and he's a lost cause. Not very trainable, but highly deadly under the right circumstances."

She laughed at that and the tension broke. We chatted for a few moments before her date appeared—a senior retired member of the organization—and whisked her away.

It was getting later and I'd had a few drinks and was feeling more relaxed. The lights lowered and the staff wheeled out a huge cake covered in pink roses. I found Clara in the corner and dragged her over to blow out the candles.

I didn't have to do much persuading. Usually she was too shy to get up in front of people, but tonight she was already drunk. Her eyes glittered and her hair was windswept, like she'd been outside.

Had she slipped away with Osian?

Ugliness reared its head and I pushed it back down. If she wanted to go make out with her future fiancé, she had every right to.

The candles covered the top tier of the cake, smoking slightly. The crowd began clamoring as she leaned over and tried to blow them out. I saw her body sway and I was up on the platform, hands around her waist, in a second.

"I'm not going to fall, Merrick," she giggled.

"Please, don't," I said. "Hold your hair back and try again."

She gathered her hair and everyone began clapping, urging her on. I felt her ribs expand beneath my hands and she blew hard, managing to take out half the candles.

"Oh God, I'm getting dizzy," she gasped.

I leaned in and finished the rest. "There you go, now have some cake, *cariad*."

Candice hopped up and started carving slices out and passing them around. As I adjusted my cuffs and alighted to the floor, I caught Osian's stare through the crowd.

Hard, cold.

Jealous?

My eyes drifted back to Clara and time seemed to slow. She was truly happy in this moment, loose with alcohol and surrounded by the people she loved most.

Glittering like a bird of paradise.

Ocean eyes alight, smile beaming, hair falling like a black waterfall down her shoulders, diamonds gleaming like starlight on her throat.

Of course he was jealous, she was worth it.

The room was getting louder the drunker everyone got. It took less than an hour for the cake to be demolished. The staff revealed an enormous champagne tower and Candice made Clara stand in front of it and get her picture taken before anyone could take a glass.

It was all a bit overstimulating. I needed a breath of fresh air so I ducked out the side door and stepped onto the lawn. Outside, it was humid, but just having some space helped clear my head.

I didn't enjoy crowds.

Feeling guilty, I stepped further into the bushes and had a cigarette. I never smoked anymore except socially. I never really had the urge. But tonight, there was a sense of confusion in my chest I couldn't shake.

It was nothing, I told myself.

Just a lot of change happening at once and Clara had been right that I didn't like it.

I finished my cigarette and went back inside. Clara was by herself at the bar, leaning on her elbow as she waited on her drink. I crossed the room and moved up behind her, reaching out to ask the bartender for another bourbon.

She looked down, not turning, and I felt her eyes fix on my hand laying on the counter. Was she looking at my watch?

Before I could react, she stepped back and pressed her ass into my groin and ground it lightly against my dick.

I froze, my ears roaring.

What the fuck?

In that millisecond, I was aware of everything. The soft curves of her ass through her skirt nestled up against my...erection.

Oh God, no, I was hard. Not just a little bit, no, I was fully hard, fully expanded. My dick crushed under my zipper and I knew she felt every inch of me.

Her body stiffened as she realized something was off. Panic spiked and I stepped back, turning and ducking into the crowd. Sliding into the shadows of the room just in time to see her turn.

Her face was flushed and her brows pulled together with confusion. She pivoted slowly, looking for someone.

For Osian?

I looked down at my watch and it all fell into place. Osian and I had worn the same watch and—like every man here—we also wore the same tux.

A muddled sense of relief flooded my chest.

She'd thought I was Osian.

But that didn't fix the very obvious problem in my pants. I needed to get to a bathroom before I made a spectacle of myself.

Luckily there was one just a few feet down the hall behind me. I ducked inside and locked the door, ripping off my jacket. My collar was soaked and the front of my pants strained.

I met my eyes in the mirror as it sank in what had just happened.

Clara had just gotten me hard. I'd lived with her for six years and never once had she given me an erection. Not when she walked into the kitchen without a bra, not when her shorts rode up and showed the bottom of her ass.

"Fuck, fuck, fuck," I breathed.

My fingers shook slightly as I undid my belt and opened my pants.

There it was, looking undeniably solid.

Alright, I needed to get rid of it fast, before anyone started wondering where I'd gone. I grabbed a handful of paper towels and closed my eyes, forcing my mind to go completely blank.

There was absolutely no way in hell I was going to let myself think about her while I did this. After all, it was just mechanics and I had nothing if not self control.

Some things were just too fucking sacred.

CHAPTER EIGHT

CLARA

I felt like such an idiot. Osian had been flirting with me all evening. Touching me, kissing my neck. Giving me the world's ugliest necklace for my gift. He'd even let his hand trail over my ass when he'd left me at the bar so I could order another Cosmo.

So why had he fled when I'd ground my ass on him then?

It didn't make sense and it was absolutely killing me. He clearly wasn't ready for that. Grinding on his dick was a far cry from letting him kiss my neck.

I'd never done anything like that before and I was sorry I had. I'd gotten drunk and misread the signals and now I needed to go apologize.

It took me at least fifteen minutes to find him in the darkened sea of bodies. He was talking to a friend, but he paused and turned to me as I drew near. To my surprise, he ran his fingers down my arm and took my hand.

"Did you get your drink?" he asked.

I nodded, leaning in so I could talk. "I'm sorry."

He frowned. "What for?"

I flushed. "At the bar a minute ago...I thought you were coming onto me so I ground on you. Like...I was just flirting, I didn't mean to offend you."

The crease between his eyes deepened. "What?"

I pointed at the bar, leaning even closer until his cologne filled my nose. "I'm sorry I ground my ass on you. I thought you were coming onto me and I was just flirting. I misread it."

He pulled back, his eyes flicking over the room. "I wasn't at the bar."

I dropped my eyes to his silver Rolex and my stomach flipped. It wasn't the same one, his had a white face and the one on the arm at the bar had been dark, velvety blue.

Oh, God, please no. I was going to have to change my name and move to Siberia now.

A hot flush roared up my neck and I let my head fall back, squeezing my eyes shut.

"Shit," I swore. "Never mind. I'm going to go get a drink. Sorry, just forget about it."

I pivoted mortified, and made a beeline for the back of the room. I had ground on some poor, but well-endowed man's groin, by accident. He probably thought I was some kind of sex pervert.

And right now he was out there in the sea of people, wondering why I had just decided to give him a lap dance without so much as a hello.

Also...goddamn, whoever he was, he was impressive. I didn't have a lot of experience with dicks, but the length and girth of his had taken me off guard.

I was a little disappointed it hadn't turned out to be Osian's.

"Clara!"

I turned to find Candice, Yale, and the Bachs standing behind me.

"Are you ready?" Candice asked. "Everyone's getting ready to play hide-and-seek."

I stared blankly. "What?"

Mrs. Bach handed me a paper tag on a little loop. "We're doing a themed game of hide-and-seek. Here, put this bracelet on, I'm about to explain it to everyone."

I slipped on the yellow rubber bracelet stamped with my name and followed them all back into the main room. Everyone was gathered around the lifted platform and the atmosphere was brimming with excitement.

"It was either this or a dinner murder mystery," said Mrs. Bach. "But I thought everyone would be too drunk for that."

"I am a bit drunk," I admitted.

"Hopefully not too drunk to hide," Candice chimed in.

Mrs. Bach alighted the platform and clapped her hands and everyone went quiet.

"Alright, we'll draw three names out of a hat and those will be the seekers," she said. "Or, as we're calling them, the James Bonds of the evening. And the rest of you are the villains. Now, feel free to go into any unlocked room, as well as outside in the yard so long as you remain within the fence perimeters. We don't want our seekers to be traipsing through the forest trying to find you."

A ripple of laughter passed through the crowd. I glanced over my shoulder and saw Merrick, leaning against the wall with his arms crossed over his chest.

Names were drawn from a hat. Caden, a woman called Megan, and her cousin, Iwan, were picked as the seekers. They were shoved unceremoniously into a closet and Mrs. Bach set a timer while everyone fled the room.

I took a moment to pry my heels off and then I padded barefoot down the middle hallway and took a left. The house was enormous and it took less than five minutes for the laughter and shrieking to die down. Silence fell.

There was a heavy door at the end of the hall and I pushed it open, slipping into the library. I could hear breathing and I knew someone had already claimed this spot, so I kept moving, taking the back door into an old servant's staircase.

The stairs wound around and put me back out into the front hallway, close to the party room.

Footsteps sounded and I saw a flash of Caden through the doorway and I dashed backwards into a room just behind me.

It was a living area with a huge, ancient fireplace. The Bach's clearly used it as a study because every surface was covered in an artifact or curiosity. I let my eyes skim over the vintage items as I padded across the Turkish rug and pulled open one of the two doors on the far end.

It was a closet and Merrick was leaning against the wall, scrolling his phone. His eyes snapped up and narrowed.

"This is my spot," he teased.

Footsteps sounded on the other side of the door. We both froze for a second and then he grabbed my wrist, tugging me through the curtained doorway into the next room.

It was a storage area with another door on the far end. Merrick's hand slipped down my forearm and his fingers slid through mine, tugging me across the floor and pulling the door ajar. It was a small closet, empty save for a broom and a mop.

We both paused, listening. It was hard to tell if the footsteps were in the main hallway or in the study.

"Come on," he whispered.

We both ducked into the closet and he pulled the door shut save for a sliver of light. I slid back against the wall, watching him as he leaned forward to peer through.

"I think we're safe," he said.

"I thought this would be dumb at first," I breathed. "But it's kind of fun."

"I'm a sucker for shit like this," he admitted.

There was a short silence and he cleared his throat, barely audible.

"Osian gave you a gift?"

My fingers came up and pinched the necklace Osian had insisted I wear. It was a smooth oval on a white gold chain with a gem of the worst shade of bile green. He'd said it was my birthstone and I hadn't corrected him because what was the point?

How he'd fucked that up, I could only guess.

"Yeah," I sighed. "I'm going to sound like a huge brat when I say this, but it's horrible."

"Can I see?"

I unfastened it and handed it over and he held it to the light. My eyes had adjusted and I could see the acute disappointment on his face. His lips parted and he released a heavy sigh.

"Jesus."

"It's supposed to be my birthstone."

He glanced up sharply. "Your birthstone is a sapphire."

"I know."

His jaw tightened, already shadowed with stubble. It always was by this time of night.

"I think I'll make him give you something else," he said, his tone cool.

"Please, it's fine. I don't want to cause problems."

"You won't have to, that's my job."

"Please, Merrick, tonight has been embarrassing enough already."

I wasn't sure why that had slipped out. He leaned against the wall, his eyes fixed on the necklace as he turned the stone over in his fingers.

"You're not having a good night?"

"No, I am," I said, cringing internally. "I just did something really embarrassing earlier and I'm trying to pretend it never happened."

There was a slight smirk on his face as he fixed his deep blue gaze on me. I hadn't realized till now, but he'd taken off his jacket and rolled his sleeves up to his forearms. It was hot in the closet and a trickle of sweat etched between his open collar.

He smelled more natural and less like the dark oak cologne he used.

"What did you do, Clara?" he asked, amusement curling in his voice.

I huffed. "Osian has been flirting with me a ton tonight and he came up behind me at the bar and I just ground a little on him. Not a lot, just like...a little bit."

He cocked his head, brow raised.

"Anyway, so, it was not Osian," I admitted in a rush. "I have no idea who it was."

He laughed softly. "That's not that bad."

"It's mortifying. You'd be mortified if it was you."

"I don't grind on people at parties."

"No, I mean, you'd be mortified if some strange woman just ground on you."

He tilted his head, studying me closely. His mouth was turned up in a smirk, but his eyes seemed so serious. All blue steel and dark, narrowed lashes.

"I'd be understanding of her mistake," he said. "And depending on how good her ass was, I'd take it as a freebie."

"Merrick!"

"Just a joke."

I rolled my eyes, but inside, I was a little thrown off. Merrick never talked about sex with me except for that night when I'd met Osian and asked Merrick about the jewelry on the drive home. And when he'd told me that any birth control I wanted was covered under his insurance.

But even then, it had been nothing more than a throwaway comment. He'd assumed I was sexually active, but hadn't pried into it.

Of course I knew he had sex. I'd met a few people I was pretty sure he'd been involved with in the past.

But never once since I'd moved in with him had he brought anyone home or said anything about sleeping somewhere else.

It hadn't occurred to me until now how strange that was. I frowned slightly, gazing at him through the dark, tracing the sliver of light across his face. He caught my gaze and his head slid back against the wall.

"Yes, *cariad*?" His voice was husky.

I shook my head.

He gazed at me from the corner of his eye for a long moment. Then his throat bobbed and he averted his gaze. Through the shadows, a glitter of sweat trickled lower until it disappeared. Beneath his clothes.

"Is anyone coming?" I whispered.

He shook his head. "Not yet."

A smile ghosted over his face.

"What?"

"Nothing," he said, shrugging. "I just didn't expect to be still playing hide-and-seek at forty-five."

"You're never too old to have fun," I said, stepping forward so I could see through the crack. The room outside was empty. I pulled back and glanced up at him. "Not that you're old."

He laughed softly. "I must seem so to you."

I shook my head. "No...you seem like a regular age...I just feel very young sometimes."

I hadn't meant for that to come out and I mentally cringed. He turned, leaning against the wall.

"Why do you say that?"

I hated talking about myself unless it was superficial things like going out to the club or shopping with Candice. Sometimes I hated it so much I felt sick to my stomach.

I swallowed hard. This was Merrick and we were alone. If I couldn't be vulnerable with Merrick, I couldn't be with anyone.

"I just missed out on a lot growing up the way I did," I said.

He was quiet for a moment, his jaw working.

"I'm sorry. I wish I could fix everything broken for you."

My throat felt tight and oddly dry. I kept my eyes lowered and shoved down the emotion swelling in my chest.

"Thank you, Merrick," I whispered. "The things you've done for me...they mean a lot."

"It's the bare minimum," he said firmly.

The air between us felt strange and a bit too dense. For some reason it reminded me of the time I'd left a hard candy in his Audi and it melted and left a pool of cherry red on his dashboard.

Thick and sticky.

Sugary sweet, fused to the leather.

It dawned on me that I was uncomfortable being so close and it must have dawned on him too because he shifted back.

Politely, like he didn't notice the hard candy dripping down the walls and pooling around our ankles. I looked at my bare feet, tickled by the mental image.

That would probably be the closest he ever got to sugar.

"You have a very active imagination over there," he said.

I jerked my head up. "What?"

"You're just over there smiling and laughing to yourself."

"Sorry, I'm kind of...still somewhat drunk."

His brow arced and we both caught the faint sound of footsteps in the front hall. They paced back and forth and faded out. He cleared his throat softly, the space between his collarbones constricting.

"Have you ever eaten a hard candy?" I asked.

His lips parted and there was a long silence. I was slowly becoming aware that the Cosmo I'd put back right before the game started was hitting my bloodstream.

My head spun pleasantly and I had the intense urge to giggle.

"I don't know."

"Really?"

He gazed at me for a long moment, face blank.

"I can't tell if you're being euphemistic," he said.

That jolted me, making me flush. If I hadn't been drunk I would have apologized and probably walked out, but I was feeling exceptionally stupid.

"What does that mean?" I pressed.

He shook his head once.

"Can I ask you another question."

He didn't say yes, but he didn't say no. He just waited. Before I could open my mouth and ask him something wildly inappropriate that I was going to regret tomorrow, the door swung open to reveal Caden.

"Tag, you're it, motherfuckers," he drawled.

"It's hide and seek, asshole," said Merrick, stepping out of the closet.

I stumbled out, blinking, and we handed our wristbands over to Caden. He had a whole collection on his arm so I guessed we probably wouldn't have long before the game wound down.

"I'm going to have a glass of wine," I said.

Merrick's hand shot out and closed around my wrist.

"No, you're going home," he said.

Caden walked away without another word, onto the next thing. I gave Merrick the biggest pair of puppy eyes I could muster, but he remained unswayed.

"You are very drunk. And tired."

"Merrick, please."

"It's past midnight."

I relented, nodding. The thought of having a hot shower and crawling into bed with some ice water did sound tantalizing.

We left the study and Merrick located Mrs. Bach to thank her for the party while I found my shoes. Then he helped me downstairs and settled me into the passenger seat of the Audi.

"Jesus, it's hot," he said, getting in and flipping on the air conditioning.

We were both quiet on the drive home. When we pulled up to the front door where he always dropped me before putting the Audi away, he put the car in park.

I watched through a haze as he reached into his pocket and held something out to me.

"What is it?" I whispered.

There was a rustle in his fingers.

"Open," he said.

I obeyed, unsure why it felt so reflexive. His fingers came so close to my lips I felt their heat and something slipped between my teeth. Hard, smooth, and spreading a sweet cherry taste over my tongue.

I smiled.

Hard candy.

He bent over the console and lifted my hand, brushing his lips over my knuckles.

70

"Happy birthday, Clara," he said softly.

CHAPTER NINE

MERRICK

I wasn't happy with how Osian had handled her birthday.

A few days after her party, I drove to the east side of Providence to one of Rhys Cardiff's new hotels. It was a garish thing, towering over my beloved city. An eyesore that bothered me every time I laid eyes on it.

He was the type to build an ugly hotel on the river just so everyone had to look at his name over the front door. Rhys was the kind of wealthy that made me want to look down my nose at him like he was something stuck to my shoe.

He checked every box. Designer clothes, fast cars, pretty women who weren't his wife. The problem was, he made a lot of money and he was a good businessman. His company was expanding into Providence whether I liked it or not so I was going to make sure the organization got a cut.

May as well get what I could out of him.

That morning I'd put on one of my custom suits and neatly slicked back my hair. Then I stared at myself in the mirror for several minutes before going to change into the kind of clothes Rhys Cardiff wore. A suit jacket over an open necked white shirt. Casual, a little douchey. Completed by the Rolex glittering on my wrist.

I looked like one of them—the kind of man I would make sure Clara never ended up marrying. Perhaps I was wrong, but Osian didn't strike me as the same sort of person as his father.

Pulling into the hotel parking lot, I put the Audi in park. My gaze caught on my watch, glittering in the sun. Mocking me with the memory of what she'd done to me at the bar. My dick twitched in my pants and I tore my eyes away.

It was an accident. That was all.

I ran a hand over my jaw and pulled the car keys free. A long time ago, Caden had pulled me aside and given me a warning about letting Clara live with me and that memory was resurfacing in the front of my mind.

"I know you're twenty-one years older," he'd said. "But you're still a man. And she's young, but she's still a woman."

"It's not like that," I'd said swiftly.

He shrugged. "Living together is a risky thing. It means you'll see her in the early morning...you'll know what she smells like when she's just out of the shower."

Something stirred in me, even then, at the idea of seeing Clara freshly out of the shower. Face bare, hair wet, staining her t-shirt. Or maybe just dripping down her naked back to the towel wrapped around her body.

"I have impeccable self control," I said firmly.

He raised a brow, unmoved. "Just make sure you set down boundaries and stick to them. Especially if you're both single."

"What do you mean?" I murmured, pretending it didn't really matter.

"I mean, one thing leads to another. One night you decide to release a little tension with each other. Doesn't mean anything, does it? Except then she's in your bed the next night and the next. And where does that go? You can't marry her, Merrick. So it ends in tears. Ugliness. Breaking her heart—"

"That's a little over the line," I'd said. "Especially for you."

I would rather die than break Clara's heart.

I adjusted my aviators, got out of the car, and strode up the front walkway. The shiny floors clicked beneath my shoes as I crossed the room, unbothered by the hostess who clearly knew who I was, and stepped out onto the patio.

Osian sat at a table with Vincent Galt and Will Donaldson, both of whom I was friends with independently of business, both in the same trade of buying and selling investment real estate. They rose as I entered, but I shook my head, sitting down at the table.

"Merrick, how are you?" Will said, sitting back and crossing his legs.

"Good, mind if I smoke?"

They shook their heads. I rarely smoked, but I was a little annoyed and I needed something to take the edge off.

I crossed one leg over the other and settled back. Boats etched their way down the river and sunlight glittered on the water. Vincent took a pack of cigarettes out, but I shook my head. I had my own, hand rolled in Providence from my favorite tobacco shop.

"What brings you out to the east side?" Osian asked.

There was a hint of wariness to his tone. Like he wasn't sure what to expect.

Good. I hoped I scared him shitless.

"I came to have a chat with you, Cardiff," I said, lighting a cigarette. I hadn't taken off my sunglasses and I could tell not being able to see my eyes was bothering him.

"Well, I'm just finishing up a meeting," Osian said.

I settled back. "Good, I'll be happy to sit in on the end of it. As one of your closest business partners and the guardian of your future wife."

That pissed him off, I saw it in the flash of his eyes. In the furrowing of his scarred brow. Vincent and Will cleared their throats at the same time and began gathering up their things.

"Let's reconvene later," said Vincent.

They exchanged a nod and disappeared. Then it was just Osian and I, staring at each other from across the table. Feeling the tension grow like ice on a windowpane.

I had picked this man out of dozens of options for Clara. She trusted me with her future, she trusted my opinion. But Osian had failed the first test and that lit my fuse. I wanted him to suffer just enough that he wouldn't make her feel forgotten or disrespected.

He needed a fire lit under his ass and I was happy to strike the match.

I hadn't intended on coming here to fuck with him, but now that he was squirming, I wasn't so sure.

Maybe I *would* fuck with him.

Give him a taste of what might happen if he put a toe out of line with Clara. I liked that, that sounded like fun.

Osian pushed back his chair. "Going to take a piss."

He ducked into the restaurant and strode across the room and disappeared into the back hallway. I stabbed out my cigarette and strode after him.

The bathroom was black marble with silk orchids along each mirror. It smelled sharp, like antiseptic mixed with male cologne. My shoes clipped on the floor as I turned the corner, heading for the urinal on the far end.

Osian stood at the one by the door. What kind of fucking psycho chose the urinal right by the door?

I unfastened the front of my pants and relieved myself. He was painfully aware of me, I could feel his discomfort. I took my time, letting him stew. Then I turned my head for the barest second, my eyes meeting his.

Looking at him like he was nothing. A roach crushed under the heel of my shoe. Then I snorted quietly through my nose and zipped my pants and went to the sink to wash my hands.

I heard his zipper and then water rushed at the far sink.

"What the fuck is going on?"

I turned, water still dripping from my hands. "I'm taking a piss. Got a problem with that?"

"Is this some kind of dick measuring contest?" he asked, moving towards me slowly.

Admirable. He wasn't running.

I cocked my head. "Me in a dick measuring contest with you? No, even I'm not that cruel."

He flushed and I saw him hold himself back. That was a delicious part about all of this—he couldn't do a fucking thing about it. He was tied hook, line, and sinker by his daddy's money. And his daddy wanted him to go through with this marriage to Clara.

"What is your problem?" he spat. "I've done everything that's expected. She got her birthday present."

I pushed my hand in my pocket, walking toward him until he was backed up to the door. His chest flushed between the collar of his shirt. I could taste his fear, rising off his body like smoke.

"The necklace you gave Clara was a fucking travesty," I said. "From here on out, any and all gifts will be run by me first. I don't care what it is. You send her flowers, ask for my approval and permission. Understood?"

His eyes narrowed and his jaw hardened.

"You're a little too protective."

"It's my job."

"Are you the reason she's still a fucking virgin at twenty-four?"

Internally, I reeled, but I kept my face blank. Clara was a virgin? Was that why she didn't use my health insurance except for her occasional visits to the gynecologist? I'd assumed up until now that she was just using condoms when she slept with men.

I'd also assumed she was just shy about openly discussing the topic of sex.

She wasn't shy.

She wasn't anything yet.

The knowledge that she hadn't had sex yet roused something ugly in me. Was she scared of Osian? Was he putting pressure on her to sleep with him? Anger simmered and I took another step toward him.

"How do you know she's a virgin?" I asked.

He shrugged. "She told me."

"Why did she tell you?"

"Because I'm going to be her fucking husband."

Those words, for whatever reason, sent a wave of anger pouring through me. It was all I could do to keep still and not let my emotions show. He pivoted and disappeared around the corner. I remained where I was, wondering why my mouth was so dry. I pulled my hand from my pocket and opened it. Nail marks, red and sharp in my palm.

Right below the silver band of my Rolex.

I ran into Vincent on my way out and we talked for several minutes. He invited me to come spend a week at his lodge in the Adirondacks . There would be a lot of our peers there, all the prominent businessmen who mattered, and it would be a good opportunity to network.

Spending a week in the mountains didn't sound bad.

"Alright," I said. "I'll be there."

"You're free to bring someone. Maybe bring a date if it'll keep you in line."

"I'm not seeing anyone right now," I said.

"You haven't for a while."

"Maybe I'm just getting too old for rampant sex."

"I truly doubt that."

I laughed, taking it on the chin. Vincent and I strolled down the front walkway to the parking lot. He pushed his sunglasses on and clicked the remote for his car twice. It beeped several yards away.

"You know, I have a niece who would love to meet you," he said.

I shook my head. "You have a niece who wants a normal man. Not the Welsh *Brenin*. Be honest."

He shrugged. "Well, If you change your mind, I'm sure she'd at least like to have a nice evening with you. That's all anyone wants anymore...just casual dating. Everyone's too scared to just commit."

"Your age is showing, Vince."

I opened my car and settled in the front seat. "I'm sure she's lovely, but I'm not looking to be in a relationship with anyone right now. And I wouldn't dream of pumping and dumping your niece."

"You're a man of integrity, if nothing else," he said.

I stopped on my way back into town at my aunt, Ophelia's house. She'd retired from active participation in the organization a long time ago and lived in a huge farmhouse outside Providence. Her wife, Daphne, was the person I owed everything to, the first person to look at me and tell me I was destined for greatness.

Sometimes that made me grateful.

Sometimes it fostered a deep resentment.

I'd never met two more different people than my aunts. Daphne was bold, adventurous, and maybe a little reckless. Ophelia was kind, dreamy, and preferred a quiet life.

She'd only been eighteen when my parents died and I fell into her care. I'd watched her grow up alongside me. My earliest memory was being in her lap, her lips pressing to my forehead and her protective arms around me.

Keeping me safe, letting me be gentle before I was forced to be cruel.

Daphne had stepped in at that point.

It was a pity that organization rules forbade her from becoming a soldier. Her progressive father had trained her anyway, but the former *Brenin* vetoed her request for a special exception to join our soldiers. So, instead, she walked away from the organization and assumed her training days were over.

And then I came along.

Daphne saw my talent early. I was a scrappy, lean boy who caused a lot of trouble. My aunts saved up to send me to a fancy private grade school. Two days in, I had militarized the six-year-olds and led a revolution in the school yard for extra recess time.

Ophelia picked me up, wringing her hands. "Honey, you can't do this. You'll get expelled."

Daphne smirked from the back seat where we sat together, her arm around my shoulders.

"I think it showed remarkable talent," she said.

"Don't encourage him," Ophelia said, sending her a glare in the rearview mirror.

But Daphne did encourage me. She took my side when I fought in school, she argued Ophelia out of punishing me for my constant distraction, and she advocated for after school activities that would help run all my incessant energy out. She could see I was different and she never once made me feel like that was a bad thing.

It was Daphne who made me who I was, who honed my skills and put me on the path to becoming *Brenin*. When Ophelia said she wanted me to leave the organization behind, it was Daphne who stood in her way.

"The boy needs to be trained," she insisted. "You can't just leave the organization. It's been a part of us for hundreds of years, it's in our blood."

"I don't want him like that," Ophelia sniffed. "Cruel and cold like the rest of the men."

"We can only do our best. But that boy's blood will tell him who he is whether you do or not."

They both turned and looked at me, eight-years-old. Eating a sandwich at the kitchen table. Sometimes I thought back to that moment and wondered what the fuck Daphne had been thinking when she looked at a little boy and decided to put him on the path of greatness.

A path that, sometimes, could be so painful.

"He's strong, smart. He could be *Brenin* someday."

Ophelia gasped, going pale. "Daphne, you know what he'd have to do to become the Welsh King. I never, ever want my son to set foot in that arena. Ever."

But Daphne defied her pleas. She taught me to fight, to shoot, to use a blade. She trained me hard through my childhood until it was time to hand me over to the base where the organization minted its soldiers.

And the rest was history.

They were both getting older and the sight gave me pause as I pulled into the drive. Daphne was graying, but she was still lean and well muscled and brimming with energy. Ophelia dyed her hair red, piling it up on her head, her brightly colored earrings dangling to her shoulders. They stood on the porch, arm in arm—a domestic oasis in the chaos of my life.

Sometimes I wondered if they'd wanted children of their own. Perhaps my sudden presence had crushed their future plans, leaving them with a little boy they'd never planned for or desired.

I'd never asked because I knew what they would say.

"Hush," Daphne would exclaim, slapping me gently on the back of the head. "You're our boy, we've always wanted you."

I got out of the Audi and climbed onto the porch, taking off my sunglasses so I could kiss them both on the cheek. Daphne leaned around me, squinting at my car. Disappointment passed over her face.

"Is Clara not with you?" she asked. "I thought she was back from school."

"She is," I said, following them into the house. "She's just not with me today. I had business on the east side."

"So what's she up to?" Ophelia asked, busying herself at the stove.

I took a seat at the kitchen table in the same chair I'd been sitting in for three decades. Worn, but clean and sturdy. Handmade with love by Daphne.

"Well, she's getting engaged next summer," I said. "So long as everything goes as planned."

They both pivoted, glancing at each other. I hated that look, the look that said they'd had a private conversation about this topic at one point.

"That's good, dear," said Ophelia, brows creased. "Who did you pick for her?"

"Osian Cardiff."

"Rhys Cardiff's son?" Daphne asked. "He's a bit...fast."

I nodded, spreading my knees and leaning back in the chair. The kitchen smelled good, like the fresh bread Ophelia was just now taking from the oven. She cut a piece and slathered it, still steaming, with butter and jam and put it before me.

I balked, instinctively glancing at Daphne. Old habits died hard.

"Honey, you know Merrick doesn't eat bread," Daphne said gently. "Can I get you some coffee instead?"

Ophelia looked so disappointed as she took the plate up that I grabbed her wrist and accepted it.

"For you, I'd eat anything," I said, patting her back.

She bent and her lips brushed the top of my head. I felt her still, holding me for a beat longer than usual. Her fingers skimmed down my side and around to my upper spine.

"Are you checking to make sure I'm not losing weight?" I asked.

She pulled back, arranging her apron. "What? Absolutely not."

"Ophelia," I said. "You're not fooling anyone. I'm a very healthy weight for my height and body type. I just had my physical the other month."

"Fine. You're just looking so lean, Merrick, and I don't like it. You can put on a little weight, it's alright."

Daphne put a stained, diner mug down in front of me, brimming with black coffee.

"You know it's not about that," she said, brushing Ophelia's arm.

"It's fine," Ophelia said, still wringing her hands. She kissed me again and went back to the sink. "You know I just worry about you all the time, Merrick, I'm not trying to get on your case."

"I know, darling," I said. "I wish I could be less worrisome."

Daphne waved a hand and sank down opposite me, her own cup of coffee in her fist. "So how's the organization going?"

"It's very good, high stress right now, but we're growing and expanding," I said. "This business deal I'm about to sign with Rhys Cardiff once Clara is officially engaged will pay for the new training base."

"I wish I could go out there," said Daphne wistfully. "Just to see it."

Ophelia sent her a sharp look. "You're retired, love."

"I know, I am."

I shifted in my chair, turning to face Daphne fully. "Ophelia will kill me, but a spot as a teacher at the base here is always open for you. You know they still call you a kingmaker."

She laughed and waved a hand airily.

"I made one king and that's enough for me," she said.

It felt good to just sit in their kitchen. We bickered good-naturedly back and forth for a bit and had a few more cups of coffee between the three of us. I told them more about Clara and Osian, but they didn't seem very happy about the match.

After a while, I pushed back my chair and stood. "I need to be getting back. Clara is probably home and she'll want to have dinner together."

Ophelia was loading the dishwasher and she glanced up casually.

"It's sweet you two spend so much time together," she said.

"We're good friends," I said. "I like her company."

She exchanged that look with her wife again, the annoying one that let me know I was out of the loop. Daphne got to her feet, moving slower than she had the last time I'd visited.

It was hard to see them age. A part of me had hoped they'd never get old, never have to leave me.

"Let me get some jam for Clara," Ophelia said. "I just picked the blackberries in the south field and made so much jam I don't know what to do with it all. I know you won't eat it, but she will."

I ignored the side of guilt she served that statement with—it was out of love and I appreciated it.

Ophelia disappeared down the cellar stairs with a basket and I stepped out onto the porch. Daphne joined me, passing me a cigarette. She made her own, rolled them herself. I accepted it and we smoked in silence for a long moment. Looking out over the rolling fields and woods in the distance.

"You're looking for something," Daphne observed.

Her dark eyes roved over my face and I felt naked. She was sharp as a razor and could read complete strangers like a book. Despite my best efforts, I'd never been able to conceal my thoughts from her piercing gaze.

"Can I tell you something?" I said softly.

"Anything."

"It's...a bit embarrassing," I said, keeping my eyes on the horizon.

She narrowed her eyes and released a stream of smoke. But she didn't speak and I was grateful for that. Daphne had never judged me, no matter how many times I'd screwed up.

And I'd screwed up a lot.

"Clara's birthday party was last week. Osian Cardiff was there and we were wearing the same watch. At one point in the night, I came up behind her to get my drink and she did something to me, thinking I was Osian."

Her brows drew together.

"She...ground on me. I disappeared before she could turn around so she doesn't know it was me."

Daphne shrugged once, her brow arced. "It was a mistake, right?"

I nodded hard. "But I...um...I had a bit of a reaction to it."

"A reaction?"

My neck went incredibly warm. "You know."

"I'm not sure—oh...oh, I see." Her mouth twitched and she shook her head, smiling. "You want to know if that makes you a bad person?"

"I stayed awake the entire night, running it through my head like a fucking movie."

There was a long silence and I started wishing I hadn't said anything. She released a heavy sigh and turned to me, putting a hand on my upper arm.

"You're not going to like what I have to say," she said. "But here goes. You're a man in your prime, Merrick, and she's a grown woman. I'm sure she's thought about you like that before."

I shook my head. "Clara and I aren't like that."

"Oh, I wouldn't be so quick to assume."

She was wrong, of course she was. Clara was innocent, physically as well as mentally it turned out, and she wasn't thinking of her guardian like that. My throat tightened and I released a heavy sigh.

"I...I don't know what to do now," I admitted. "I think I might be attracted to her, but it could also be that...well, I haven't been having sex. For a while."

"Do you love her?"

A shock moved through my chest, unsettling me to my core.

"I love her in a platonic way," I said. "But nothing else."

She didn't believe me, I could see it in the sharp twist of her mouth.

"Does it hurt to look at her?"

She laid her worn hand on my chest, right over my heart. It was comforting and my throat tightened even more. I let my eyes drop to the floorboards of the porch. Ones that I'd run over a hundred times in my bare feet as a little boy.

"Does what hurt?"

She patted my chest. "Does it hurt here when you think about her?"

I swallowed with difficulty.

"Sometimes. But I don't fucking know why."

She heard the catch in my throat and she hugged me, nestling her head against my chest. For a fleeting moment I wished I was young again and my aunts could just handle all of my problems.

But I was a man, molded by fire. Hardened by steel.

I kissed her head and untangled myself just as Ophelia emerged with a basket of jam for Clara. I accepted it and waved goodbye and disappeared down the driveway.

Still just as confused as before.

That night, I took Clara out to dinner at our favorite restaurant in downtown Providence. She was talkative, telling me how Osian wanted to take her out to see a movie at the historic theater next week.

Then she told me a salacious story about how she'd caught Candice making out with Yale in the back of his car. Parked out in the street and everything.

Could I believe it? Candice was just in denial, wasn't she?

I was quiet, watching her in the soft candlelight. In the distance, the river lapped at the shoreline and all around us people chatted among themselves. A night bird wailed. A ship sent the hollow echo of its horn over the water.

Life moved on. Oblivious to how an accidental touch had thrown my entire world off balance.

Across the table, Clara glittered in a pink sweatshirt and black leggings, dressed down for our outdoor dinner. As always, her makeup was done and tonight she wore that shade of lipstick somewhere between red and dark pink.

Like she'd bitten into a ripe blackberry and the juice stained her lips.

Sweet and tart.

As she talked, I became slowly aware of the feeling Daphne had been looking for when she laid her palm on my chest. A tightness beneath my ribs. A little ache where my calloused heart beat fast.

Does it hurt when you look at her?

Yes, yes it did.

CHAPTER TEN

CLARA

Osian picked me up at eight the day he'd promised to take me to the cinema. Despite pretending all week that I was looking forward to it, I had mixed feelings about the date.

He'd been so handsy during our first meeting, and that had been with his parents and Merrick in the same room. I was dreading how it would be when he got me alone in his car.

It was stupid, people went out on dates alone all the time.

It took me almost an hour just to pick an outfit that didn't feel like I was showing too much skin. I finally decided on a vintage style sweater, cropped jeans, and sneakers. I finished it off with a touch of lipstick, but no jewelry.

Turning in the mirror, I looked myself over. Good, it was conservative, but pretty.

Merrick was in the kitchen on his laptop, working quietly, when Osian arrived. I could tell he was dying to walk into the hallway and rake Osian over with that death glare.

"Please, be good," I'd begged him earlier. "I think he's terrified of you."

"Good," said Merrick. "I hope he pisses his pants."

He didn't look up from his computer to see me roll my eyes and flounce out of the room.

Osian walked into the hall, looking rich and careless in his expensive clothes. The curl over his eyebrow was in top form tonight. He probably used gel to work it into that perfect shape so it would hang just right.

The idea of him fussing with his hair tickled me.

He bent, cradling my elbow, and kissed my cheek. It didn't feel intrusive as I'd expected...it just felt normal. Like I was a regular girl going out on a regular date with a nice guy.

My stomach did a little flip. It was a new experience being touched by a man.

"Is Merrick here?" he asked stiffly.

"Um...yeah," I said. "Did you want to talk to him?"

Osian gave a quick nod. I hesitated, but he didn't explain, so I went to the kitchen. Merrick glanced up, stretched his long legs out and cracked his neck.

"I thought you were leaving," he said.

"Osian wants to speak with you first," I said.

His jaw worked, but he didn't say anything, he just walked past me into the front hall. I came around the corner and they both looked at me and then at each other.

"Do you mind to wait in your room, Clara?" Merrick said.

He had his stern face on, the vaguely paternal one. A hint of rebellion rose in me and I stalled, frowning.

Osian was going to be my fiancé next year and Merrick was my guardian. Whatever they were discussing likely had to do with me and I hated that they didn't consider me serious enough to be included.

"Clara," said Merrick.

"Why?" I cocked my head. Challenging him.

"Not everything is your concern."

Osian was getting uncomfortable. He shifted his weight, pushing his hand into his pocket. There was a little bit of confusion in the power dynamic. I could feel it.

Osian would be my husband someday and, according to organization rules, he would be my male guardian. But right now, in this moment, I was Merrick's ward.

And, on top of that, Merrick was *Brenin*.

He held the ultimate trump card.

I could tell that bothered Osian. His jaw tensed and he looked away.

Oddly enough, I found I was enjoying this a little bit. Watching them measure their metaphorical dicks against each other. Even though I knew Merrick was going to win out in the end. He always did.

"Is this about me?" I pressed.

"It's not women's business," said Osian shortly.

"If it concerns me, it's my business."

Merrick's jaw twitched and he crossed to me, cradling my elbow. I didn't want to look like a child being dragged from the room so I went with him as he ushered me down the hall. We paused outside my bedroom door and I sent him a heavy glare.

"Do we have a problem, *cariad*?" he said quietly.

I crossed my arms. He was a lot taller than me...how had I never noticed that he practically towered over me? His body was far broader than I remembered. In fact, it seemed to fill out a doorway despite his graceful build.

I was caged between his chest and my closed door. His gaze bored into me, waiting for me to answer.

I'd never noticed up until now, but he had such an intense stare. Made all the more stark by his thick, black lashes.

His lips parted.

My teeth began working that spot in my mouth again. I was fighting not to have another of those odd, intrusive thoughts about him, but it was almost impossible when he was so close I could feel his body heat.

It occurred to me as I looked up into his familiar face that there was a side to Merrick that was completely unknown to me. A side to him that he concealed behind closed bedroom doors.

I'd watched a little bit of porn before out of curiosity and I'd read a few smutty romances. I wasn't born yesterday, I knew what people did in bed with each other.

Out of the blue, it was hitting me that Merrick did all those things. He fucked, he talked dirty, he moaned, he got vulnerable and naked.

And yet...it was unimaginable.

"Clara?"

The word shot through me like cold water and I jerked my face up to his, my cheeks heating.

"What the hell is going on with you?"

I turned on my heel and shut myself in my room. Merrick didn't pursue me, he just went back down the hall. I heard their voices rising and falling and then Osian knocked gently on my door.

We watched a movie together in an almost empty theater. Then I let him kiss me in the car behind the building.

My body stayed quiet, hyper aware of how he responded. He tasted a bit like mouthwash, it was on the back of his tongue when he pushed it past my teeth. Gagging me a little.

He didn't seem to mind that I was slow to relax. It was more about him and what he was doing to me than anything else.

There was a kind of confusing violence to his arousal.

He kissed me and he wanted more. More of my mouth, more of my tongue. He started on my neck with fluttery kisses and ended with bites that stung. He sucked the skin above my neckline and left a purple mark. That was a little exciting.

He rolled his seat back and pulled me onto his lap. His eyes glinted in the dark, his face half lit by a streetlamp.

"Can I take your sweater off?" he panted.

For a moment, I considered saying no. But then I remembered the realization I'd had in the hall.

I remembered that Merrick fucked and, for some reason, that made me a little angry.

"Yes," I whispered.

My sweater slipped over my head and fell into the passenger seat. Baring my upper body. My heart began pounding as his eyes fell on my lace bra. Just thick enough to cover my nipples.

"Fuck, your tits are bigger than I thought they'd be," he breathed.

He didn't ask permission when he took my bra off, freeing my breasts. I didn't stop him. My heart was fluttering too fast and my mouth was dry. The lace cups fell away and his eyes widened slightly.

I was a C cup, so I wasn't exactly huge, but then I wasn't really small either. My nipples were a pink-brown color. The soft skin of my breasts was pale and showed the network of stretch marks and blue veins beneath.

He looked hungry.

A little shiver moved down my spine. Not a nice one.

His eyes met mine and he brushed back my hair, holding it in his fist at the nape of my neck. My left breast tingled as he cupped it. Working the sensitive nipple with his thumb. It was overstimulating and I writhed slightly, wishing he would stop.

"I'm going to give you the first piece of jewelry next month," he said.

Sweat started in the middle of my naked back.

"I can't stop fucking thinking about it," he panted.

"About what?" I managed.

He bent and kissed my breast. "Getting all my jewelry on you. Every piece."

I gasped as his mouth closed over my nipple. Sucking and pulling back with a sharp pop.

"You're so hot," he murmured. "Fuck, baby girl, you've got the perfect body. Tight, just the right amount of ass and tits."

That bothered me, not because I hated my body. It was fine. Did I sometimes wish it was different? Of course, but that was normal. No, his words made me uncomfortable because they made me feel small.

Pinned in his fist and helpless to move, but not in a nice way.

He nuzzled my neck, his breath hot in my ear.

"I want your clit pierced for me," he breathed. "I can't stop thinking about my diamonds tucked between your legs. I'll bet you have the tightest, sluttiest pussy."

Oh. My. God.

I swallowed hard to keep myself from gagging. He pulled on my hips, shifting me closer, and I felt his erection under his pants. Hard and terrifying.

My whole body pulled back. Closing up like a sensitive plant. The space between my legs was about as wet as the Sahara Desert.

Red flags were popping up like fireworks in the back of my brain. It wasn't that I was offended by his comment. It was the way he said it. Like my vagina wasn't attached to a real human. Just a perfectly shaped place for him to get off in.

My stomach twisted.

I thought I knew why Candice got uneasy around him now. The man she'd lost her virginity to was rough and selfish. He'd pushed her face into the bed, told her to get on her knees. He'd taken her virginity the only way he knew how, the way the world had taught him.

Then he'd put on his pants and left.

I was worried Osian would do the same. And my heart couldn't take that.

"You okay?"

I blinked and Osian's face swam back into view. He'd stopped kissing my neck and he'd pulled back. Thank God.

"Can...can I go home?" I whispered. "Sorry, I'm...we're moving a little fast."

His lips pressed into a thin line and he shifted back in his seat. I could tell he was disappointed as he helped me back into my clothes. Of course he was. As always, the threat of Merrick loomed heavy over me.

Touch her and die.

We drove home in silence and I let him kiss me briefly. Then he walked me to the door and I let myself in, locking it behind me.

The house was dark and I knew Merrick was probably already asleep. I worked my shoes off and went to my room to shower. Then, hair wet and dressed in a baggy sweatshirt that reached my knees, I padded into the kitchen for a drink.

I took my wine out into the front room and turned on the lamp. From up above, there was a scuffle. Then I heard Merrick's even tread on the floor.

Down the hall.

Down the stairs.

He appeared in the doorway, one hand rested on the wall. I paused, mid swallow, and gazed at him in the darkness.

He wore a white t-shirt, tight over his torso. His lower half was covered in a pair of gray sweatpants.

Thin gray sweatpants.

My whole body tensed.

I'd never seen him in casual pants before and I was struggling not to stare. The problem was, I could see the lean ridges of his pecs and abs right over the waistband. And lower...well, there was a faint rise beneath his pants. Like he wasn't wearing boxer briefs, like he'd just rolled out of bed and pulled on his sweats.

"Are you alright?" he said.

His voice was husky and his hair was rumpled. He'd been sleeping and I'd woken him. Guilt twinged in my chest.

His eyes softened as he gazed down at me and a lump rose in my throat.

The waterworks started and I blinked rapidly, dipping my head and taking a sip of my wine. I heard him move across the carpet. He knelt before me so we were eye to eye.

His hand came up. Warm. So big it engulfed the side of my head.

He brushed back my hair and tilted my chin up.

"Clara, you can always talk to me," he said softly. "About anything."

I swallowed hard, choking back everything I wanted to say. Pushing down all my fear, all my secrets. The pink V card in my wallet, the terrifying future looming over me.

The problem was, it was too big. It just crawled back up my throat and came spilling out along with my tears.

"I'm scared," I whispered.

His mouth parted. "Why?"

He was the perfect listener, attentive and quiet. I felt the dam burst and I spilled out everything to him.

Face burning, I told him I was a virgin and that Candice wasn't. I told him about the man she'd slept with and how she'd felt after. I told him I never wanted to feel like that, but I was worried Osian might be the sort of person who would make me.

Even though I had no real reason to believe he would.

His face never changed. When I was done, the room went completely silent. My whole body burned, itching for him to speak. After a while, he released a breath and met my gaze.

There was violence in his eyes. Tempered, bridled. But there all the same.

I blinked, taken aback.

"Merrick," I whispered.

He rose and paced across the room and paced back. Then he went to the bar cart in the corner and poured a drink.

"He stopped when you asked him to, right?" he said evenly.

"Yes, Osian hasn't done anything," I said. "That wasn't the point of what I was saying. He respects my refusal and he hasn't pushed me to do anything I didn't consent to."

He raised the glass to his mouth. Usually I could read Merrick pretty well, but there were so many mixed signals coming off him I didn't have a hope of understanding what was locked inside his head.

"I understand what you're telling me," he said. "You've been taught that sex is unsafe. That it's...rough."

I swallowed.

"I'm sorry for that, Clara. You shouldn't have to fear intimacy."

I emptied my wine. If I hadn't been so tired and tipsy, I wouldn't have had the courage to ask him the question bouncing around in my head.

"Is it for you?"

My voice was barely audible, but he heard me. And he froze. The bare skin at the base of his throat flushed. His chest expanded, filling out his shirt even more. Showing every curve of his pecs.

"What?"

Tears threatened to fall. Pushing against my lids.

"Are you rough when you sleep with women?" I whispered.

His mouth parted. An eon passed in the front room of Merrick's house. He worked his jaw, glancing down and back up again.

"Do you want the honest answer to that?"

"I want the truth."

"Sex is complicated, Clara," he said, his voice hoarse. "There are a lot of different ways to be intimate with someone. I'd like to think that I'm gentle. I...I like giving pleasure over getting it. But there have been times in my life when, under the right consensual circumstances, I have been quite...rough."

I swallowed, unsure what exactly he meant.

"But rough sex isn't appropriate for someone's first time," he said firmly. "Do you know the man Candice slept with?"

I nodded.

"Who was he?"

"Am I signing his death sentence by telling you?"

"I just want to talk to him."

"You should ask Candice about it then."

His broad jaw worked, dusky with stubble. In the darkness, when he turned his head, his profile was stark. Strong chin, straight bridged nose, thin mouth, thick lashes.

"Please don't say anything to Osian. This is my problem, not his," I whispered. "I just need to deal with my own shit."

He hesitated, eyes fixed on me.

"Sometimes I just need someone to listen, Merrick. I'm not looking for you to fix my problems."

His lids flickered. "I know, *cariad.*"

That single word tamped down the anxiety in my chest. I rubbed the tear trails from my face and got up, walking my wine glass to the kitchen. He followed me, leaning in the doorway. His face was shadowed. Unreadable.

I felt his gaze bore into me as I pulled the dishwasher open and started loading it. Steam clung to my face. Soothing the reddened skin. His eyes followed my every move, but he resisted the urge to tell me I was loading the dishes wrong.

"Do you want to come to upstate New York with me this week?" he asked.

I straightened. There was something in his voice. Temperance. Strain, like he was walking a fine line.

"Why are you going there?"

"Vincent Galt is having some people up to his lodge," he said. "I'll have some business meetings, but I should have some free time. You can do what you like. Drink Cosmos and soak in the hot tub."

Yes, God, yes, I wanted that. Of course I did. Somehow, without even having to speak my desires aloud, he understood them.

I nodded hard. "Yeah, I would like that. A lot."

CHAPTER ELEVEN

MERRICK

I didn't kill the man who had taken Candice's virginity, but I did make him regret his choices. Yale knew his name and he knew the story. He didn't have any problem spilling who it was—not one of my men—and I paid him a visit.

He worked in the same complex as Gretchen. I didn't hurt him, I just sat him down and asked him a few questions. Then I had him put his hand on the desk. Palm down, flat. I traced the shape of it with a knife into the wood. Leaving a reminder for him to think twice next time.

He whimpered.

That was fine, I was into that.

Adrenaline always got me hyperaroused, hyperfocused. I needed to work it off before I went home to Clara.

So I went to the warehouse and beat the shit out of the standing bag. Exhausted, I showered in the locker room in the private area. There was no one around so I indulged myself and jerked off. It was nice while it lasted and my brain behaved itself and stayed blank. But as soon as I was done, I felt antsy again.

Clara was already packed when I got back. Her berry pink and black striped bags were piled by the door. I passed by them and walked into the kitchen to find her making a thermos full of coffee and peppermint cream.

Her damp hair was tied up on top of her head, but there was a tendril tickling the nape of her neck.

Caden had been right about one thing.

I could look at her wet hair and know exactly what it smelled like.

Dark jasmine.

She was quiet on the drive to the landing strip where I kept my private plane. I glanced at her a few times. She looked so sleepy and cozy, curled up with her empty thermos in her lap.

God, I loved just existing in her vicinity.

Without thinking, I reached out and patted her knee. Her head swung around and she fixed wide, dark eyes on me. There was a moment of silence. The radio murmured, too low to be intelligible.

"Are you alright?"

She nodded.

"Just tired?"

She shook her head. "I'm...just having some trouble adjusting to everything. I never really had to think about what came next when I was in school. I just took it day by day. But now...now I have this whole future planned out. It's weird for me."

"I understand."

I wasn't sure why I'd said that because it wasn't really true. I had always been the master of my ship.

Clara had never had the luxury of choosing anything. Growing up, she was forced to be obedient and quiet. Barely looked at as more than a piece of furniture. As my ward, she was spoiled with luxury and given anything she desired.

But she wasn't really free.

The lodge was half empty when we arrived around nine that night. Vincent Galt greeted us on the porch, shaking my hand and brushing his lips over the back of Clara's fingers.

"Miss Prothero," he said, cocking his head. "You are stunning. Osian is a lucky man."

She flushed slightly, but kept her chin up. "Thank you, sir."

97

"Oh, no, call me Vince," he said. "We'll see a lot of each other over the next week. You'll love it up here in the mountains, it does a person good. I always tell my wife there's nothing that can revive you like fresh, mountain air."

"It's lovely," Clara said, letting him usher her into the front room of the lodge.

It was a huge space with three stories and vaulted ceilings. The interior was perfect for business with its classy, cherry wood tables and black leather couches. I was glad to see the hot tubs steaming outside and the bar along the far wall.

"I'm going to go meet up with my wife for a late dinner," Vincent said. "But I'll see you tomorrow morning."

He kissed Clara's cheek and shook my hand again. Before he left, he flagged down an employee and had them carry our bags down the hallway.

I moved to the front desk, Clara just behind me. There was a severe looking woman standing behind the computer. When she noticed us, she fixed a plastic smile on her face and straightened her spine.

"I have two rooms booked for the week," I said. "We're part of the conference."

"What name was that, sir?" Her voice was clipped.

"Merrick Llwyd. L-l-w-y-d."

"Oh, I see." Her eyes dragged over me, clearly familiar with who I was. The lines of her face softened. "Alright, let's get you checked in then, Mr. Llwyd."

Her fingers flew over the keyboard and her brows drew together.

"Alright, so it looks like we actually just have the one suite booked for you," she said.

"Come again?"

Her eyes bounced between Clara and I. "The note on your file says Mr. Galt requested a room to be booked for Mr. Merrick Llwyd and a female companion. I think our booking team assumed you would be...um, well, wanting to be roomed together."

Clara's brows shot up, but she kept her eyes ahead.

"It's fine," I said. "Let's just add a second room onto the booking."

Her glasses slipped down her nose as her fingers clicked over the keyboard again.

"We are fully booked, sir," she said, her voice thin. I could tell she was nervous.

"How big is the suite?" Clara piped up.

"It's almost fifteen hundred feet, so pretty big," the woman said. "There is a second bedroom, but it only has a twin bed."

Clara turned, chewing her lip, and looked up at me for approval. I considered it for a moment, unsure how to proceed. If there were two bedrooms, it wouldn't be all that much different than our arrangement at home.

But everyone would know we were sharing a suite.

They would talk.

But what was the alternative? Grimly, I turned back to the clerk and nodded.

"It's alright," I said. "We can make it work."

The clerk dragged her eyes back and forth between us and nodded slowly. "I apologize for the mistake, sir. We didn't understand what the situation was between you and your...friend."

"Thank you," I said briskly. "And she's my ward."

The clerk glanced up, clearly confused.

"He's my guardian," Clara said, jerking her head at me.

"Oh," the woman said. "Actually, I do need to see both your IDs."

That was odd. I kept silent while Clara passed her ID over the counter. The woman looked over both our cards and handed them back. She finished our paperwork and gave us our keys. I took them with relief, glad the awkward encounter was over.

"What was that about?" Clara asked as we boarded the elevator.

"It was just a booking error," I said.

"No, why did she want to see my ID?"

I sighed. "I think she was concerned that maybe you weren't here voluntarily. I should have clarified that you were my financial ward."

Clara's jaw dropped. "I'm twenty-four."

"I know that, we both do. But she probably sees a lot with the lodge being just an hour from the highway. I imagine a lot of rich assholes come through here with less than pure intentions."

"Ew, men are the worst," Clara said, stepping out into the hall.

"Unfortunately, you'll have to meet some rich assholes this week," I said. "So please be vigilant. And don't fall for it when they or their sons go after you, because they definitely will."

"Even knowing I'm marrying Osian next year?"

"If they have any knowledge of the organization, they'll know you're unattached until the last piece of jewelry," I said, unlocking the door. "And if they're not privy to that, they won't know of Osian."

I pushed open the door to a sizeable suite with a kitchenette. There was a bedroom door on each side with a lot of space between them, a few couches, and a rug.

This wasn't so bad, there was enough room to give us the privacy we needed. It wasn't like we'd be sharing a wall.

"I'll take the twin," she said, pushing open the right hand door. "Oh, look, it has a bathroom with a jet tub."

If she was happy, I was happy. I circled the room, checking the locks absently and running my fingers over the windowsill for cracks. Everything seemed secure. I did a quick walk-through of Clara's room to make sure it was safe and went to unpack.

I'd just gotten out of the shower and put on a t-shirt and sweatpants when I heard a timid knock on my door. Clara stood outside, wearing a tight t-shirt and loose pajama pants. Her hair was in a messy bun on top of her head, little tendrils brushing her shoulders.

"Can I order room service?" she asked, holding out a menu. "It says they have chocolate mousse."

"You may have anything you like," I said. "Just charge it to the room. I'm going to do some work and go to bed. I have several meetings I need to prepare for tomorrow.."

She nodded and disappeared into her room.

I propped myself up in bed and put my reading glasses on. The screen of my laptop swam in my vision. I attempted to sort through my emails, but the words blurred.

Why hadn't she worn a bra under her pajama top?

Did she want me to see the little rise of her breasts? Was she trying to get me to look at her nipples pushing through the fabric?

No, I was the one being stupid. She just felt safe, she trusted me.

The next morning, it dawned on me that with the exception of a handful of older women, Clara was the only woman at the lodge. We had breakfast in the dining room and every eye fell on her as I walked her to the table. I wasn't sure she noticed.

She was distracted by the view from the window and crepes stuffed with Nutella, strawberries, and whipped cream. I watched her as she ordered a latte with whipped cream and pink sprinkles and drank it with her pile of crepes.

There really couldn't be a taste profile to that meal other than pure sugar.

Contented with being boring, I had my usual. An egg white omelette, one slice of whole wheat toast, a half of an avocado, and black coffee. I'd eaten the same breakfast for the last fifteen years and if it wasn't broken, I wasn't about to fix it.

Vincent and his wife, Adele, joined us halfway through. Adele was a refined woman, originally from a wealthy family in England. She was tall and beautiful, with black hair she kept in a demure bun and a lot of big, chunky diamonds on her hands and wrists.

She was one of those rich women who was always busy whenever I talked to her, but I was never actually sure what she did.

Clara must have realized at some point that she was surrounded by a sea of testosterone because she looked relieved when Adele sat down beside her. She offered her a shy smile and they began chatting.

"Is Clara the youngest woman here?" I asked quietly, turning to Vincent.

He nodded. "Gene Barrister is supposed to bring his daughter up at the end of the week. But for right now, yes."

Adele turned to Clara. "Do you want to go to the spa after this? There's enough testosterone in this lodge to fuel a rocket jet. I need some girl time."

"I'd love to," Clara said. She glanced up at me, waiting for my approval.

I gave a quick nod. "You may do as you please, Clara."

Vincent and Adele exchanged a glance that annoyed me. Like they were silently judging the fact that Clara had asked my permission.

"Would you like me to have dinner with you tonight?" Clara pushed her chair back and stood, setting her napkin aside.

I nodded. "Yes, just be back at the room at five."

She left with Adele and there was as short silence as Vincent and I finished breakfast. Then he stood and picked up his jacket, slinging it over his shoulder. I followed him out of dining room toward the meeting lounge.

"You should start seeing someone," he said lightly.

"I know you're trying to set me up with your niece."

"No, it's not that."

"What is it then?"

Vincent paused, glancing down the hall. "You're an important man who has a lot of meetings and dinners to attend. Most of those social events are set up for men with wives or partners."

"What's your point?" I asked. "I've always been single."

"No," Vincent said firmly. "Clara fills the social role of your partner."

I opened my mouth to retort and stopped, unsure what to say.

He was right.

"In every wealthy family, there's a woman the man can bring to parties and dinners," he said. "Sometimes it's the eldest daughter, but usually it's the wife. But...Clara is neither of those things."

"You've been listening to gossip," I said.

Vincent's jaw worked. "There's definitely some talk."

My patience was rapidly waning. I jerked the door open and stepped into the lounge. Vincent followed at my heels, unperturbed.

"What do they say?" I ground out.

The door swung open and a crowd of men filed in, holding coffees and chatting among themselves. Vincent cleared his throat and sank into a chair by the window and I sat down beside him.

There was a tense silence between us.

"What do they say, Vince?" I asked softly.

He blew out a short breath. "They say you're sleeping together."

Disgust curled in my chest. "I've never once touched her."

"I believe you."

"Why does everyone think that?" I snapped.

"Because, as I said, she fulfills the empty social role your wife should fill," Vincent said. "You're going to run into trouble with Osian Cardiff, I promise. He's *supposed* to be marrying Clara, but you're out here with her on your arm like you *are* sleeping with her. Eventually he's going to start feeling insulted."

"I'm not fucking scared of the Cardiffs."

"I have money invested in your hotel deal with them too."

He had a point.

I wasn't sure what else to add to the conversation, but luckily the awkward silence was filled as a mutual friend sat beside us and the meeting began.

I had a harder time than usual concentrating.

CHAPTER TWELVE

CLARA

I spent most of the first day in the spa with Adele. She was an elegant woman who intimidated me a little at first, but I warmed up to her quickly. She was at least fifteen years younger than Vincent and I was dying to ask their story, but I felt it was rude for our first meeting.

Instead, I let her ask about my life. About college, about my impending engagement. We lay on our backs as the masseuse worked on our legs and mulled over the latest organization gossip.

After our massages, we went to the sauna.

"Vincent is in the organization," said Adele, leaning against the wall. Heat made dewdrops gather across her bare skin. "I wasn't. It took me a long time to adjust."

"I think Merrick keeps a lot of things about the organization from me," I said. "He's very protective. Sometimes maybe too protective."

"I didn't know much about it when I married Vince." She smirked, her eyes distant. "I was so confused when he brought my father a diamond bracelet. So was my father."

"I had no idea about the engagement jewelry," I admitted. "Honestly...it's intimidating."

She lifted a brow. "I was livid when he told me about the piercing. I slammed the car door, told him to go fuck himself. But I warmed up to the idea."

I cringed, squeezing my legs together. "Merrick said you could swap out a nipple piercing if you wanted. I think I might do that."

"I...well, how honest do you want me to to be?"

Despite my earlier embarrassment about the subject, I recognized this as my opportunity to get first hand information. I wasn't going to waste that.

"I'd like to know what I'm in for."

She wiped back her soaked hair. "Well, I ended up loving my clit piercing. It made me a lot more sensitive, which was something I struggled with."

"I do too," I admitted quietly.

She studied me for a long moment and I shifted, looking away. She had a keen, matronly gaze that seemed to cut right through me to my core.

"You haven't had sex, have you?" she asked, her voice gentle.

I shook my head.

"I wouldn't have it pierced until you start having sex," she said. "If you wait for your wedding night, do your nipple for your engagement. Once you learn what you like, then maybe then you can let Merrick pierce your clit."

Heat shot down my spine and I flushed. The sauna felt like it was a million and ten degrees.

"You mean Osian," I said quickly.

"What?"

"Osian will be my fiancé."

It was her turn to be embarrassed. She waved a hand, searching for words.

"Sorry, I just got confused because you said Merrick's name earlier," she said. "Of course I meant Osian."

"It's fine."

There was a short, uncomfortable silence and then I decided to take the plunge and ask her how she met Vincent. We talked about

105

their age gap briefly. It didn't seem to bother her at all. Then we had mimosas while we had our hair and makeup done.

Before we parted ways in the hallway, she paused in her doorway.

"Don't do anything for a man you don't want to," she said.

"What do you mean?"

"It...you don't seem all that thrilled about Osian. I'd hate to see you pressured into a marriage you aren't happy about."

I swallowed the lump in my throat. "I just need to get to know him better. He seems nice enough."

She nodded and I unlatched my door, stepping inside.

"A little age gap isn't anything to be afraid of," she called, disappearing into her room.

I was about to call back that Osian wasn't much older than I, but then I remembered I'd already told her that. So what was she talking about?

Merrick didn't return until late that evening. He apologized for his lateness and disappeared to get dressed in his room. I sat at the table and waited for him in my little black dress and pink handbag.

The room smelled like his cologne.

Rich, like dark oak.

He stepped out, clipping his cuff links. He wore a dark blue suit that fit his body perfectly. Of course it did—only custom-made everything for Merrick Llwyd.

My stomach twisted as I remembered Adele's mistake. I knew it was an accident, what she'd said, but that didn't take the mental image out of my head.

Merrick on his knees in front of me with his hands on my thighs.

Parting them.

No, that was not a helpful thought. I squeezed my eyes shut and shook my head, jumping to my feet. When I opened them, he was staring at me with a crease between his brows.

"Are you...alright?"

"Yeah, sorry. Let's go eat, I'm starving."

He locked our door and I teetered on my dangerously tall heels. There was no way I was getting to the dining room without help.

Merrick sensed that and offered his elbow, letting me curl my arm around his so he could lead me down the hall.

He pulled out my chair. The dining room was dim with flickering candles. Every table was full around us and I felt a few curious eyes. Scalp prickling, I glanced over the room.

Maybe there was more than a few stares.

I looked down at my black dress. The hem had ridden up to the middle of my thigh. Slipping my hand down, I yanked on it. The collar pulled down below my breasts and I clapped a hand over them, pulling it back up.

I gave up. If something was going to show, I'd rather it be my legs than my breasts. At least those were under the table.

Merrick cleared his throat. He was leaning back in his chair, the wine menu in one hand. His deep, blue gaze was fixed on me over the table. Taking in my every move.

"Am I embarrassing you?" I asked quietly.

"What?" He frowned. "No. Why ask that?"

"I mean, my clothes."

His jaw worked and I could tell he was picking his words carefully.

"I think you're a beautiful woman and you shouldn't feel self-conscious about what you choose to wear."

He was lying, I could tell. But he'd been raised by two headstrong women and he was too well trained to speak his mind on such a dangerous subject.

Also...beautiful? He'd called me beautiful.

I should have let the whole thing drop. The problem was, I wanted the real answer.

Our waiter arrived and we ordered a bottle of wine and a starter. When he'd disappeared, I pushed my chair in and leaned on the table. Merrick stayed as he was, legs crossed.

"I want the truth," I said.

"About what?"

"Do my clothes embarrass you?"

That stubbled jaw started working again.

"I'm not embarrassed," he said. His voice was low, sitting deep in his chest.

"Okay, then—"

"Sometimes, they make you more...noticeable."

I froze. Alright, so that made me feel much worse. Blinking quickly, I took a sip of ice water, stalling.

"Do they make you uncomfortable?"

He was having an incredibly difficult time with this conversation. He shifted in his seat and cleared his throat.

"Uncomfortable isn't the right word," he said. "I feel...aware of you in a way that is different than...than the way I usually feel when I'm around you."

His gaze was rock solid. Boring into me over the table. He'd said his piece and he wasn't backing down from it.

"Okay," I said, still processing. "I'm sorry, I think."

He shook his head, his gaze flashing. "Never apologize for your body. My feelings are my own to deal with."

His feelings? My eyes darted up, throat dry. Pulse increasing.

"You may dress exactly how you choose, Clara," he said. "Do you understand?"

I nodded, wordless.

"If anyone treats you disrespectfully because of it, I'll deal with them. It's your body and you have the right to do what you want with it."

I needed to lighten the mood. He was tense, all strung up and on edge. I was painfully aware of myself and how there was a strange ache between my legs.

Taking a deep breath, I released a shaky laugh.

"So if I can do what I want, can I get a tattoo?" I asked, smiling.

His brow shot up. "Over my dead body."

"So I can have piercings, but not tattoos?"

"The piercing is traditional, Clara," he said. "It's different."

"You have a tattoo," I pointed out.

His hand flexed, fisting. The veins below the tattoo above his wrist stood out for a second.

"Just because I do something, doesn't mean you should do it too."

"Oh, so do as I say, not as I do?"

"Exactly."

The waiter returned with our wine. He poured a tiny bit and let Merrick taste it, waiting for his nod before filling both our glasses. The waiter left with our orders and I settled back in my chair. Making sure to keep my thighs closed and my ankles locked.

I wasn't wearing panties. Not because I was trying to be seductive, the dress was just too thin for it.

Suddenly, I felt out of my depth. Maybe I shouldn't have come to the lodge with Merrick. I glanced over the room, taking in all the suits and shiny watches. There was a handful of women, but most of them were older than me, and they were all elegant in their classy dresses.

I was the only young woman here and I stuck out like a sore thumb. It didn't help that I was drawing attention to myself by wearing skimpy clothes.

I took a sip of wine and realized the glass was empty.

Merrick glanced over as I refilled it, but didn't say anything.

By the time our meal was over, I was thoroughly tipsy. I felt stupid for drinking too much, but I also felt a lot less anxious so I wasn't sure I regretted it. Merrick ushered me into the hallway and pulled me to a halt.

He knelt in front of me, balancing on one knee.

I froze. "What are you doing?"

He glanced up. "Taking off your heels so you can walk."

I felt stupid all over again. His lean hand gripped my ankle and lifted it. I flailed and my hand came down on his shoulder, gripping it. His head was bent, light glinting from his black hair.

I wondered how many other women had had the privilege of having the Welsh King get down on his knees and take their heels off. It had to be a lot because he was quick. Like he'd had a lot of practice.

His expert fingers flicked the strap, pulling back. The heels came off in his hand and he rose smoothly.

"Alright, let's get you in bed."

He began striding down the hall, my heels hanging from his fingers. I stood there. Paralyzed and drunk, staring straight ahead. It wasn't a good combination.

The reality of what he'd said at the table was hitting me like a ton of bricks. Sinking into me, soaking me to the core.

He'd become aware of me, he'd noticed my body. It had made him feel things he didn't normally feel.

My mind went back to my birthday when we'd hid in the closet. When he'd gazed at me through the dark with a trickle of sweat etching down his neck.

When the air had felt so sticky and sweet it practically pooled around my ankles. I'd asked him if he'd ever tasted hard candy and he'd said he didn't remember, but he'd had one in his pocket. The exact kind I liked, that I always kept in my purse.

Merrick never ate sugar. He'd kept one in his pocket because once upon a time I'd left mine in his car and left a mark on his leather upholstery. Because he knew I liked them.

My head hurt. What did all of this mean? Was I just stupid drunk or was the wine freeing my forbidden thoughts? Making connections I didn't have the courage to make sober?

I dragged my eyes up to him. He stood in the middle of the hallway, waiting for me to move. Up until now, I'd felt twinges of puzzling feelings towards him, but I'd always thrown them out right away. I'd always corrected myself when I noticed his abs under his shirt or accidentally stared at his mouth too long.

But not tonight—tonight I looked him up and down and took my time with it.

He was, objectively, gorgeous.

Midnight hair, impossibly tall, and lean and muscular. Built for sin, made to be enjoyed. I knew absolutely nothing about sex, but I knew I could do dirty things to a body like his.

I could objectify it, pleasure myself with it. Drag my nails all over those lean muscles and suck bruises into his neck. Trace my tongue between his pecs, between his abs, and down to the forbidden place under his belt.

He'd asked if the hard candy was a euphemism and it hadn't been at the time. But it was now.

He was probably sweet and hard at first. But I knew he'd melt on my tongue and drip down my throat by the end.

A thrill moved down my spine and heat radiated from my cheeks.

He was the most delicious man I'd ever seen.

And yet, I'd missed it for six years.

"Clara!"

His voice, harsher than I was used to, yanked me back. I blinked rapidly, my face burning.

"I'm sorry," I gasped, hurrying past him.

"I think you need a full glass of water and a Tylenol before you go to sleep," he chided, completely oblivious.

There was a frantic pulse between my tingling legs. He ushered me into the suite and I stumbled into the bedroom and shut the door. On the other side, I heard him searching through the cupboards.

My heart pounded.

This couldn't change anything.

Yes, for the first time, he had turned me on and made me want him.

But he was old enough to be my father and I was supposed to be marrying someone else next summer.

CHAPTER THIRTEEN

MERRICK

She was asleep by the time I brought her a Tylenol. She lay on her side, her cheek against her arm. Her lashes were dark against her cheeks. Her body rose and fell, little snores whistling from her nose.

Her dress was rumpled, hitched several inches above her knees. Her bare thighs were lovely. Soft, slightly rounded, with a little line of muscle up the side.

I stalled, feeling intensely guilty.

She wasn't my type. Perhaps that was why I hadn't noticed her body until recently. Her figure was petite with some curve to her ass and breasts. Made to be enjoyed, but not by me.

My chest tightened.

I had set her up with Osian because it was a good match. She'd always have money and he would treat her well.

But it also meant that he got to be the man who shared all of her milestones. He would pierce her, he would marry her, he would get her pregnant.

She would be Mrs. Clara Cardiff.

I swallowed past the dryness in my throat. I had to be alright with that, I had to make peace with letting her go after all this time.

I had to be able to honestly hand her over on her wedding day.

And yet...fuck, that was going to hurt.

I'd never hear her pad down the hallway and into the kitchen, her hair messy and her eyes puffy from sleep. I'd miss her constant chatter in the evenings while I worked. I'd miss her prying me out of my chair so I could fetch her wine from the cellar because she was afraid of spiders and the dark.

Those were the parts of living with her I loved the most.

The unpolished moments.

I forced myself to move my feet and leave the room. But I could have sat there and watched her sleep all night.

It was a cool, clear, Autumn day outside the next morning. I changed into shorts and a t-shirt and strapped on my exercise watch. There wasn't a gym at the lodge, just a pool and a weight room, but there were miles of running trails.

The lobby was almost empty. I passed through it and moved down the front steps and crossed the parking lot. The sun had just crested the horizon and the trees were touched with gold.

The air was purer up in the mountains. Maybe I would buy a cabin in New Hampshire.

But what was the point of that? Once Clara was gone, it would just be me and all I did when I was alone was work. When she had been away at college, I became an extreme workaholic, but when she was home, I found myself not wanting to go into the office.

She made me want to be home.

I located the trailhead and headed south at a slow jog. Just getting my heart pumping and clean air in my lungs was helping flush the last few days out of my system.

I was pretty confident at this point that bringing her here was a mistake.

There were too many men and we were being watched too closely for my liking. I'd attempted to do something nice and give her a respite, but instead I'd kicked a hornet's nest. Now we were the subject of speculation.

As if on cue, my smartwatch beeped and I paused, glancing down to see Osian's name blink on the screen.

Why the fuck was he calling?

I ran a hand over my face to clear the sweat and tapped my earbud. "Hello," I said coolly.

"Do you have Clara with you at the lodge?"

"Why?"

He huffed and I heard a door slam and footsteps, like he'd just walked out onto a sidewalk. "I was just at your house and no one was there so I asked Caden and he said you were gone on business with Vincent Galt. I know he's at the lodge, so I'm asking if she's with you."

I bit back the urge to roll my eyes.

"She's here."

"Why?" he snapped.

That was a loaded question. I bent, stretching back and looking up at the trees overhead.

"She wanted a break from Providence."

"And she couldn't take a girl's trip with her friend or something?"

"Do you even know her best friend's name?"

"Of course I do," he said, slamming a car door. I heard his engine purr and it sounded like the call switched to Bluetooth. "As her future fiancé, I want to make it clear that this kind of thing can't continue."

Oh, someone had decided to grow some balls. Very cute.

"She's not your fiancé yet," I said coolly. "And if you don't step it up, she may never be."

He laughed shortly. "Like you're going to give up more than a billion dollars a year to your organization for some pussy."

Shock rippled through me and I was genuinely speechless for a moment. Not because I'd never heard that kind of talk before, but because he had the nerve to talk about Clara that way to my face.

I took a deep breath and let my anger simmer low.

"No one is getting pussy," I said evenly. "You are not her fiancé until I accept the last piece of jewelry and she agrees to be pierced. Until then, she is free to travel, she is free to fuck, she's free to do as she likes."

"You're too indulgent with her," he snapped.

"You are rapidly falling out of my good graces, Cardiff."

There was something in my voice that made him shut up for a moment. Then he cleared his throat and released a sigh.

"I think we got off on the wrong foot. Clara is very beautiful and I'll admit I get jealous, but it's not coming from a bad place. I'm looking forward to marrying her."

That was more like it. Maybe Osian Cardiff was more than just a spoiled, nepotism baby. I certainly hoped so.

"I understand where you're coming from," I said.

"If you could please respect the fact that I am going to be her fiancé, I would appreciate that."

"Again, I understand where you're coming from."

He released a slow, hissing breath.

"I am trying here," he said coldly. "You're making this a lot more difficult than it needs to be."

"Is this because she won't fuck you?" I asked, before I realized what I was saying.

There was a short silence.

"She'll fuck me eventually, she's just shy," he said evenly.

Oh no, I didn't like that.

"If you put any pressure on her to do anything she doesn't want, I will beat you to a pulp with my bare hands. I've done it before, twelve times, and I don't mind doing it again," I said. "Not even your daddy's money will be able to put you back together again."

"You're a fucking psycho," he spat.

"I can be," I said. "But only when provoked."

I clicked my earbud, hanging up.

My body was soaked with sweat by the time I'd run all the aggression off and my mind was clearer. I hadn't handled that well and I was going to need to reach out and make things right when I got home.

I wanted to keep him scared so he didn't disappoint her, but I didn't want to lose this deal. I needed this money for the training base.

He was right—it was important.

CHAPTER FOURTEEN

CLARA

Word got around that I wasn't Merrick's and I started getting a lot more attention by the middle of the week. At first, it was intimidating, but then I got used to it.

I had to admit that it was nice to be distracted by handsome men that wanted to flirt with me and buy me drinks.

It distracted me from Merrick. I'd never felt his presence the way I felt it now. Perhaps it was just because we were being forced to share a suite. But he was everywhere.

The shower in my bathroom broke and it took the lodge a day to get it working again. I had to use his bathroom to shower that day and I left rattled.

I wasn't sure why. The only thing in his shower was a bottle of body wash that smelled like him.

His razor was on the sink beside a bottle of aftershave. On the chair beside it sat his folded sweatpants. He was so clean and minimal, and yet...I felt him everywhere.

We ate at the restaurant for dinner almost every night. My body was a traitor and I found myself losing focus when he talked.

Distracted by how tall he was, how deep his voice was, how his eyes lit up when I said his name.

It all felt dangerous.

So I put a little distance between us, especially at night. Here at the lodge, I didn't want for distractions. After dinner, I'd go down to the outdoor bar in my swimsuit and some eager man would buy me a Cosmo. He'd linger, sometimes soaking in the hot tub next to me, and we'd chat.

It turned out it was a lot easier to flirt after I'd had a few drinks. So I indulged myself because it felt good. The compliments, the flattery, the endless drinks.

None of them tried to sleep with me though. I didn't have to ask why. Even though I was technically single, Merrick still hung over me like a threat.

Don't cross the Welsh King.

These men liked the fantasy of me, but none of them had the guts to actually do anything about it.

On Friday evening, Merrick had a dinner meeting that I couldn't attend because it was organization business. I went to the spa in the afternoon and got waxed and then had the most relaxing massage I'd had in a long time.

I put on my last clean swimsuit—a tiny, velvet pink bikini. I'd debated even bringing it because it left nothing to the imagination.

But I was feeling bold and I looked good, so I put it on and covered it with a short, silk robe. I padded barefoot out the side entrance of the lodge.

Through the window, I could see all the men in suits at the bar. Merrick was barely visible, but I could just make him out. Looking breathtaking in a tailored black suit and one of his custom gold watches. He was leaning on the bar, Vincent Galt at his side, talking with an older man I didn't know.

My stomach did a desperate, little flip.

There was a handful of younger men at the bar. The kind of people Osian would hang around with. Rich, ivy league, already hooked into their father's businesses.

Confident in Merrick's protective shadow, I skipped past them to the bar. The bartender handed me my Cosmo as soon as he saw me coming. He was a sexy, tattooed, blond man in his early thirties who bought me more drinks than he charged to the room.

Tonight, he was extra attentive. I leaned on the bar and sent him a shy smile and he winked.

"I get off in ten," he said. "Join me in the hot tub?"

I nodded, feeling naughty even though I had no reason to. I was still single and Osian was still sleeping with other people. I deserved to have a little fun before my engagement.

Making sure he was watching me, I grabbed my usual spot at the hot tub. For a moment, my fingers hesitated over the tie of my cover up.

I was almost naked beneath it.

A secret thrill went down my spine and I unfastened the robe, letting it fall to the patio. I knew the bartender was looking at me— along with the rest of the men at the bar—and the realization made my core tingle.

If I hadn't had the unspoken threat of Merrick hanging over me, their attention would frighten me.

But it was just exciting.

I slipped into the steamy water and sank down, keeping my breasts visible. Through the window, Merrick and Vincent had migrated to the opposite side of the room. Merrick had his back to me, oblivious.

Good, this wasn't any of his business.

The bartender arrived a few minutes later with his friend, a lanky, dark haired man. They were both in swimming trunks and I couldn't keep my eyes from lingering over their abs as they sank into the water.

Very nice.

"I'm Liam," the bartender said. " I never formally introduced myself."

"Travis," the other man volunteered. "I work the bar sometimes too."

"Clara," I said, smiling innocently.

Liam raised a brow, glancing down at my breasts in my wet, velvet bikini top. "You here alone, Clara?"

I nodded.

"Really? Cause I've seen you around with Merrick Llwyd," Travis said. "You're fuckin' hot, but I'm not about to mess with Llwyd's girl."

"Fuckin' suicide," Liam agreed, looking starved as he studied my chest.

"I'm not Merrick's," I said.

For the first time, Merrick's protection annoyed me. If I'd wanted to, I probably could have swiped that little pink card my first week back if it wasn't for Merrick. Even the organization adjacent men were scared of him.

"So why'd you come with him?" Travis asked.

I took a sip of my Cosmo, watching as Liam broke open a packet of cigarettes and handed one to Travis. I disliked the smell so I'd never tried one before, but they did look sexy smoking them. Liam winked at me and blew white smoke from his nose.

"Merrick is my guardian," I said.

"Shit," said Liam. "How old are you?"

"Twenty-four."

They both sighed with relief.

"I'm from the organization," I said. "But you already know that if you're aware of who Merrick is. Not many women live without a financial guardian in my world. Merrick is mine. I live with him and he pays for everything for me."

"So you must be a spoiled girl, huh?" Liam said.

"I know what I'm worth." I cocked my head.

They both laughed and shifted closer in the tub. I felt Travis's knee press against my thigh and I glanced at him from the corner of my eye. He winked and held out his cigarette.

"I don't smoke," I murmured.

"Try it," Liam urged.

I let Travis put his cigarette to my lips and I breathed in, knowing better than to fully inhale. When I pulled back, there was a little sliver of pink lipstick on the paper. He locked eyes with me as he put it back to his mouth.

I blew out the smoke. It didn't taste like much.

"Good girl," said Liam. "Not so bad, huh?"

I shook my head, sipping the last of my Cosmo. It tasted a little stronger than usual and I wondered if Liam had added extra vodka to it. My head felt light, but in a pleasant, dreamy way.

We chatted for a while. Liam told me he was from Sidney, Australia and he went to the university on the Canadian border. Travis was done with college and retired from a short football career after an ACL injury. They were both delicious and attentive, refilling my glass, getting me ice water, and letting me smoke from their cigarettes when I wanted.

After a while, I was feeling tipsy and bold enough to ask the question on my mind.

"Do you two do this a lot?"

Liam cocked his head. "Do what?"

"Sleep with the same girl," I said. "You're both flirting with me for a reason."

Travis laughed. "She's onto us."

Liam's mouth broke into a wide grin. He was beside me now, my legs draped over his beneath the water. His hand had been working the string of my bikini bottom for a while. Just wrapping it around his finger. Barely touching my skin.

"We're not going to fuck you, baby," he drawled.

I frowned. I hadn't intended on sleeping with anyone, but it bothered me they weren't even going to try.

"I'm not a fucking idiot," Travis said. "Merrick Llwyd took down twelve men with no gun, knife—no nothing. Everyone respects the fuck out of him."

I pushed my lower lip out. "Yeah, whatever. That's what they say anyway."

Liam ran his hand down my thigh to my knee. "You still have your cherry, don't you, princess?"

I gasped. "How dare you!"

They both laughed and Liam bent, kissing the side of my neck. Right below my ear. A shiver moved down my spine.

"Relax, baby," Travis said. "It's just a bet."

I glanced from one to the other. "You made a bet that I was a virgin?"

They looked a little embarrassed, but Liam nodded. Travis reached down and picked a bottle of coconut rum from the patio and pulled the cap off. He took a drink and passed it to Liam.

"I doubt Merrick lets you go out without a tracking collar on," Liam said. "He's not going to let you sleep around."

I paused, staring straight ahead. Through the window, I could see Merrick in a crowd of other suits. I knew it was him by the light glinting from his hair. Black like the iridescent feathers of a raven.

It hit me then what they were trying to say. Up until now, I hadn't realized it, but despite all his talk about autonomy, Merrick was still just as misogynistic as the rest of the men I knew. He just didn't realize it.

My pink V card wasn't in my purse.

It never had been.

No, it was tucked away in Merrick Llwyd's custom leather wallet.

Anger surged through my chest. For all his talk about equality, I was still under his lock and key. Even the most intimate parts of my body weren't mine to use as I pleased.

"I want to go," I said, standing. "I drank too much."

"Hey, hey, sorry if we upset you," Liam said. "We didn't mean it."

I shook my head, climbing out of the hot tub. My legs felt wobbly as I balanced on the patio boards and looked around for my robe.

"Hey, sweetheart, let us get you another drink," Travis urged.

I shook my head, padding around the tub, trying to find my gown. "Did you take my cover up?" I snapped, whirling on them.

Both looked completely confused. Liam, to his credit, got up and helped me look but the robe was gone. Travis leaned over the side of the tub, staring down.

"I think it fell through the cracks," he said.

I knelt, peering down between the boards. There was my pink silk robe, lying in the dirt down below, far out of my reach.

Fuck.

"That had my room key in the pocket," I said, sniffing.

"Have the front desk make you another," Travis said.

"Yeah, it's okay," said Liam. "Let me get my shirt for you and walk you in."

They could both tell I was upset and they were being too nice. For some reason, that made me even more angry. If it wasn't for Merrick, I would have let these men kiss me and buy me drinks until I was brave enough to let them put their hands under my clothes.

After all, Osian was back home sleeping with anyone he pleased.

Why shouldn't I?

"No," I snapped. "Merrick has my extra room key in his wallet."

I whirled and marched to the upper deck. Every line of my body was exposed, the pink velvet stuck to my breasts.

Every single man fell silent as I strode by them. I could feel my bikini bottom riding up my ass. The only thing it was successfully covering right now was my pussy.

No one said a word, but of course they didn't.

Fucking Merrick.

The front doors to the lodge swung open and I marched through. Wading my way through the sea of suits and ties. If I hadn't been tipsy, I'd never have had the courage to walk into a roomful of business men barely clothed.

But right now, it felt like the perfect fuck you.

Merrick was at the bar, his back to me. As I drew closer, the chatter died down around me and heads turned. Gazes dragged over my body. Confusion and little flickers of desire moved through the sea of eyes.

Vincent saw me first and he elbowed Merrick hard.

"What is..." Merrick said, turning.

I walked right up to the Welsh King and he looked down at me and his mouth parted. His face changed slowly, going completely blank except for his eyes. Those burned like blue flame. Fixed on me, a crease deepening between his brows.

Shadow crossed his face and a flicker of anger came with it. Like a storm just breaking over the horizon.

I tilted up my chin, holding out my palm.

"Room key, please," I said sweetly.

CHAPTER FIFTEEN

MERRICK

I felt Vincent's elbow dig into my ribs, cutting my conversation short. I turned abruptly, annoyed.

"What is...."

Before I could finish my sentence, I saw what everyone was staring at.

Clara.

She wore the most fucking ridiculous pink, velvet bikini I'd ever seen. It was just two strips of ruched fabric over her breasts and pussy. Tied with a few fucking pieces of string.

And it was soaking wet, stuck to her like a second skin. I could see the faint outline of her hard nipples under the velvet and when I flicked my gaze down, I saw the crease of her vagina.

And if I could see it, so could everyone else.

Blood rushed in all different directions, confused about whether it should be in my head or my groin. My entire body locked as I watched in horror as she marched up to me and put her hand out.

"Room key," she demanded. "Please."

I didn't want to make a scene, but I couldn't just hand over the key and go back to a room full of men who had all seen her almost naked. The entire room was full of sharks and they were eating her alive with their eyes.

I cleared my throat, keeping my face blank. Then, a tempered smile locked in place, I took off my jacket and draped it over her shoulders.

She narrowed her eyes at me. I bent so I could whisper in her ear.

"Get your ass upstairs to my suite," I said. "Now."

I'd never spoken to her like that before. Ever.

Her eyes widened, wiping that smug expression from her face. Her mouth pushed together in a mutinous pout. She knew she was in trouble and I could see the regret in her eyes.

She turned on her heel and practically ran from the room. I passed Vincent my drink.

"Excuse me," I said, teeth gritted.

"Shit," he said softly.

Avoiding dozens of stares, I walked through the crowd and turned the corner into the hallway. She'd taken off the jacket and she was walking fast towards the back exit.

"Clara," I snapped.

She paused, glancing over her shoulder. Her hair was wet and it stuck to her upper back.

"I said, my suite."

She hesitated.

I clicked my fingers, pointing at my door. "My suite. Walk. Now."

She obeyed, her head down. I shut the door and flicked the lock.

Dead silence fell.

I'd never felt more conflicting emotions in my life. She had embarrassed me in front of people who mattered. Perhaps she'd endangered some of my business deals.

But none of that hit me as hard as the realization that I wanted to pull down her wet bikini bottom, bend her over, and spank her ass until she begged for...what?

For me to stop?

For me to fuck her?

My palm itched and I clenched my fist. Her eyes were big and she was chewing the inside of her mouth. I could tell it was finally hitting her that I was actually upset.

125

She was also playing me. Making puppy eyes, big and round with wet lashes.

"Merrick," she whispered.

I put my hands on my hips and cleared my throat.

"I should punish you for that stunt," I said.

My voice sounded so fucking hoarse. Why had I said it like that? I sounded like the beginning of a porno.

Pull it together, Merrick.

"I'm sorry," she blurted out. "I don't know what got into me. I had too much to drink or something."

"No, you're sorry you're in trouble. You'd walk out there in front of everyone practically naked in a heartbeat if I let you."

Something about what I said triggered her. Her brows creased and her lower lip pushed out. Flames crackled in her eyes.

"Stop trying to control me," she snapped.

Oh, that pissed me off. Heat surged and I jerked my tie off and rolled up my sleeves. Sweat trickled down the back of my neck. Was the heat turned all the way up?

"Clara, I let you do whatever you like," I said. "What more can you possibly want?"

"I could have slept with not one, but two men tonight if it weren't for you," she said, trying to toss back her wet hair. "But I couldn't swipe my V card if I tried because everyone is just so fucking scared of Merrick Llwyd."

"Good," I snapped. "You don't need to sleep with every man who buys you a drink."

She gasped. "Are you calling me a whore?"

"No, I'm telling you that no man in this lodge is worthy of fucking you. So I don't regret scaring them off."

She lost it, throwing her hands up.

"Then who, Merrick, is worthy of fucking me?"

I hesitated because the truth sounded ridiculous. No one was worthy of fucking her, not even Osian. No one had hands worthy of touching her body or a mouth that deserved to kiss hers. She was too fucking perfect, too precious.

I swallowed.

"I am trying to be the better man here," I said. "But I am struggling."

"Oh, I know," she retorted.

I moved toward her and she backed up, sitting down hard on the couch. Her fingers, manicured and painted a glittery pink, dug into the cushions. I sank into a crouch before her, looking up into her face.

She glowered, pouting.

"You embarrassed me tonight in front of people I have good relationships with," I said. "Traditional people who won't appreciate what you did."

Her jaw worked. "I was angry because I hate that no one will touch me because they're so scared of you."

Yes, they were, and for good reason. I would kill anyone who treated her cheaply and think nothing of it. And I didn't regret a fucking thing.

"Why do you want them anyway?" I asked. "They're assholes."

She squirmed. "I wanted to know what it feels like. I just want to feel good too. Why is that a bad thing?"

It wasn't a bad thing. Wanting to feel good in bed was a natural human desire, but I didn't want some random man to do that with her. Just the thought made the blood pound in my head until my ears roared.

It hit me like a ton of bricks.

I wanted to be that man.

Shaken to the core, I took a beat to get my thoughts straight. Then I rose and took her smooth, warm chin in my fingers. She looked up at me and I thought I saw her breath hitch as I stroked her face with my thumb.

"Those men won't make you feel good, Clara," I said gently. "You know that."

Her lips parted. I felt her heartbeat, throb like electricity through the air.

"Do you?" she whispered.

"Do I what?"

"Do you make women feel good?"

The truth was yes, I did. There was nothing I enjoyed more than giving oral. I loved the taste of it, the musky smell of it, the silkiness of a woman's sex against my mouth. I lived for the rush of orgasm, the begging, the whimpering, the crying out for God.

I could get off just from eating pussy. I had before, on purpose and more than once.

I cleared my throat as I felt my cock twitch in my pants. I needed to change the subject now.

"I'm not discussing my sex life with you," I said, not unkindly.

"Merrick—"

I released her and went to the bedroom to retrieve one of my shirts. She was standing there, her arms wrapped around her body, chewing on her mouth when I got back. I passed the t-shirt to her and she took it gingerly.

"Cover yourself with this shirt and go to your room," I said. "I'm going to fix the mess you made downstairs. I'll be back at eleven and I expect you to make a full, sincere apology to me."

Her lower lip trembled and I had to steel myself. She needed to learn that there were consequences to her actions.

"But—"

"Clara," I said. "Go to your room now."

She wanted to argue, I saw it flash in her eyes. Instead, she made the smart choice and pulled the t-shirt on and flounced into her bedroom. I took a moment to gather myself and realized I was hard.

Fuck, had she seen that?

What was wrong with me that she had gotten me hard? With the exception of her birthday party, she'd never once aroused me that much. And yet, I was throbbing against the zipper of my pants.

Maybe it was just the thought of eating pussy that had gotten me so hard.

I went into my bathroom and shut the door, despite being alone. There was something shameful about the erection I had. Because despite what my brain told me, my body knew that it was Clara, my ward, that I was hard for.

I took my phone out and halfheartedly found some porn.

But I didn't fucking want porn.

I turned my phone off and set it aside. I met my own gaze and made a choice, a pact with myself, that I would indulge myself this one time. And never again.

My hand braced against the door frame and I unzipped my pants. My eyes closed and I let my brain take over, showing me what I desperately ached to see.

Clara on her back, her soaked bikini sticking to her body.

My hands slipping under the strings. Tugging the flimsy fabric aside. Revealing her soft pussy, nestled between her thighs. Bare from laser. I knew she'd gotten laser hair removal because I saw her credit card bills.

Fuck, I paid her credit card bills.

I paid for her pussy to be all soft and naked.

Her bills came right to me, stacked up on my desk. I tried to give her privacy, but I still saw what I was paying for sometimes.

A bill from her favorite lingerie store.

Another from a sex toy shop. That one had said exactly what she'd bought. A little pink rabbit vibrator.

I'd signed off on that bill and tried not to remember that I knew, but it was burned into my brain. The image of her manicured fingers between her thighs, that pink vibrator against her clit.

She probably whimpered when she came, biting her lip to keep quiet.

I wondered how many times I'd worked upstairs in my office while she pleasured herself in her bedroom. What a waste when I could make her come so much harder and so many more times.

What a fucking waste I hadn't touched her yet.

CHAPTER SIXTEEN

CLARA

I cried the moment I was safe in my room.

Of course I knew Merrick could get angry. Everyone got angry at some point in their lives. But I'd never actually expected to witness it, much less have it be directed at me.

It wasn't even that bad. He'd never once raised his voice or said anything cruel.

It was the disappointment at the heart of his anger that hurt the most.

Stripping my cold, wet swimsuit, I crawled into bed. He'd been gentle and kind for so long that I'd forgotten he had teeth.

I was dangerously close to seeing another side of him that I wasn't ready for. A little thrill of fear moved down my spine, coupled with something else.

Was that desire?

I froze, face buried in the pillow.

Did I actually want him? Or was I just flustered?

I turned it over and over in my head and came up with nothing. My body was betraying me again, shooting off signals I didn't understand. I washed my hair and put on a pair of shorts and a tank top and crawled back under the covers.

It was only ten. I still had another hour before Merrick would be back, expecting me to apologize for embarrassing him. I chewed the inside of my mouth and stared up at the ceiling.

The clock ticked and one minute passed. The digital clock on the bedside table was thirty minutes off. I checked my phone. No, they were both off by a minute. It was nine-fifty-nine.

I got up and blow dried my hair and curled it in soft waves for tomorrow. Then I tied it up in a loose bun to protect it and went and sat on the edge of the bed.

It was ten-fifteen.

I chewed my mouth again, a bit of blood spreading over my tongue. That spot on the inside of my lip was sore and raised. A scarred mess.

He was doing this on purpose. Making me wait so I had to stew over my sins. It was the kind of thing my father had done. Never hitting me, just making me sit there for hours wondering if he would finally lose it.

Except with Merrick, it was different. He would never lose it with me, of that I was positive.

My phone pinged and I snatched it up, fingers shaking. It was Candice, responding to a text I'd sent her earlier before the hot tub. She was asking when I'd be home tomorrow and if we could go out to the club.

I hesitated and a little thrill of rebellion went through me.

Sure, let's go out. I'll be back around three.

Okay, what are you doing right now?

I considered lying, but it was Candice. She knew me better than that.

Merrick is pissed at me and I'm waiting for him to get back from his meeting.

There was a short pause. Then:

Merrick is pissed? What did you do?

I explained in a page-long text, including that he was expecting me to apologize, and sent it. Her typing bubble wobbled for a long time before her text came through.

Damn. He actually sounds like he is pissed at you. That's really weird, I don't think I've ever seen him mad about anything.

I know.

We talked about it for a few minutes longer and got nowhere. We were both confused by his anger because all we'd ever known was the gentle side of him.

Laying aside my phone, I rolled onto my side. The clock blinked almost eleven. My heart pumped a little faster as the minutes moved by, this time too quickly. My phone pinged, flashing a message from Candice.

Let me know what happens.

The lock to my suite whirred and the door pushed open. I sat up quickly, but didn't dare get off the bed. In the living room, he sighed and I heard his coat fall to the couch. The door to the mini fridge opened, a glass clinked.

"Clara."

I remained still.

"Clara, come out here, please."

Heart in my throat, I padded barefoot to the door and peeked around the corner. My whole body tensed and then warmth pooled in my hips. Sudden and unexpected.

He was leaning on the kitchen counter, propped on his elbows. A glass of clear liquid, probably vodka, sat before him. His white shirt was open at the collar and the sleeves were still rolled halfway up his forearms. I'd never seen that many buttons undone before. In fact, I'd never seen his chest at all.

Why would I have? He was always careful to wear a shirt around me.

His eyes flicked to me and held. His dark hair, normally slicked back, was loose. Some of the natural wave was coming through, a shock of it hanging messily over his forehead.

I wondered what it felt like.

Would it curl around my fingers if I played with it?

He cleared his throat, his eyes not wavering.

"Come here, Clara."

My heart thumped so fast that my ears roared with the pressure. I pushed the bedroom door open slowly and crossed the room. He didn't turn, but his hand dipped into this pocket.

He took out a watch and laid it on the counter. I leaned in to look and my whole body went completely still.

It was a silver Rolex with a dark blue face.

Heat radiated from my face, spilling through me until it reached the bottoms of my feet. *He* was the man I'd ground my ass on at my birthday party.

Oh my God.

Before the mortification could set in, a single thought filled my brain. Merrick was packing. But of course his dick was huge, it was probably a prerequisite for becoming the Welsh King.

Trying not to look down at his groin, I lifted my burning face up and locked eyes with him. His mouth parted, showing a sliver of his tongue and teeth. I stared at it, transfixed.

"Clara," he said.

"I'm sorry," I whispered. "For grinding on you. I had no idea it was you. And I'm sorry for embarrassing you tonight."

He ran a hand over his jaw, his fingers scratching on his dark stubble. I took a step back as he turned, unfurling his six-foot-five body over me. He smelled less like cologne tonight and more like...Merrick.

If someone could bottle that smell and sell it, they'd make millions.

"I wasn't embarrassed," he said.

His voice was hoarse and low. A rumble in his throat.

"You said—"

"I know what I said," he blurted. "I know...I know that's what I should have felt. But I was...jealous more than anything."

I gaped at him. "Why?"

"Because they all saw you like that." His eyes dropped, falling over me quickly. My heart pounded. "Because you are my ward, the Welsh Princess, and no one deserves to see you like that."

It wasn't what he wanted to say, I felt it in the tremor of his voice. I swallowed, heat pulsing deep inside me. Every rational part of my brain begged me to hold back, not to touch him.

But the little rebellious bit of me, the part between my thighs, had taken control.

I reached out. He started when my palm touched his chest, inhaling sharply. His skin was scorching hot. His heart hammered under the thin cloth.

The world spun.

What was happening to us?

"*Cariad*," he whispered.

"Merrick."

The watch skittered from the counter and fell to the ground. His hand was on me, on the back of my neck. All rough and lean and strong.

His other hand slid down my spine and gripped me through my shirt. Fingernails dragging up the cloth. His palm searing my naked lower back.

Everything was happening too fast. Like a blurry movie. His body pinned me against the counter and I felt his erection for a breathless second.

Hard at his hip, pushing into my lower belly.

But it was nothing compared to the searing, euphoric heat of his mouth coming down on mine.

For a second, there was nothing. Just space and darkness.

Then my brain exploded. Every strand of DNA erupted like fireworks. Gold and silver bursts in a cold, endless galaxy. A shower of meteorites across a universe made for only us.

This was chemistry. This was rare, like a once in a lifetime eclipse. Written into the beginning of the world for this moment in time— this indescribable moment when Merrick Llwyd kissed me.

Every part of my body and mind unwound itself to nothingness so the Welsh King could write himself into my cells, into my neurons, into the breath from my lungs.

We spun on and on like this, his mouth hot and firm on mine. Kissing me with aching slowness. Like he wanted to spend the rest of his life locked in my arms with our breath mingling and fireworks burning somewhere far away.

Limp, I let my lips part. And his tongue swiped against mine.

Desire woke, hot and wild. Filling my core and tightening it like a coil of pure heat.

This was the lust that made people do stupid things and fuck up their entire lives over a single person.

I knew because I was right there, ready to lose it all tonight.

He pulled back for the barest second to kiss my neck. His mouth burned like a brand.

"Fuck," he said hoarsely. "Fuck me and then forgive me, *cariad.*"

Delirium was making me high and desire making me stupid. A low whine burst from my throat at his words. At his desperation. His hands slid over me, touching my throat, my ribs, my stomach, my thighs.

Never over the places that needed touched the most.

He was holding back.

I didn't want him to hold back, I wanted it all.

"Yes," I breathed, delirious from his kisses. Feathery down my neck and bare shoulder. He paused, pressing his forehead to my neck. Hot breath spilling over my breasts.

"Goddamn it," he swore softly. "No, no, I'm sorry."

"Merrick—"

"I can't do this, *cariad,*" he said, his voice strained. "I shouldn't be here. I should never have come here tonight, I knew what I was going to do. This isn't how we are...we're not like this."

"Why?" I breathed.

He raised his head, running a hand through his hair. He was drunk on me, disheveled from my touch. Another button had popped open and I could see the dark hairs on his chest.

My core pulsed.

"I'm old enough to be your father," he said grimly. "I'm your guardian."

"It doesn't matter," I said. "Merrick, I want this."

He shook his head once, his eyes clouding. What we'd done was hitting us both hard. Filling the room with cold awkwardness.

The Welsh King had kissed me.

And that single touch had destroyed any hope of a platonic relationship. Even now, just looking at him, my body was on fire. The places where his hands had been felt raw and empty.

The places he'd been would never be the same again.

He took a step back. "I have to go."

"Why?"

"Because if I stay any longer, I'll stay the night."

Stay the night, please, stay the night.

A million images flashed through my brain. Merrick in my bed, naked and warm. His bare chest, speckled with hair, against my back. His hands on me, his mouth breaking me into a million pieces.

Making me feel things I never thought I would.

Desperate, I crossed the kitchen and gripped the front of his shirt. Pulling him down until I could stand on my toes to reach him. Our mouths drew together like magnets.

Our kiss was more intense this time, more focused. Building on itself. Our mouths moved together in perfect tandem. Kissing, licking, biting, sucking. Tongues brushing in bursts of sweetness and heat.

I pulled back just enough to speak.

"Please, stay the night, Merrick."

His jaw worked. "If I stay, I'll take everything."

"Then take it."

"Fuck, you don't know what you're offering."

"Yes, I do," I insisted. "Take me to bed...take my virginity. I want you to have it, it's yours."

He laughed once, hollow and pained. "I'm not worried about your hymen," he whispered. "I'm worried about your heart."

That stopped me in my tracks.

"My heart?" I faltered.

He brushed back a free strand of my hair. His palm was so warm and lean against my cheek. I wanted to bury my face in it, to bite it, to lick it.

"We both care for each other," he said. "I don't want to ruin our friendship. I have to protect you and ensure you have a good future. Fucking you doesn't factor into that."

I caught my breath, trying to control myself. Fuck friendship. How was I supposed to live after his kiss? How was I supposed to let Osian kiss me knowing how much better it could be?

I knew now that Merrick's kiss was a beautiful, world altering event. Like the birth of a star in a cold galaxy. A burning meteorite streaking through the night sky.

So intense and then over in a second.

Leaving me permanently altered.

"I...I can't just go back to normal after this," I whispered. "You had to feel what I felt."

He swallowed, avoiding my eyes.

"Merrick, don't lie to me, please."

"I felt it." His jaw worked. "But now I feel the weight of my responsibility towards you."

He pulled back, gently moving me aside. The moment was over and now we were standing in the shrapnel. Trying to figure out what came next.

"You were jealous," I said flatly. "You have been for a while, I saw it the night you introduced me to Osian."

Something dark flickered in his eyes. The silence lay thick over us, like dust settling.

"Osian Cardiff will make a good husband," he said slowly. "He'll give you the future you planned."

My fingers curled and I swallowed, my throat painfully tight. Tears threatened to gather on my lashes. Merrick released a slow sigh and bent, picking up his watch and putting it on.

He went to the door, his head bent.

"We're leaving first thing in the morning," he said. "We'll get breakfast on the way."

He walked out into the hall and I heard him double check the lock. I stood there, my arms wrapped around myself. Toes curled on the cold linoleum. Body shaking from the sudden loss of heat in the room.

Legs wobbly, I made it to the bed. As I sank down, my phone pinged. I swiped the screen to see a text from Candice.

So? Was he mad? Are you grounded or something?

I swallowed hard. I'd never, ever kept anything from Candice before. We were always completely honest with each other, even when it didn't cast us in the best light.

But how could I tell her I'd kissed Merrick? That we'd talked about having sex. That I'd begged him to take my virginity and he had refused. That the world would never be the same.

My fingers shook as I typed out a text and sent it.

Nothing, he wasn't mad. I just said I was sorry and now we're back to normal. A lot of drama for nothing.

CHAPTER SEVENTEEN

CLARA

The drive to the airport and the plane ride home the next morning were agonizing. Merrick looked rough, his hair tousled and his face unshaven. I'd never seen him like this. It was a little scary.

He settled into the seat opposite me and flipped his laptop open. His sunglasses were reflective, hiding his eyes completely. I couldn't tell what he was feeling and I wasn't about to ask.

I wanted to say something, but I couldn't think of a single thing. So I sat there in silence, my body coiled up in the seat. After a while, he put his laptop away and shifted, spreading his knees.

I glanced up, wondering if he would speak. Instead, he leaned back in his seat and turned his head to the window.

Dead silence reigned until we got back to the house.

He entered the hall, standing aside to let me go first. The house smelled cold and musty from being empty. I took my suitcase from him and began dragging it down the hall.

"Clara."

My heart fluttered. I stopped walking and looked back. He'd taken off his sunglasses and hung them on the deep V of his button up collar. Right where a few dark hairs appeared beneath the white fabric.

"Osian wants to see you," he said.

The last person I wanted to see after last night was my future fiancé. I was in a mood and all it would take was one stupid comment for me to blow up.

"I'm going out clubbing with Candice," I said.

Not waiting for his response, I tossed my hair and dragged my suitcase down the hall and slammed my bedroom door. I stood still, waiting to see if he'd come after me.

But no, his dress shoes clipped up the stairs to his room. Then he slammed his door and something hit the ground hard. Like he'd dropped his suitcase.

My stomach flipped. I'd never heard Merrick slam a door before.

The sound opened the floodgates again. I ran a hot bath and cried in the tub for a while. A few hours later, he revved the engine of the Audi outside and I listened as it disappeared down the drive.

How was I supposed to process this?

Merrick was supposed to be my safe place. My harbor, my protective force. But in a single moment, we had ruined six years of friendship.

Now we both knew that we wanted each other and nothing could ever be the same again.

Numb, I took a shower. Then I turned on music and did my makeup and hair. In the garage sat the brand new car he'd gotten me. Reminding me that no one had ever treated me better than fucking Merrick Llwyd and no one ever would.

Teeth gritted, I drove myself to Candice's house and we went to the club.

She could tell I needed to just drink and dance instead of talking. So we both did a line of shots and went out onto the floor.

The music pulsed, pounding through my veins like a drum. Filling my ears, throbbing in my chest. At some point in the night, Yale appeared in the crowd and coaxed Candice into dancing with him. Or rather, dancing on him.

I was out, making my way to the other side of the floor. Preferring to be alone than watch them grind on each other.

I stayed in the middle of the dance floor, almost crushed by the sea of bodies. I was drunk on Cosmos, drunk on desire, drunk on rage. So I danced because I knew I was beautiful and desirable.

Sweat made my body glitter melt. My mascara smudged. A stranger danced with me for a brief moment, holding my hips between their palms. They took my hands and held them above my head, spinning me into the darkness.

Then they were gone, disappearing abruptly like they'd been scared off.

My scalp prickled and I glanced up to the balcony overhead. I swore I saw Merrick standing over me. Watching me twist and curve in my tiny pink dress.

Fuck him. He didn't own me.

When I lifted my eyes again, he was still there. Definitely flesh and blood. Leaning on the railing, watching me with those burning cobalt eyes. All sexy and mysterious with his shirt open at the collar.

Taunting me with the forbidden things beneath his clothes.

I swayed my ass, turning slowly to give him the best view. Even from so far away, I saw his eyes change. Darkness creeping into the corners.

I was way too drunk to make good choices, so it wasn't a surprise that I didn't. I lifted my pink manicured fingers to make a V and flicked my tongue through them once. His brow rose sharply.

In retrospect, I wasn't confident I knew what it meant, but I'd seen Yale do it before and it got a reaction out of Candice.

It definitely got a reaction from Merrick.

He turned on his heel and began descending the stairs. My heart began throbbing and I danced backwards, keeping my eyes on him. Making sure I didn't lose his tall figure as he waded into the crowd.

Light flashed and the bass shattered my eardrums. He was trying to get to me, but the crowd was too tight. I lifted my hands, dancing slowly, seductively. Teasing him, getting him even angrier than he surely was already.

"What's wrong?" I mouthed, smirking.

He cocked his head. "Come here," he mouthed.

I shook my head.

He lifted his brow, giving me a do-it-or-else look. I swung around, still dancing to the beat, and began moving away from him. After all, what was he going to do to me?

Punish me? Spank me? The thought was thrilling in my intoxicated state. Desire surged between my thighs and I realized with a jolt that my panties were wet. I glanced over my shoulder and shook back my hair. He was a little closer, a driven expression on his face.

Like he was angry and starving all at once.

I hoped he took me out to his car, put me over his lap, and spanked my ass with his bare hand—his stupidly sexy bare hand with those veins that went down through his knuckles.

God, how had I never realized how gorgeous he was?

I spilled out onto the sidewalk, barely getting two steps before his hand closed around my wrist. He pulled me against his body and all the air shot from my lungs at the impact. His forearm locked over my stomach like an iron band.

My God, he was brutally strong.

"Merrick," I gasped.

He didn't speak. Instead, he lifted me into the air. Like I weighed nothing. Spun me, and tossed me over his shoulder. Cool air hit my ass as my dress rode up. Leaving my lace panties exposed.

Thank God I'd decided to wear underwear.

His rough palm brushed over it, tugging the skirt down to cover me. His touch shocked me, like a live wire, sending tingles to the bottoms of my feet.

There was something so angering and arousing about being manhandled like this. I squirmed, kicking halfheartedly. Unsure if I wanted him to keep manhandling me or put me down.

"Hold still," he said shortly.

His grip tightened. He was ridiculously strong. But then, he had killed twelve men with his bare hands...at least that was the story. But I hadn't mentally translated that into an inhuman level of strength.

I hard the Audi door open and he dumped me unceremoniously into the back seat. Then he stepped back and I heard the child locks click. Fury boiled in my chest. My fists clenched and I struggled to my knees to look through the window.

He was standing on the curb, talking on his phone. Unbothered.

I flipped him off. His brow lifted, but that was it.

Burning with embarrassment, I sank into the middle seat and crossed my arms. He paced back and forth outside for a minute longer and then he got in the car.

There was a long, long silence.

The engine purred under his foot as he pulled out into the street. His hand hung on the top of the wheel like he didn't care. In the rear view mirror, I saw his gaze fixed pointedly ahead.

The dashboard beeped.

"Put your seatbelt on," he ordered.

I obeyed, but with my lower lip pushed out. So he knew I was pissed.

We drove in silence all the way home. He circled the Audi and pulled open my door, stepping aside.

"Go inside," he said.

The world spun and I wobbled as I crossed the driveway in my towering heels. He unlocked the door and took my upper arm gently and guided me into the kitchen.

The bright kitchen light blinded me for a second. I blinked, rubbing my swimming eyes. He still hadn't shaved his stubble and it was stark against his skin. The few silver hairs made him look distinguished. Like a real gentleman.

He set a bottle of Tylenol and a glass of water in front of me. Then he pulled out the kitchen stool, indicating I should sit.

I obeyed, taking a slow sip of water. My palms felt sweaty and my head spun. The silence was deafening.

Why wouldn't he crack? I'd kill for just a bit of a smile.

He pushed his hands into his pockets. I looked down, tracing the muscles in his exposed forearms down to where his wrists disappeared into his pants pockets.

"Let's have a talk, Clara," he said.

I nodded once, keeping my eyes down.

He cleared his throat. "Please look me in the eyes while I'm speaking with you. I am your *Brenin*."

My jaw went slack. He'd never pulled the Welsh King authority card with me before, ever. A little hurt, I dragged my gaze up.

"You drink too much," he said.

This time, my jaw fell open. I drank too much? Me? How dare he say that when he came home every day and had a glass of whiskey?

"You drink too," I pointed out.

"I have a drink every other weeknight, equaling exactly one shot glass of high quality whiskey," he said. "On weekends, I allow myself one day where I can have no more than three drinks."

I just stared at him, too drunk to comprehend.

"You're getting messy," he said. "You've gotten drunk with Candice numerous times since you got home. You're hungover in the morning and you sleep till noon on those days."

My throat tightened. He didn't sound like Merrick anymore. He sounded like my fucking father.

"You're going to cut back on your drinking," he said firmly. "To two days a week. Otherwise, I'm putting a limit on your credit card."

That was over the line. I mouthed silently, so shocked I couldn't think of words. He put his hands on his hips, his jaw set and his eyes stern.

"I...how dare you?" I whispered.

He stepped back, pacing. His hands still on his slender hips.

"How dare I...what?" he said, his voice low. "You are a beautiful, talented woman and you're fucking around and using my money to do it. Don't think I didn't see every damn thing you did at the lodge."

"What does that mean?"

"You spent almost every night drinking with men," he said. "And, I hope to God, it never got further than that."

I set down the water and kicked my heels off. Anger erupted in my chest and I took a step toward him. Fists clenched.

"Why? Why couldn't I have taken it further, Merrick?" I said softly.

144

He hesitated.

"You've always told me I could do what I wanted with my body. You gave me access to any birth control I wanted. You told me that there was nothing wrong with sex as long as it was consensual," I spat. "So why did I embarrass you by flirting in a hot tub?"

His cobalt eyes burned, rimmed with those black lashes.

"Because you're not like other people," he said. "Because you're the Welsh Princess."

"Oh," I said, laughing shortly. "This isn't about me. This is about you and how you fucking look to all your little subjects."

"No, this is about you not living up to your potential. Not realizing your worth."

"You sound like a tool, Merrick," I snapped.

"Clara, that's beneath you," he snapped right back. "I'm not trying to sound like your father, but—"

"Then don't," I shouted, bringing my palm down on the table. "Don't talk to me like you're my father because you aren't. He's dead, Merrick, he's fucking dead and I'm better off for it. I don't need you turning into him."

I wasn't sure why I said it. Perhaps because it was such a relief to admit it in such straightforward terms. My father was an ice cold, patriarchal tyrant and I'd hated living under his thumb. I didn't regret speaking the words aloud, but I did regret the look that passed over Merrick's face.

I'd forgotten my father was his closest friend.

Ashamed, I took a sharp breath. "I'm sorry. I didn't mean it."

"I know you meant it."

"Still...I never meant to hurt you that much."

He ran a hand over his face, rubbing his stubble. "You have every right to feel whatever way you do about your father. I have good memories of him, you don't. Our feelings are both legitimate."

I sank back onto the stool. "Why are you so reasonable? It's annoying," I whispered.

"Intensive practice."

The silence in the kitchen was deafening. He finally released a sigh and began making a pour-over. He poured my favorite creamer into the steaming cup and put it in front of me.

"Drink," he said. "You're going to hate yourself tomorrow."

I obeyed, already feeling a little better.

"I'm not withdrawing my request," he said.

"What?"

"Any drinking that isn't a glass of wine while out to dinner will be limited to the weekends."

"Two days a week? That's it?"

"That's it."

"Three maybe? Friday, Saturday, Sunday?"

"Two days only."

I huffed into my coffee, rolling my eyes. He remained unswayed. I glared at him subtly as he pushed his sleeves up further and began loading the dishwasher. He was precise in everything he did, setting every dish in its proper place.

He wiped down the counter, not missing a single spot.

"Merrick."

He glanced up. "What?"

"What does that gesture I made at you mean?"

He started laughing and stopped abruptly when I frowned. There was a short silence and he cleared his throat. Leaning on the table, his shirt gaping briefly.

"It's an obscene sexual gesture," he said.

"Oh. I thought it was kind of like the middle finger. I saw Yale do it to Candice and she got really pissed."

"It simulates cunnilingus."

"What?"

He lifted his fingers and my heart stopped as he made a V over his mouth. I forgot how to breathe. My fingers tightened around my mug so tightly I worried it would shatter. His lips parted and his tongue flicked out.

"Oh," I breathed. "Now it makes sense."

He grinned in a flash of white. His fingers dropped.

"Do you like that?" I asked before I could lose my nerve.

"Like it?"

"Do you enjoy going down on women?"

He was at a loss for words, his lips parting.

"You admitted you wanted to sleep with me. You kissed me," I said, heart thudding. "And now you can't even answer that question."

His lids flickered and his eyes burned, narrowing.

"You're not asking if I like going down on women," he said. His voice was thick, edged with rich darkness.

"Yes, I am."

"No, you're asking if I would enjoy going down on *you*."

The world spun around us and I ached for him. Dying to feel that universe shattering touch once more. His stare was like a laser beam, so intense it scorched me to my core. Making me pulse and my panties dampen.

"I have my doubts Osian will ever do that for me," I said.

"He'd better."

"I...I don't want him to. I mean, I don't care."

His jaw tensed, working slightly. We were both quiet, breathing hard. Unsure and fighting against our desires. He cleared his throat and to my shock, sank to his knees before me.

My God. The Welsh King on his knees.

He looked up, cocking his head. "You are asking me to perform oral sex on you."

I felt my eyes widen. "Do you always say it like that?"

"How?"

"So...clinical."

He bent his head and kissed my knee and the skin beneath his lips tingled. The wave of heat that erupted in me sent sweat trickling down my spine.

"Fine," he whispered. "You're asking me to eat your pussy until you come all over my mouth."

The world broke, it shattered, it erupted. To hear that kind of talk from Merrick...that was a cataclysmic event.

My sex throbbed against the stool.

I knew it. I knew he wasn't just classy suits and perfect manners. I knew that beneath it all, he had a side to him that did filthy things in the dark.

I let my head fall back. If I hadn't been still drunk, I wouldn't have had the courage to pound the last nail in my coffin.

"I don't want my first time to be with Osian," I whispered. "I want *you* to take my virginity. So show me how good it can feel. You always tell me that it's your job to set the standard for how I should be treated. So do it. Fuck me, Merrick. Take me upstairs to your bed. Just this once."

CHAPTER EIGHTEEN

MERRICK

I did take her to bed, but not mine. She was still drunk when I closed the door and strode down the hall. Blood pumping, pooling in my groin. Ears roaring from the pressure.

I didn't sleep that night, even after a long shower. An hour after waking, I found myself staring at my therapist through the haze of steam rising from my hot coffee.

Morning sun cut through the shades.

Making patterns on the floor.

Gretchen Hughes was organization adjacent so she knew who I was and what kind of life I led. And she specialized in my particular issues.

Adult attention-deficit hyperactivity with a side of obsessive-compulsive disorder. Not my cocktail of choice, but the one the universe had seen fit to serve me.

Luckily, I was doing well. After fifteen years of seeing Gretchen once a week and an extraordinary amount of discipline and hard work, I was the best I'd ever been. I had the tools I needed to deal with it, I knew my triggers, and I was able to see warning signs before they escalated.

"Why the emergency session?" she asked. "Are you having issues?"

I looked down at the teacup of espresso. Everything in Gretchen's house was pretty and delicate. From her handwoven rug, to her silk curtains, to the cups she always served my coffee in.

I glanced up, steeling myself. Gretchen knew more about me than anyone. I'd confessed my darkest secrets and my most potent weaknesses to her. Her methods were unorthodox so we kept them under the table. I visited her in her home office and paid her in cash.

She told me the uncomfortable truths I needed to hear.

But only if I did the same.

She narrowed her eyes, cocking her head. Her hair was blonde and silvery, straightened to a silky curtain around her face.

"Edwin."

My jaw twitched. Fuck, I hated when she called me by my first name. Especially right now, with everything I was going through with Clara.

"Can *Edwin* be off limits for today?"

She sighed. "Fine."

We were both quiet as she waited for me to speak. She adjusted her seating, crossing one leg over the other. This morning she wore white heels to match her long, elegant dress.

"You never told me why you hate your name so much," she remarked.

I cleared my throat. "It's Clara's father's name."

Her brow arched and she scribbled something on her yellow pad.

"I thought you liked him," she said. "Why not use the same name?"

"I stopped using Edwin because it was easier for us to work together and I never thought it fit me well."

"And now that he's passed?"

I cleared my throat. "It's confusing for Clara."

She made another note. Her eyes locked on me again.

"Do you see yourself as paternal towards Clara?"

I shook my head.

"Are you sure?"

I checked in with myself and shook my head again. "No, I never have. I'm her guardian, her protector, but I've never felt that way towards her."

Her lids flickered. "You're here about Clara today?"

She was so goddamn perceptive it made me wonder if she were psychic sometimes. I shifted, crossing my legs to match hers. Sometimes I mimicked her slightly because it helped me stay on equal footing.

"I am."

"Alright," she said crisply. "First and foremost on your mind then? Add context after."

"I almost fucked her."

Gretchen was a veteran, but her jaw still went slack for a second. She rearranged her face quickly and made a short note.

"Context?"

I told her about going up to the lodge and how Clara had walked into my meeting in her bikini. That fucking wet, velvet bikini. How I'd gone to her room later with the intention of scolding her and I'd kissed her instead.

And confessed to wanting to sleep with her.

I finished and took a sip of coffee. She made a few notes, her glossed lips pursed. Then she put those piercing eyes back on me. I jiggled my foot, caught in her headlights.

"I feel like there's some context missing," she said.

"There isn't."

"You scolded her. Told her you would be back at eleven. Went back out to finish your meeting. And then...what? Suddenly got horny right before you saw her again?"

I took another sip of coffee and my foot jiggled faster. She raised a perceptive brow and I adjusted my legs. Letting them stretch out so I could cross them at the ankles.

Fuck it. Gretchen knew all my worst secrets.

"I got aroused when I told her off the first time," I said. "So I masturbated to the thought of her. I thought it would be a harmless, one time thing. I think it was a mistake."

Her face didn't change.

"You don't usually come to me about your sex life," she remarked. "Clara means a lot to you."

"Yes."

"You're afraid."

I cocked my head, waiting for her to explain.

"You're afraid of hurting her."

"I am."

"So why are you here today?"

"I went to the club last night to check over some of my books. We'd just gotten back from the lodge, I told her to see Osian, but she said she was going out clubbing with Candice. She was alone, dressed in this tiny, glittery dress. Drunk, that was obvious. So we made eye contact and she made an obscene gesture—"

"What gesture?" Gretchen's mouth twitched.

I gave her an example.

She smirked. "Oh, she's got a bit of sass."

"You could say that."

"What happened?"

"I hauled her ass home and sobered her up. She admitted she didn't know what that gesture meant so I told her and things escalated. She told me she wanted me to go down on her and...other things."

"What things?"

"She doesn't want to lose her virginity to her future fiancé," I said hoarsely. "She wants me to take it."

There was a short, shocked silence. Gretchen chewed her glossy lower lip. Her silver pen spun in her fingers.

"I said no, obviously. She was tipsy," I amended. "And even if she hadn't been, I'd have said no."

"Do you ever talk about sex with her?"

I shrugged. "Occasionally."

"Have you told her about your sex life?"

I shook my head.

"You never discuss your past partners?"

I shook my head again.

"Why not?"

"I didn't think it was appropriate to talk to her about my sex life at all. And I think I was right, considering all it took was a single conversation about oral for her to beg me to fuck."

Her brow arched. "So what it sounds like to me is that you've always felt that there was some...chance that you might find her attractive. Otherwise you wouldn't have put up so many boundaries with her around...sensitive topics."

She was right, of course she was. I got to my feet and crossed the room to refill my espresso. The machine hummed and the scent of coffee filled the office.

"When was the last time you had sex?"

I calculated. "Three years and two months."

"Really?"

"Unless you're counting oral. I had a threesome last year."

"Why?"

"The threesome? It was for political purposes. I needed to make an alliance. I needed the people I was working with to think I was being benevolent. I had a threesome with a diplomat and his wife. I goaded the husband into feeling like he had blown the whole deal and then I offered them five percent. They took it."

"Everyone plays checkers while Merrick Llwyd plays chess," she remarked. "So did you get sexual release during this threesome?"

I shook my head. "We both went down on his wife. That was it."

"So it's been over three years since anyone focused on your pleasure?"

"That's correct."

"Why?"

"I don't want to bring strangers into the house with Clara living there. She deserves security and safety."

"I see."

I sat back down with my espresso and Gretchen made a lot of notes. Her manicured hand flew over the yellow pad. I shifted, uncomfortable with the silence.

"What does that tell you?" I asked quietly.

She flipped her pad closed. Her eyes locked on mine.

"That you care very, very deeply for Clara."

I swallowed, my throat tight. "I know."

She stood, smoothing her dress down, and crossed the room to the table. I watched her idly as she filled a glass with water and took a sip.

"I told her she could only drink on weekends," I said.

Gretchen lifted that lethal brow again. "How often does she drink?"

"About four times a week. To excess."

"You're being a little hard on her."

"Considering that Edwin was a recovered alcoholic, I think not."

Gretchen zeroed in on me, eyes narrowed. "If you don't want her to see you as similar to Edwin Prothero, don't act like you are," she said flatly. "I have a sneaking suspicion that daddy issues aside, she's not interested in being around a man who reminds her of her emotionally neglectful father."

I swallowed my pride and bit back my words.

"Getting drunk and clubbing four times a week isn't something to tie yourself in knots over," Gretchen said. "She's not an addict. She's just a young woman without direction."

"You're right," I said with difficulty. "I'll apologize to her."

"Good boy."

I couldn't keep back my smirk. "Oh no, I'm not one of your other clients. Don't *good boy* me, Gretchen."

She jerked her head at the door. "Then go on, get out. I have a client who appreciates it coming in ten minutes. And it's probably one of your rich and powerful peers, so better hurry."

It was probably better that Gretchen didn't officially practice anymore. Being a therapist by day and a dominatrix for Washington's elite by night wouldn't have gone over well with the board of psychiatry.

"Can I ask you a question? Just a question, I don't need judgement or advice," I said. "I only want your opinion."

She nodded, sobering at my serious tone.

"What if I were to give into her and be the first man to touch her?" I asked softly. "Would that be so bad? It would ensure she had a good first experience."

Gretchen's mouth thinned and she took a deep breath and released it.

"It would," she agreed.

"What are the risks of doing that?" I wondered aloud.

When Gretchen spoke, her voice was as cool and light as a snowflake.

"I think, Merrick, that the odds that you hurt her are very high," she said. "She loves you, maybe not romantically yet, and she trusts you with everything she has. You taught her how to value herself. Getting her heart broken by the only man she's ever trusted will ruin her completely."

I drove myself home, knuckles white on the steering wheel.

CHAPTER NINETEEN

CLARA

I didn't know what I expected to happen, but it wasn't for things to just go back to normal. The day after I'd begged Merrick to take the little pink card from his wallet and use it, I woke to find him acting like nothing had changed.

We had dinner together with a few of his friends, including Gretchen Hughes who I didn't know well. It made me a little jealous, seeing him surrounded by beautiful, successful people, although I wasn't sure why.

It wasn't like Merrick was mine.

He drove us home and said goodnight, leaving me standing in the hall. Completely confused.

His refusal to acknowledge what had happened hurt. Enough to keep me in my room, curled up. Miserable and hiding under the covers.

Over the next few weeks, I let Osian take me on a few dates. We had gone out a total of six times when he asked me to sleep with him.

Miserably, I said yes. Not because I wanted to, but because I was too nervous to refuse him.

He took me back to his apartment. It was luxurious, deep in the heart of downtown Providence. My heart hammered in my chest while we had dinner and a glass of wine.

My palm was slippery as he led me back to the bedroom.

It was a clinical space, like he never spent any time there so he hadn't bothered to furnish it. The bed was white, the walls gray, and the floor bare. The complete opposite of Merrick's house.

He shut the bedroom door and pulled me close, brushing back my hair. His mouth skimmed down my neck. My stomach fluttered as he turned me around and unzipped my dress.

The kiss he pressed in the middle of my back felt lifeless.

Nothing in comparison to Merrick's mouth.

I tried to get into what he was doing, but my body felt cold and heavy. He pulled his shirt off and I traced his stomach, wondering why the sight of it did nothing for me.

His fingers skimmed down my lower belly and slipped beneath my cotton panties. My hips tensed and my thighs locked together. Blocking him.

Nope, no, this was not going to work tonight.

"Please," I whispered. "Sorry, I don't know about this."

He was very close and I caught the flicker of irritation in his eyes. His hand closed and pulled back. Relief flooded me. There was always a little doubt that he would stop when I asked in the back of my mind.

"What is it?" he said quietly.

I sensed his impatience in the ridge of his dick under his boxers. Wriggling my hips, I pulled away just enough so we weren't touching.

"I'm not ready," I said. "You haven't even given me my first piece of jewelry."

He sighed, rolling over and sitting up. I turned to look at his naked back.

"I submitted it to Merrick for approval," he said.

"Wait...really?"

He glanced over his shoulder, looking more annoyed than ever. That contemptuous gaze bored into me, making me squirm.

"He hasn't approved it yet," he said. "Apparently he needs more time to consider if it's worthy of you."

"How...how long has he been considering."

Osian sighed again. This time he was quiet until he'd put his clothes back on. Then he flipped the light switch and ran a hand through his dark curls.

"Three weeks."

That was strange, considering that Merrick had made it clear he approved of Osian. It also gave me a little thrill. Something was holding Merrick back, something he didn't want to discuss.

I sat up, pulling the sheet to cover my body. "Okay, let me talk to him."

Osian sighed, leaning in the doorway. "Are you on birth control?"

I stared at him. "Um...no."

He rolled his eyes slightly and turned around, disappearing into the main room. Bewildered, I pulled on my clothes and went after him. He was in the kitchen, pouring a drink.

"Can't you just use a condom?" I asked.

He glanced at me over the rim of his glass. His scarred brow crooked.

"I can use a condom," he said. "But I don't know about anyone else."

My stomach went cold. "Excuse me?"

He shrugged. "We're not exclusive yet. Not until Merrick approves the fucking jewelry."

"You know I'm not sleeping with anyone."

"I am. Fucking other women."

I swallowed, expecting that statement to hurt even though I'd heard it before. Surprisingly, it felt like nothing.

"Okay, that's fine. I know we're not exclusive until you pierce me."

His jaw worked. "Are you still virgin?"

His attitude was pissing me off and I considered lying to him. Just to see his reaction. But I also didn't want to deal with the inevitable tantrum he would throw if he knew I'd let someone else fuck me.

I nodded.

"For now," he said icily.

"What the hell does that mean?" I snapped.

"Why do you think Merrick won't approve my jewelry?"

"I don't know. I said I would ask."

He bolted the glass of vodka and refilled it. I shifted, uncomfortable with the amount he was drinking. He fixed his narrowed eyes on me, leaning against the counter.

"Has Merrick ever tried to fuck you?"

I gasped. Dead silence reigned as I gathered myself.

"We aren't like that, Osian," I stammered.

"Then why the fuck did he follow me into a bathroom and threaten me? Why has he been breathing down my neck since I met you?"

"Merrick is my guardian."

"That doesn't mean he won't try to fuck you."

I drew myself up, done with the conversation. He saw the anger in my eyes and he balked, clearly realizing he'd gone too far.

"I'm leaving," I said.

"Fine."

"Okay."

He emptied his second glass and picked up his phone. "I'll call a car for you."

I shook my head.

"No, thanks. Merrick will come and get me."

Osian's eyes flashed, seared with heat. He leaned on the counter, still shirtless, and cocked his head. There was an unexpected ugliness in him that unsettled me.

"Does Merrick usually fuck women young enough to be his daughter?" he said coolly. "Or is he just making an exception for you?"

"You're drunk," I snapped.

He snorted. I grabbed my coat and purse and left the apartment. Slamming the door. My eyes were wet as I rode the elevator to the first floor. I caught a glimpse of myself in the door.

Makeup smeared, eyes red.

I couldn't see Merrick when I looked like this, all sticky and swollen from tears. He wouldn't react well to Osian making me cry. I was already juggling too much drama and I didn't need to stoke the flames over something this trivial.

Especially because this engagement meant so much to Merrick financially.

I called an Uber instead.

Then I went out to the club with Candice. This time, I couldn't get Merrick's face out of my mind. Disappointed, concerned. So I drank just enough to get me loose and dancing and cut myself off after that.

I was a little tipsy when I got back to the house. It was almost midnight so I stripped off my heels and scampered silently up the stairs. Merrick never went to sleep before one in the morning so I knew I could still talk to him about the jewelry.

His bedroom door was open. I frowned. Merrick never left his door open. He was anal about making sure doors were shut and locks were secured. Even inside the house.

I pushed it ajar and found the room completely silent and empty.

Alright...that was really strange.

My chest clenched. Had something happened and he'd left in a hurry?

No, if it was really a big deal, he would have called me. I felt around for my phone and remembered I'd left it on the hall table.

Damn it.

I stepped into his room to make sure it was really empty and my eyes fell on a beam of light coming from the bathroom. My heart stopped and I wobbled, putting out my hand to steady myself.

I lost my balance and sank to the ground. Frantically, I scrambled to my feet and looked up. Praying that if he was in the bathroom, he hadn't heard me fall.

Fuck. Me.

I could see in the bathroom, directly across the spacious floor to the clawfoot, hammered brass tub in the far corner. It was classy, like the rest of his dark oak and multi-paneled mirrored bathroom. And it was definitely not empty.

Merrick was in it, hazy through the steam. Or was it smoke? His naked arm hung over the edge, a cigarette in his fingers. His head was back, eyes closed. The shadow of stubble was stark over the lower half of his face and his hair was rumpled, more curly than usual.

My God, he had shoulders for days.

Tanned, muscular, a brush of freckles over his skin. His exposed neck was just...beautiful. Lightly dusted with stubble under his chin and over his jaw.

Speaking of hair...he had the perfect amount trailing up between his pecs. I couldn't see much lower than the middle of his chest, but...God, it was delicious.

My nipples tightened beneath my tiny dress.

He released a sigh and every nerve in my body stood to attention. Then his opposite arm lifted from behind the tub and he took a drink from...a *beer*?

Merrick didn't drink beer.

And he definitely didn't drink cheap beer either. Yet, here he was looking exhausted and partaking of what he would consider pure trash. I'd seen Merrick smoke a cigarette on occasion and that always shocked me. But this was on another level and it felt more intimate than seeing him naked.

The world had gone mad.

I remained rooted to the ground. Unsure how to get myself out of his room.

He sighed again, leaning forward, and stood abruptly. Panic burst in me and my heartbeat exploded. I saw a glimpse of his bare chest and his abs, glittering with water. Dusted with dark hair. Ridged all the way down to his...no, I was absolutely not letting myself look down there.

A little shriek split the silence. Was that from me? Panicking, I clapped my hands over my face.

The beer bottle fell to the ground.

Smash.

"Clara!"

I kept my eyes firmly shut. "I'm sorry, Merrick. I thought there was someone in the house because the door was open. I'm so sorry, I'll leave."

But I couldn't leave because my eyes were shut and I couldn't open my eyes because Merrick was *naked*. I heard the towel rack clatter and his footfalls on the floor.

"Can I please open my eyes so I can leave?" I whispered.

"Hold on."

There was a short silence. The most uncomfortable of my entire life. The door creaked.

"You may open your eyes," he said.

I obeyed gingerly. He'd turned on the bedroom light and I could see every inch of him in high definition. Big, strong shoulders. A delicious flat stomach. A trail of hair going from his navel down to the towel around his waist.

"Clara," he said.

"I'm so sorry, Merrick."

His lips parted and his eyes ran over me briefly. Then his hand came out and took hold of my jaw between his finger and thumb. Bending my face back and looking into my eyes.

"Are you drunk again?"

I shook my head. "No, I only had a bit to drink with Candice. I promise. She can back me up."

He gave me a look that made me feel small. Brows lowered, eyes stark, energy boring into me. Then he cleared his throat and blinked rapidly.

"I'm going to go," I whispered, turning on my heel.

His hand closed around my elbow. I froze, my body going still. His palm was hot, searing me up my arm. All the way to the center of my heart. Thumping wildly against my ribs.

Fuck...please touch me. Touch me like you touched me that night. Make the fireworks go off again, make meteorites shower across the sky.

"Why did you walk into my room?"

He spun me and I gasped, stumbling back. He still had that intense, focused stare trained on me. Brows drawn together. Mouth parted, a sliver of bottom teeth visible.

"I..I'm sorry, I came to ask you about Osian's jewelry," I whispered.

He took a step nearer and his palm slid up the side of my neck. Stars burst behind my eyes. My chest tightened. My heart felt raw, fluttering hard.

"What about it?"

"He said, um, he said you didn't approve it."

He shook his head once, brow creased. "No, I didn't."

"Why?" I whispered.

His thumb dragged over my cheekbone. A burning trail in its wake.

"Because I haven't decided what to do with you yet."

I swallowed with difficulty. Being in his stare like this was agonizing. Like standing on a dark road with blinding headlights trained on me. Locking every muscle of my body.

"Do you think your father would want this?" he asked.

"I...my father isn't here."

He cocked his head. "It doesn't bother you? I was his closest friend."

"Should it bother me?" I whispered. "I don't owe him anything."

He pulled his hand back. Of course he did. Merrick was always in control of himself. Always perfect, always the Welsh King before anything else. Out of nowhere, anger flooded my body down to the soles of my feet.

"Fuck you," I said softly.

His brow arced.

"Fuck you," I repeated.

"Clara—"

"No," I said, drawing back. "Fuck you, Merrick Llwyd."

His eyes flashed and narrowed. "Watch it, Clara."

"No," I said, my patience ending abruptly. "I won't beg for you, if that's what you're trying to get me to do. I'm not one of your women who are just so honored to sleep with the *Brenin*. I care about you, I want you, but I'll be damned if I ever humiliate myself on my knees for you. So, if you're planning on acting like a teenager who can't make up his mind about what he wants, I suggest you fuck yourself and be satisfied with that."

His throat flushed. His cobalt gaze was dark and wide.

"Don't play with me. I am no one's toy," I whispered. "I'll never fuck anyone who doesn't want to fuck me back just as badly. I know my worth because you showed me it."

"Clara, you—"

"Listen to me," I snapped. If I was going to go down, I was doing it in style.

His jaw worked. "Go ahead."

"I'm not asking you to marry me, Merrick. I'm asking you to teach me how to fuck before I marry Osian. That's it. But if you don't want that, there are a dozen men in your nightclub right now who would be happy to do the same."

Blue flame blazed. "So why haven't you fucked one of them instead?"

"Because I trust you," I breathed. "But I won't beg for you."

His hand shot out, seizing my wrist. Our eyes locked.

"Good girl," he said softly.

A rush of warmth pooled in my chest and seeped down to my core. "What?"

"You are the Welsh Princess and you don't beg for any man," he said. "And that includes me."

"But...you still won't sleep with me," I whispered, my mouth dry.

Something passed over his face I didn't recognize and his eyes dropped. Then they flicked up and the intense longing in them caught me by surprise.

"You have no idea how much I want to say yes," he said hoarsely. "So fuck it. Yes, I want to sleep with you, *cariad*."

CHAPTER TWENTY

MERRICK

I sent her downstairs to change while I put on a pair of sweatpants. Faintly, I heard the sound of her shower running. She would be in the kitchen waiting for me in a few minutes.

The odds that you hurt her are very high.

I closed my eyes. Let my head fall back.

Fuck.

I ran my hand over my hair to tame it and left the bedroom in just sweatpants. She'd already seen my bare torso so there was no point in hiding my body. The damage was done. We were past that point.

She was in the kitchen, her wet hair stuck to her upper back. She wore a cropped shirt and plaid shorts that rode up her ass a little. I crossed the room, my eyes glued to her body.

Unashamed this time.

She turned and my eyes fell to her bare, lean belly. There was a piercing on her navel, diamond and gold. I reached out and touched it and her stomach clenched.

"When did you get your stomach pierced?" I asked.

"This summer in England."

I sank to my knees to get a better look. She backed against the sink, her fingers digging into the counter's edge. White knuckles and pink fingernails.

It was late, we were both exhausted. Our guards were down. We were already going to have regrets in the morning.

Bending, I tongued her navel gently. Flicking her ring.

"Oh my God," she moaned.

"Yeah, you like that?"

"Yes, I don't know why. It just feels good."

I nuzzled her stomach and pushed the tip of my tongue into her naval. Her hips rode against my chin. Just a little, like she was shy about her neediness.

"Is this weird for you?" I asked softly.

She shook her head. "It feels good when you touch me. It feels right."

It did feel right, despite all the warning bells going off far away. Very, very far away.

"Did you know your navel has nerves that go down to your clit?" I murmured.

"No, I didn't know," she gasped.

I flicked her ring with my tongue. She gave the sweetest, little moan. Feeling bold, I pushed my tongue into her navel again and thrust gently. Like I would if I were eating her pussy.

She whimpered.

Fuck, that went right to my dick.

Still tonguing her gently, I looked up and we locked eyes. My hands tightened on her hips, my fingers pushing beneath the hem of her shirt. I wanted her so fucking badly, but we had to be careful.

"May I take your shorts off?" I murmured.

She bit her lip, chewing the inside of her mouth. She probably had a sore from how much she did that.

"It's okay if you're not ready for me to see you in your panties."

"No, it's just...I don't have any on."

My erection throbbed, heavy in my sweatpants. I stood and her eyes dropped like a stone. Her lips parted and her jaw worked.

"You are...large," she breathed.

"Thank you."

"How...how big is it?"

Instead of answering, I gently took her wrist. I drew her hand toward me slowly so she had time to pull back if she felt uncomfortable. Our hands cupped my cock in the hot space between our bodies.

Her fingers flexed, gripping me hesitantly. Her pupils widened.

"I can feel how warm it is through your pants," she said, not taking her eyes from my groin.

"I'm very hard."

"I can tell."

Swallowing past my dry throat, I stepped back to put some space between us. She stood watching me as I made us both a cup of coffee. Her mouth turned up in one corner when I added her favorite creamer to her cup.

"Thank you," she said, accepting it.

"You're welcome. Now, we should probably lay out some boundaries and expectations," I said.

"Why?"

"You said you wanted me to teach you how to fuck."

"I do."

She took a step closer and her palms slid up my chest. Fingers flexing just enough I felt her nails. Her lashes were heavy and her eyes pulled me in.

Her body melted into mine, her hands gripping my forearms. My entire being tingled and pure fire seeped through my veins. Arousal coiled down my spine, getting me painfully hard again.

Our mouths moved together eagerly. Tongues brushing, breath mingling. When she drew back, we were both panting.

"We need boundaries," I said. "Rules. I can't hurt you."

"What kind of rules?"

I rested my chin on her head, looking out the kitchen window into the dark.

"We need to keep this separate from the rest of our lives. I won't fuck you here in this house," I said. "I'll take you somewhere."

"Alright, that makes sense."

"And I don't want anyone to know, I don't want this to ruin your reputation. Not Candice, Yale, or Caden. And absolutely not Daphne or Ophelia."

"I agree."

"Or Osian."

She drew back, her brows creasing. "He's going to know someone slept with me eventually."

"We'll cross that bridge when we get to it. Also, in the spirit of total honesty, I've told my therapist about what happened at the lodge. And the rest of it."

Her lids flickered. "The rest of it?"

"That you asked me to have sex with you."

"Oh. What did she say?"

"She said...there was a high chance that you would end up hurt if I slept with you," I admitted. "She doesn't think either of us can do this without getting attached to each other."

"We're already attached to each other, just not like that. I think we're safer the way we are than if we weren't friends. I mean, look at us talking through this like adults."

"We are adults." I studied her skeptically. "And I always talk through things before I have sex with anyone."

"Does that ever put a damper on things?"

"No, I need to know where I stand with people. Especially strangers."

She started chewing the inside of her mouth again. I brushed the backs of my fingers over her chin and her eyes flicked to mine. A bolt of pure electricity heated the space between us.

"Do you know where you stand with me?" she breathed.

"I like to think I do."

"You are the most careful man I've ever met."

I laughed and stepped back. "Thank you. I think."

It was very late, but neither of us were tired. I made another pot of coffee—decaf this time—and went to the living room. She stayed in the kitchen for a moment longer and appeared with her evening bowl of ice cream drenched in chocolate syrup.

I stretched out in my chair and she hesitated a few feet away. Her eyes lingered on me, but she didn't get any closer. Her knuckles were white around her bowl.

My chest ached. She wanted something, but she was afraid to ask for it.

"Clara," I said. "What is it?"

"May...may I sit with you?"

I glanced down at the chair. There was really only room for one person. Then it hit me and I melted and held out my arm. Her shoulders sagged with relief and she was by my side in a second, climbing carefully into my lap.

She settled back, curled up with her side against my chest. "Do you want some ice cream?"

I shook my head.

She put the spoon in her mouth, flipping it upside down to curl her tongue around it. Getting every bit of chocolate.

"Have you ever sat in anyone's lap before?" I asked carefully.

Her eyes darted to mine and dropped down.

"No."

"Not even your father's when you were little?"

She shook her head, eyes still locked on her bowl. "He wasn't really like that. We never hugged or anything either."

There was a bit of chocolate on the corner of her mouth. I brushed it off with my thumb and she flushed. Pink stained her neck and cheeks.

"Has anyone ever told you they loved you?"

"Like...romantically?"

"No, I mean in any way."

She thought about it for a second, putting the spoon back in her mouth. When she released it, it made a little pop.

"Candice and her parents," she said. "Owen and Catrin told me they loved me a lot. And of course Candice does all the time."

"But not your father?"

She laughed shortly. "My father would have curled up and died before he said he loved me. We just weren't that kind of household. It's no wonder my mom got out when she had the chance."

That caught me off guard. She never talked about her mother, probably because she had so few memories of her. I kept quiet, giving her space to continue if she felt like it.

Apparently she didn't because she shrugged and put more ice cream in her mouth.

"Anyway," she said, swallowing hard. "It doesn't matter."

I traced down her spine until I got to her bare lower back. She slowed and I felt her breathing speed up a little. I swirled my fingertip over the little dimples above her ass.

"So this is the first time you've ever sat on anyone's lap?"

She nodded.

"How is it?"

Her eyes went distant and she snuggled closer to my chest. "It's nice. You feel warm...strong. Safe."

"You're always safe now."

She nodded once and I felt her pull into her shell. Dismissing all of the hurt I knew lay beneath her surface. Upstairs, the grandfather clock chimed two in the morning.

She sat aside her empty bowl and laid her head on my shoulder. I let my arm slide around her body, holding her against me. Stroking through her damp hair.

Her breathing deepened and her body went limp.

CHAPTER TWENTY-ONE

CLARA

When I woke, he was gone and it was early morning. I could hear a faint whirring sound from the lower floor and I followed it down to the gym. He was running on the treadmill. Shirtless, glistening with sweat. Earbuds in and eyes locked ahead.

It blew my mind that I'd slept in the arms of this man.

I padded across the floor and he saw me, hitting the red button. Suddenly shy, I crossed my arms over my chest. I hadn't worn a bra last night and my nipples were hard under my shirt.

He popped an earbud out. "Good morning."

"Hi," I said softly.

"I have to go into the office in a minute, but I was up early taking care of some things. I found a beautiful house in the New Hampshire mountains and I'd like to take you there. If you still want me to fuck you."

I did my best not to blush, but the heat swept through me all the same.

"Yes," I whispered. "Did you rent it out already?"

"I bought it. This morning."

I gaped at him.

"You bought a house just to have sex in?"

He stepped down from the the treadmill and put his earbuds in his sweatpant's pocket. He didn't seem phased. Like it was normal to just buy a house to fuck in.

It wasn't normal, at least not for Merrick. He was a careful, classy spender. He drove an expensive, custom car, but it was the only car he owned. He had quality, tailored clothes, but not many of them.

He repaired his things when they broke, invested in quality products, and never flaunted his wealth.

I was the only thing he splurged on. When it came to me, he swiped credit cards and signed contracts like it meant nothing. My toes curled, heat bubbling in my stomach.

"Why did you buy a house instead of renting one?" I asked.

A smirk played on his mouth. "I don't like being interrupted during dinner. Or dessert."

Inwardly, I flailed. Praying I wasn't blushing.

"I don't think anyone would have noticed us in a rental in New Hampshire," I said quickly.

"I want you to have the privacy and comfort you need for your first time."

He'd done it for me. Of course he had. A lump rose in my throat and I blinked, looking away. Why was he so damn kind to me? Surely there was a side to him that wasn't so...well, everything my father hadn't been?

"Thank you."

He started up the stairs and I followed him to the kitchen, watching while he got a glass of water. He was still sweating heavily and I found myself staring. Admiring the droplets running down his abs. Staining his sweatpants.

"Are you on birth control?" he asked.

Startled, I shook my head.

"Alright, I can use a condom."

A pang shot through my chest. I knew it was stupid, reckless, foolish, but I wanted him bare. I wanted to feel the heat of his skin fill me. I wanted him to come inside me so I could have the whole experience. Start to finish.

"I'll get on birth control," I said quickly.

His brow arced. "I don't know about that."

"Why?"

He cocked his head, thinking hard. "Alright. If you go on the pill we can forego the condom. I've been tested since...the last time I had sexual contact with anyone."

I nodded, unexpectedly jealous.

He emptied his glass, kissed my forehead, and strode out of the kitchen. I stood there, fists clenched, heart pounding. There was a sweet, hot ache between my legs.

I didn't have to be anywhere for a little while so I padded quietly down the hall to my room. I slid the lock down and climbed into bed. Flushed, I took my vibrator out and pulled my shorts down. Spreading my thighs. Slipping my hand between them.

A bit of silky wetness stained my fingertips. My heartbeat fluttered against my ribs. Loud in my ears.

I closed my eyes. Into my mind swam the image of Merrick between my legs, sheet pulled up to our waists. Moving slowly against my body. Pleasuring me, filling me. Skin on skin, breath mingling. Low, husky moans spilling from his mouth and onto my neck.

Nothing between us, just our desperate bodies in the dark.

My spine arced. The wave hit me before I was ready and I cried out.

When I resurfaced, I was panting hard.

Sweaty, flushed, and stunned.

A week later, I found myself on my back with my legs open in the gynecologist's office. Merrick hadn't asked me any questions, he'd just made an appointment on the recommendation of his doctor. It should have annoyed me, but it didn't. I liked that he was handling things.

It made this awkward, pre-sex period easier.

"So you're planning on becoming sexually active soon?" the doctor said, pulling on her gloves.

I nodded, keeping my eyes ahead. "Yes, in the next month."

"Well, congratulations," she said pleasantly. "And it's good you're coming in beforehand. It can help ease your fears around your first time to get an exam and have your questions answered."

"Thank you," I said.

It felt incredibly weird to be talking casually with her while she had her head between my knees. I flexed my cold toes in the stirrups.

"Is this your first time coming in?"

I considered lying, but decided against it.

"Yes, I didn't think I needed to before now," I admitted.

"Well, moving forward we want to see you every few years," she said cheerfully. "And if you have issues with your birth control, of course we can help out too. If you're planning on becoming pregnant, we have a specialist who can answer your questions about fertility."

"I'm not," I said quickly.

She nodded. "You have time."

We were quiet as she examined me and did a pap smear, which hurt more than I'd expected. She prescribed me the pill and I sat up, covering my lap while she sanitized her hands.

"Did you have any questions?" she asked.

"Um...I was wondering what pain level I should expect," I said. "For the first time, I mean."

She crossed her arms. "It's hard to say. Sorry, I'm sure you'd rather hear a solid answer. But that can depend on the skill of your partner. Is this also his first time?"

I shook my head. "Definitely not."

"Do you trust him?"

I didn't hesitate before nodding. "Yes, I know he's careful and patient."

"Good, that's what matters most. I would recommend using a vibrator with him, or yourself, before foreplay. You need to make sure you're really relaxed. Have him take it slow, let him focus on you."

A shiver went down to my core. Nervous anticipation.

Merrick appeared to pick me up from my appointment. My doctor was still standing in the lobby, talking with the nurse when he arrived. He wore a classy, blue suit and his aviators. The sight made my core clench and the doctor's jaw fall slack.

I crossed the room and he bent, kissing my temple.

"How was it?"

"Good, she's putting me on the pill."

It was late so he took me out for dinner. We had sashimi in a private room at one of Merrick's favorite restaurants. Then we went home and parted awkwardly in the hallway.

I asked to sleep in his bed a few days later.

He refused.

"If you sleep in my bed, Clara, I'll fuck you," he said hoarsely. "And I swore I'd take care of you. Accidentally getting you pregnant doesn't factor into that."

I knew he was right, but I was dying to be near him. Just to feel his heat and fill my senses with his dark, oak scent.

It tortured us both to be so close, but still so far.

So close I could almost taste him.

I had to endure seeing Osian at a dinner for one of his father's business deals. He was as brash and arrogant as ever. His hand lingered on me all through dinner. Fingers closed on my thigh like he owned me. Like he'd already pierced me.

Eyes possessive.

After the meal was over, he asked Merrick to speak alone. They went into the hallway while I waited by the door. I could just make out the rise and fall of their voices. Too low to really hear.

They were discussing me.

Of course they were.

I trusted Merrick, I had no other choice. But I wished I could be part of the conversation.

After several minutes, Merrick strode down the hall. The look in his eyes caught me off guard.

Hard. Dark. Possessive.

My core clenched, a little thrill of fear going down my spine. He put his hand on my lower back and ushered me out the front door and into the Audi.

I curled up in the seat, arms folded in my lap.

His hand flexed on the steering wheel.

"Did you kiss him?" he asked.

I glanced over, noticing the hard line of his jaw. Was he angry with me? I hadn't done anything wrong by kissing Osian.

"Yes," I said carefully.

"Did you like it?"

"It was...alright."

"What else?"

"What do you mean?"

"Did he touch your breasts? Your pussy?"

I gasped, taken aback. His eyes were still straight ahead, his face obscured in darkness as we drove.

"He...um, he took my bra off and touched my breasts," I said. "But I kind of freaked out when he tried to put his hand into my panties, so he stopped."

"Fucker," said Merrick softly.

I couldn't believe it. Merrick wasn't jealous of anyone. He was the Welsh King, the top of the food chain. I turned in my seat.

"Do I need to remind you that you picked out Osian for me?"

"No, no need to remind me. I'm painfully aware of that."

"He's not a bad person."

"He's got room to grow."

"Merrick."

He was quiet for the rest of the drive home. When we got inside, he helped me out of my coat. Then his hand closed around my wrist and he spun me around. Pulling me against him.

His mouth came down on mine.

His body pinned me to the wall.

Hot, heavy, suffocating.

Like being sucked down by a wave and enveloped in an ocean of the sweetest heat.

His hands were in my hair, bending my head back. Sliding down until they were under my clothes, kneading my hips, my thighs. He kissed me hard, bruising my lips. His tongue pushed between my teeth, to the back of my throat.

When he pulled back, a bit of hair fell over his forehead. I reached up in a daze and brushed it back.

"Merrick," I breathed. "You are jealous."

"You're enough to make any man jealous," he said darkly.

He brushed his mouth across my forehead, searing my skin. The breath he released sounded more like a groan. Then he was gone, striding down the hallway. Disappearing into the shadows. Leaving me to sleep alone once more.

CHAPTER TWENTY-TWO

MERRICK

I had excellent control, but with Clara, I didn't trust it. I'd never wanted anyone as much as I wanted her in those days leading up to our weekend in New Hampshire. I'd never felt so out of control, like she'd ripped the wheel right out of my hands.

Like I was falling.

She started taking her birth control the day after her doctor's visit. She told me when she took her first pill, like it was a big milestone.

"Thank you," I said.

She frowned. "Why are you thanking me?"

"For handling the prevention part," I said. "I wouldn't mind wearing a condom with you, but I...I'm...fuck, never mind."

She cocked her head, chewing her mouth. "What?"

Heat pooled at the base of my spine and gathered in my groin. She was standing in the hall, just outside my door. I took her upper arm and pulled her close. Allowing myself the pure luxury of kissing her soft mouth.

So fucking sweet. She moaned softly and her hands curled in the front of my shirt. Playing absently with the hair on my chest as her mouth moved against mine.

Reluctantly, I pulled back.

"I can't wait to feel you bare."

She nodded, tucking her hair back. Dipping her chin.

"You're such a good girl," I praised, softly stroking her chin.

She had an immediate reaction. Her cheeks and throat flushed and she dropped her eyes. Working that spot inside her mouth again.

"Do you like that?"

"Like what?" Her voice was raspy.

"When I praise you."

Her palms slid up my chest. Resting on my pecs, stroking me through my shirt. Then moving higher and locking around my neck. She looked up at me, like we were a real couple.

"I do," she said softly. "I'm just not used to it."

Recklessly, I leaned in and kissed her hard.

"This weekend, I'll call you a good girl all night if you want," I murmured. "Praise you for every time you come on my mouth."

"Merrick," she breathed.

Our heartbeats were loud in the space between us. I kissed her hairline, breathing in that scent like a drug. "No sex until this weekend. Go back to your room and go to sleep."

Her lower lip pushed out. "I swear you're just teasing me."

I turned her around and gave her a little push into the hall.

"Go to bed," I said. "Goodnight, Clara."

I put Caden in charge of my business and Yale in charge of organization affairs for the next week. They both had questions, but I kept it firmly vague.

I had a business deal that was private in New York, I told them. I'd be gone for ten days at most. Clara was feeling stressed out and she was going to spend some time in the country with Daphne and Ophelia. That last lie was probably safe because my aunts rarely interacted with anyone from the organization anymore.

A cold front moved in Thursday night and the weatherman called for heavy snow in the New Hampshire mountains.

I didn't tell Clara.

The day finally came and I couldn't get back from work fast enough. She appeared in the kitchen, already dressed in a black sweatsuit, and dragging her suitcase. I had just finished making a thermos of coffee for the road.

Our eyes locked and a wave of something I had no name for passed between us.

"Are you ready?" I asked.

She nodded hard.

I loaded our bags into the rental sedan and she curled up in the seat beside me. Dark hair spilling over her shoulders. Lips colored berry purple. Long, red nails gripped around the thermos.

I settled into the driver's seat.

What was I doing?

My hand hesitated over the key and my fist clenched. She leaned forward, her brows drawing together.

"Are you okay, Merrick?" she asked softly.

I turned the key and the engine purred. "Yeah, making sure we brought everything."

She kept her eyes locked on me as I shifted to look behind us and backed the car up and pulled down the drive. We were both quiet on the way to the halfway point. Maybe I was paranoid, but I wanted to switch cars halfway there. Just in case.

When we pulled up, she jumped out and grabbed her purse.

I leaned across the seat and popped the glove box. There was a pistol in a holster stored there. Her jaw dropped as I took it out, removed the holster, and pushed the naked gun under my belt.

"What are you doing?"

I stepped out of the sedan. "I'm always armed, Clara."

"Really?"

I raised a brow as I took her suitcase and ushered her across the parking lot to the SUV parked in the far corner beneath the floodlight. She kept looking back at me, her glittering fingers still clutched around the thermos.

Who did she think kept her safe? I didn't have security guards in my home, just at the perimeters of the yard. I slept with a gun holster on the side of my bed. When I left the house, I carried beneath my jacket.

I'd seen enough shit not to, but Clara hadn't and she didn't understand.

She got into the SUV and I loaded the bags and settled into the driver's seat. Without thinking, I pulled her to me and kissed her mouth. Peppermint cream and coffee mingled on my tongue. My hand came up to cradle her head. Her breathing came fast and she moaned.

She *moaned*. So fucking soft and sweet in her throat.

A little sound of longing.

When I pulled back, her eyes were dazed. We both laughed, unable to pretend any longer that there wasn't something special about a kiss like that.

Fuck, I was going to hurt her, wasn't I?

We got to the house around five that night. Her eyes were wide as she took in the spacious structure built into the side of the mountain. Hundreds of miles of pine trees spread out in a green sprawl over the valley below.

The sunset would be breathtaking from the bedroom.

I carried the suitcases up the steep stairs and unlocked the door. She waited obediently in the hall while I did a full walk through of the house. Checking behind every curtain, in every closet, testing every lock.

She was staring out the window in the front room when I returned. This side of the house looked north, giving us a picturesque view of the mountains and a bubbling spring. Birds gathered on the front porch, fighting over an empty feeder.

Clara was chewing her mouth, looking out. I took her hand, letting the suitcases stay in the hall, and led her upstairs to the second floor.

The house was modern with big windows and light wood furnishings. The ceilings were lofted and the floors made of warm pine. Reminiscent of a Swiss chalet.

We moved silently into the bedroom. The bed was enormous and covered in a heavy, down comforter. The far wall was completely made of glass and looked out over the pine forest.

Under the overcast sky, it felt private despite the whole room being open.

Like the world had given us a hidden place.

A place for us to discover the secret parts of each other.

"Do you like it?" I asked.

Her eyes were wide and her mouth parted. She slipped off her shoes and padded across the floor. She paused before me and glanced down, curling her toes.

"Is the floor heated?"

"It's supposed to be," I said. "Can't have you getting cold feet."

She smiled and her eyes went distant.

"You bought this house just for this weekend?"

I nodded. "You asked me to show you what it was like to be treated the way you deserve. So here you are."

A smile broke, the light flooding back into her face as her confidence returned. She flung her arms around me, hugging me tightly. Whispering her thank yous into my chest.

"Let's talk," I said.

She looked up. "About what?"

I sat on the edge of the bed and pulled her to stand between my knees. A bit of dark hair fell across her cheek. I brushed it back. So fucking soft.

"Do you want this to be like we're together?" I asked. "Touching, kissing, no boundaries on being naked? Or do you want me to fuck you under the covers and sleep in the other bedroom?"

"No," she said in a rush.

I raised a brow.

Her soft palm slid down my jaw, rasping against my stubble. She bent and her mouth brushed mine. Pressing to me, kissing me slowly. Giving me a taste of her tongue.

Her fist closed in my hair, pulling me back.

"Fuck," I breathed.

"I want you all weekend. I want to sleep in the same bed, I want to shower together. I want...I want to see you naked in the kitchen. Making me coffee and breakfast."

My cock throbbed, begging to be let out of my pants. She still had ahold of my hair. Keeping me in her grasp. Our eyes locked and flashed.

"You first," I said.

"What?"

"You can cook too. I want *you* naked and making me breakfast in the kitchen," I said, my voice dropping to a growl.

"Hmm, no," she said. "I thought you said I was a princess and princesses don't cook."

"Do kings cook though?"

"This one does. He cooks the best Sunday roast I've ever eaten."

I shifted, but she kept her fingers in my hair. She was playing with me, I saw it in her eyes. Baiting me to drop my guard and give her the pushback she wanted.

"Getting a bit bossy, *cariad*."

She shrugged. "You sure you don't like it?"

I rose and slid my fingers into her hair, fisting my hand and drawing her head back. Her pupils blew and her breasts heaved beneath her sweatshirt.

I bent, my lips brushing her ear.

"Do you want spanked?" I breathed.

Her chest rose and fell, spine bent back. Gaze fixed on me. I knew that if I put my hand between her legs, she would be soaked for me. Heat coiled in my groin, making me pulse.

"Yes, please," she whispered.

It was so unexpected that I laughed and released her, letting her skip off to the bathroom. She was a handful, I was finding that out quicker than expected.

And yet...I liked that.

CHAPTER TWENTY-THREE

CLARA

He'd thought of everything. The house was fully stocked with food, drinks, fresh linens and towels. I ducked into the shower to wash away the four hour drive and change into a casual pair of shorts and a tank top.

When I got downstairs, the spacious kitchen smelled like steak and caramelized onions. He stood at the counter, shirtless and in sweatpants. Popping the cap from a bottle of red wine.

My heart stilled and restarted.

God, it hadn't even started and I was already dreading for the weekend to be over.

Oblivious, he poured a splash of wine and sipped it. His eyes lit up.

"That's very good," he said. "Come taste it."

I joined him, taking the glass and having a sip. From the same place his mouth had touched.

"I like it."

He flashed his wide smile and went to the stove. I pulled myself onto the counter and filled my glass, my bare feet hanging down. I took a sip, glancing subtly at him.

That was a sight I could get used to.

His back muscles were impressive. Moving under his smooth skin as he flipped the steaks and took them off the stove. That dusting of freckles over his shoulders was so sexy. Like a bit of vulnerability in the expanse of his perfect torso.

He brought me a plate of steak, caramelized onions, and roasted carrots. I watched him, suddenly shy at his big, half-naked presence, as he cut a strip of meat and speared it on a fork.

"Open," he said.

I obeyed. He grinned and put a piece of the juiciest, tender steak on my tongue. I wasn't the biggest fan of steak, but Merrick could make just about anything delicious. I closed my eyes, unable to hold back the moan.

"Good girl," he said softly.

"Oh my God," I breathed. "That's amazing."

His lids flickered, dark lashes flicking over those deep blue eyes.

"I hope you make that sound when I put my cock in your mouth," he said.

I coughed, almost choking. Swallowing with difficulty.

His hand came up and ran down my side to my hip. Gripping me hard. His other hand lifted and he touched my lower lip with his fingertip.

I parted for him. Eyes locked on my mouth, he pushed his finger onto my tongue.

"Suck it," he breathed.

I obeyed, unsure if I was doing it right. I must have been because he groaned quietly and began moving his finger back and forth over my tongue.

Like he was fucking my mouth with it.

Heat pooled heavily between my legs and an ache I felt down to the bottoms of my feet started in my core.

"Fuck, you're a natural," he praised.

"Thank you," I said, muffled by his finger.

"Have you ever given head?"

Heat crept over my face. "No."

"Good."

I felt that dark jealousy creep in, shading his eyes. He pulled his finger out and a sudden sense of loss filled me. The sensation of having him inside me was heavenly. So dirty and so right. Even if it was just a finger in my mouth.

I didn't want it to end.

He cut another piece of steak and ate it. Then he fed me the third piece and let me lick his fingers. And suck the tips clean while his heavy eyes bored into me.

Never missing a thing.

When the plate was empty, he refilled the wine glass and put me on my feet. He took my hand and led me from the kitchen. My heart began pounding. Beating in an odd, disjointed rhythm.

The reality of what we were doing was hitting me slowly. Like a slow motion crash.

Merrick was going to sleep with me. My guardian, the man who'd taken care of me for six years. The Welsh King, the most notorious man on the Eastern Seaboard.

My Merrick, the man I trusted more than myself.

We were going to take our clothes off and have sex with each other. The idea was unfathomable.

And yet, it was about to happen.

Unsticking my dry tongue from the roof of my mouth, I swallowed. I kept my eyes down as he ushered me gently into the bedroom. The door shut with a finalizing click. Bathing us in the pale starlight over the pine forest.

He turned on the lamp in the corner and set the wineglass down. His eyes were moonlit pools and I saw something there that was new to me.

Pure vulnerability, desire, and something like awe.

"I want to go down on you, *cariad*," he said. "That's the first thing I want with you, it's all I've been wanting. I need to taste your pussy before I go fucking insane."

There was a short, shocked silence. Heat plummeted to my core.

"May...may I change?" I asked.

My voice was raspy. He nodded once and I ducked into the bathroom. Shutting the door and releasing a breath.

Fuck, I was out of my depth.

He would be waiting and I didn't want him to think I was getting cold feet. I wanted this more than I'd ever wanted anything. And I knew I could trust him to get me through it.

I showered again, paranoid that I wasn't clean enough to have a man put his face between my legs. Then I brushed out my hair and put on a little lipstick and mascara. Just enough that I felt pretty.

I wasn't comfortable wearing lingerie with him yet. It felt too intimate. Instead, I slipped on a pair of cotton panties and a t-shirt.

Then I padded out into the bedroom before I lost my nerve.

He was sipping wine, standing by the window. Sweatpants hanging off his hips, profile stark against the pale light.

I cleared my throat. He turned and his whole body froze. His eyes flicked down and up again. Barely looking where he set it, he put the wine down and crossed the room.

His big, lean hand was in my hair, gathering it in a gentle grip. Pulling my head back so he could kiss my mouth. Making my knees go weak and my core pulse.

"Fuck, you're so beautiful," he murmured.

Before I could respond, he picked me up in his arms. Easily, like I weighed nothing. Automatically, my arms slid around his neck and my legs curled around his waist. Holding him close.

His mouth brushed mine, coaxing my lips apart. When he kissed me, I heard the faint sound of fireworks and the dull roar of the ocean, crashing waves of heat through my body.

He was taking his time with me. Letting his tongue barely dip into my mouth before kissing me so slowly I felt everything. All the way down to the deepest point between my thighs.

I moaned, digging my fingernails into him. Raking over his freckled shoulders. He spilled me onto my back on the bed and climbed atop me. Mouth on my jaw, on my neck. On my breasts through my thin shirt.

My God, that felt so good. Even through the fabric, his mouth was heavenly.

My head fell back as he nuzzled between my breasts. Sparks danced in my eyes. Making the dark ceiling pop and writhe overhead.

His mouth moved, finding my nipple through my shirt. A low moan escaped his throat and his hips began moving, pushing his erection into my thigh. Grinding it absently on me. He took my covered nipple and worked it with his mouth.

"Oh my God," I gasped.

He pulled back, brushed my hair from my face.

"Do you need to slow down?" he breathed. "I'm getting carried away."

"Please don't stop," I begged. "I want you."

He shook his head. "I don't intend on fucking you tonight, *cariad*."

Wait...what? I stared up at him, confused. He sat back on his heels and his hands drifted down over his lean stomach. Down to the tie of his sweatpants at the end of that trail of dark hair.

Was he wearing underwear?

"I think we should focus on just exploring tonight," he said. He pulled the string on his pants. Unfurling the knot. "I'll eat your pussy...make you feel good."

He slid his thumb under his waistband and pushed down, revealing a strip of boxer brief. I was breathing hard, my eyes fixed to his waist.

The V of his lower abs flexed. His cock twitched beneath his pants.

"May I see it?" I whispered.

The corner of his mouth turned up and he got to his feet and pulled his sweatpants off. Revealing his muscled body and the clear outline of his erection under his boxer briefs.

Transfixed, I pushed myself up and reached for him. My hand hesitated over his lower stomach. I glanced up, waiting for permission.

"Go on," he said. "I want you to feel comfortable enough to explore my body and get used to it."

Grateful, I skimmed my fingertips down to his waistband. Underneath the fabric, his cock twitched. I stared at it, at the wet stain at the tip of the long ridge.

"What is that?" I asked softly.

He glanced down. "Pre-cum. It just means I'm aroused."

"How...how much comes out?"

"Maybe a few drops, it depends."

I touched the wet spot and his lids flickered, mouth parting. He twitched again and his head fell back, his throat bobbing as his chest heaved once.

"Can you...take your boxers off and lay down?" I asked.

His cobalt eyes flared and his fingers slid down, hooking the waistband. Tugging it down around his thighs until it fell to the floor. My eyes fell and my stomach fluttered.

My body burned, tingling all over.

He was perfect. Thick, long, the dark hair on his groin neatly trimmed. He was everything I'd imagined he would be...except for one thing.

"You have tattoos right above your penis," I said.

He looked down. "Yes, I do."

He was amused by my reaction. I gazed at his cock, transfixed, as he moved past me to the bed. He lay on his back, propping his head and shoulders up on the pillows against the window.

Feeling bold, I climbed on my hands and knees to him. Hesitantly, I straddled his left leg and lowered myself onto his thigh. His skin felt warm and firm and I had the sudden urge to rub myself on him.

"What do they mean?" I asked softly.

"They're status symbols," he said. "I got the bottom ring when I became *Brenin*. The short, broken lines are for...other things. Then the thickest line is done for every decade in power."

"What are the short lines for?" I pressed.

"Never you mind."

I frowned, annoyed. He was protecting me, keeping me ignorant of something ugly. I could tell. Deciding now wasn't the time to press him, I skimmed my fingers down his stomach.

Stopping right above his cock.

His lids flickered and the lines of his muscled torso relaxed. Gathering my courage, I wrapped my fingers around his cock, right below the head.

"Oh fuck," he said in a rush.

He pulsed, hot and silky under my fingers. I'd thought about what cocks felt like, but this was so much different. He was twitching and his heartbeat thrummed under my grip. The rounded head was flushed and there was a bit of wetness at the tip.

"Can...can I lick it?" I asked.

His hips jerked and his lids flickered.

"Jesus," he breathed. "Yes, please."

Heart pounding, I braced myself on the heel of my hand and bent until he was inches from my face. He smelled good, like warm skin and soap.

And Merrick—intoxicating, dark oak. Solid and safe.

I put out my tongue and touched it to his tip and his cock twitched. His eyes were so bright, burning like blue flame. Locked on my face like there was nothing else in the world but me.

Feeling bold, I flattened my tongue and dragged it up his hard length. From the base all the way to the head where he tasted so good. I licked him again, like he was hard candy that would melt under my tongue.

Salty, clean, hot.

How many licks to get to the center of the Welsh King?

The thought made me want to giggle, but I was too horny to let myself get distracted. My core pulsed, hot and needy. There was a slippery sensation growing between my legs and a building pressure deep inside.

Mind blank, I put the head of his cock into my mouth and sucked. He groaned, the most delicious rough and deep sound. Almost like a growl. A tendon in his neck flexed. I swirled my tongue up the underside of the head, trying to get all the salty, sweetness of him.

"*Cariad*," he breathed.

Experimentally, I pushed it a little further back on my tongue. He responded with another heavy moan. His hips worked slightly as I pulled back. Letting his cock slip from my mouth with a small pop.

"How was that?" I asked softly, suddenly shy.

He sat up abruptly, pulling me into his lap. His cock pressing against my inner thigh, wet from my mouth. His lips met mine, kissing me briefly before moving up to my temple. His arms were firm, holding me to his chest.

"Merrick," I whispered. "What is it?"

His hand closed in my hair, pulling my head back. There was unreadable emotion surging in his eyes.

"You're so fucking perfect," he breathed.

I chewed my lip. "Would you like to take my clothes off?"

CHAPTER TWENTY-FOUR

MERRICK

I had my hands under her shirt before she could finish her sentence. Peeling it from her, freeing her breasts. Perfect breasts that needed to be in my mouth. In my hands, in my face, on my dick.

Everywhere and anywhere I could get them.

Her breasts were breathtaking, perfect in every way. Maybe a C cup, it was hard to tell. Teardrop shaped with pale veins like a patchwork over her skin. Small, light brown nipples that hardened to peaks under my gaze.

Mind blank, I put one in my mouth and swirled my tongue over it, making her gasp. My teeth grazed the tip and her spine arced. Her head fell back and that beautiful waterfall of dark hair fell in a tangle down her back.

"Merrick," she moaned.

My tongue curled on her nipple and flicked gently. Her hips worked, her sex damp through her cotton panties.

Fuck me, I needed to see her pussy. The last month had been torture and I finally had her in my bed. I couldn't wait any longer.

She yelped as I flipped her onto her back. A little tremor moved down her stomach. I slid my fingers along the underside of her thighs and up beneath her panties and tugged them down.

"Spread your legs for me, *cariad*," I said.

"Merrick." Her dark eyes flicked to mine.

I kissed the underside of her knee, licking her soft skin. Biting the inside of her thigh and kissing up to the bare mound of her sex. I could see the little line of her pussy, but not what was between it. Not what I really needed to see.

"Are you comfortable?" I asked, forcing myself to hold back.

She swallowed. "I'm just nervous."

"Why?"

She chewed her mouth, eyes big. Her upper body was propped up on her elbows as she looked down at me.

"What if you don't like it?" she whispered.

I brushed my jaw over her knee, stubble rasping. "There is no world in which I won't be completely infatuated with what's between your legs."

I applied light pressure to the inside of her knee, but she resisted.

"There's something else."

Pausing, I met her gaze. There was a flush on her cheeks and she was chewing hard on her mouth.

"I don't orgasm very well," she admitted. "Like, it's hard to get there."

How would she even know? A vibrator was purely mechanics. It wasn't the slow build of arousal, the teasing, the soft touches. The hours spent on making her thighs slick with desire before I ever touched her clit.

The going to the edge again and again until there was no choice but to fall.

And fall again and again. Until we lifted our heads and realized the sun had already risen.

"So you use your fingers and your vibrator on yourself and you struggle to finish?" I asked.

She nodded. "I can finish maybe half the time."

I stroked up her leg, cradling it.

"Let me make you a deal," I said. "We're just going to relax tonight and if you come, I'll reward you for being a good girl. And if you don't, I'll also reward you for being a good girl and letting me try."

She smiled hesitantly. "Okay, that would be good."

"Yeah?"

"Yeah." She nodded.

She sank back into the pillows, eyes on the ceiling, cheeks flushed. I expected her to lose her nerve, but she didn't. She just spread her legs wide and there she was, inches from me.

Heat shot down my spine and I felt pre-cum slip from my cock. There wasn't a single thought in my brain, just the driving need to touch, taste, kiss, and savor her pussy.

She was bare from laser—I knew that already—and her sex was a soft pale brown with a hint of blush.

I slid down, pushing my arms under her thighs to draw her close to my face. Her muscles clenched and a glittering diamond of arousal appeared at her entrance.

Without thinking, I bent and touched the tip of my tongue to it. Sweetness blossomed in my mouth and I couldn't bite back the groan of satisfaction. She breathed out sharply as I made a V with my fingers and parted her gently.

Her labia was short and her clit completely hooded. I licked my fingertip and gently tugged the skin back to reveal a discreet, little nub flushed dark red. She was already turned on, her sex a little flushed, but she wasn't wet enough yet. I wanted her dripping by the end of the night.

"What are you doing?" she whispered.

"Admiring you," I said. "You're lovely."

She gave a nervous, breathy giggle and her pussy clenched. "Sorry, I don't know why I laughed."

I skimmed my fingertips down either side of her pussy. "You're just nervous. Try not to be. You're alright and I'll talk you through it so there's no surprises."

"Thank you," she whispered.

I bent and kissed the rise above her sex. "I'm going to warm you up. I'm going to kiss your perfect thighs until you're begging me to eat your pussy out. Then I'll use my tongue around your clit until you're ready for my mouth on it."

She moaned and her hips stiffened as I bent and began kissing her inner thighs. Her skin was velvety soft and smelled faintly of jasmine. It was so sweet, but nothing on the natural scent I kept getting from her pussy the closer I got.

Her hips began working and I slid my hands down, gripping her thighs to hold her steady.

"Please," she breathed.

"Please...what?" I murmured. "If you tell me exactly what you want, I'll do it."

"I can feel my heartbeat in my clit...I need your mouth on it."

I shifted my mouth up so my breath washed over her most sensitive point.

"Are you going to keep your legs spread for me so I can eat?"

"Oh...oh God...yes."

I let my mouth fall on her clit, covering it in hot wetness, but not moving. She was writhing now, her breasts heaving, her hips grinding against nothing.

"Merrick...fuck, please just lick it," she begged.

I complied, keeping my tongue soft and wet as I dragged it over her pulsing clit. Her whole body shuddered and her hands slid into my hair and clenched.

"That's my girl," I breathed. "You lie back and let me pleasure your perfect, little pussy the way you deserve."

This was the moment I'd been waiting for and I was going to draw it out as long as possible. If it took all night for her to come, that was fine by me. All I needed was to get my face and my mouth between her legs and savor her like a fine wine.

This was my element.

A descent into my personal paradise.

She moaned as I experimented with her clit until I found the spot that made her thighs clench and her eyes roll back. It was on the underside, slightly to the right. When I licked that with steady pressure, not changing my pace, she was incoherent.

She begged, she shuddered, she built, she panted, she raked me hard with her fingernails.

But she didn't come.

"Merrick," she finally gasped. "I need a break."

I lifted my head, thoroughly drunk and not ready to stop.

"Is there anything I could be doing better?" I asked, resting my chin on her lower belly.

"No, you are amazing," she said sincerely. "Your mouth is...magic. It's just what happens sometimes...I think maybe nerves."

"Would you be open to letting me put my fingers in you?"

Her brow arched and she chewed the inside of her lip.

"Why?"

"Maybe it'll get you over the edge."

She nodded hesitantly and sank back down, shifting her hips and spreading her legs again. I liked that she was getting more comfortable with me.

"I'll start with one," I said, running my fingertips over her wet arousal.

I bent and spat gently on her opening, working the extra wetness over her pussy. Then I parted her so gently and breached her opening with the tip of my middle finger. Her slick muscles clenched and I paused, feeling them pulse around me.

"All good, baby girl?"

"Yes," she breathed.

I pushed in further and she clenched, pulling me in halfway. She was hot, soaked, and incredibly tight.

"How does it feel having my finger inside your pussy," I whispered.

She just nodded hard and I laughed under my breath and slid it the rest of the way in. She gasped and I let her adjust for a moment before I began looking for *that* spot.

"You tell me when I find your G-spot," I told her.

"How am I supposed to know?"

"You'll know."

I propped myself up on my elbow so I could watch her face. She had her eyes closed and her lips parted. Her hands were on her breasts, gently kneading them and circling her nipples with her nails.

I had a sudden, intense image of my cum splashed across those breasts. Across her pretty nails and hands. Dripping from her hard nipples.

Fuck me.

I shifted my hand a trace lower and her eyes flew open.

"Oh my God," she gasped.

Triumph blossomed, making me throb harder. I circled the spot once and began caressing it gently up and down, working it in slow, even motions. Her hips shook and her spine lifted off the bed.

"That's it, *cariad*, think about how much better my cock is going to feel on this spot."

She moaned and I slid between her legs, taking my finger from her pussy. I wanted an orgasm from her tonight and I was willing to start from square one again if that's what it took.

I warmed her again, coaxing the spark of her arousal back into a flame. She was frustrated and her thighs were tense, so I flipped her onto her stomach and began gently rubbing her lower back with my thumbs.

"What are you doing?" she said, her voice muffled.

"Getting you to relax," I said, bending to kiss just above her ass.

"May I have a glass of wine? Maybe that'll help."

I glanced over at the half glass still sitting on the bedside table and decided against it.

"I think it's better that I just take the time you need to get you relaxed," I said. "You may have some wine when you're done, if you still want it."

She huffed and I brought my hand down on her ass. It rippled, giving me a breathtaking view. I slapped it again and she moaned, grinding her hips.

"You like it when I spank you?" I asked.

"It feels good...the vibrations."

I flipped her onto her back and licked over her breasts, sucking her nipples. She moaned and I traced my mouth down her stomach and settled between her legs once more.

"I'm going to warm you up a little more," I said. "You be a good girl and play with your tits for me and let me do the rest."

She complied. I worked over her thighs with my mouth and tongue, getting closer and closer to her pussy every time. She shook as I moved nearer and the entrance of her pussy was soaked by the time I got to it.

This time, I slid two fingers into her, watching her face closely for signs of discomfort. But she just moaned and whimpered, her fingers working her breasts and teasing her nipples.

My tongue found that sweet spot and began working it gently while my fingers plied her from the inside. There was a specific rhythm I'd picked up on over the years and I let myself fall into it with gradual intensity.

Time meant nothing. She tasted so good and her pussy was silky on my tongue. Her muscles were tight, coiled like a spring around me. I had my eye on the prize and I wasn't stopping for anything. There was nothing in the world more important than getting her to orgasm.

I wasn't sure how long it took before she went stiff, but suddenly, in the depths of the dark room surrounded by her taste and scent, I felt the energy in her body shift.

She'd stopped just building and now her desperate hips were preparing for the inevitable.

It took everything I had to keep a steady pace.

"Merrick," she moaned. "Oh, God, Merrick...I think I'm going to come."

She pulsed hard twice around my fingers and cried out, her resistance snapping as she fell over the edge.

"Oh God," she gasped. "You're...you're making me come."

She lost it after those words, her spine locking and legs shaking, a little gush of wetness spilling out around my fingers. Her hands left her breasts and reached up to grip the pillows.

Nails tearing at the fabric. Pussy pumping around me. Mouth stuttering and open in a silent cry.

Fuck me, she was wrecked.

And so was I. My cock was painful, somewhere below, and my jaw ached, but there was no way in hell I was getting off her until she pried me away.

In the dark, with her taste seeped into my pores, I entertained a single thought.

She was the last person I wanted to go down on ever again.

I'd achieved paradise.

CHAPTER TWENTY-FIVE

MERRICK

Her body slowed and her eyes flew open, dazed. My stiff jaw popped, but I barely noticed.

Her scent was soaked into my skin. Her taste was on my tongue, in the back of my throat. Triumph burned in my chest and in my groin. Begging for a release of my own. I bent and kissed her swollen clit and she whimpered.

"That's a good girl," I said softly.

I glanced at my phone and the screen lit up. It was almost two in the morning.

I'd eaten her pussy for over two hours. And every minute of it had felt like paradise, even when my tongue cramped and my jaw locked. It still felt like the best fucking way I'd ever spent the night.

Even for just one orgasm, it was worth it.

"I'm sorry it took so long," she whispered.

"Don't apologize," I ordered, pushing myself onto my knees. "Just let me come on your stomach."

Her eyes widened and she nodded, her fingers twisting in the sheets. I ran my hand over her slick pussy, gathering her wetness, and wrapped my hand around my cock. Jerking it slowly with my eyes locked on her face.

Watching her take in my pleasure.

Her eyes were fixed to my erection. Her pretty tits rose and fell, her stomach muscles tensing. She was still aroused, transfixed by the sight of me jerking myself off.

Fuck, that felt good.

Pleasure surged down my spine and I came hard, gritting my teeth. All the tension I'd built up while eating her came rushing out of me as I painted her lower belly with my cum.

Marking her. Making her mine.

I let out a soft groan at the sight of her on her back with her legs spread. My release on her skin, pooling in her pierced navel. Her dark hair spread over the white pillows. Stark in the pale moonlight coming in through the window.

A soft warmth blossomed in my chest.

More potent than arousal.

"Merrick, are you okay?" she whispered.

I shook my head once. "Yes, sorry. You're just so fucking sexy like that. All covered in my cum."

I bent and she leaned up, her arms locking around my neck, and kissed my mouth. When she drew back, she had a smug, satisfied look on her face.

"I can taste myself on your lips," she said.

I kissed her again, already hard. If she wasn't still virgin, I'd have parted her legs and fucked her slowly. Made love to her for the rest of the night until we passed out from exhaustion.

Fucked. That's what I meant. Not made love.

I pushed myself up into a sitting position and ran a hand through my hair to push it back. For a moment, I fought the urge to look back at her. Things were moving fast. I knew they would.

But it was making me nervous.

Clara was in my bed.

Edwin's daughter. The woman I'd promised to protect. I'd had my mouth on her, my fingers in her pussy, my tongue down her throat.

But I hadn't put my cock in her.

There was still time to turn back.

I didn't want to, despite my guilty conscience. There was a darkness throughout whatever it was I felt for her, gnawing away at my hesitation. It turned me into an ugly, jealous man. A man who secretly thought I had a right to her firsts before anyone else.

Not because I'd done anything to earn it. Just because she was too fucking precious to let another man put his mark on her like that.

Maybe it was alright this week to be a little ugly and jealous with her. After all, if the man she married wasn't possessive of her, he was letting her down.

Without warning, I pushed her back against the bed. Pinning her by the hips. She gasped and went still, eyes wide. Giving into me so easily. My mouth trailed down, dipping into her navel, tasting myself off her belly.

Teasing the gold ring. Taking it in my teeth and tugging it gently until her eyes rolled back.

Gently, I parted her legs, spreading her open. She was still swollen and glistening with arousal, drenched from what I'd done.

Fuck, that sounded so dark. So satisfying.

I spread her pussy open with my finger and thumb and licked her clit. Keeping my tongue soft and wet because I knew she was sensitive. Her spine arced, her hips grinding up on my mouth.

Dark jealousy rose in me like a wild animal. Clawing to be free, begging to do terrible things on my behalf.

I sucked harder, keeping my head down and my eyes lowered. I wanted the hood over her clit pierced with my diamond. Not Osian fucking Cardiff's cheap shit. No, solid gold and the rarest diamond I could get my hands on.

Marking my property.

Fuck, why was the thought so exhilarating? Like a drug right up my spine, buzzing in the base of my skull.

I raised my eyes to hers and she gasped and her face went sober. She saw what I felt, it was painted all over my face. For the first time, I didn't back down and hide it.

Instead, I slid my hand up between her breasts. To her perfect, silky neck. My fingers locked around her throat and her breasts heaved. Her nipples went hard and I moved over her, my mouth grazing them. Nipping her skin and making her whimper.

Our eyes locked, my hand still around her throat.

"Merrick," she whispered.

"For the next week," I said, "this is mine."

CHAPTER TWENTY-SIX

CLARA

My pussy throbbed and my hips worked up against him of their own accord. This side to him was seductive and terrible at the same time. Dark, jealous Merrick scared me, but not as much as he aroused my body.

I'd never imagined he had it in him.

Of course he did. After all...Merrick had killed twelve men with his bare hands. At least, that was what everyone said. That was the rumor that circulated.

That he was a monster deep down when he needed to be.

Brutal. Deadly. Merciless.

And yet, I'd never seen that side of him. My Merrick was gentle and patient with me. Indulgent to a fault.

His eyes flickered beneath his lowered lashes. Thick and dark like his creased brows. His thin mouth was set like stone, his jaw tensed and shadowed with stubble. Still a little wet from being between my legs.

His naked body pinned me to the bed and his grip was firm on my throat. Pinning me like an animal about to devour me whole.

I shivered down to the soles of my feet.

He bent, his hand shifting to my jaw. His mouth burned over mine, and despite my churning emotions, I moaned against his kiss. When he pulled back, it hit me what he'd said.

"A week?" I whispered.

He lifted his head, fixing his gaze out the window. "There's a winter storm coming tonight. We'll be snowed in for at least a week."

I stared, stunned. "What?"

"You heard me, *cariad*."

Indignation rose in my chest and I squirmed fruitlessly under him. "You knew. And you didn't tell me."

He was in a mood, not jealous anymore. Something else, something I was equally unprepared to deal with. He shifted his hips and pushed his naked erection against the inside of my thigh. Grinding my leg like he was trying to prove a point.

Our eyes locked.

"Stop humping me," I said.

He froze. "What?"

"You're humping me," I said, swatting at his shoulder.

He burst into laughter and fell onto his back. The spell was broken and when he rolled onto his side, the old Merrick was back. His finger slid up between my breasts and tilted my chin back. He kissed my mouth discreetly.

"I'm going to shower," he said.

He stood, naked and breathtaking. I pushed myself up into a sitting position, forgetting I was also naked, and swung my legs over the side of the bed. His eyes skimmed over me and his cock went hard again.

I hadn't realized it had a hair-trigger on it.

"Hold on, I'm not done talking to you," I said. "You could have just asked me to stay a week, I would have said yes."

He shrugged. "That's why I didn't bother asking."

I found I didn't mind. The last thing in the world I wanted was to leave this fantasy.

He wiped me down with a warm washcloth and I pulled on one of his t-shirts and climbed back into bed. He went into the bathroom, leaving the door wide open, and turned on the shower. I lay curled against the cold window, listening to the wind pick up outside, and watched him stand beneath the streaming water.

Lathered in soap. Water glistening on his body. Streaming down between his abs.

I could get used to this.

He must have come to bed at some point because suddenly I was awake with bright light piercing my lids. There was a heavy weight draped over me. A naked arm lay over my body. Fingers hung loosely before my eyes.

I'd never imagined being crushed by over two hundred pounds of warm, lean muscle could feel quite so good.

I stayed still for a moment, thrilled just from being in bed with him. I'd wanted this so badly for the last few weeks. It was every bit as perfect as I'd hoped.

Outside, the wind howled. I dug my way up from the swathe of white blankets and peered out the window.

The whiteness was blinding. He hadn't been lying about a winter storm. As far as I could see, coating the pine forest, was at least three feet of snow. Down below, the SUV was just a bump in the drifts.

Excitement thrilled through me and I squeezed out of his grasp. He mumbled in his sleep and rolled onto his back. The cover had fallen down to his hips, revealing the most delicious line of black hair disappearing beneath it.

My core pulsed and I shifted my hips.

I was slippery already.

My fingers pushed beneath the oversized shirt I still wore and cupped my sex. I was tender from his mouth and fingers, but not enough to dampen the heady pulse in my clit.

I wanted him to put his mouth there again.

Gathering my courage, I climbed back into bed and straddled his hips. His lids fluttered and opened. Ignoring my shyness, I pulled the shirt from my body and let him take a good look.

His cock hardened beneath my thigh and he groaned.

"Fuck, you're going to keep me hard all week," he said, his voice husky with sleep.

"Are you complaining?"

"No," he said shortly. "Get up on my face."

I hesitated, confused. "What?"

Not standing on ceremony, he gripped my hips and dragged me up his chest and over his shoulders. So I was on my knees over his face, my hands splayed on the cold glass for support. I felt my thighs tense and I shifted back, sitting on his chest.

"Let me go wash," I whispered.

His fingers tightened and he lifted me easily, setting me over his mouth again. His tongue swiped out, licking over my wet entrance.

"If I wanted you to wash, I would have asked you," he said.

"Merrick—"

"I want to taste pussy, not soap," he said. "Now do as you're told and put your cunt on my mouth, *cariad*."

My God, he could say the dirtiest things. Heat curled and burned in my core and I gave into him. Sinking down.

His tongue dipped into me and I arched as he pushed it in halfway. It didn't hurt, it just...stretched. The way his fingers had.

My hips loosened as he pumped his tongue gently. Then the tip curled and he pulled back. He repeated the motion again and again, turning me sightly to get me from different angles.

What was he doing?

My hand clapped over my mouth. He was licking the wetness from inside my pussy. Getting all of it before it even left my body. A hot blush curled up my throat and stained my face.

I wasn't going to stop him. He was enjoying himself immensely, I could tell by the rise under the blankets.

He pulled his tongue from my pussy and shifted me up. It took me a second to realize he was going lower. My thighs tensed and I jerked back, falling on my backside on his chest.

"What are you doing?"

He sat up, shifting me into his lap. "I'm sorry, I got carried away."

I stared at him, mortified.

"Were you trying to lick me...back there?"

He nodded, completely unembarrassed.

"I was, but I should have asked you first. You just seemed into it so I thought I would keep going."

We stared at each other and I felt my cheeks burn.

"Why...why would someone want that?" I whispered.

I felt stupid for not realizing that was a thing that people did, but not enough to forego questioning him. He'd opened the door and I needed answers. Especially because...well, I sort of wanted him to do it to me.

Not now, but maybe before the end of the week.

"You're sensitive there and it feels good," he said. "I enjoy it because it's intimate. And you have a fucking beautiful ass that makes me want to put my whole face in it."

I fought the urge to fan myself.

"But I went too fast," he said, pushing me off his lap and rising. "Let's have breakfast since it's already noon and then we'll mess around in bed some more. And I'll go slow. How does that sound?"

I nodded, watching him pull on his sweatpants.

His dark hair was tousled, the natural wave coming through. The stubble on his jaw was longer and showed a few more grays than usual. He ran a hand over his hair, brushing it back, and walked out of the room.

I pulled on a skimpy crop top and matching sweatpants and padded barefoot to the kitchen. It turned out that the entire floor was heated, not just in the bedroom. I slapped my feet on the stairs, soaking in the warmth.

He was by the stove, turning the burner on. Flipping the pan in his hand before setting it down. Drizzling the oil and cracking eggs.

My toes curled.

Here I was safe. Protected by the one person who would never let me down. I walked up behind him and pressed a kiss to his naked back.

"*Cariad*," he said, turning.

"Merrick," I whispered, looking up at him.

He bent and kissed my mouth and molten lava rushed through me. When he broke away, the tension was so thick I thought he was going to turn off all the burners and haul me upstairs.

Instead, he slapped me across the ass.

I jumped, gasping. A grin flashed over his unshaven face, lighting it up.

"Make some coffee," he ordered.

"Merrick!"

He leaned in, mouth brushing my temple. "It's lucky the floor is heated because if you don't start doing as you're told, I'm going to make you get down on your knees in this kitchen and take my cum down your throat for breakfast instead."

My jaw fell open.

Oh my God, he was filthy.

And I loved it.

Heart thumping, I did as he asked. I felt his eyes on me as I made two cups of coffee and handed him one. Watching as he took an experimental sip. His jaw worked and he set it aside.

"It's good," he said. "You've got room to grow, but luckily you have me to teach you."

"Oh, really?" I rolled my eyes.

He made a platter of eggs and sausage and we ate together at the table. I asked him if we had enough food for the week and he said yes, of course he'd planned for longer if necessary. There were even extra clothes in the closet upstairs.

"What if the pipes freeze?" I asked.

"They won't," he said. "It's not that cold."

I went outside to the porch to check his theory. He followed me, lounging in the doorway. His eyes washed out in the bright light. Snow sticking to the front of his sweatpants and melting on his bare chest.

I pushed on a pair of boots by the door and stepped out onto the porch. It was covered in snow and my shoes made wide, flat prints. Marring the perfection.

"You look lovely," he said distractedly.

Heat blossomed between my thighs. We were alone in the silent forest, with no one for miles. The only sound was the snow falling gently. I turned, looking back at him, and slipped the straps of my crop top down.

Baring my breasts to the wintry air.

His breath sucked in sharply. His eyes lit up like blue flame and his lids lowered. Heavy with lust.

My fingers drifted down, untying the waist of my sweatpants.

He was right, it really wasn't that cold.

In fact, I felt like I was burning up.

My sweatpants fell, baring my ass and pussy to the cold. In the intense light, I could see every vein, every imperfection, every stretch mark on my body. But I wasn't embarrassed because if anyone would accept me, it was Merrick.

He had always accepted me.

"Come here," he said.

His voice was almost a growl. Sitting heavy in his chest.

I shook my head. He took a step, but I held up my hand.

One hand slid down my cool skin and pushed between my thighs. I was slick and pulsing, right on the edge. Perhaps it was because he'd eaten me that morning, but I hadn't come. Or perhaps it was how intense the cold felt on my nipples.

But I knew right then that if I touched myself, I would come.

He was watching me, every nerve in his body tense like an animal ready to pounce. His brows were lowered and he was on the verge of panting.

Beneath his sweatpants, his cock was fully hard.

My other hand slid up and cupped my breast, pinching my cold nipple. Rolling it. Kneading the soft flesh. My fingers pushed up against my entrance, gathering my arousal, and began rubbing my clit.

"Fuck me," he breathed, pupils blowing.

He was transfixed. Watching me touch myself shamelessly. Out in the open, under the sky. With snow on my skin, teasing my senses and making me so sensitive.

The familiar hot coil started in my hips and my stomach tightened. My fingers moved faster and I took my other hand and spread myself open so he could see my clit. Exposing it to the cold air, sending tingles down my thighs. So he knew exactly what he did to me.

His hand slid down under his waistband and stilled, wrapped around his erection. Too distracted to even touch himself.

I let myself moan as I got closer, whimpering so he could hear just how good it felt. Wetness stung my thighs, prickling as it mingled with snowflakes. Pleasure built and built under my touch, threatening to consume me whole.

I was on the edge. Lost in a whirlwind of heat and cold.

High from teasing him, from how badly he wanted it.

My orgasm hit me in a wave and I cried out, my voice muffled by the snow. My toes curled in my boots as I fought to remain standing. It pulsed through me, ebbing acutely the way it had last night under his tongue.

He couldn't take it anymore. His body moved fast, closing the space between us. His hands were on me, lifting me and carrying me inside while I was still coming. Pulsing, arcing, shaking in his arms.

My cold body contacted the heated floor in the living room. He was on top of me, pinning me to the thick, white rug. His eyes consumed everything, filling my vision until there was nothing in the world but him.

His hand was on my cold thigh, lifting me as he slid between my legs.

"Tell me not to," he begged under his breath.

I shook my head.

He shuddered and his cock touched my sex, hot and punishingly hard. Dragging over my soaked opening. He bent and kissed me, his mouth open and his tongue filling me with his taste. Licking, biting, sucking the way he had the first time he'd kissed me at the lodge.

I was still coming, just a little, and I knew he could feel the tremors moving down my stomach.

"I'm going to fuck you, *cariad*," he said.

"Please," I whispered.

"No going back from this," he said through gritted teeth.

He slid into me and I cried out, shocked by the sensation. For a second, there was a bolt of pain and then I was full, so full that surely he wouldn't fit. But he just kept going, guiding his cock into me until my legs shook against his sides.

It was too much, he was too much.

My fingernails pierced his ribs as he ran out of room. There was an intense pressure somewhere deep inside, like I needed to give way around him, but I wasn't able to. It made me want to whimper, to squirm.

That dark possession stole over his eyes as his hips rocked against mine. Keeping me pinned to the floor, our bodies locked.

I had never imagined it would feel like this.

Like being complete. Like that meteorite I'd felt when he kissed me the first time kept burning on and on instead of sputtering out.

His arm slid up and gathered my body against his chest. Then, with a ripple of pain, he dragged himself out and pushed back in. My muscles loosened a little as he began thrusting gently, going even further every stroke.

Until he was seated in me. All the way to the hilt of his cock, to the dark hair on his groin.

"That's a good girl," he said against my neck. "Feel the way you take me? All the way until your pussy is full."

I panted, my lower back arcing. Giving him access to every inch of space.

"You make me fucking lose my mind, *cariad.*"

The ghost of a smile passed over my mouth. It was a power trip seeing the Welsh King like this, desperate and on the edge of losing control.

"You love having me wrapped around your pretty little finger," he growled. "Let's see how you like being wrapped around my cock."

Yes, please, I was pretty sure I would like that. He shifted, pulling my leg around his waist. His hips shook slightly as he adjusted himself. He was trying to hold back, to be gentle, but I didn't want that right now.

I wanted all of him.

Inside me, dripping down my thigh like melted hard candy. How much fucking to get to the center of the Welsh Princess?

"Please," I breathed. "It doesn't hurt."

The discomfort had eased. Instead, I was filled with the most intense, sweet pressure that reached deep in my belly. But I could take it. The entrance of my pussy clenched around him as he pulled out and thrust back in, sending butterflies through my stomach.

"How long?" I whispered.

His mouth was on my throat. "What?"

"How long have you wanted this?"

He kept fucking, driving his cock into me with hard strokes, but he didn't answer for a moment. Then his teeth scored my neck and I gasped, whimpering past my clenched jaw.

"Too long."

Yes, God, that was what I wanted to hear. His hips worked harder, pounding into me until the room was filled with the wet sounds of our desire. He slowed for a few minutes and his hand came up and gathered my wrist, pinning it back against the rug.

Our eyes locked. Dark hair fell over his forehead. His mouth parted and a sliver of his bottom teeth flashed white.

"I'm going to fill you with my cum," he breathed. "This is your last chance to stop me."

I shook my head.

"Come in me, Merrick," I begged.

His eyes rolled back. "Oh, fuck, beg for me just like that."

I tightened my thighs, holding him against my hips. He fucked hard with short, shallow thrusts. His jaw was clenched and his eyes were alight. Filling my vision with nothing but blue fire.

"I want your cum inside me," I panted. "Please."

"Fuck, yes," he groaned. "Fuck, baby, take every fucking drop in your tight, little cunt. I want it dripping down your fucking legs."

His groin pushed up against my clit, still sensitive from my orgasm. His eyes closed and his hand tightened on my wrist. His thrusts moved even faster and the pressure inside me intensified.

Sending an ache through my lower belly as I fought to accommodate him. I needed him to finish soon or it was going to start hurting.

His hips stuttered and I felt his cock twitch.

"*Cariad*," he breathed, barely audible. "My God...*rwy'n dy garu di*."

Warmth blossomed deep in my lower belly. The pressure increased as he rode me with short, erratic strokes. My eyes closed, remembering how he'd painted my stomach with his cum last night.

That was happening right now. Deep inside me.

He was filling me with his desire. Marking me, making me his the way I'd dreamed about.

My fingernails dug into him as he finished with a deep shudder that moved down his entire body. He stilled and his head fell to my chest. I slid my fingers up his side to his throat, letting my fingers rest over his pulse point.

His heart was beating like a drum.

"What did you say just now?" I whispered. "I don't speak Welsh."

"Nothing," he murmured. "I was cursing."

"Why?"

He kissed my forehead. "Because you felt so fucking good."

He reached between us and I felt him pull from me. When he sat back on his knees, he'd already tucked himself back into his pants. There was a faint pink smear on the side of his hand.

I pushed myself up on my elbows. His eyes fell, glued to my pussy. His hands were gentle as he pushed my knees open fully. I'd expected him to regret what he'd done, but the look in his eyes was almost...satisfied.

I shivered deliciously.

"I meant to take you in bed," he said. "The way you deserve."

"It was good," I said, suddenly feeling shy.

"Did it hurt?"

"Just a little."

He lifted me to my feet and tugged my crop top straps back over my shoulders.

There was a pale pink stain on the floor where we'd laid together. Not very large, but enough to make me blush.

"Sorry," I said softly. "I bled on the floor."

He bent and pressed a kiss below my navel. A shock of heat traveled down to my tender core and I squirmed, suddenly wanting to do it all again. Now that I'd felt him inside me, all my fear was gone.

My pink card was swiped.

CHAPTER TWENTY-SEVEN

MERRICK

I'd never been so glad that she didn't speak Welsh than right now.

Why had I said that?

My post-orgasm clarity returned like a wall of bricks. I cleaned her with a warm, damp cloth and tugged her sweatpants up over her hips. She watched me, chewing that damn spot on the inside of her mouth.

Her eyes were wide, glassy. Her lower lip was swollen.

She looked good like this. Just-fucked and satisfied.

We went back into the kitchen and she got a glass of water. There was a long silence as she sipped it, clearly stalling. I washed my hands, letting the blood and cum disappear down the drain.

Evidence of what we'd done.

She set aside her glass and slid up against me, wrapping her arms around my waist. Her head settled on my sternum, nestling against my naked chest. My hand hovered, hesitating, over her hair.

I bent and breathed in. Sweet, dark jasmine.

"Do you really not speak Welsh?" I asked.

She shook her head.

"Why is that?"

She shrugged.

"Your father never taught you?" I pressed.

She pulled back, laughing. It was short and humorless. "My father never taught me anything."

I kept quiet for a moment, watching as she started making another round of coffees. She was lovely, washed out in the bright, snowy light. Her cropped shirt hung off one shoulder and her baggy sweatpants were rolled around her hips.

Under her clothes, I'd put my signature on her body. Between her thighs, she was forever altered by me.

Why did that feel so good? I should be ashamed of myself. I stepped up behind her, running my fingers through that silky hair. She paused, letting her eyes rest out the window. There was a group of deer at the edge of the woods. Rummaging under the snow for frozen green.

"I never talk about my father because he was your closest friend," she said.

Her voice was different. Detached.

I traced her spine to the small of her back. "That shouldn't stop you."

"I never understood it."

"Understood what?"

She turned and braced the heels of her hands on the sink. She did this thing with her hip when she was gearing up to have an honest talk. I dropped my eyes.

She was doing it, popping her left hip out.

I fought the sudden urge to slide my hand under her sweatpants. Cradle that hip. Or maybe slip my fingers between her legs and feel the wetness I'd left there.

I dragged myself back to reality. She was watching me, her chin jutted.

"I never understood why you were friends with him."

I considered it for a moment. This was tenuous ground.

"I met him at a point in my life when I needed direction," I said. "He was older than me and he'd been through the military so he was disciplined. I...I owe at lot of my own ability to be so disciplined to him. He kept me focused. And he helped me militarize the organization and gain a lot of ground along the East Coast."

"But did you ever spend time together outside work?" she pushed.

"No, but then all I did was work and sleep."

She blinked rapidly. I could tell this conversation was incredibly difficult for her. It made me want to take her in my arms. Soothe her, hold her against my chest.

But she didn't need that. She was trying to say her piece, I could tell.

And she deserved a place to do that.

She swallowed, shaking her head. "Nothing. Never mind."

She turned to slip away, but I slid my arm around her waist. Holding her between my body and the counter. Her eyes narrowed as she fixed them on me.

God, she had a withering glare when she needed it.

I brushed her cheek with my thumb, cradling her head. "Talk to me."

"Okay." She swallowed hard. "My father wasn't a good person. You are. I don't understand how you ever tolerated being friends with him."

"He never did anything to me," I said. "It wasn't until he left you in my care that I got an inside look at his family life. What did he do?"

She swallowed and tears brimmed. Threatening to spill down her cheeks. A cold sense of dread simmered in my stomach and I had to take a deep breath to calm myself.

"Did he...did he do something to you?" I asked.

My voice cracked. I cleared my throat and she frowned, clearly confused.

"What?"

"Did he molest you?"

"No," she said quickly, shaking her head. "No, God, no. It wasn't like that. He was just so cold and distant. Even when I was a little girl, begging him for a hug because I was afraid at night. He never let me play with anyone but Candice because he respected her family.

He didn't let me have any fun...or just let any happiness into our house period."

"That's...difficult," I said, my muscles loosening.

She laughed again. Short and without humor. Her arms crossed over her chest.

"He made me wear the ugliest clothes," she said. "All I wanted was a pretty dress like the other girls at my school. But he put me in these horrible, beige dresses. He didn't want me being a slut, is what he said."

She rolled her eyes. I kept quiet.

"It was a weird thing to say to a ten-year-old," she said. "And I wasn't allowed to even eat normally. No sugar ever. Not even on my birthday or Christmas. It was like...it was liked he enjoyed controlling me and denying anything that might make me happy."

I'd known Edwin was a strict man, that he never indulged himself. I'd picked up some of his traits. We'd both eaten the same, stripped back, austere foods.

I just did it for different reasons.

"Does it trigger you that I eat like him?"

Her jaw worked. "Not really. I thought you did it because you like having rippling abs and looking like a Greek god at forty-five."

I laughed aloud and her shoulders relaxed.

"You think I look like a Greek god?"

She blushed and poked my stomach. "I mean...you look pretty good."

I bent to kiss her forehead. I wasn't ready to get into the real reason why I'd adopted some of Edwin's eating habits. She wouldn't understand what it was like to live with compulsions and avoidance the way I did.

She wouldn't get how everything was contaminated. Potentially lethal. How just having my hand touch a dirty countertop meant I couldn't pick up my cup of coffee.

Fuck. Was I slipping? Did I need to see Gretchen when we got back into Providence?

Better to be proactive than reactive. I'd learned that a long time ago.

"You look pretty good yourself," I said.

"Thank you." She cocked her head, that little smirk playing on her mouth.

"Are you angry with me for being friends with Edwin?"

"No, I just never got it."

"I think Edwin was a much different man at work than at home," I said carefully. "I never witnessed what you did. And I also wasn't his daughter. You needed love and affection, but I needed discipline, his expertise."

She chewed on that spot on her mouth, her eyes on me. Narrowed in thought. Then she went to the fridge and took out a jar of chocolate syrup and a bottle of whipped cream.

I watched, unsure what she was doing as she filled her cupped hand with whipped cream. There was a gleam in her eyes and before I could react, she smeared the cream all down my chest. Over my stomach. Tugging my pants down to right above my cock so she could wipe it over my lower abs.

"Playing with your food?" I asked.

She pushed two fingers into the chocolate syrup and drizzled it over the mess she'd made of my torso. It was cold as it etched down my abs to my waistband. My sweatpants were fucked.

"Have you ever wondered why I eat a bowl of ice cream every night," she said, licking her fingers.

Slowly, her red nails darting into her mouth and out again.

"No," I said huskily.

She bent and her hot tongue slid all the way from my lower stomach to my chest. Fuck me, that went all the way down my spine to my cock. It throbbed in response to her touch. Begging to be inside her again.

Her tongue darted out. Curling over a drizzle of chocolate, flicking it into her mouth. Dragging over the whipped cream, leaving a bit of white on the tip of her nose.

She lapped at the melting cream and sugar, eyes fixed to mine. Her red nails dug into my sides, all messy and beautiful.

I slid my hand under her chin, pulling her face up.

"I think," I said softly, "that the clinical term for what you have is daddy issues."

"What makes you say that?" she whispered.

"What are you doing right now?"

She ran her fingertip over my stomach and popped it in her mouth.

"Licking whipped cream and chocolate off my dead father's friend," she said, rolling her eyes. "Because I never got to have sugar or go out with boys. Because I'm a spoiled, resentful brat."

That surprised me. The last part. The first part was spot on.

"No, you're not," I said firmly. "I don't want to hear you talk about yourself like that again. Understood?"

She stilled, her fingertip pushed in her mouth. I slid my hand around her head and fisted it, holding her steady by the hair.

Her lids lowered, her eyes going hazy. Her breasts heaved under her thin shirt. I knew she was getting wet between her legs and my cock was begging for more of what she'd given me this morning.

"I understand," she whispered.

"Good. Now go to the bedroom and turn on the shower."

Our coffee sat forgotten on the countertop. She climbed the stairs quickly ahead of me, her ass swaying. There was a little wet spot between her legs where my cum had soaked through her pants.

Beautiful.

We both dropped our clothes on the bathroom floor and stepped into the shower together. Her nipples were hard peaks, begging to be touched.

I pulled her near in a sharp gesture and closed my mouth around one. Giving her a taste of my teeth. The yelp that escaped her was so satisfying. That yelp became a moan as I kissed up her neck.

Her fingernails dug into my lower back.

Fuck, she scratched hard. I was going to be painted with marks before the week was out.

"Are you too sore to take me again today?" I asked.

221

She shook her head frantically. "No, I want it."

I dropped to my knees before her and lifted her leg to drape it over my shoulder. Her body swayed and her hand clenched in my hair.

It hurt, but in the best way.

The first swipe of my tongue over her clit made her latch those nails into my shoulders. She tasted of arousal and faintly of my cum.

Good, I wanted that taste between her thighs every minute of this week.

Her stomach clenched as I licked around her pussy, building her arousal slowly. She was slick by the time I got to her clit. A shudder moved through her body.

I kept going, sucking her clit into my mouth and pleasuring it with firm, circular motions. I felt the orgasm in her body, tensing her hips, making her grind against me.

She whimpered, she begged, she said my name over and over.

But she didn't come.

"Merrick, let's do this later," she said finally, her voice fragile. "It's not working."

I pulled my head from between her legs. She was flushed, not just with arousal. It hurt to see her embarrassed because she didn't need to be—it wasn't her fault. I rose and kissed her hard. Letting her taste the silky wetness from her pussy.

"Let me try something else, alright?" I said.

She nodded, chewing her mouth.

I unfastened the shower head and adjusted it to the center jet. Then I pulled us both to our knees, tucking her body beneath mine. Letting my hard cock rest against her ass and her slick pussy.

"Take the shower head," I told her.

She obeyed, wrapping it in her hesitant fingers.

"Aim it at your clit and find where it feels good," I urged, my mouth against her ear.

She did as she was told and I felt her body jerk. Tensing and shivering. I gathered her against me and cupped her soft breasts. Playing with her nipples lightly, keeping her on the edge, but not overstimulated.

When she was used to this, I could overstimulate her all night. Make her come until she was spent.

But right now, we were in the learning curve.

"Does that feel good, *cariad*?" I asked.

She nodded.

I nuzzled her neck and gently scored it with my teeth. Her thighs shuddered and I knew she was building. Really building this time.

"You've been such a good girl for me already," I said, keeping my voice low and husky. "You're so pretty when you come and you taste so fucking good when I lick all that wetness from your perfect, little pussy."

"Oh my God," she panted.

"You want that? You want me to lick all the wetness from your pussy when you finish coming?"

"Yes, please...please."

"Maybe if you keep being a good girl, I'll show you what it's like to get your pussy fucked from behind. You'll get down on your knees like a pretty, little whore and let me use you, won't you, *cariad*?"

"Oh God," she burst out.

"Yeah, you want that? You want me to use you like a whore?"

She stiffened when I called her a whore. Then she came, her whole body shaking uncontrollably under mine. Her fingers loosened and she dropped the shower head, but I caught it and trained it back on her clit.

A cry burst from her and her spine arced, her head falling back to my shoulder. Face turning up so her eyes could fix to mine. Big, desperate, pupils blown.

"Merrick," she begged. "Enough. It's too much."

I slid my hand up between her breasts and gently gripped her throat. Holding her back against my chest.

"No, no, you'll take it until you're done," I soothed. "You're a good girl and good girls deserve to come hard."

She shuddered and pulsed until her body went limp against me and I flicked the shower off. She was quiet as I dried her off and carried her to the bed. Spilling her naked, beautiful body out onto the white sheets.

"That was amazing," she said, eyes glazed.

I knelt over her. "I aim to please."

"Well, I am very pleased."

I laughed and bent to kiss between her breasts. "I'm going to eat you out again."

Her legs clenched, drawing up to her chest. "Please, don't."

"You need it."

"I've had it twice, almost three times, since we got here."

"Not enough. You need eaten out regularly. Preferably twice, maybe three times a day. And by someone who knows what they're doing."

"Oh, so...you?"

"Yes," I said. "Me."

She giggled and that sound was a shot of adrenaline down my spine to my cock. Without thinking, I flipped her onto her hands and knees and pulled her to the edge of the bed.

She gave a sharp gasp and stilled. Waiting like such a good girl.

My God, she took my breath away. I ran my palm gently down her side and gripped her round ass and squeezed it. Then I slapped it lightly to watch the recoil shiver down her thigh.

Fuck, that made me hard.

"You sure you're not sore, *cariad*?" I asked.

She nodded. "Please, I want it again."

I kneaded her ass a little harder, marveling at how soft it was. How different it looked from my hand. Hard, scarred skin over my knuckles against untouched silkiness.

"Merrick," she whispered.

"Yes, *cariad*," I murmured, distracted.

She wriggled her hips, pushing back against my hand.

"Please. Fuck me."

She broke me, shattered my reservations. Wrapped me around her little finger. I pulled her near and brushed my cock against her silky, wet entrance. Gripping it by the base and rubbing it over her clit.

"Fuck, yes," she moaned.

I bent and kissed the middle of her back and she shuddered. Then I went to the dresser and took out a bottle of lube. It was cold, so I warmed it in my palm for a moment. Then I worked it over her hot entrance, dipping into her for a blissful second. Relishing when she clenched around my fingers.

"Am I not wet enough?" she whispered.

"You are," I assured her. "But I know you're sore. And you're about to get even more so, so let's minimize the damage."

She kept still as I lubed my cock and took her by the hips, lining myself up with her entrance. There was a moment of resistance and then I slid into her tight pussy and she gasped aloud.

I clenched my jaw. My vision flashed.

Fuck. Me.

She was so perfect, so wet, so silky. Like falling into heaven.

A quick descent into paradise.

I couldn't keep my hips still any longer. They pulled out and began driving my cock into her pussy. Gentle at first so she could accommodate me. Then going harder, faster, so I could enjoy the way her ass shook when I slammed into her.

It had never felt so easy and good before. I'd spent my life treating sex like an art, a skill. Something I did with deliberation so I could give my partner the best experience. I'd never really let go with anyone.

But with Clara...my brain went completely blank and my animal urges took over. Just as they had when I'd taken her virginity on the living room floor.

She gasped as I pushed her further up the bed, on my knees. Our bodies locked together. My hand slid up between her breasts and gripped her throat. My other hand braced against the window. My cock pulsed deep inside her, begging for me to satisfy us both.

Beneath me, she whimpered.

And I fucked her. Hard and rough the way I craved. She cried out, but not for me to stop. For more, begging for me to go harder and faster. So I did. Filling the room with her whimpers and the sounds of our bodies meeting.

"Flip me over," she gasped. "I want to look at you."

I obliged, pulling her close by the thigh and pushing back inside her. Her eyes widened, her pupils blown. Her peaked nipples were pink from being played with in the shower.

I bent and licked one, sucking it briefly. Her lashes fluttered.

"You're so fucking good for me," I breathed. "You know you're such a good girl, don't you?"

She bit her lip, panting. Eyes rolling.

"Tell me," I ordered, pounding into her pussy. "Tell me you're a good girl for me, *cariad*."

"I'm a good...girl for you," she managed.

"Fuck, yes," I moaned. "Is that what you want? You can be anything you want with me, princess, so how about you be my whore?"

Her hips bucked, stuttering, and her eyes rolled back. I evened my hips, reeling it back a little until I was pumping into her with smooth, long thrusts. Making sure she felt every inch of me.

Our eyes locked and I thought I saw a hint of hesitancy in her face.

Maybe I was going too hard.

I bent, kissing her forehead and her mouth. Brushing back her hair so I could cradle her face.

"You're doing such a good job," I breathed. "Look at you, it's only the second time and you're taking me so well."

"Oh my God," she whispered. "When you talk like that...it makes me so wet."

I knew, I could hear it when I pumped my hips. Short thrusts, angling so I was hitting her G-spot.

"I can feel it. I can feel how wet you are for me."

I took a beat, drawing out until a strand of arousal connected our bodies. My hand drifted down, breaking the thread. Rubbing it between my fingers before guiding myself back into her and slamming in hard. This time she winced and I went still. Goddamn it, I'd hurt her. I'd gone too rough too fast.

"Are you alright, baby?" I smoothed her hair back and cradled her face.

"I might need you to finish," she said, barely audible.

"Do you hurt?"

"I'm getting a little sore," she admitted.

"I can finish myself."

I started to pull out, but her legs locked around my lower back, keeping me inside. Her expression was fierce as she shook her head. I had to bite back my smile.

"No, I want you to come inside me."

"I'll go hard for a minute and come. Alright?"

She nodded. I slid my arm under her upper back and pulled her against my chest. Our mouths met as I kissed her, pounding into her pussy. Sweat gathering on my lower back.

She shook in my arms as she kissed me. Tongue brushing mine. Nipping at my lower lip. Parting her mouth so I could suck the tip of her tongue.

Slowly, keeping a steady pressure as I fucked her. My orgasm shot down my spine and I lost control, emptying everything I had into her pussy. Pleasure surged like a wave. Drowning me, making my vision flash.

I groaned against her mouth and she whimpered.

This was perfection. Tangled up with her. Her taste on my tongue. My cock buried all the way as I pumped my cum into her pussy.

It hit me in the middle of my orgasm that this was the best sex I'd ever had. Nothing fancy, no frills. Just plain missionary. Just kissing and fucking in bed in the middle of the afternoon.

And it was absolutely mindblowing.

The only thing that would have made it better was if I knew where we were going from here.

CHAPTER TWENTY-EIGHT

CLARA

He kissed me slowly, keeping me cuddled to his chest. I was warm and limp, the muscles between my thighs satisfied. His big, warm body was wrapped around me and the hairs on his chest tickled my cheek.

It was bliss. Especially with the soft, late afternoon sun coming in through the window. Making patterns on the bed.

He stirred after a while, kissing my head. "Are you alright, *cariad*?"

"Never better," I said dreamily.

"I think I'll clean up and shave," he said.

He pushed upright and swung his legs over the side of the bed. Cracking his neck as he rose to his feet. I sat up and his cum trickled down the inside of my thigh.

"Can I shave you?"

He paused in the bathroom door, eyes narrowing. He was looking at me like he didn't trust me to wield a razor by his throat.

"*Can* you?"

"I can shave myself," I said. "I used to shave my pussy before I got laser and that's a lot more complicated than doing a man's face."

He relented and I got up, padding past him gleefully. He caught me on the ass, slapping me hard enough to make it smart. I yelped and swatted at him and he gripped my wrists. Pulling them behind my back.

Kissing my neck.

"Be good," he ordered.

When he let me go, my heart was pounding. Every touch, even when he was playful, set me on fire.

I washed and while he showered I found his razor and set up a station in the kitchen. When he came downstairs in just his boxer briefs, I had a bowl of warm water, shaving cream, and a towel laid out.

"I didn't realize I was dealing with an expert," he said.

"I know a lot of things," I said. "Stick around and I'll just keep surprising you."

He hooked his finger under my bra between my breasts and pulled me close. All the air left my lungs. He kissed me slowly, his mouth almost overwhelming me with the sensations it evoked.

"You surprised me upstairs," he said softly. "You've done so well for me, *cariad*."

Heat flared in my stomach, seeping to my toes. I curled them.

"Thank you," I whispered.

"I want one more orgasm from you today," he said. "Tonight."

"I'll do my best."

He scored my neck gently with his teeth. He liked doing that, like he was laying claim to me. Putting his mark on my skin.

"Sit down," I ordered.

He obeyed and I stepped between his knees and pressed the warm towel to his jaw. We were both silent as I prepped him. Our breaths loud. The clock ticked over the stove.

Somehow this felt just as intimate as sex.

"Tilt your head back."

He complied, exposing his neck. I spread the shaving cream carefully over his skin down to the middle of his throat. Then, keeping my fingers steady, I shaved him in smooth, short strokes.

It was hard to maintain focus with him so near. Especially when his eyes never left my face.

The silence ticked on and on, but it never became suffocating. Instead, it felt safe. I settled on his knee, in his lap. Working the last part of his jaw to make sure I got every bit of stubble.

"Can I ask you something?"

"You may."

"Well, I opened up to you earlier, so I think you owe me a little honesty," I said.

"You're making me nervous," he said lightly.

I looked him in the eyes. "Did you really kill twelve men with your bare hands?"

His face didn't change. It stayed all sexy and serious, his broad jaw clenched. His throat bobbed. My stomach dropped and I began panicking, worried I'd offended him.

His mouth curved into a tight smile.

"Why would you worry about something so dark right now, *cariad*?" he said smoothly. "There's so many better things to think of."

His hands gripped my ass and hips, sliding up. Circling my waist. Then he pushed his face between my breasts and rubbed it hard, covering me in shaving cream.

"Did you just *motorboat* me?"

He swatted my ass, making it jiggle.

"That'll teach you to mind your business," he said, not unkindly.

He pinched my thigh gently and I yelped. A hot blush swept up my neck and wiped my mind clean as he pulled me close again. Kissing my mouth slowly as he absently pushed his fingers in the shaving cream on my chest.

Kneading my breast lightly. Tugging my nipple between his fingers.

Making me forget.

I shoved him back playfully and he grinned, eyes flashing.

"Be a good girl and finish what you started," he ordered.

I kept shaving him, pretending to concentrate fully on what I was doing. But my mind was still drifting back to my question. Back to his refusal to answer.

But he didn't really need to answer for me to get an affirmative response.

His silence was enough.

When I was done, he leaned over the sink and looked at himself in the window. He tilted his head, gazing at his reflection while I waited for his verdict.

"Very good," he said.

His praise made me glow. He went upstairs to shower and put on sweatpants. I turned on the radio and switched it to a classic rock station. When he returned a few minutes later, I was heating up leftovers and having a glass of wine.

He circled my waist, spinning me to face him. "Dance with me, *cariad*."

We danced in the kitchen to muffled strains of "Moondance" by Van Morrison. It felt like a dream, having my head against his naked chest. His lean hands on my back, his fingers threaded in mine.

I closed my eyes and pretended the week never had to end.

I burned the leftovers and endured his teasing while he made spaghetti and garlic bread. We ate at the kitchen table, me sitting on his lap again, and had a glass of red wine with a fancy label I couldn't pronounce.

Outside the snow kept coming down. Filling up the endless landscape with pure white. Burying the car in the parking lot, rising in drifts against the doors.

I hoped it snowed forever so we never had to leave.

We loaded the dishwasher together and I watched him wipe every crumb from the counters. As he always did. Then he had a rare cigarette, lounging in the front doorway. He didn't look cold even though he was shirtless and surrounded by a pine forest covered in snow.

He just looked perfect.

Cobalt blue eyes, dark, dark hair, freckled shoulders.

Snow melting on his chest.

"Can I try it?" I asked, joining him.

He held the cigarette out, between his finger and thumb. I took a quick puff and started coughing. His grin flashed and he pulled me against him.

"Never change, Clara," he murmured.

He kissed me and it ruined me like usual. But what did it matter when I was ruined for him already? One day in and my hair was permanently tangled in his fingers. My mouth burned constantly from his kisses. My hips ached for him.

I was well and truly fucked.

Literally and figuratively.

CHAPTER TWENTY-NINE

CLARA

It was almost three in the morning when I woke abruptly. The bed was shaking and I could hear heavy breathing.

Panicked, I rolled over and clicked the light. The pale lamp bathed the bed in a golden glow and I could just make out Merrick. On his back, body shivering, eyes half open and rolling back and forth.

"Merrick," I gasped, scrambling upright.

He jolted, flipping over and rolling on his knees in a fluid, practiced movement. His hand shot behind him and pulled a gun from beneath the bed.

My whole body went ice cold. Our eyes met.

"Clara," he breathed.

"You were dreaming," I whispered, eyes filling with tears. "But it looked scary and you were panting in your sleep."

His shoulders sagged and his eyes shut for a second. Then he laid the gun in the bedside table drawer and held out his arm.

I hesitated, still shivering.

"I didn't know you had that there," I said.

"It's my job to protect you," he said. "I'm always armed when you're around."

I nodded, swallowing past my thumping heart. I understood, but I just didn't like it.

"Come here, *cariad*," he said, gathering me around the waist and pulling us both back down beneath the covers. "Hush now, you're shaking."

"You scared me," I admitted.

I felt him swallow. "It was only a nightmare."

"Do you get those a lot?"

"Not that I can remember," he said slowly, stroking my hair. "But I haven't slept with anyone in a long time, so I don't know."

I pushed my face into his warm chest and listened to his heartbeat. It was steady now, thumping comfortingly in my ear.

We didn't talk about it the next morning, but the following night, around one, he shook me awake. I was dead asleep, my whole body warm and limp beneath my heap of covers.

"What is it?" I murmured.

His hand slid down my naked side and pushed between my thighs. "Can I go down on you?"

I cracked an eye. "I'm not sure I can orgasm...I'm barely awake."

"You don't need to," he said, sliding under the blankets.

Confused, I pushed the covers down until his head was exposed. His eyes were heavy, but there was a hint of unease to them. Like there had been after his nightmare.

Had he had another one?

"Are you okay, Merrick?" I asked, my voice cracking.

He nodded, running his nose across my pussy.

"You always taste so good," he murmured. "It's calming. Grounding."

I slid my hand down and stroked through his hair and his lids fluttered. His eyes closed as his mouth moved over me and his arm came up and pulled the covers over his head.

"Go to sleep, *cariad*," he said, muffled.

I lay on my back and felt his mouth work between my legs. After a while, he slowed until it was just languid caresses. Then his jaw, scratchy with stubble, sank against my inner thigh. His breathing evened and I peeled back the covers to find him asleep.

Big hands gripping my hips. Face buried against the heat of my pussy.

When I woke, he was still sleeping in the same place, but he was snoring a little this time. I bit back a giggle. It was kind of cute the way he was curled up between my legs. Too large to fit properly.

He stirred, eyes opening. He blinked twice and I saw realization sink in as he focused on me up above him.

"I haven't slept that well in a long time," he said hoarsely.

"You slept with your face between my legs," I said. "I don't know how your neck doesn't hurt."

He ran his finger over my entrance and it came away glistening. Our eyes met and he pushed himself up onto his hands and crawled over me.

"You got me so hard it hurts, baby," he breathed.

"You teased me all night," I pointed out.

He gripped my ass hard and slapped it, making me yelp. All the anxiety of the last two nights was gone and I didn't dare bring it up again. He could be so guarded.

"You can't fuck me until you make me French toast," I yawned, wriggling out from beneath him.

He made a grab for me, but I slipped away and tore down the hallway and stairs and spilled into the kitchen. His footfalls followed me and his muscled forearm wrapped around my waist as I ran past the sink. Yanking me against his naked body.

"You're being a bad girl this morning," he said.

"Oh no," I breathed. "Cry about it."

I expected him to turn me around and kiss me or spank my ass and carry me back to the bedroom. Instead his hand wrapped around the nape of my neck and bent me in half over the sink. Pushing all the breath out of me.

Two fingers filled me and flicked my G-spot hard.

"Oh God," I whimpered.

His grip tightened, holding my face into the sink. I was aching between my legs like I'd never ached for him before. The cool air against my wet pussy was making me so sensitive that my clit was throbbing.

"What? She can dish it out, but the poor thing can't take it?" he murmured.

"Fuck you, Merrick," I goaded.

His fingers withdrew and his cock slammed into me, filling me with every inch of it in a single moment. My eyes rolled back and I cried out, biting my lip.

His big, lean fingers tangled in my hair and kept my head pressed down. The sink was cold against my bare stomach and the cabinet door pressed into my shins. I'd have bruises tomorrow.

I was crazy about his gentle side, but this...this scratched an itch deep inside and I wanted more of it. I whimpered, moaned, begged, and told him how big he was and how I loved taking him like this. Urging him on.

He'd done his fair share of praising me and it turned out it felt good to return the favor.

"That's right," he said, jaw gritted. "You take the whole thing."

He gathered my wrists in his grip, held them behind my back, and fucked me hard. The sound he made when he came echoed in my head. So satisfying, somewhere between a growl and groan.

Then he cleaned me up, brewed my favorite coffee, and put me on the counter to watch while he cooked. He made me French toast naked and fed it to me and told me all the things I wanted to hear. How pretty I was, how good I felt, how hard I made him come.

And somewhere beneath it all, I felt the undercurrent of his darkness.

Buried deep, deep inside.

CHAPTER THIRTY

MERRICK

I knew I only had her for the next week so I didn't waste my time. We fucked in the mornings, in the kitchen, before lunch, in the shower, in bed again for an afternoon nap. At night we went upstairs after dinner and I kept her up until well after midnight.

Her birth control was working overtime and my dick was raw by the end of the fourth day, but that didn't stop us.

It felt like a marathon, but I was so addicted I couldn't stop. I wasn't sure I'd ever had this much sex in my life at one time. That was saying something because I'd put in a lot of time in my twenties and thirties.

I wasn't sure what it was, but the quality of the sex we had was better than anything I'd experienced.

It was intimate and breathless.

It felt so safe and easy.

I forgot all about performing or fulfilling fantasies. I just made her come until she couldn't come any more and then she did the same for me. Then we ate and slept and did it all over again.

On our fourth day there, we had a late lunch and she fell asleep around five. I carried her upstairs, stripped her naked, and tucked her into bed. Then I went downstairs to use the gym and have a shower in the hall bathroom.

It was almost nine when I finished some work on my laptop and went up to the bedroom. It had finally stopped snowing the sky was clear through the glass wall over the bed.

In the starlight, I could just make out her form. Curled up on her side, dark hair splayed out over her pillow. Naked arms tucked against her breasts.

I stripped and slid between the sheets. The sight of her made my chest ache, a soft, nostalgic emotion that welled up like water.

A feeling my people had a word for.

Hireath.

A place I'd never been, a place I longed for more than anything. A future I could have, but knew I would never get.

"Merrick," she murmured.

Her voice was thick with sleep and her eyes were black in the starlight.

"Clara," I whispered.

There was a soft, expectant silence.

"I want you," she said.

I eased her closer and moved atop her, sliding between her smooth thighs. She moaned softly as I spat into my hand and worked it over her pussy.

The welcoming heat of her body enveloped my cock and sent a soft glow up my stomach. Up into my chest.

My eyes had adjusted to the dark and I could make out her face, below mine. Her lips were parted and her eyes were big. Soft like a deer's, watching me like I was the only person in the world.

Like she felt this fragile warmth too.

"Merrick," she breathed. "I need to feel you move inside me."

I bent and kissed her throat and she tilted her head to give me access. Her lovely neck tasted so sweet, like her naked skin without any of the scent from her soap and lotion.

My hips began pumping, taking her with gentle strokes.

We both gasped audibly at the sensation. Tingles like electricity moved up from my groin and my stomach muscles clenched.

My mouth found hers and sparks burst through my whole body. Her fingers skimmed up and cradled my head. Nails digging into my scalp just a little. Our lips singed, moving as slowly as my hips.

There was nothing in the world but this woman. Nothing but darkness, starlight, and her soft mouth against mine.

Nothing to hold us down to earth.

We spun into space, into a galaxy where there was just our bodies wound together. A slow awareness settled in the back of my mind. This wasn't fucking and it wasn't sex either.

It was something else.

Something so sweet that it melted on the back of my tongue and filled my veins with slow fire.

When she pulled back for a breath, her eyes were glazed and she was panting. I buried my face into her neck and kissed her down shoulder. Gently taking her nipple in my mouth and sucking as I pumped my hips between her spread thighs.

"Oh my God," she breathed.

We were both delirious with the pleasure surging through our bodies. It was building in my spine, like waves on the shore. Growing more intense with every stroke.

"Merrick," she whispered.

I moved my head, my mouth brushing her chin.

"*Cariad?*"

"I love having you inside me," she said softly. "When you go slow like this, I...I can feel everything."

She moaned as I worked my hips, brushing against her innermost point. Her pussy moved in rhythmic pulses in time with my thrusts. Hot, wet, perfectly blissful.

"I love being inside you too," I murmured.

Our eyes locked in the dark and our bodies rocked softly together. She lifted her chin, trying to reach my mouth.

I gave it to her, letting her kiss me with desperate, little strokes.

My hips shuddered and I came hard and slow, unable to hold myself back. Her fingers gripped the back of my neck, winding in my hair. Holding my face to her breasts as I emptied myself into her body.

Sealing us together.

"Oh my God," she breathed. "I've never felt anything like that before."

Cold moved through me like a gust of wind. It wasn't supposed to be like this. She had a future, her whole life ahead of her. Planned out exactly the way she'd dreamed.

That future didn't involve me.

I was supposed to be an experience. Just pleasure and fun.

Nothing more.

I pulled back, untangling our bodies, and stood. For the first time in a while, I was speechless. Completely off guard. Just standing there with my chest heaving, trying to find the right words.

The words that would put a wall up between us.

But they weren't there.

She pushed herself up, holding the sheet to her chest. "Merrick," she whispered.

I cleared my throat. "Clara."

Her eyes were wide, but this time it was with something else. Her lashes glistened.

"What was that?"

I opened my mouth, still too stunned to speak. I knew what that was. We both fucking knew what that was.

She cocked her head, waiting for me to say something. I snapped to life, pulling on my sweatpants and pushing my cigarettes into the pocket.

"I...um...I'm going for a smoke," I said hoarsely.

I felt her eyes on me as I fled the room. It was cold out, but it helped me steady my hands so I could light my cigarette. I stood on the porch, shirtless, but barely cold. My skin tingled from her touch. Her scent was all over me.

Dark jasmine.

My mouth still tasted like hers. I darted my tongue out and flicked it over my bottom lip.

My hand shook as I put the cigarette to my mouth.

I was smoking too much.

Twenty-six years ago, I'd stood at the center of an underground arena. I'd dug to the depths of myself and accepted that I wasn't likely to live till the evening.

Then I'd fought for my life and they made me the Welsh King.

I didn't want Clara to live in my world of blood and duty. I wanted her to live free, without the constraints of being married to the *Brenin*. She'd outlined exactly how she wanted her future to unfold to me years ago and I took that seriously.

She'd said she wanted to marry a man like Osian Cardiff so she could be a beautiful, careless trophy wife. So she never had to go back to the dark, utilitarian world she'd grown up in.

The cigarette burnt my lips, barely more than a nub in my fingers. I flicked it away and went into the dark hall. Locking the door.

Checking it once. Twice. Three times. Then four.

Fuck, I'd messed it up. It had to be in groups of three or it wasn't right.

One, two, three.

Four, five, six.

Seven, eight, nine.

I turned and walked down the hall and paused. Releasing a breath as I pivoted and stopped myself.

Images of Clara dead, throat slit in our bed upstairs, flooded my mind. All because I hadn't checked the locks properly.

Gritting my teeth, I strode back down the hall and tapped the door just above the lock. I couldn't touch the actual knob, otherwise it was fucked up and I had to count by threes again.

I could see it was locked, but the impulse to check it was out of control. I closed my eyes and took a deep breath. Calming my mind, forcing the images from my brain.

I tapped the door three times, took a long look at the lock, and turned on my heel.

My body froze up again, barely a step down the hall.

Goddamn it. I closed my eyes, envisioning Gretchen sitting in front of me. Face calm, eyes steady and comforting.

"It's not real," she said softly. "Trust yourself, Merrick."

But...it was real though. People died by home invasion all the time and I was a prime target as the Welsh King. Maybe I should barricade the door and install another lock in the morning.

A bolt that I could see all the way down the hall.

I took a deep breath and closed my eyes. Searching for my pulse in the darkness as I forced my breathing to slow.

One, two, three.

Four, five, six.

Seven, eight, nine.

Before my brain could start working, I strode into the kitchen and took the stairs two at a time.

For a second, I thought I was free. I was almost to the bedroom door when the panic set in. Before I knew what was happening, I'd swung around and I was back downstairs. Walking down the hall with my heart pounding in my chest.

No, I wasn't going through this tonight. Not with Clara upstairs. I needed to stop this before it got bad again. I whirled, completely misjudging how close I was to the wall, and struck a picture frame with my elbow.

It fell, the glass splitting in half. The sound echoed down the hall.

I snapped out of it, sliding to my knees in the hallway.

I'd fucked everything up.

Her footsteps sounded above me, pattering down the stairs. Her pale face appeared at the end of the hallway and then she was running to me. Falling to her knees, cradling my elbow.

Uncurling my hand, looking for an injury.

"I'm fine, Clara," I said, forcing my voice to steady.

She gripped my wrist, her eyes locking on mine.

"I think you need to start being truthful with me," she said.

CHAPTER THIRTY-ONE

CLARA

He looked cornered.

Trapped.

My chest tightened as fear rippled through me. I'd never seen Merrick like this and it threw everything off balance. Merrick was supposed to be the strong one, the Welsh King without a single crack in his armor.

I sent him upstairs to take a shower and I made him a drink with his favorite whiskey. I had a feeling I was going to need something too so I prepared an enormous bowl of ice cream with chocolate sauce.

He was sitting on the edge of the bed, flipping through his phone. He looked normal, except for the faint bruise on his forearm.

I set his drink down and knelt on the floor before him. Taking his hand in mine and flipping it over. Our eyes met and I kissed the scratch just below his elbow.

The corner of his mouth turned up, but his eyes were sad.

"I'm okay, I'm not out of control," he said evenly. "It just happens sometimes."

I hesitated, worrying that he would think I was prying. But part of me didn't care if he did.

"Do you have a name for whatever happened in the hallway?" I asked.

He jerked his chin. "Sit on the bed and have your ice cream."

I obeyed, crossing my legs and cradling the bowl in my lap. He propped himself up against the window and took a sip of his whiskey. His eyes were reflective as he gazed up at the ceiling.

"Gretchen Hughes has been my therapist for a long time," he said. "Growing up, Daphne and Ophelia could tell there was something going on, but it wasn't until I met Gretchen that I got a proper diagnoses."

He paused and I let him sort through his thoughts.

"I have adult ADHD, which is totally manageable for me. The kind I have isn't that bad," he said. "However...I also have OCD, which is harder for me to control. Sometimes it's hard to figure out what is causing what. It was a problem for a while, but Gretchen worked with me intensively for years and I've been really good."

Cold settled in my stomach.

"I triggered you, didn't I?" I whispered.

"No," he said swiftly. "I have a pretty good handle on it, but that doesn't mean it's gone. It's just something I live with."

I thought back over the almost six years I'd shared his home. He had his quirks, but I'd never translated that into an actual diagnosed issue. Feeling guilty for having missed so much, I reached out and put a hand on his leg, rubbing his thigh gently.

He glanced down and shifted the drink in his hand over his lap.

Oh. My. God.

"Do you have a boner?" I said.

He shook his head. "No."

"You absolutely do."

"I do not."

"Merrick!"

He pulled his hand back. "Okay, fine. I do. I got distracted."

I rolled my eyes and he adjusted himself. The mood slipped back into being sober.

"Can you tell me what you do that I might have missed?" I asked.

His jaw worked.

"There's the obvious things. I like things clean, orderly. I have my things made custom because they have to be exactly right. My clothes have to be made with certain materials that won't distract me. The locks...they have to be checked and fully secured."

"Okay, those make sense," I said carefully.

"I eat the same things every day because a lot of foods cause kind of a...revulsion," he said. "I work out a lot because it calms my symptoms. I keep my space clear and clean, my food simple, my schedule rigid, because it frees up my brain so I can use my energy in other areas, where I need more mental focus."

My chest hurt.

I'd never realized it till now, but I had it so easy. I could just live without struggling with everything in the world around me.

"Can I ask a stupid hypothetical?"

"Sure."

"If there was an apocalypse and you couldn't do all those things...would you just shut down?"

"No," he said. "I wouldn't have a problem. In fact, I do better in crisis situations than ordinary life. I think that's what makes me a good *Brenin*."

"That...that doesn't make sense."

He shrugged. "No. It doesn't, but there's a lot of things about having these diagnoses that don't make sense."

I wasn't sure what to say, so I kept quiet.

He released a short breath. "I had a lot of problems with impulse control when I was younger, I was very disorganized, struggled with regulating myself, but I'm a lot better with those things now."

"You're very disciplined," I murmured.

"I have to be," he said firmly.

"I'm sorry."

He frowned. "For what?"

I stroked down his thigh to his knee. "I'm just sorry that all these things that come so easily to others are such a struggle for you. I wish I could fix it for you."

His jaw worked. "It's the OCD that gets me. That shit can get dark."

"What...what do you mean?"

"I struggle a lot with obsessive thoughts about violence," he admitted. "Not committing it, but of it happening to the people I love. I check the doors, the windows, I sleep with a gun by my bed. But when I go to sleep at night sometimes I have to fight these images of horrible things happening to you."

I slid closer to him, running my fingers up his spine. Kneading the muscles of his neck.

"I'm safe, Merrick," I whispered.

"I know that here," he said, touching his temple. "But I don't believe it here." He touched his chest.

"Am I the only one who worries you?"

He shook his head. "I have trackers on Daphne and Ophelia's phones, as well as Yale and Caden's. Don't worry, they consented to it."

I chewed my mouth until that metallic taste blossomed on my tongue.

"The cleaning thing...I thought you just liked things being clean," I said, feeling stupid.

"It's more to do with contamination," he said. "What if I make you coffee and the pot is dirty and you get mold poisoning and die?"

"Um...Merrick, I don't think that's going to happen."

"I know that in my head," he said. "But there's always that torturous, tiny possibility that I'll gamble on everything being alright and lose."

I gazed up at him, my chest aching. "I'm sorry this is a struggle for you, Merrick," I whispered. "I don't know how to say the thing that I want to say."

"Just say it."

I chewed my lip, blood like metal in the back of my throat.

"I like you," I said. "To me, you will always be perfect. But that doesn't mean that I'm not sorry that you have to struggle. Does...does that make sense?"

His eyes went soft and he pulled me into his lap, cradling my head against his chest.

"It makes perfect sense, *cariad*," he murmured.

Neither of us felt much like talking anymore, so we finished our whiskey and ice cream. I lay beside him, curled in the heat of his body. Feeling his chest rise and fall. His breath kissed over my face and his fingers stroked through my hair.

"Clara?"

I kept still.

"Yes?"

"I killed twelve men with my bare hands in the arena so I could be the Welsh King."

There was faint tightness in the center of my chest and nothing more. The soft caress of his hands overwhelmed everything. Even fear.

"I thought so," I whispered.

He kissed the back of my neck and his breath burned to my core.

CHAPTER THIRTY-TWO

MERRICK

We didn't speak of the intense sex or my confession again.

Instead, we kept going on the same trajectory. Fucking, eating, and fucking some more before passing out in bed. It was easier to talk with our bodies than our mouths.

Although, I did let my mouth do a lot of the talking between her legs. Her pussy made all the noise in my head stop. It focused me. Gave me something that was positive and without pressure.

It was beautiful. Slightly pink with a freckle on the hood of her clit that I hadn't noticed until halfway through the week. I kissed it every time I took her panties down. And every time, she shuddered and squirmed.

She wasn't judging me or making me perform. And she didn't mind that sometimes when I woke, unable to sleep, all I wanted was to put my face between her legs until I passed out.

The snow melted and there was light flooding. We stayed an extra day and didn't bother to put our clothes on. I kept her on her back with her legs open. Taking my mouth, my cock, my fingers. Her spine rolling through her orgasms until she begged for mercy.

Then it was all over.

Then, without warning, we were home. Standing in the cold hallway with our suitcases.

In shock.

"I...I'll go unpack," I said.

She made a noise in her throat and I turned at the end of the hall and looked back. Her eyes glittered with tears and her knuckles were white. Gripping her suitcase because she had nothing else to hold onto.

"Merrick."

"Clara, we promised," I said.

"I don't want to sleep alone."

I took a breath, forcing my feet to keep still. If I took her in my arms, it was all over. I would take her up to my bed and fuck her, kiss her, and tell her I would never let her sleep alone again.

"Clara," I said, my voice tight. "I can't be the only one who breaks this off. You said it was just for the week. We both have to hold to that."

She swallowed, nodding.

"You told me six years ago what you wanted and I promised to make that a reality for you," I said. "We had our fun. It's time...it's time to get back to the real world."

Her lip trembled. "I hate this part," she whispered.

"I hate it too. I'm going to unpack and then I have to be in at the office," I said. "I'm sure Candice is dying to see you."

The house was silent after she'd gone to her room and that silence drove me out of my mind. I showered even though I hated to because the last remnants of her scent were gone now.

I met Caden at one of our secondary warehouses. He'd just spent the week with Trystan, the head of our training base in Wyoming. Things were going according to plan, except work had stalled until we could have the next shipment of building materials brought in.

"We need more money," Caden said, staring out over the harbor.

We stood along the shore, outside the warehouse. Inside, I could hear the faint hum of machinery, dulled by the ocean roaring against the rocks. Caden stood in his leather jacket, his face pale from the cold. That cigarette hanging from his lip.

"I'm getting it," I said.

He gave me a sharp glance.

"Where the fuck were you?" he said.

"Watch it."

He swiveled, shifting his weight to one leg. "You left Yale and I in charge of the first meeting with Trystan in weeks. And what business meeting could be more important than the business you're doing with the Cardiffs?"

I cleared my throat. "It was important too."

"So the story's changing," he said shortly.

Caden's eyes narrowed, washed out to pale blue in the insipid light. "Did you have Clara with you?"

"Enough," I said firmly.

His gaze bored into me until I turned away and strode back into the warehouse. I heard his boots crunch on the gravel behind me.

"You're fucking her," he said, through a haze of cigarette smoke.

I spun around. Livid, but successfully keeping it locked away under a calm exterior.

"Do we have a problem, Caden?" I said.

His mouth thinned. "I apologize, sir," he said flatly.

I nodded curtly, striding through the warehouse to the other end where I'd parked the Audi. My phone buzzed as I got into the car and an alert popped up for Clara's location.

She was on her way to Candice's house.

I sank back into the front seat. My body was raw from the last week. Forever altered by her touch. But it was my brain...and my heart that were having the most trouble recovering.

I had no idea what I felt for her, but I did know that the last thing in the world I wanted was to give her up.

CHAPTER THIRTY-THREE

CLARA

The day after we got home, I went over to Candice's house. Her parents were home, having coffee in the kitchen. Owen was a burly man with a pleasant face and a head of silver hair and Catrin was willowy and soft-spoken. I'd spent a lot of time with them over the years, especially while my father was still alive.

I stopped to talk for a minute, feeling guilty although I wasn't sure why. Catrin offered me a hug and brushed my hair back, looking me over.

"You look great," she said. "You're really growing up."

"Thank you," I said. "I had a really relaxing week with Daphne and Ophelia."

"Oh, how are the aunts? I haven't been out that way in ages," Owen said. "The last time I saw Daphne she said they were redoing the kitchen."

"Yeah, they're really good," I said, forcing myself to stay relaxed. "The remodeling is going well. They both said to say hello when I saw you next."

"Did you get any snow out at the farm?" Catrin asked.

She paused at the counter, her hand on her hip. Jewelry glittering on her manicured hand. She always looked so elegant and poised, not at all like Candice, who did everything she could to be the opposite.

"Yeah, a bit maybe," I said nervously.

There was a clatter from behind me and I breathed an internal sigh of relief as Candice appeared. She hugged me from behind and scoped out the room, going to the cabinet to grab a bag of chips.

"You want something to drink?" she asked.

"I'll take iced tea," I said.

"How's Merrick?" Catrin said. "I haven't seen him around for a week."

Into my mind flooded a hundred images from the last week. His tongue dragging down my stomach to my pussy. His eyes burning from between my legs as he made me come on his mouth.

Heat surged and I felt it creep up my neck.

No, no, not now.

"He's fine," I said quickly. "I haven't really seen him. He had some business out of town or something."

Candice grabbed my wrist and pulled me towards the stairs. "You can get caught up later, mom."

Up in Candice's room, I checked my reflection in the mirror. The heat had drained from my face. But there was something on my shoulder. Frowning, I leaned in and tugged my sweater aside.

My jaw dropped.

At some point, he'd given me a hickey. It must have happened the last day we were there and I hadn't noticed.

"Oh my God," Candice said, smirking. "Do you have a hickey?"

"No," I said, covering it.

She bounced off the bed and pulled my sweater down, spinning me to face the mirror. Our eyes locked and slid down to the mark on my collarbone.

"Did you have sex?"

My stomach twisted. I was such a liar, such a bad friend.

"No," I managed. "It's nothing. I just saw Osian yesterday and we made out for a bit. I'm...trying to get used to it."

Candice narrowed her eyes, making me feel like I was being X-rayed.

"Have you seen his penis yet?"

"Candice!"

She started laughing and climbed back onto the bed, opening the chip bag. I yanked my sweater up and joined her, crossing my legs.

"Are you having sex?" I said.

Her brow arced. "Who would I be having sex with?"

"You know who."

She shook back her hair and rolled her eyes, looking annoyed. "I wouldn't sleep with Yale if you paid me. He's dead to me."

There was a cold current through her voice that made me pause.

"Did he do something?"

She huffed, wrapping her arms around her chest. Candice was tough, she was outspoken, she rarely let herself be vulnerable. I'd picked up that last trait from her. But now, her eyes were hurt.

"He said I'd never be taken seriously as a lawyer because my tits were too big," she said quietly.

My jaw went slack. Candice was a slender woman with a skinnier waist than mine, but she was easily four cup sizes bigger. Three years before I ever went through puberty, she was crying and trying to cover up with giant sweatshirts.

Now, she'd just given up. Her parents refused to let her get cosmetic surgery so she'd just learned to live with it.

But I knew it was her biggest insecurity.

"You're going to law school?" I asked. "I had no idea."

She shrugged, picking her cuff. "I was thinking about it. I'm pretty argumentative, might as well get paid for it. I had lunch with Merrick's lawyer and he's pretty interesting so I thought maybe I'd try to get into the University of Georgia."

"So...you should do it," I said.

"Now I feel kind of stupid," she mumbled.

I shook my head. "Because of something Yale said? He's stupid, don't think about him."

"No," she said firmly. "It wasn't just about my boobs, although he's right. I've had guys make gross remarks about them for years. But he wasn't saying that...he was basically saying that no one in the organization would take me seriously as a female lawyer."

"That's not true," I said. "Merrick would never let anyone treat you badly because you're a woman."

"Merrick can't follow me around everywhere. He can't make these men respect me."

I climbed onto the bed and settled cross-legged. "Have you sat down with Merrick and talked about what the real prospects for law school are? If I didn't know about it, surely he doesn't."

"Neither of you know," she said, running a hand over her nose. "Both of you have been really busy for the last month."

"I'm sorry," I said quickly. "I suck as a friend. I've been busy with the engagement stuff, but it's not an excuse."

She sniffed loudly, pushing her shoulders back. "It's fine, it's not important. Maybe I'll ask dad or Merrick to start arranging someone for me instead of going back to school. Honestly, that's probably more realistic."

"Are you happy?" I asked quietly.

She paused, her lips parting. "I mean...I guess. Are you?"

My mind filled with the memory of waking up beside Merrick, of feeling his hot weight draped over me. Of watching him cook, of showering with him, of stargazing on the porch while he had a cigarette.

"I am sometimes," I whispered.

Her gaze went flat. "Do you still think your original life plan will make you happy? Being a rich, organization wife and having kids."

I nodded, but deep inside, I wasn't sure.

"Maybe I'll try that too," she sniffed.

"So...is that it? You're not even going to talk to anyone else about this?"

"No, it's just fucking depressing and I want to talk about something happier right now." She rolled her eyes. "Surely you have some gossip for me? Did you really just sit around with Merrick's aunts and do nothing all week?"

There it was, that guilt like a knife in the pit of my stomach.

"We spent a lot of time talking," I said. "Daphne always has a lot of insightful things to say about...well, everything. Ophelia was caught up with all the house renovation so she was busy most of the time. Oh, and I went on birth control."

Candice sat up. "What? Why?"

I wasn't sure why I'd said it. Probably because she would notice me taking it sooner or later.

"Osian seems like he's expecting me to have sex with him before we get married," I said slowly. "I just...I really don't want to get pregnant."

That wasn't a lie, it was just avoiding the truth.

Candice chewed her lip and wrapped her arms around her knees. She gazed at me for a long moment.

"You don't seem very excited about Osian," she said.

I shrugged. My throat felt tight. I took a chip from the bag but it tasted like dust on my tongue.

"He didn't do anything to me," I said. "He's just...kind of a douche."

"Have you told Merrick how you feel?"

"What would it do? We both made a deal with the Cardiff family and Merrick's good name and business is riding on it. And...I don't have an actual excuse. Like...he hasn't done anything bad to me," I said, struggling to find the words. "He just...he just...I don't know."

Her brows creased. "You can be honest with me. Tell me."

I thought back over all my interactions with him, my stomach cold. "He just acts kind of entitled about my body. Like...just because I'm marrying him someday doesn't mean he has a right to me...right?"

"No, of course not," said Candice.

Her eyes flashed and narrowed. I could tell she was gearing up to utterly loathe Osian for the rest of her life.

"Before I went to Merrick's aunt's house, I told Osian I would sleep with him," I said. "We went to the bedroom and everything was fine, but then he tried to put his hand in my panties and I

255

freaked out. I told him no and he stopped. But he was pissed off and he started accusing me of sleeping around."

Her lips became a thin line. "I'll fucking kill him."

"Candice, please, don't."

"Okay, fine. But you have to tell Merrick."

"Tell him what?" I said, chewing my mouth hard. "That I agreed to fuck Osian and he stopped when I said to stop? That's the thing...he hasn't done anything that I can say clearly is wrong."

"You can still tell Merrick he gives you a bad feeling."

I started pacing the room, my arms crossed tightly. "No, that's stupid. I agreed to this and I have to go through with it."

Candice got to her feet and took me by the elbows, turning me to face her.

"Okay, deep breath," she said.

I obeyed, inhaling and exhaling.

Her crystal blue gaze locked on mine.

"I want you to think really hard about your answer because I'm about to ask you something serious. Okay?"

I nodded. My tongue tasted like blood, but I didn't stop chewing.

"Do you think that Osian would ever put his hands on you?"

Shock rippled through me at her words. I opened my mouth to speak and closed it.

"Think really carefully," she said, her voice soothing.

I closed my eyes and ran through all our interactions again.

And again.

Candice was waiting when I snapped my lids open. My chest burned, all twisted and tight. Tears threatened to slide down my cheeks.

"I don't have a reason to think he would," I whispered. "But I don't know."

"What are your instincts telling you?" she asked.

I shrugged, helplessly. "Not to trust him."

"Okay, you have to talk to Merrick."

"Candice—"

"Clara, your body is telling you it doesn't feel safe with Osian. You have to listen to it."

"Things just aren't that simple."

She fell quiet and released me. There was a defeated look in her eyes that only made me feel more guilty. At that moment, my phone pinged on the dresser and I went to check it.

It was a text from Merrick.

Dinner tonight?

My heart skipped a beat and my hand shook as I swiped the screen. Why did he want dinner with me? Was he rethinking things?

No, he had said things would go back to normal.

And this was normal. Merrick took me out to dinner all the time. I forced my breath to slow as I typed out a response.

Sure. Where?

The bubble appeared, rolling for a minute.

The Italian place on the east side of the river that has the drinks you like.

You don't like that place.

Who says?

You said it was unhealthy.

There was a long pause and then:

I'll pick you up from the house at seven.

My heart beat oddly for the rest of the afternoon, but I pretended it was nothing. I drove home from Candice's house and showered. Then I obsessed over every dress in my closet for the next hour even though I knew exactly what I was going to wear.

A little black dress. Tight around my body. Coming down to the middle of my thigh.

Black high heels, a little velvet bow above my ankle.

I put on berry pink lipstick and fluffed my hair. Downstairs, the front door opened and I heard him in the hall.

"Clara," he called. "I'm ready, so just lock the doors when you're done. I'm going to make a phone call in the car."

"Alright, I'll be there in a minute," I yelled.

I grabbed a black velvet handbag and left the house, punching in the code. He was leaning against the Audi, one foot crossed over the other. As I descended the steps, he paused mid-sentence.

Then he gave me the up and down glance. Quicker than a flash.

Warmth burst in my chest. I waited for him to open the door and I climbed into the passenger side. He hung up the phone and got into the car.

There was a long moment of silence.

The air was so thick I could feel my heart thumping. Like a vein pulsing between our bodies.

He pulled the car out onto the darkening road and we headed towards the highway. Everything in me was dying to say something to break the silence, but I couldn't think of a single word.

We pulled up outside the restaurant. He helped me out of the car and guided me inside to his table in the corner.

I said something stupid about how the river looked beautiful at night with all those boats.

He said it did, but he didn't take his eyes off me.

I ordered two Cosmos and drank the first in less than a minute. He noticed, but he didn't say anything. The waiter brought him expensive whiskey, a single shot in one of those classy, crystal glasses.

It rested in his fingers.

His sexy, lean fingers with those square tips that had been inside me just days ago.

Heat surged up from between my thighs. My head swirled from the Cosmo, making me painfully aware of his gaze on me.

Who even had eyes that blue with lashes that dark?

It was fucking ridiculous.

"Did you have a good day with Candice?" he said.

I stared at him. "How did you know I was with Candice?"

"I have a tracker on you."

I leaned back in my chair and tossed my hair. Of course, in the back of my mind, I knew Merrick wasn't going to let me run around

Providence without keeping tabs on me. But it was still fucking annoying.

"Why would you care where I've been?" I said, giving him a sweet smile. "Since we're not anything to each other."

"I'm your fucking guardian."

His eyes flashed, not out of anger. More out of...grumpiness? I studied him. That was a bit odd, Merrick wasn't one to succumb to melancholy.

I cocked my head. "Feeling grouchy?"

His brow crooked. "No."

"Hmm."

I kept my brow arched as I sipped from the straw. Merrick scowled and I could tell that little *hmm* bothered him. There was a long silence and his jaw went tense.

"What, Clara?"

"Nothing," I said, shrugging. "You were just less grumpy when you were getting laid."

His lips parted and his eyes crackled.

"Behave yourself," he said.

"Why?" I said, deciding that if I was going to kick this hornet's nest, I was going to kick it hard. "Is this easy for you? We were fucking less than seventy-two hours ago and now you're just going to pretend we can go back to...to this?"

"We have to, Clara," he said.

I shot to my feet and strode down the hall to the bathroom. I felt his eyes on me as I disappeared behind the door.

Heart pounding, I leaned on the sink. My eyes stung, but I was more angry than anything else. I hated how calm, how detached he was, when all I wanted to do was curl up and cry.

Instead, I ducked into a stall and wriggled my skirt up around my waist. Underneath, I was wearing a tiny, black lace thong that barely covered anything. I worked it off and balled it in my fists, smoothing my skirt down.

His eyes snapped to me as I crossed the room, heels clinking. The restaurant was full and everyone was focused on their own tables.

No one but him noticed me walk up to our table and put my hand on his arm.

"How much is that whiskey a glass?"

His eyes narrowed. "Around three hundred dollars."

"For that little bit?"

"It's very good."

I dropped my panties into his glass. We both sat there in stunned silence as they sank to the bottom. A scrap of lace in amber.

I couldn't believe I'd done that.

Fuck it, he was being an asshole. Circling the table, I sat down and crossed my arms. Training my eyes out the window. The waiter appeared and put our food down, but didn't say anything about the panties in Merrick's whiskey.

I dragged my eyes up to his and they were burning. His face was carved from stone. The skin between his collarbones was flushed.

He lifted the glass and took a sip and set it aside. Between my legs, my pussy was slippery. I swirled my spaghetti and took a bite.

"How's your food?" he asked lightly.

"It's good," I said. "How's your whiskey? Apparently it's expensive."

He leaned on the table, resting his chin in his fingers. There was a faint smirk on his mouth.

"Would you believe me if I told you it tastes like your cunt?"

I gasped, blushing to my roots as I whirled to check if our neighbors had heard him. No one was paying attention, thankfully.

"You're being vulgar," I hissed.

"You are being incredibly difficult," he said. "You need an attitude adjustment, *cariad*."

"Oh, I expect you think that's your job?"

"No, but if it involves spanking your ass, I'd be happy to help."

"How dare you!"

He turned and lifted his hand to the waiter, who hurried over to our table. He bent and Merrick said something to him and his eyes widened.

I sat there, mouth open, as the waiters descended on the tables and everyone got up and walked out. Merrick remained as he was, one leg crossed over the other, his whisky with my drenched panties in his hand.

Not a feather ruffled.

The waiters disappeared as well and we were alone in the middle of the dark restaurant.

Oh fuck, I'd forgotten he was the Welsh King.

Merrick was gone and in his place was a powerful man with a face of stone and a stare that could burn down the world.

My core pulsed rhythmically and my heart pounded. Was it possible to be scared and aroused at the same time? Apparently it was. I wrapped my arm around my body, but I couldn't tear my eyes from him like this.

Sitting there like he owned the world.

Like he owned me.

"Come here," he said.

My body tingled as I rose and went to him, my fists clenched. He looked me up and down.

"Take your heels off and kneel," he said coolly.

This was a side to him I'd never seen before. And it was mesmerizing.

I took my shoes off and sank down, sitting back on my heels. He shifted his chair to face me and set his whiskey down. His two fingers dipped in and lifted my soaked thong.

"Open your mouth."

I hesitated, but the look in his eyes made me obey. He took the panties in his fist and brought them dripping to my lips. His fingers clenched and whiskey streamed onto my tongue.

Scorching down my throat. I coughed.

"Swallow," he said. "You made a mess, you clean it up."

I obeyed. Caught under his spell.

"Take your dress off."

CHAPTER THIRTY-FOUR

MERRICK

What the fuck was I doing?

Her eyes were so dark and big as her fingers struggled to get her zipper down. It peeled away, revealing her breathtaking body underneath.

She didn't have a bra on under that tiny dress. Her nipples were hard. I slid my eyes over them, down the gold ring on her navel, to her sex tucked between her thighs. There was a faint glitter of arousal at the crease of her pussy.

"You need fucked, but I said I wouldn't fuck you," I said evenly. "Come here and sit in my lap. Touch yourself until you finish on me."

Her pupils dilated and she moved toward me like she was in a trance. I kept my eyes on her face as she straddled me, filling my lap and wrapping her legs around my waist.

Our eyes met, the space between us tense.

"Put your hand between your thighs," I whispered.

She obeyed and her head fell back. A heavy sigh released from her lips and her spine arced.

"Does it feel good for you?" I breathed.

"Yes," she moaned.

"Do you like touching your pussy in my lap?"

Her lashes fluttered. "Fuck...yes."

I let myself stroke her silky thighs, sliding my hands up over her hips. Her fingers worked quickly and her stomach tensed, a faint wet sound coming from between us.

"Tell me," I urged. "Tell me how it feels."

Her lids flickered, her eyes rolling back. "I feel so safe."

"Enough to come for me?"

"Yes, sir," she gasped.

My other hand came up and cradled her head, bending her so she had to look me in the eyes. She was panting, her stare glazed.

"Don't call me sir," I whispered. "Say what you really want to say."

It was rare that I allowed anyone to make me their fantasy. But I had no self control when it came to Clara. I knew that we were playing with fire, but I was drunk on her, ready to get hurt just to feel her trust.

She kept touching herself and her lips moved, but no sound came out.

"I can't hear you," I said softly.

She swallowed and her mouth parted.

"Daddy," she whispered.

I brushed her hair behind her ears. "I'm here, *cariad*."

Her eyes closed and her head fell back again. Lovely throat curving, breasts pushed into my face. Her fingers slowed as she played with herself and I realized she had her fingers in her pussy. Working that sweet spot from inside.

"Do you like calling me that?"

She bit her lip, nodding.

"Don't be embarrassed." My voice was thick. "Call me whatever makes you feel safe. Tonight I'll be anything you need me to be, baby girl."

She gasped, hips grinding in my lap. "Then, yes, I want to call you daddy."

My resolve shattered. I felt it crack like a physical sensation. What did it matter anyway? What was one more time with her when we'd fucked so much over the last week?

My hand shot out and gripped her wrist. Eyes locked, heart thumping, I pulled her hand from between her thighs. She whimpered softly and I took her fingers in my mouth and licked them clean.

Sweet tartness blossomed over my tongue and any shreds of my resistance faded. Reckless, I pushed two fingers into her soaked pussy and found that sweet spot. Her lids flickered and her head fell back as she surrendered to me.

My mouth brushed her throat, kissing her softly.

"Come for me, baby girl," I breathed. "I paid for every plate in this restaurant to leave twice over. This is the most expensive orgasm you've ever had so let me make it fucking good."

Her breasts heaved and her hips shuddered. Slippery wetness dripped down my knuckles. My thumb found her swollen clit and worked it in slow circles.

She tightened around me, gripping me like a vise. Her slick muscles pumped around me, getting tighter and tighter, but never releasing.

Her body was shaking, unable to get over the edge. I slowed my pace and took her left nipple in my mouth. Her eyes flew open and her throat and cheeks flushed dark pink as she let out a desperate wail.

But she didn't come.

"I'm sorry," she gasped. "I can't get there."

"Hush," I said, standing with her in my arms.

I spilled her onto her back on the table and buried my face between her thighs. My fingers stroked inside her hot, slippery pussy and my mouth found that little bud above it.

It was hot on my tongue as I sucked it in slow, building pulses. I quickened my fingers and started licking her as I sucked and she exploded. The cry that burst from her as she broke apart was heavenly. I pulled back and straightened, heart pounding.

I needed to keep myself under control or I was going to fuck her on the table right now.

"Not here," I whispered.

She pushed herself up and blinked, her mascara smudged beneath her eyes. I picked up her dress and helped her into it. Her gaze bored into me as I slipped her heels on and pressed a kiss to her ankle.

Her toes curled.

"I liked calling you daddy," she said hesitantly. "I don't know if I'd want it every time. But it was nice."

"You can call me daddy anytime you feel like it."

Her mouth curved into an uncertain smile. Then it faded as we realized we'd done the very thing we had promised we wouldn't.

She slipped off the table and sat down. I returned to my chair and sank into it, pulse still racing. There was a long silence and she picked up her Cosmo and drained it.

"You're going to say that this has to be the last time, aren't you?"

I cleared my throat, looking around at the wreckage of the table. She was poised, her glittering fingernails digging into the edge of the table.

"I was going to say that until you're officially engaged to another man, you belong to me," I said.

Her gaze snapped up. "Wait...what?"

I raised a brow. "You don't want that?"

"No...I do," she stammered. "I just...what about Osian? He's going to want to sleep with me at some point. Do you care?"

Jealousy ripped through me and it was all I could do to keep my face blank. Or at least I thought I had. She balked, shrinking back into her seat.

"What?"

"You just...you look scary when you make that face."

"What face?"

She chewed her mouth. "The face where it looks like you want to kill twelve people with your bare hands again."

"Tell Osian to stay off you until the wedding," I said. "Say you changed your mind and you want to wait until your wedding night to sleep with him. Or I can tell him."

"Please don't. I can do it." A bit of crimson stained her lower lip. "He's going to be pissed when he finds out I'm not a virgin anymore."

265

"I'll handle it."

She watched me with wide eyes as I called out the red faced waiter and paid the bill for the entire restaurant. I wasn't sure if she was anxious or aroused. Her cheeks flushed as I held out my hand and she slid her fingers through mine.

She stayed quiet while I led her out to the car and drove her home. As we pulled up the driveway, I slid my hand over the console and stroked her leg. Gripping her thigh. Her breath caught and she shifted her legs apart.

"Osian isn't a virgin and he isn't abstaining," I said. "I see him at my clubs, picking up women, all the time. Just because you're a woman, Clara, doesn't mean you have to adhere to a different standard."

"I don't want to sleep around," she said hoarsely. "I just want to sleep with you. In your bed."

CHAPTER THIRTY-FIVE

CLARA

When we got home, I turned to go shower in my bathroom and he grabbed my wrist and spun me around. I fell against his chest and his fingers buried in my hair.

His mouth grazed mine, hot and smelling like whiskey and Merrick.

"Just where the fuck do you think you're going?" he murmured.

"To shower."

I made to kiss him, but he pulled back until he was barely out of my reach. Denying me, teasing me.

"You can shower in my bathroom."

"It doesn't have my things in it."

"Use mine then."

"Sure, if I want to have a huge breakout tomorrow. I need my things, not yours."

He relented and I ran barefoot down the hall and into my bathroom. It took me almost an hour to shower, wash my hair, do my skincare. Faintly, I heard him checking the locks and windows as he did every night.

His footfalls disappeared upstairs. I tied my hair up in a loose bun and dug through my clothes to find something nice to sleep in.

Instead, I came up with one of his t-shirts. My fingers ran over the soft cotton and my stomach fluttered.

Breathing deeply, I pressed my face into it.

Dark, crisp oak.

My core clenched, roused. I pushed the t-shirt back into my drawer, wanting it to be my secret for when this was over. Instead, I put on a cropped tank top and ruffled shorts that barely covered my ass.

He seemed to like when I wore that combination.

I grabbed my little bag of nighttime things and padded down the hall and up the stairs. At the top, I hesitated, unsure.

What if he'd changed his mind?

Gathering my courage, I knocked on his door and he opened it. He was wearing nothing but his boxer briefs. My breath caught as I looked him up and down, my eyes lingering on his groin.

I could make out the faint outline of him.

Even unaroused, it was sexy. Like a promise.

He hooked his finger under my waistband and pulled me into the bedroom and pushed me back against the door. My bag fell to the ground and his mouth found mine and consumed it.

Stars burst to life behind my eyelids and I squeezed them shut. My body melted into his hands, big and lean against my back.

He picked me up and we fell into bed in a breathless tangle. His cotton sheets were cool against my back and his bed smelled just like him. All smoky and sexy and male.

Hands shaking, we took what little clothes we wore off and tossed them over the side of the bed.

His naked body settled over mine, hot and lean between my thighs. We kissed slowly, our mouths tangled and our tongues tasting of each other. His hand was on my throat, barely touching my skin.

He didn't need to. Just the suggestion of his warm, perfect hand was enough to keep me right where he wanted me.

We made out like we were starving until I felt drunk. My breasts heaved. I was aching and slippery between my legs. I needed the perfect stretch and heaviness of him inside me now or I was going to go crazy.

"Fuck me," I breathed.

His jaw tightened and he gripped me and rolled onto his back. I swayed, but he kept me steady. Positioning me on his hips and taking his cock by the base. He slapped my clit with it once, smirking. Then he dragged the head over me, gathering my arousal.

I twitched at the contact, begging him with my eyes. Pleading with him to fill the emptiness between my thighs.

His eyes glittered, his chest heaved. One hand on my hip and the other on his cock, he guided it into me in one, slow thrust.

My eyes rolled back and my nails dug into his stomach and chest. Thick, hard warmth filled me to my deepest point. Scratching that itch so perfectly I whimpered, wriggling my hips to get him as deep as possible.

"Beautiful," he murmured distractedly. "Look at you."

I ground my hips, pleasure making me frantic and weak all at once.

"Yours," I panted.

"Mine."

His voice came out low and thick, like a growl. Our eyes locked and I began riding him slowly, palm flat on his lean stomach.

"Touch yourself while you fuck me, *cariad*."

I'd never done this, but as soon as my fingers found my clit my entire body lit up. This was it, this was the way my body wanted to come. I should have tried this a lot sooner.

Right away, I felt an orgasm building deep inside. A hot itch of pleasure, coiling tighter and tighter, threatening to break. Blossoming in my hips like lava pooling and bubbling.

"That's a good fucking whore," he breathed, thrusting gently in time with me. "You come for me just like that."

My hips shuddered as pleasure hit me like I'd never felt before. Slow, throbbing ecstasy. Twisting my spine, making me stop riding and just shudder on top of him. Gripping his cock hard enough to make him clench his jaw.

He flipped me on my back, braced his elbow on the bed, and fucked me. Hard and fast as I finished coming around him.

I was an incoherent mess, still pulsing. Hair tangled, lashes wet, lips swollen. He finished with a groan, back arcing in, eyes closing. His jaw tensed and he throbbed inside me, warmth blossoming in my innermost point.

Our bodies stilled.

"Are you alright, baby?" he whispered.

"Yes," I breathed. "That was amazing."

We both gasped as he stirred and pulled from me slowly, leaving me tingling. Then, eyes on me, he moved down my body.

My thighs clenched.

"What are you doing?"

"Eating your pussy."

My body tingled, completely overstimulated. I'd never had two orgasms in a row, so close together, and I doubted it was even possible.

"It's too much," I breathed, falling back against the pillows.

He didn't think it was too much. His hot mouth came down on my clit, building me slowly with the lightest strokes. Nipping, flicking, sucking me. Eating my still tingling sex until I felt another orgasm rushing down my spine.

I wound my fingers into his dark waves and let the ceiling swim overhead.

My clit was swollen and overstimulated. But I still came, so hard I barely felt the pleasure. Just the waves as my inner muscles clenched and my thighs locked around his head. Bucking my hips against his mouth.

Then, he did it again.

I was whimpering, begging him for mercy in the same breath as I begged him to keep going. My fingers pulled at his hair, trying to get his mouth off my clit, but he just held my wrists down.

"If you really don't want this, use your words and tell me," he breathed. His tongue flicked me and I yelped. "But I don't think you want me to stop."

I bit my lip until blood spotted my tongue. He pulled another orgasm from me, this one weaker, but lasting so much longer. Then he flipped me over and told me to hold onto the headboard and sit on his face.

When I came again, my legs giving out under me, I heard him groan.

Deep and heavy, his body shuddering.

Panting, I looked over my shoulder and a ripple of surprise broke through the haze.

He had finished on his stomach.

I whipped back around, shocked. He moaned from somewhere down below, muffled by my pussy. My glittering, red nails dug into the oak headboard right before my eyes as I processed what had just happened.

He'd come just from going down on me.

My nipples peaked and, despite my exhaustion, arousal surged in a hot wave down my spine and pooled in my hips and thighs.

"You really love eating pussy," I whispered.

He lifted me off his face and ran a hand over his jaw, cleaning the arousal from his skin. He looked drunk and thoroughly satisfied. Not embarrassed at all.

"I really fucking do," he panted.

He pulled me to him, kissing my mouth. I tasted us together on his tongue and it made my head spin. My sweetness and his saltiness mixed in the back of my throat.

He was gone when I woke and it was almost ten. There was a notecard on the bedside table and our clothes were folded on the chair. He'd even attempted to make the bed around me, tucking the sheets over my body.

I smiled, sitting up. Wincing at the soreness between my legs.

The world felt right. Like I was where I belonged.

I flipped open the card and written in his sharp, rigid handwriting, it said:

Don't forget, no drinking except on weekends.

I rolled my eyes and got up, dropping it in the trash. There was something else on the table, propped up on the lamp. A velvet pouch with a little emerald clasp.

I shook it out in my hand and my stomach sank. It was a fine, silver bracelet with my initials on the clasp. There was another note inside, but the handwriting wasn't Merrick's. It was loopy and messy.

Please accept this as a token of our future commitment.

—OC

My eyes smarted and my hand shook as I sank down onto the bed.

Why had Merrick chosen to accept the first piece of jewelry now? Why had he ruined everything when he could have put it off and let me pretend this never had to end?

I gripped the bracelet, looking for somewhere to put it. I didn't want it in my room, but I couldn't get rid of it because Osian would expect to see me wearing it.

Merrick could keep it for me.

Blinking hard to hold back the unexpected tears, I tugged open his dresser drawers, but they were full. The closet door was shut, but I doubted Merrick would care if I went inside so I pulled it ajar.

And stopped short.

There wasn't a single shirt, suit, or pair of shoes inside. Instead, it was a dimly lit room with locked cases on the wall. Full of guns of all shapes and sizes. Black and silver wicked looking things that made my pulse still.

Just like the ones my father had kept in his office.

My throat was dry as I swallowed, stepping into the closet and letting the door swing shut. I flicked the light on and my mouth went dry.

He was the Welsh King, the head of a mafia organization. He was a very classy and intelligent criminal, but he was a criminal all the same.

So why did this surprise me?

I didn't have to ask myself twice. I knew why the sight of weapons triggered me so badly.

Merrick was my home. My safety. But he also reminded me of my father and that was a hard pill to swallow. Not in essence, but in the hidden parts of him that surfaced now and then. The guns, the scars, the self denial, the flicker of cruelty behind his intense gaze.

My eyes were wet as I paused before a display case full of knives. On the top was a short blade in an open velvet box.

I lifted it, gripping the hilt in my fist. There was curling script down the blade and my family crest at the base.

Edwin Gethin Prothero.

My father, the man who shared Merrick's first and true name. Two Edwins against the world.

My throat tightened. They had been brothers in arms. I knew they'd fought alongside one another to take all the territory below Boston and keep the Irish at bay.

They had shared their lives for fifteen years. Broken bread together, drank together. Probably slept with the same women.

My shaking finger slid up the blade and blood broke from beneath the skin. Just a few drops. Dripping down my palm to my wrist.

"Clara."

I turned, a tear leaking from my lashes. Merrick stood there looking so goddamn handsome in his burgundy shirt. His mouth was a thin line and his eyes burned. Flame so hot it was blue.

"I thought you were at work."

"I came back to get my wallet."

My fingers tightened around the hilt of the blade. It shook as we both gazed down at it.

"Why do you have this?" I whispered.

His hand curled around my elbow, but I didn't let go.

"Edwin gave it to me before he died," he said.

I pulled back, suddenly angry although I wasn't sure why. That intense stare fixed on me as I took a deep breath. Blinking to keep the rest of my tears back.

"This is mine," I said. "It has the Prothero family crest on it."

"These knives were left to me."

I dropped it with a clatter and turned to go, but he seized my wrist. Blood stained his fingertips and his lips as he lifted my hand and kissed my palm.

His tongue darted out, tasting my blood. Licking it from my skin. Our eyes locked and our breath came short and fast in the silence between us.

"Anything I have is yours," he said. "If that's what you need to let him go."

"I've already let him go," I said. "It's you that can't. I won't do this, Merrick, I won't have the ghost of my father in the room with us. If you want me in your bed tonight, take his shit out of this room."

It was cruel and I saw the pain in his eyes for a moment before he dropped them. He swallowed and I could make out the pulse in his throat.

"Edwin made me who I am," he said.

"I know," I said. "I can tell."

CHAPTER THIRTY-SIX

MERRICK

I beat the shit out the punching bag that morning.

In the training warehouse, it was fucking cold. But I didn't feel anything as I stood there, shirtless, and let the sweat fall like rain.

I know, I can tell.

Despite how my chest ached, I stuck to my schedule and ran through the training with the younger men at the gun range. We had to keep moving forward, growing and getting stronger. The minute I took my foot off the gas was the minute I conceded my territory.

My organization was known for having the deadliest soldiers and I needed to have the firepower to back that up. So I drowned myself in my duties as *Brenin* and hoped the sweat would somehow wash me clean.

I was still broken that evening as I showered at my office and changed into a suit. Clara was supposed to have dinner with Osian and I had an appointment with Gretchen.

It was for the best.

Gretchen made a pot of blooming jasmine tea and poured me a glass of her best whiskey. I accepted it without protest. She could always tell when it was going to be a tough session.

"Did you break it off?" she asked softly.

I shook my head, jiggling my foot.

"Alright, tell me the worst and we'll work backwards like we always do."

We were sitting on opposite ends of the room. She wore her terrycloth, white bathrobe and sat facing me. Tea in her lap. I was as I always was—in a custom suit with one leg crossed over the other.

"Okay," I said. "I slept with her again and she told me I was like her father the next morning."

"Ouch," Gretchen said. "Do you mean, she said it as in...she's not attracted to you?"

"No. She woke up the next day and found Edwin's knife and my weapon case. I had to come back to get something and I found her. She was...very upset. For some reason, she said the knife was hers and I told her that it was all I had from her father, that he had made me the man I am."

Gretchen's jaw worked. "Alright."

"And she said that she could tell."

Silence settled over the room. Then she cocked her head and made a soft sound in her throat.

"What?" I asked.

"Has she ever called you daddy during intercourse?"

I wasn't surprised by her words. Gretchen had always been forthright.

"Once. Last night I went down on her while we were out to dinner and she seemed like she wanted to, so I encouraged it."

"You...did that while you were *out* to dinner?"

"The room was empty."

"I see." She pursed her lips, nodding. "How did that make you feel?"

I took a slow sip and let the whiskey burn my throat. My head fell back on the couch and the ceiling filled my vision.

"Good," I said. "I felt like I was doing something right. Like she was protected and safe."

"Did she like it?"

"I think so."

"I see."

Gretchen scribbled something in her notebook and took a deep breath. Like she always did when she prepared herself for dropping a bomb on me.

"You're a fixer, Merrick," she said. "You always have been. You feel guilty that you had such a positive experience with Edwin while, unbeknownst to you, he was hurting someone you care deeply for. You are trying to fix this for Clara and you have been for a long time."

"I've only ever tried to treat her the way she deserves."

"By giving her everything her father never did."

I winced.

"Clara actually seems like she's dealing with her trauma remarkably well. In her mind, as far as I can tell, Edwin is dead and buried. What's done is done and she's just trying to heal from it."

I cleared my throat. "I think that's an accurate assessment."

"So why can't *you* let him go?"

There was a long silence as I thought it over carefully. Gretchen poured herself more tea and fixed her eyes back on me. Not letting me off the hook.

"Because I was so confident I knew him," I said. "Because...I knew Edwin had a daughter and I never bothered to meet her until he was dead. Because...I could have intervened, talked to him. Instead, I just let her get hurt."

"Hindsight is twenty-twenty," she said. "And you, Merrick, despite being the Welsh King, are only human."

She was right. Of course she was. That was why I paid her an enormous amount of money.

"But...why did she call me daddy?"

Gretchen tilted her head. "Because you are a powerful, older man who takes care of her and makes her feel safe. I have some serious doubts that she mentally associates that word with Edwin."

That was a whole new perspective I hadn't considered.

"That...actually makes a lot of sense."

"I always do." She stood up. "I think Clara has a need for a man who provides her those things, but she's not looking for a father. She just wants an older man who makes her feel safe, who won't hurt her or let her down."

"I can give her that."

"You already do."

The ache in my chest eased. Gretchen released a deep sigh and ran a hand over her hair, tucking it behind her ears.

"Merrick," she said carefully. "I know you've considered Edwin to be the person who saved you when you were at rock bottom and who kept you going. But what if that wasn't true?"

I felt my brow crease. "What?"

"Well, Edwin passed away during the span of time while you were seeing me and I can attest that you didn't fall apart. It might be time to think back and see if maybe Edwin didn't save you."

There was only one other person who could have saved me, but I wasn't allowed to talk about them to Gretchen. Everything would have been so much simpler if I wasn't carrying so many secrets.

"Who saved me then?"

"You did."

The thought had never occurred to me and it was startling. I froze and let it sink in, washing through me. I wasn't sure if I trusted it to be real, but if it was...it felt good. It felt like finally taking back control.

"You have an idealized idea of Edwin in your head because you believe he pulled you out of addiction all those years ago," she said.

"He did," I said forcefully.

"You weren't an addict, you were undiagnosed and self-medicating," she said sharply. "You put in the work, you sat here in my office, you killed your demons."

"So you're saying I spent fifteen years being friends with a man and I never really knew him? You think he gaslit me for a decade and a half?"

"I think that if you talked to other people who knew him, you might get a different story of who he was."

I cleared my throat. "What does that mean?"

She hesitated, like she wasn't sure if she should speak.

"Why did his wife leave him?"

"No one knew why Efa left," I said.

"Divorce isn't common in your organization. Efa risked a lot walking away and never returning and she gave up her only child."

"She was a coward and she abandoned her daughter."

The words sounded harsh coming from me and I regretted them. I could tell Gretchen didn't like them either.

"You told me that your aunts were friends with Efa once," Gretchen said carefully. "Maybe ask them if they know why she left. But I am warning you that you might not like what they have to say."

"You seem confident their split was Edwin's fault," I shot back.

"You're getting defensive," she scolded. "I've worked with a lot of clients over the years and I've learned a thing or two. Edwin respected you, but you were his equal. Clara wasn't and she was neglected."

"Maybe he just wasn't a good father."

"Perhaps. Most women won't talk publicly about the abuses done to them in private because there's an unfortunate sense of shame about it. That goes for wives and daughters."

I stared up at her, my mind whirling. I knew all of these things, but I'd never put the pieces together like that.

And now that Gretchen had, I realized I didn't want to know the truth.

"My head's kind of fucked right now." I cleared my throat. "Can I think about this and we can talk more next week?"

"About talking with your aunts? Of course," she said. "There's no real reason to except for your own healing. Edwin is dead and he can't hurt anyone anymore."

"He may not have hurt anyone."

"He may not have. Efa may have fallen in love with someone else or simply been overwhelmed by having a young child and never got support."

"Edwin never hurt Clara," I said slowly. "He was just a cunt. She told me."

"Neglect is a form of abuse."

279

"I know."

Gretchen released another long sigh. There was a long silence and I rose and set aside my empty glass.

"I need to go home and face the music," I said.

"Are you going to sleep with her tonight?"

"Sex or just sleeping?"

"Either."

"I don't know. We'll see if she'll have me."

She walked me to the door and I let her hug me briefly. She had a comforting, flowery smell that reminded me of Ophelia. As she pulled back, she cupped my cheek.

"I care about you, Merrick," she said. "I want more than anything to see you happy. But it's going to break your heart when Clara marries Osian."

My tongue felt dry. "I know. But I can't give her the future she wants."

I drove home and parked the Audi in the garage beside Clara's car. The front hallway light was on. She was home, probably in her own bed.

Tiredly, I let myself in and went to the kitchen, but stopped in the doorway. Clara was at the table with a coffee and her laptop. She wore one of my t-shirts and knee socks. No panties, I could see a sliver of her pussy between her thighs.

"Clara," I said softly.

She looked up. "Where were you?"

"I had work," I said, deciding to be truthful. "Then I had an appointment with my therapist."

"Oh," she said, surprised. "I was out with Osian."

"Yeah? How did that go?"

"He was in a bad mood, but when he saw the bracelet he seemed fine," she said. "I told him I wanted to wait until our wedding night and he wasn't happy about it, but he agreed."

"Oh," I said. "That's good."

She slipped from the stool and crossed the room and slid her palms up my chest. Her eyes locked on mine, soft and vulnerable.

"I'm sorry for this morning," she said. "My father is a sore spot for me. I reacted badly. You don't have to move any of your things."

"I understand," I said. "I'm sorry too."

"You didn't do anything wrong."

I took her in my arms and kissed her mouth, tasting peppermint coffee and whipped cream. My dick twitched despite my best efforts to control it. She felt it and she pulled back, smirking.

"Where am I sleeping tonight?" she whispered.

"My bed," I said, kissing her forehead. "Where you belong."

We went up to bed and moved through our nighttime rituals. Like we'd been together forever. She snuggled up under the covers and I slid in beside her and pushed her shirt up. Running my hand down and working the tight muscles in her lower back.

She let out a little sigh, curling deeper into the pillows. I buried my nose in her hair and closed my eyes. Blocking out everything but her warmth and the scent of jasmine.

"I know this has to end," she whispered sleepily. "But before it does, I want to know what it would be like to be yours. Just so I can remember later when it's all over."

"You *are* mine," I murmured after a while.

She hadn't heard me. She was already asleep.

CHAPTER THIRTY-SEVEN

CLARA

Christmas and New Year's came and went, but Merrick was always busy during those months so I only saw him once or twice a week. Then it was February and Merrick said something about business slowing down until April. I didn't ask him to explain because it gave me exactly what I craved.

Merrick, all to myself.

Osian decided he was going with his father to do a tour of their family businesses overseas early in the month. He'd be gone for twelve weeks, learning the ropes. I suspected it was less about training to take over the business and more about getting his dick wet all over Europe.

Maybe it would have bothered me if I wasn't spending every free minute in Merrick's bed.

Before Osian left, he had a private meeting with Merrick. They talked for a long time and he left seething. I tried to get Merrick to recount the conversation, but he refused.

It was organization business, he said.

That was code for it's-about-you-but-I-don't-want-to-talk-about-it. I wasn't stupid, it was clearly about my engagement. Merrick was refusing to accept the second piece of jewelry and Osian was trying to use his father's money to threaten him.

But Merrick didn't threaten easily. He told me later that the necklace was singularly unimpressive. Merrick gave it back and told him to return when he had better taste.

Osian left for Europe with his tail tucked between his legs.

"Picking out a set of jewelry isn't rocket science," Merrick said that night, wrathfully typing on his computer in bed. "You'd think I'd asked him to bring you the moon."

"What would you buy me?" I asked. "If it was you."

"Something better."

I spent Valentine's Day alone only to have him come home at the end of the day with a bag, and a round, paper box. He was fully dressed in a suit and tie, looking so good I wanted to rip his clothes off.

I was already in his bed, makeup off and hair tied up. Retainer in.

"I'm taking you out," he said, spilling the boxes onto my lap. "We leave in an hour."

"Where—where are we going?"

"Never you mind," he said. "Just pack an overnight bag with clothes for warm weather."

"It's forty degrees outside," I said.

"Trust me, *cariad*."

He was in a good mood, I heard it in the spring in his step as he disappeared into the bathroom. I packed my overnight bag, but I loitered, shy about opening the gifts until he returned.

He appeared in the doorway, crossing his arms.

"Go on then," he said.

A thrill went through me as I popped the top of the box. Inside was the most beautiful bouquet of pink and black roses. It was his staple and it never failed to make my heart do a little flip.

"They're beautiful," I said, smiling.

"I'll have the housekeeper cut them," he said. "Now open the other one because we need to get going."

I untied the bag and pulled out a tissue wrapped bundle. It unrolled in my hands and the softest, red lace panties and bra tumbled onto the bed.

Lava pooled down my spine, bubbling in my core, spreading down my legs. He had bought me lingerie. No one had ever bought me lingerie before and I hadn't realized how much of a turn-on it would be.

My heart was going so fast. I lifted the garments, my face heating.

"They're beautiful," I whispered.

He moved closer, taking my chin and tilting it up. His eyes skimmed my face and a slow grin broke over his face. He was so fucking pleased with himself.

"Oh, that's good to know."

"What?"

Instead of speaking, he slipped his hand under my sweatshirt and into my panties. His ring and pointer fingers parted my folds gently and his middle finger dipped into my drenched pussy. My lower back arched.

He kissed my forehead. "If getting romanced makes you this wet every time, it's nothing less than princess treatment from here on out."

My cheeks burned.

"You've always treated me like a princess," I admitted. "But not like this...this is different."

"Nothing less for you, *cariad*."

He pushed his middle finger into me all the way and stroked that sweet spot on my front wall. Slow and deep, keeping a gentle pressure where I needed it most.

"If you don't stop, we'll never leave," I gasped.

He laughed softly and pulled his hand free, licking his fingers clean. Our eyes met and heat sparked, filling the air with electricity.

This man would be the death of me.

"Open the rest," he said.

I obeyed, letting a silky, red dress and a pair of red bottomed shoes spill out. The lining of the dress was short and tight and it had a draping, transparent skirt that reached the ground.

"It's beautiful," I breathed.

"Not as beautiful as you, Clara."

I looked up at him and there was a long silence. In it, I felt all the things we were both too afraid to say. The weight of knowing this had to end.

"Put it on," he ordered. "I want to watch you dress."

He wasn't in the mood to be disobeyed and I wasn't in the mood to disobey. Something about him walking in here knowing exactly what he wanted me to wear and where he intended to take me had sparked an unfamiliar desire to be submissive.

Usually, I liked challenging him.

But not tonight.

Tonight he was in control and we both knew it.

He sank into the chair in the corner, one leg crossed over the other. Eyes glued to me, dark lashes heavy.

"Strip for me," he said. "Put what I bought for you on."

My hands tingled as I took my clothes off and slid on the delicate lace. It settled perfectly on my hips and breasts. Exactly the right size. The dress settled over it like it was made for me.

He rose and joined me before the mirror. Gathering my hair and kissing the back of my neck, sending shivers down my spine. He zipped the dress closed and his eyes met mine in the mirror.

"You are beautiful, Clara," he said softly.

I wanted to thank him, but I was too breathless to speak.

His mouth burned the side of my neck in a slow kiss and my head fell back against his chest. My lids closed.

"You wanted to know how it feels to be my woman," he murmured. "Let me show you tonight."

I snapped my eyes open. Hanging from his lean fingers, just before my eyes, was a delicate gold chain with a single, glittering diamond.

He brushed the hairs falling over my neck aside and clasped it. It slid down and rested above my cleavage.

"I want you spoiled, *cariad*," he breathed. "I want my diamonds on your pussy."

It didn't hit me what that meant until we were in the car, driving into the dark.

Piercings.

No, that couldn't be right. Merrick knew that part of me was reserved for Osian's jewelry.

I glanced sideways at him. He looked like sin in that black suit, fitted to his body. My throat tightened. I was so fucking obsessed with this man it felt like a physical ache sometimes.

We pulled up to his private plane. My skirt whipped around my legs as he helped me across the tarmac and up the ramp. Then we rose above the city and I watched until the light became blips in the darkness.

He poured himself a whiskey and me a glass of golden champagne. He sat back, crossing one leg. I curled up under his arm and he stroked down my back. Gathering up my transparent skirt and sliding his hand beneath it. Against my bare thigh.

"Maybe I'll just tell the pilot to keep flying," he murmured. "Take you to Paris and never come back."

My heart thumped, off beat.

"We can't," I whispered.

"I know."

I glanced up at him. He really had the most beautiful eyelashes I'd ever seen on a man. Long, thick, dark, making the beautiful cobalt blue of his irises so striking it still distracted me after all this time.

I was giddy on everything—the night, his gifts, the diamonds, him in that suit, the champagne just hitting my brain.

"You're so pretty," I murmured.

He laughed. "Thank you."

"Do people ever compliment your eyes? Like, when you're just out having lunch or shopping?"

"It happens. They catch people off guard."

"They look good on you," I said seriously. "It's like you're wearing guyliner."

"Come again?"

"You know...eyeliner for men."

"Ah, thank you, I guess."

I snuggled against him, taking a sip of champagne. "You're so perfect."

There was a long silence and he cleared his throat. "I'm a work in progress, *cariad*, as we all are."

There was a note of sadness in his voice I didn't like. I'd brought him down and I regretted it. My hand slid up his thigh and I traced over his groin with my fingernail.

He went hard instantly, shifting his hips.

"You're horny," I said.

"We haven't fucked in three days," he said. "I've been busy."

I knew instantly what I wanted to do for him. We'd been sleeping together for weeks now, but he had never asked me to perform oral on him. It wasn't for lack of wanting, I knew that. He had enjoyed it when I'd put him in my mouth the first time he made me come.

I suspected he didn't want me to feel pressured.

My heart picked up as I leaned forward to set my champagne aside. I caught a glimpse of my hands, decorated in diamonds and gold.

They looked mature and elegant. Like a woman who knew what she wanted. A woman who made a powerful man want to open his wallet.

God, that made me want to suck him off even more. We were alone, but I still felt vulnerable as I slid to my knees between his shoes. He tensed, his eyes widening. His fingers tensed on his glass, knuckles going white.

"What are you doing?" he breathed.

"It's Valentine's Day," I said. "There's something I've wanted to do for a while and I'd like to do it for you tonight."

He looked like he had a million things to say, but he just nodded. His eyes dazed like he'd never seen anything so beautiful as me on my knees. It was a powerful feeling.

My fingers ghosted down his zipper and up to his belt. Working it open so I could open his pants. His chest heaved and he set aside his glass. His hands moved to help me and I swatted them away.

"No," I whispered. "This is all mine tonight."

287

A smile ghosted over his face as he eased back, spreading his knees. I pulled his underwear down and his cock sprang free. Hard, glittering at the tip, and tattooed with those mysterious lines. His gaze darkened with arousal.

I wrapped my fingers around him, relishing his warmth. Our eyes met and my nipples ached as I began jerking him slowly. His jaw went tense and he mouthed a silent profanity under his breath.

"Hold my hair back," I said.

He gathered it in one hand, wrapping it around his fist. I took a slow breath. I could do this, I knew how to do this. I just had to trust myself.

Bending, I let the tip of his cock slip into my mouth. Salt and Merrick filled my senses. Eagerly, I pushed down and immediately realized how dry my mouth was from anticipation.

I pulled back and licked my lips and pushed him back in, letting my mouth slip down over his length.

Much better.

I paused for a breath. He felt big in my mouth, much larger than I remembered from the first time. In fact, there wasn't a lot of room left for me to move my tongue. I pulled out again and licked him from base to head.

All around, up every side.

Stalling for time so I could figure this out.

"Doing alright, baby?" he asked. He sounded amused.

I frowned. "I'm fine, thank you."

His next words were cut off with a groan as I took him in my mouth again, letting him push all the way back. His cock was wet and it slid in and out easily so I did that and he groaned so it must have been right.

"Close your lips," he murmured. "Suck it gently."

I pulled him out. "I can take it, I can do it."

"I know you can take it for me, *cariad*, but I'm communicating what I like to you."

"Oh," I said. "Okay, that makes sense."

His cock filled my mouth and I closed my lips around it, sucking gently as I moved my head up and down. His thighs went tight and his fist spasmed, pulling my hair a little painfully.

The muscles in his forearm clenched, pushing me down an inch or two.

"Good girl," he praised softly. "You're doing so well."

His words were simple, but they hit me just right. Warmth glowed in my chest and heat bubbled deep in my core. He felt so good on my tongue, so soft and hard and slightly salty.

My lips tingled and my jaw ached, but I didn't care. I just wanted to feel him lose control. To reward me with his cum down my throat.

I needed to know how many licks it took to get to the center of the most powerful man on the Eastern Seaboard.

Quickening my pace, I grasped him by the base and worked him with my mouth and my hand at the same time. He swore audibly and his other hand slid around the back of my head. Guiding me up and down in quick strokes.

"I'm going to come," he breathed. "Stop me if you don't want it in your mouth."

I sped up and his hips jerked as he groaned aloud. He twitched, gently pressing my face into his groin, and his taste spread over my tongue in slow pumps.

Salty, almost soapy, with a hint of sweetness.

Fucking addicting.

His hands eased and I slid his softening cock from my mouth. Our eyes locked and I swallowed his cum. Apparently it didn't take that many licks to break the Welsh King into pieces.

"Fuck," he said.

He was in awe. A sense of power swept through me and I flushed with pride.

"This is without a doubt the best Valentine's Day I've ever had," he said.

"Why did you never ask me for that?"

He pulled me to my feet and fastened his pants, taking me in his lap and settling me to face him. His thumb came up, wiping the corner of my mouth.

"I wanted you to offer it," he said.

"I was scared," I admitted. "You're big."

"You did really well."

"I'm sure I have room to get better," I said. "I'll have to practice more."

He kissed my mouth, slow and deep. Then he let me off his lap so I could fix my hair and makeup in the bathroom. I was flushed, my pussy slippery under my dress as I applied lipstick.

The plane alighted about an hour later and I was confused to find that we were on a landing strip in the middle of nowhere. I let Merrick help me down and lead me across the pavement to a second plane.

"Are we going somewhere very far away?" I asked.

"Yes," he said. "And no."

I climbed up the steps, his hand on my lower back the whole way to keep me steady. We both stopped short in the doorway. His mouth brushed the back of my neck.

"Happy Valentine's Day, *cariad*," he murmured. "Let's have dinner together."

The interior of the plane was lit with a soft glow. There was a table set with glasses and on the far end of the room, there was a queen bed made with silk sheets.

"It's beautiful," I said, turning to kiss his mouth. "Why did I get dressed up if we weren't going out though?"

His eyes lingered on my face and fell, moving down my body slowly. Like he had all the time in the world to look.

"That was all for me," he said.

I couldn't keep from giggling like an idiot as he pulled me across the room and helped me sit. The doors closed and we held tight as the plane rose and leveled in the sky. Then there was nothing but the soft rush of the engine and his eyes burning before mine.

He had me right where he wanted me and I wasn't fighting it. I was still giddy from the champagne and flushed with arousal from giving him head.

We ate oysters, chilled with lemon. I'd never had them before and I wasn't sure how to do it, so he pulled his chair close. His hand hovered on the back of my neck as he tilted my head back and brought the shell to my mouth.

"Swallow," he said, breath hot on my neck.

I let it slide down my throat, enjoying the taste of ocean and lemon on my tongue.

"It's good," I whispered.

He eased the strap of my dress down, baring my shoulder.

A hot tingle moved down my spine and burned in my core as his mouth kissed up to the base of my neck. I gripped the front of his suit, trying to steady myself.

His lips parted, his tongue flicking out, burning beneath my ear.

"Are you trying to seduce me, Mr. Llwyd?" I gasped.

"Me?" he murmured. "Never."

He shifted me to face away and his mouth grazed the nape of my neck. I shivered as he kissed every bump of my spine so softly it made me want to squirm. All the way to the top of my zipper.

"Can I try something new tonight, baby?" he asked.

"What is it?"

His mouth grazed the side of my throat. "Just trust me. All you have to do is tell me to stop and I will."

I nodded and he lifted me to my feet and led me to the bed. On the floor was a velvet bag and from it he pulled three dark red silks. My heart skipped.

"What are those for?" I whispered.

"Later," he said. "Stand here, don't move."

I obeyed, fingers clenched. He noticed and he gently worked them open, his thumbs massaging my palms until I relaxed. Then he turned me to face him and slid down to his knees.

My heart did a backflip. His head was bowed, completely absorbed in what he was doing. Almost like it was a meditation.

His middle finger contacted my calf and he dragged it up. So soft and gentle.

My core tingled.

"Lift your skirt, *cariad*," he murmured.

Fingers trembling, I obeyed, holding it to my waist. Baring my lace panties to him.

He bent and pressed the softest kiss right below my navel. The heat of his lips shot to my core and I pulsed. Then he dropped my skirt and turned me back around.

He unzipped my dress and kissed every inch of the skin between the zipper. So softly, like little flutters down my spine. It felt like forever before he finally eased the rest of the dress down and helped me step out of it.

Our eyes met as he stood.

"Lay back," he said, his voice hushed.

Why did this get my heart hammering faster than any of the rougher sex we'd had? I nodded wordlessly and sat, shifting up the bed until my head was on the pillow.

He knelt over me, a red satin tie in his hand. His eyes trailed over me in the matching lingerie and I felt the hunger in his gaze. Like a tangible ache.

"I'm going to tie these around your wrists," he said. "They'll be loose enough to get out of if you need to, but all you have to do is tell me to stop. Tell me you understand?"

I nodded, mouth dry.

He lifted a finger and tapped his mouth. "No, say it out loud."

Heat radiated up my throat. "I understand."

"Perfect," he said. "The third tie goes over your eyes. Are you comfortable with that?"

"Yes," I said quickly.

"Good girl," he said. "The only thing I need from you tonight is that you use your words to tell me your boundaries. I get to control your pleasure, I control the speed, I control the outcome."

I nodded.

He circled the bed and began securing the ties. "I need to hear it verbally. Try again."

"Yes, I understand," I said clearly.

He sent me an approving look that made me shiver, offering him a small smile. He tied both silks around my wrists and brought them tight enough my arms were pulled out and up, resting on the pillows. They felt firm on my wrists, but not restrictive.

He knelt, still fully dressed in his suit. One knee on either side of my waist.

The rise beneath his zipper was impressive.

But not frightening the way it had been when Osian had touched me. Perhaps because I knew Merrick only ever used his body to make me feel good, to praise me, to reward me.

The red silk slipped through his fingers. Catching on the calluses on his palms.

Then he slid it over my eyes and secured it. Pressing me back against the pillows with darkness all around.

His weight lifted from the bed.

There was a moment of nothingness...then his fingertip ran over the top of my foot. Circling around my ankle and under the bridge.

Oh God, I felt that where it mattered.

My toes clenched.

He clicked his tongue. "No, don't curl your toes. Stay relaxed for me."

"I'm ticklish," I protested.

"No, you're not," he said, stroking the tips of my toes. "You're trying to stay in control. Keep your foot relaxed when I touch it."

I took a deep breath and forced my body to relax from top to bottom. This time when he ran his fingertip up the bridge of my foot, I managed not to curl my toes and squirm.

"Good girl," he said. "It feels good, doesn't it?"

"Yes," I gasped.

His finger left my foot and his mouth replaced it. Kissing up over the top and working his way over my ankle and up. My heart was pounding in my ears by the time he kissed the underside of my knee.

His tongue slipped out, leaving a little wet spot.

My leg jerked. I'd done so well up until that point, keeping my body relaxed and still. But his tongue had sent me over the edge.

He hushed me softly and kissed just above my knee.

The way he was touching me was driving me to distraction. I'd never been so aware of every nerve and where it connected, every inch of skin, than I was right now.

My breasts felt hot and tight beneath the cups of my bra and my nipples tingled against the lace. Between my thighs, I felt wetness seeping into my panties. Stinging my skin.

As if on cue, his fingers skimmed between my breasts. There was a faint click as he unhooked it and slid the cups back.

I felt his gaze, even though I couldn't see it. And it felt like sweet fire moving in a slow flush over my skin.

Leaving me so sensitive before he ever touched me.

Hot breath ghosted over my left nipple and the tip of his tongue circled it. So gently it was scarcely a real touch. He repeated the motion again and again, around and around. Until my ears roared and I trembled trying to keep my body still.

He lowered his mouth fully over it and sucked.

My spine arced and a whimper forced itself from my throat. He sucked a little harder and released it, licking once and then withdrawing.

"Does that feel good?" he asked softly.

"Yes," I gasped.

His hand cradled my face, his rough thumb dragging over my mouth. "Should we check and see if you're wet yet, *cariad*?"

"I'm soaked," I breathed.

His hand skimmed down to my thigh and parted my legs. It slid up and hooked my panties aside. There was a short silence and I started getting worried.

"What's wrong?" I whispered.

"Nothing," he said. I detected vulnerability in his voice, like a catch. "It's just...beautiful."

"Oh," I whispered. "Thank you."

He cleared his throat. "But not wet enough. I'm going to take your panties off and have you spread your thighs. Then I'm going to start all over again and when I can see you drip for me, I'll let you come."

I gasped. "Merrick, please."

His weight lifted from the bed and his fingertip touched the bottom of my foot.

Fuck.

He was true to his word. I was shaking by the time he got to my knee again and my lower lip was hot from being bitten. He got to my breasts for the second time and took his time there. Teasing my nipples until I was audibly whimpering. My fists clenched around the silk ties.

"Should we check again, baby?" he breathed.

I had no words, just a desperate moan. His weight left the bed and he was silent for a moment.

"Fuck," he whispered. "Good girl."

My lips trembled. "Is it what you wanted?"

"It's everything I've ever wanted," he murmured. "Now I'm going to make you come and if you need me to stop, just tell me to stop."

"How many times?" I whispered.

"Until I'm satisfied," he said. "Then I'm going to fuck you and it'll be a little rough, so make sure to use your words if you need them. Tell me you understand."

"I understand," I gasped.

That first slow lick over my pussy was a quick descent into paradise. Better than any first bite of ice cream or first taste of candy I'd ever had. As deliciously decadent as the Welsh King himself.

I came.

Never in a million years did I think I would ever be able to come from one touch, but it was happening right now. Pleasure burst through my core and I cried out, my spine arcing as it washed down my hips and thighs.

"Fuck me," he swore, burying his face between my legs.

He made me come again and again until I wasn't sure where the pleasure started and where it ended. It just kept coming, ebbing up and down. Sometimes so intense it made me beg and sometimes just a little swell and then a burst.

It broke me. Leaving me sweating, my fingers aching from yanking on the silk ties.

When he finally took the blindfold away, my eyes were popping with stars. I blinked hard, focusing on his face.

It was intense. Maybe a little frightening.

He still had his button up on, but it was open at the collar. Rumpled like his dark hair, hanging over his forehead. His five o'clock shadow had come in strong, frosted with a little gray, and he had that dangerous glitter in his eyes.

It made me feel small that I was naked and he was fully dressed. But in the most delicious way.

I swallowed, my lips parting.

He rose and moved to the wall to my right. There was a panel with a knob, which he turned, flipping it to reveal a full-length mirror.

"What is that for?" I asked hoarsely.

He began untying me. "It's for the Welsh Princess to watch herself get fucked like a whore."

Oh.

My stomach clenched as he pulled me upright, my thighs shaking. He turned me around and pressed me to my hands and knees. My necklace unstuck from my damp chest and hung between my breasts. My mascara had melted beneath my eyes.

It was intimidating to see him, kneeling behind me fully dressed.

"Do princesses get fucked like whores?" I whispered.

His eyes contacted mine. Dark and dangerous. He reached between us and I heard the hiss of his zipper.

"Yes," he said firmly. "Princesses get spoiled until they're soaking wet and then they get fucked to sleep. How does that sound, *cariad*?"

He pushed down the front of his pants, unleashing his cock. It hit against my wet entrance and a jolt of arousal tore through me.

"Good," I gasped.

I was soaked, but I was also so tight with arousal that when he sank into me I cried out. Not from pain, just from the intensity of it.

He didn't stop, he just pushed in until he was seated with his groin pressed against my ass.

Sweat slid down his throat. Soaking his open collar.

His eyes never left mine.

"Can you take it?" he asked.

I nodded hard. The last thing I wanted was for him to stop. My inner muscles were dying for him to move, begging to feel the power of his hips drive his cock into my body.

His palm slid around to my lower belly and up between my breasts. Bending me up, lifting me onto my knees. Keeping us locked together as he pulled me against his chest. His hips drew back and slammed in, sending shockwaves through my core. I whimpered, screwing my eyes shut.

His mouth was inches from my ear.

"Watch," he ordered softly.

I obeyed, gaze falling on our bodies in the mirror. My stomach and breasts were slick with sweat and I was pressed to the front of his shirt and pants. Part of me wished he was naked and the other part loved that he was still fully dressed.

His hips pumped and his other hand came up and slid into my hair, making a fist and keeping my head in place.

"Look," he murmured, his voice husky. "Look at that fucking beautiful woman on my cock."

I whimpered.

The corner of his mouth turned up. "Tell me whose pussy this is."

"Yours, daddy," I whispered daringly.

His jaw tensed and he groaned deep in his throat. "Are you going to let daddy fuck you the way he wants, princess?"

I nodded frantically, eyes wide, my lower lip pinned so hard under my teeth it ached. I didn't have time to speak because he was fucking me hard and fast. I'd heard the term 'getting railed' before, but I hadn't experienced it firsthand until right now.

And I loved it.

His jaw clenched, his eyes burned. He kept me back against his chest, my spine arced. His hand moved from my breasts to my jaw.

Holding me by the face and the hair so I couldn't move. Shock after shock of pleasure burst in my hips as he fucked with short, hard strokes.

"You're taking it so well, baby girl," he praised, releasing me and pushing me back down to my hands and knees. He braced his palm on my shoulder and gripped my hip with his other hand to hold me steady.

Stars burst behind my eyelids. The Welsh King knew how to fuck hard.

It was good that he'd made me come and gotten me wet before he fucked me like this, because he was relentless. Pounding into me until I was incoherent and then pushing me onto the pillows to take me again.

His palm slid up my throat and cradled my chin and his two middle fingers pushed past my lips. Filling my mouth until my throat tightened, threatening to make me gag.

He withdrew abruptly and flipped me onto my back.

"It's not enough," he whispered. "Just fucking. I need you so badly, darling, I need to be in every part of you."

I knew what he meant, but I wasn't ready for that. Throat dry, I shook my head.

"Not your cock," I whispered.

His mouth brushed hot over my forehead as he slid his length into my soaked pussy easily, pressing his groin up against mine. He sat back on his heels, taking me with him, and wrapped my arms around his neck.

"My fingers?" He was barely audible.

I nodded, face brushed into his neck.

His hand slid down, his big hand with square fingertips and lean fingers, and grazed the place where we connected. Stroking where my pussy enveloped his cock. I shivered involuntarily as it moved back, taking my wetness with him.

His hips worked, fucking up into me. The bed creaked, the room filled with our heavy breaths. I squeezed my eyes shut and clung to him as his middle finger applied light pressure against my asshole. Circling gently as he kept fucking me.

It slipped inside and I couldn't bite back a gasp.

"Oh, good girl," he panted. He pushed to his middle knuckle.

My nails dug up his back and left red streaks over the freckles on his shoulders.

He tipped our bodies, his finger and his cock still inside, and we fell back onto the pillows. Our eyes locked and there was a frantic whimpering sound. It took me a moment to realize it was coming from me.

"Take my tongue," he breathed, mouth grazing over mine. "Take all of me, in every part of you."

My lips parted and I closed my eyes, giving into him. Letting his finger slide into that part of me until I was filled, letting his cock pump in and out of my drenched pussy, letting his tongue consume my mouth.

He just kept going. And going. Riding my hips, tongue-fucking my mouth, finger pumping into my ass. Until there was nothing but my cries and his harsh groans, until he saw me wince.

Immediately, he pulled his finger out and shifted his face to my neck.

"No, don't stop," I whispered.

"Can you finish taking me in your pussy?" His voice was muffled as he kissed my breasts.

"Yes, daddy," I gasped.

"Hard, baby?"

"Hard."

My spent body was completely relaxed as his hips began pounding slow and deep against mine. So spent that when he finally finished with a sound of deep, feral satisfaction, almost an hour later, I was asleep in seconds. I barely felt him undress and slide into bed before everything spiraled into darkness.

CHAPTER THIRTY-EIGHT

CLARA

I woke slowly, my body deliciously sore. My eyes felt sticky and my throat was raspy. My arms ached as I pushed myself upright.

The floor was littered with our clothes. His dark suit and my flimsy lace undergarments.

I turned, taking in his sleeping form. He was on his back, my red nail marks stark on his chest. His eyes were closed and he looked almost...innocent.

Fuck that, after last night I was convinced this man didn't have an innocent bone in his body.

He'd done the dirtiest things to me last night. He'd called me things that should have made me cry, but made me come instead. He'd seduced and conquered me like he did everything else.

I sank back into the bed and he stirred, rolling to face me. His lashes fluttered open and his eyes skimmed over my body. I looked away, heat creeping up my cheeks.

"*Cariad*," he said huskily.

He propped himself up and wrapped an arm around my waist, pulling me to his chest. His eyes were concerned.

"Did I hurt you?"

"No, no," I breathed. "It was just a lot."

The old Merrick was back. Gentle and worried about me. He tugged the sheet down and his hands skimmed over my body. Coming to rest on the tiny bruises scattered on my thighs.

"Fuck," he swore.

He looked genuinely upset. I gripped his stubbled jaw and gently kissed his mouth.

"If I had wanted you to stop, I would have told you to," I said.

He nodded and I reached up, stroking my fingers through his hair. His shoulders relaxed and I bent and kissed his mouth. The raw feeling between us faded and he pulled me into his arms. Our bodies melded, warm and languid.

I didn't want to move. I just wanted to stay here and feel him breathe.

"Alright," he said finally. "We're here, so let's get dressed."

He set me on my feet and began putting on his pants and shirt. I slipped my lingerie back on, but it seemed a bit embarrassing to walk out in my dress from last night.

"Is there a robe or do I need to do the walk of shame?" I asked.

He pulled a drawer at the end of the bed out and tossed me a wad of white cloth. I unwrapped it to reveal a...swimsuit cover up?

"It's a bit cold for this, no?"

His mouth turned up and he crossed the room, hitting the button. The door hissed open and I blinked in the bright light. I padded to his side and gasped, elation sweeping through my chest.

Miles and miles of blue. Churning, roiling, smelling of salt and freedom. Pale yellow sand stretched out as far as I could see. And an enormous, Grecian style compound in the distance.

I whipped around. "Where are we?"

He kissed my temple. "Paradise."

"No...really. Where are we?"

His jaw worked. "It's an island. That I own. But I use it for business so I'm not going to tell you what it's called or where we are."

He could be so stubborn. I gave it up and pulled the cover up over my lingerie and practically ran down the ramp.

The sun burned overhead and the sand was hot under my feet as I tore across the beach to the water. He followed me, at an easy pace. A confident pace I knew so well.

Euphoria filled my chest. Built up from the last several weeks and the chaos of last night. There was no one around but two men from the crew and a bodyguard by the plane. I pulled my cover up off and ran into the ocean.

"Clara Prothero," he called. "Cover yourself."

I didn't want to. I was almost naked and free, the sun and wind kissing my skin. It had been a long winter with the threat of Osian hanging over my head.

Here, in paradise, Osian seemed like nothing more than a bad dream.

But Merrick...he was real. And he was coming right towards me. Walking into the shallow water in his shoes and snatching me around the waist. Pulling my wet body against his chest, his eyes lit up.

"Get your perfect ass inside," he ordered.

"Merrick, I want to swim," I begged. "Please."

"You may. In your swimsuit."

"Merrick—"

He turned me around and picked me up, slinging me over his shoulder. The world flipped upside down and I hung there, in shock, as he walked me up the beach, through the garden, and into the compound.

Inside, it was beautiful and austere. The air conditioning was running full blast and my wet skin prickled as he marched me down the long hallway and up the stairs. We turned a corner and he pushed open a set of double doors to reveal a bedroom that looked out over the water.

The bed was low and wide, surrounded by mosquito netting. There were plants on the balcony that opened out to an infinity pool.

I gaped at the view, forgetting that he was behind me, his grip still hard on my wrist.

"Let's get cleaned up," he murmured against my neck.

Before I could speak, he ushered me into the bathroom and turned on the spacious shower. The water poured down from the ceiling, already steaming.

I bent and started working my wet panties off. Out of the corner of my eye I saw his hand come up and then it cracked across my ass. Hard enough I shot upright, whirling.

"Merrick!"

"It looked like it needed spanked," he said, flashing a grin.

My pussy pulsed, roused by the sting. I huffed and pretended to be offended as I unhooked my bra and stepped into the water. Turning my back to give him a prime view of the handprint.

He dropped his clothes onto the floor and joined me. Shaking his wet hair back and running a hand over his head.

"I have to confess something," he said. "I'm here for business too."

"I kind of thought you might be," I said. "Once I realized this was clearly a private island on international waters."

His mouth twitched. "What is it you think I do?"

I shrugged. "Mafia stuff. Probably threatening people and taking their lunch money. I don't know."

He laughed, a deep, rich sound. "No, not really."

"So...what do you do?"

"I make lots of money so I can spoil you."

I rolled my eyes and turned around, handing him a bottle of shampoo. He began massaging it through my hair gently, taking his time. His fingers felt heavenly.

"We'll be alone until tomorrow night," he said. "There will be a lot of guests. I was thinking of sending you home before then."

"Why?"

"There will be a lot of men here. Some of them aren't the good kind."

"They won't touch me if they know I'm yours."

He went still for a moment. Then his fingers slid down my neck and began massaging my lower back.

"Is that what you want, *cariad*?" he asked, his voice low. "For everyone to know who fucks you?"

A shudder moved down my spine and through my hips as I remembered how hard he'd taken me last night. The things he'd said in the dark still rang in my ears.

"Maybe," I whispered.

His fingers stilled in my hair. I turned, letting the water pour down. Bubbles streamed down my back as I looked up at him. So handsome, droplets of water dusting his chest and stomach.

"Are you mine?" I breathed.

His throat bobbed. "For as long as possible. If you still want me after last night. I warned you that I have some rough edges."

I settled my body against his, every curve and line fitting into the dips in his chest and stomach. We felt so perfect together. Infinite, unshakable.

"Those are the parts I want the most."

He slid his palm up my back and tangled it in my wet hair. I shifted so I could look up and his eyes sobered and he released a small sigh.

"You may stay."

CHAPTER THIRTY-NINE

MERRICK

If I hadn't been so spent from last night and this morning, I'd have taken her to bed again.

If I could have, I'd have canceled the auction tonight, ordered everyone away. I'd have spent the morning, the afternoon, and the night in bed. I'd kiss every inch of her body and apologize for how rough I'd been last night.

"Are you?" she'd asked weeks ago. *"Are you rough with the women you sleep with?"*

I winced as I strode down the hall. I was almost at the end, preparing to turn the corner, when Caden appeared like a jack-in-the-box. Springing up out of nowhere with that smug smirk on his face.

"Did you fucking bring Clara here?" he said, his mouth jerking up in the corner.

I turned the corner and kept walking. He fell into step beside me.

"Don't start," I said.

"Has it occurred to you that you could just have her," he said. "I've seen how she is around you. She's practically putting herself on a silver platter."

I glanced sharply at him.

"Fuck Osian Cardiff," said Caden.

I stopped in the middle of the hall and I turned to face him.

"The Cardiffs are offering equal to my net worth," I said, my voice low. "What kind of *Brenin* would I be if I turned that down? And what kind of guardian would I be if I robbed her of the future she's been planning for six years. She told me what she wanted and I promised her I would get it for her."

"Maybe she'll change her mind."

I cleared my throat. "I don't know if I can trust that she knows what she wants."

Caden's brow arced. "Why?"

"Because...of course she's bonded with me," I said, voicing one of my deepest fears for the first time. "I'm the only man who hasn't treated her like shit."

There was a short silence.

"Okay, I get that," said Caden slowly.

"Anyway," I said briskly. "There's nothing going on between Clara and I. Understood?"

"Yep, yeah, nothing going on," Caden said, rolling his eyes.

We didn't speak of it again. There was a lot of prep that needed to happen before guests started arriving and the auction began. I kept myself busy for the rest of the day and tried not to think of her.

That night, I found her in the bedroom in a shimmery, silver dress that showed the outline of her body through the thin fabric. Underneath, I could barely make out her black lace bra and panties and the gleam of her pierced navel.

My dick twitched.

She'd let her hair fall naturally in waves around her shoulders. I ran my fingers through it and closed my fist. Forcing her to look up into my eyes.

"You be a good girl tonight," I said.

She rolled her eyes.

"No, I mean it, Clara," I said. "This isn't like back at home. There are powerful men who have no qualms hurting people. Including women. You stay in my sight all night, don't drink too much, and don't flirt with anyone."

She swallowed, her lids flickering.

"Maybe it would be better if they knew I was yours," she whispered.

I shook my head.

"I'm not fucking up your future."

There was something heavy in the air. I felt it like a brewing storm as I led her down the hall to the first floor crowded with people. The disco style lights were lowered, glitter moving slowly over the floor as they rotated. The fountain in the center of the room bubbled and music thrummed in the background.

She stopped short. Her eyes widening.

"Are those...dancers?"

I let my eyes run over the women. They were perched on a dozen pedestals, lights burning behind them to create silhouettes. Their bodies moved slowly, sinuously.

It was too dark to tell, but I knew they were naked.

"Merrick," she breathed.

"It's alright," I said. "They're professionals and no one is allowed to touch them."

"What...what are they here for then?"

I guided her into the crowd and headed for the bar. "Most of these men are here to make sales with me. I keep them on the edge, get them hot and bothered, and have them make decisions while they're distracted and horny."

She gaped at me. "Merrick Llwyd, always playing chess while everyone else plays checkers."

I let my head fall back as I laughed. "My therapist says that to me too."

She ordered a Cosmo and I had a shot of tequila. Before anyone could look our way, she took me by the tie and yanked me down. Her mouth tasted like lime and lipstick.

And a bit like tonight was going to be giant fuck up.

CHAPTER FORTY

CLARA

He assigned Caden to watch me. It was annoying that I had to have a babysitter and I didn't know Caden well so he wasn't any fun. I sat at the bar and scowled at him over my drink. He caught my eye and gave me a long stare.

He was a strange man, usually quiet, but occasionally as sarcastic and cutting as a steel blade. I'd heard a rumour he was a magician before he met Merrick and he'd stolen ten million dollars from the biggest bank in England. That was stupid and obviously false, but it was exciting to think about.

Feeling reckless, I slid up beside him. He glanced at me, his eyes cutting.

"Hey," I said. "I know Merrick has you clocking me."

"That right?" he drawled.

In my already tipsy state, I found his English accent fascinating. It wasn't one I'd ever heard before meeting him.

"Where are you from?" I asked. "I never asked you."

He cocked a caustic brow. "Providence. Rhode Island."

"So...can I ask about your accent?"

"I grew up in Sheffield."

I considered him, my vision wavering. Maybe I'd had too much to drink up front. I should probably get something to eat to balance it out.

"Do you have a girlfriend? A boyfriend?" I asked.

He shook his head. I studied him. He was attractive, but I wasn't attracted to him, which was weird because he kind of looked like Merrick. But it still seemed crazy to me that he wasn't with anyone.

"I can find you one," I said confidently.

"No, thanks," he said. He pushed off the bar and took me by the elbow, hauling me through the crowd to the side door.

He pushed it ajar and ushered me out onto the balcony. I stood there, confused, as he lit a cigarette. He breathed it out and ran a hand over his head, smoothing back his hair.

"Why are we out here?"

"Because I want a smoke and I have to watch you."

"Oh, okay."

I drained the rest of my drink and took his, wrinkling my nose at the smell of vodka. At least, I was too drunk now to care what it tasted like. I shot it and his brow curved. A faintly sour expression seeped over his face.

"Are you sleeping with Merrick?" he asked.

Every nerve in me froze. "What?"

"It's a simple question." He leaned in. "Are you sleeping with Merrick?"

"No. What?"

He rolled his eyes, expelling a stream of smoke from both nostrils. I squinted, watching him, but he seemed disinterested in continuing the conversation.

"Are you a magician?" I asked.

His eyes locked on mine.

"You're a dumb bitch when you're drunk," he said.

I gasped. "You asshole."

"I kill people for Merrick for a living," he said. "Did you think I was going to be a gentleman?"

"Jesus," I breathed. "I guess we've never really spoken much so I didn't realize how much of a dick you can be."

He laughed, a short, caustic bark. When he spoke, his voice was a derisive drawl.

"Sweetheart. We're all dicks here. Don't let Merrick pull the wool over your eyes."

"Wow...you really are a massive asshole."

He shrugged, expelling more smoke. "Did he tell you what the tattoos on his dick mean?"

"No," I said, before I could catch myself.

"Ha," Caden said. "Knew you were fucking him."

I went bright red and whirled, swaying slightly, and reached out to grab the doorknob. His hand closed on my wrist and he turned me around. There was a warning light in his eyes.

"Be a good girl," he said. "Stay put and listen to Merrick."

I wanted to punch him. Or push him off the balcony.

"How many lines does he have?" Caden asked, letting me go and pulling out his pack of cigarettes. This time he gave me one too and I breathed it in just enough to taste it on the back of my tongue.

"How do you know about them?"

"I have them too, we all do," he said. "Just different ones. Now, how many?"

"I didn't count them," I whispered.

"Twelve. I have the same status rings. But not the lines."

"Okay. So?"

"How many men did he kill in that arena again?"

The world slowed and a sick feeling rose in my chest. My palms felt slippery and my legs weak.

"Twelve," I said hoarsely.

His eyes were cold. "You shouldn't be here," he said. "You don't know anything about the world you were born into and it'll shock you enough to leave him when you finally see it."

"I know he's not...normal," I said.

"What do you think it does to a man to be put into an arena and made to fight for his life with nothing but his bare hands?" Caden drawled. "Hours in there, like an animal. And then to have the most intimate part of you tattooed with a reminder of it so you can never forget?"

My stomach twisted. Was I going to throw up?

"Why are you telling me this?"

"Because he's in love with you," Caden said. "I saw it happen slowly over the last year."

My head spun, the alcohol inside me bubbling.

"You are going to fuck him up," he said. "It's my job to protect him and right now, you're the greatest threat."

Hot tears brimmed over and slid down my neck.

"I don't mean to," I gasped.

His hand shot out and gripped my upper arm.

"If you care about Merrick, you will get yourself out of your engagement and marry him," he said. "Because Merrick is one heartbreak away from becoming a monster and losing everything we've built for the last decade. I won't let that happen."

"Caden," I whispered, my voice thin. "I can't do that. Merrick will lose the deal with the Cardiffs and I know he needs it."

"I'll figure out another way to get those funds," Caden said.

"Please," I said. "Stop."

He released me and stepped back. I brought my cigarette to my shaking lips and inhaled all the way. A buzz blossomed at the base of my skull.

"This is going to end badly if one of you doesn't make a choice soon," Caden said, his voice softer.

I turned on my heel, flicking the cigarette at his feet, and ducked inside. I had no idea if he was following me or not, but I didn't care. I elbowed through the crowd and ran down the hall, jerking open the door to the women's bathroom.

I stopped short. Adele stood there, texting on her phone. She looked ravishing in a floor length, black gown, diamonds glittering on her ears, her throat, and her wrists.

"Clara," she said. "I had no idea you were here."

Wordless, I hugged her. She stiffened in surprise, but when she heard me hiccup, her arms melted around me.

"What's wrong?"

Tears slipped out, fast and hot. I pulled back, trying to dab my eyes without ruining my makeup. She pressed her mouth together and went to get me a tissue.

"Nothing," I said. "Just...men."

She tilted her head. "Osian isn't here, baby."

My throat tightened with a fresh sob.

"It's not Osian," I whispered.

She took my hand and pulled me into the dressing room off the side of the bathroom and locked the door. Then she took a tissue and dampened it with cold water and I kept still while she dabbed my makeup.

I told her everything. It was stupid, she was the wife of one of Merrick's colleagues. But somehow I knew I could trust her and this would stay between us women. There were some things that were sacred.

I didn't leave out a single detail, including the night on the plane. Voice steady, I told her how he had seduced me, how he'd fucked me like he owned every part of me, how he'd left me marked by his desire.

I told her what Caden had said to me on the balcony—that Merrick was one heartbreak from becoming a monster.

"I've known Caden for years," she said. "Don't take it too personally. He's just like that."

"An asshole?"

"Yeah, unfortunately," she said crisply. "But...listen, baby, Merrick is a good man. And...sometimes good men have dark sides to them."

"I know," I whispered.

"He's a good man who does bad things."

"I'm trying to wrap my head around that concept," I said. "I feel like I'm drowning. I spent the last six years thinking he was so gentle and kind."

She nodded understandingly. "He is, just not how you think."

"What am I supposed to think?"

She took a deep breath and washed her hands, patting her cheeks with cold water. Then she turned to face me, putting her hands on my shoulders.

"The darker parts of people aren't the parts to be afraid of," she said. "It's the weak men, the ones who won't accept their darkness, that we should stay away from."

I swallowed.

"Like Osian?"

She patted my upper arms. "I couldn't say this at the lodge, but, darling, you need to get rid of that man."

"Merrick has a really big business deal with the Cardiffs."

"You are more important in the long run."

"It's more complicated than that." I took a deep breath, still fairly drunk, but feeling more in control. She accepted my weak smile, tilting my chin up.

"Vincent will be looking for me," she said. "Are you going to be okay?"

I nodded. "Yeah, sorry for having a breakdown."

She hugged me tightly.

"Now, go try and have a bit of fun," she said. "Safely."

I left the bathroom and watched her join her husband at the bar. Vincent slipped his arm around her waist and his mouth lingered over hers before kissing her deeply.

My chest ached. Would I ever be in their shoes? So in love for more than two decades?

My eyes skimmed the room, desperate for Merrick. He stood on the other side of the room, talking to a group of men in suits. Svelte, radiating that magnetic energy from every pore. In his element.

I shivered despite the sweat dripping down my spine.

"Clara."

I spun and found myself face-to-face with the last people I expected to see.

"Travis," I said. "Liam."

They looked fancier than I'd ever seen them in black suits and slicked back hair. Liam had a Cosmo and a whiskey in his hand. He held out the former to me and I accepted it, surprised.

"Why are you two here?"

Travis looked a little sheepish. "Well, we actually do a fair bit of business with the organization," he admitted.

"Our company purchases...things from Merrick," Liam said. "I just do the bartender thing for fun, to get women."

"Oh?"

"Yeah."

There was a long silence as I waited for them to elaborate. They both got more and more uncomfortable, shifting their feet.

"Want to do shots?" Liam said.

I stared at him and my spine relaxed, pushing aside everything I'd just told Adele. She was right. I needed to have some fun tonight.

"You know what...yes, I'd love to do shots with you," I said.

They both flashed elated grins and we lined up along the bar in the corner. The bartender was a handsome, tattooed man with a silver eyebrow piercing. When he saw us sit down, he raked his eyes slowly over Travis and Liam.

"You alright then?" he asked, meeting my eyes.

"Yeah," I said, offering him a sweet smile. "I'm all good."

"What can I get for you?"

"I'll have lemon vodka."

He brought a round for all three of us and we tapped our glasses and shot it down. The vodka burned, settling in my stomach. Washing away my nerves.

Maybe I did have a problem.

"Want another round?" Liam said. "It's all on my tab."

I nodded. The lights were dim and the music thrummed gently in the background. I could make out faint strains of "Cornerstone" by the Arctic Monkeys and it was putting me in the dreamiest, drunken state.

We had a cigarette out on the balcony. If I hadn't been so inebriated I might have noticed a change in Travis and Liam. Neither of them were flirting with me the way they had at the lodge.

But I was too tipsy to notice. After we had a smoke outside, I went back to the bar and the tattooed bartender asked me if I'd ever had a blowjob shot. I gaped at him, blushing to my ears.

"No," I stammered.

He set a shot glass topped with whipped cream in front of me. "If you can take it all in one go, it's on the house."

"Okay," I said, sitting down. "What do I do with it?"

All three men laughed uproariously and I felt my blush creep down to my neckline.

"You put your hands behind your back and take the glass in your mouth and tilt your head back fast," the bartender said. "And then swallow it, sweetheart, and it's free."

He was definitely flirting with me...or maybe he was just trying to get tips. Nonplussed, I tucked my hands behind my back. My entire body prickled as I felt their eyes follow my every move as I fitted my mouth around the rim of the glass.

The energy around me shifted. Everyone nearby sobered and I felt them move back. Making way for a more magnetic, imposing presence.

A hand slid up my back and gathered my hair.

"Tilt your head back."

My core clenched. I knew that deep, pleasant voice anywhere.

I obeyed, drawing my head back. The liquor went down my throat and I swallowed with difficulty, the glass suddenly cumbersome between my teeth.

A hand cupped my chin and lifted the glass from my lips. Lean fingers set it aside and turned me to look up into his deep blue gaze.

"Having fun, *cariad*?"

Oops, he'd told me not to drink too much. Guiltily, I nodded.

"You're very drunk," he said softly. "And you are also making me very jealous. Lean back against the bar."

I looked around, confused. Liam and Travis had stepped away, watching with eyes wide. The bartender crossed his arms, his brow raised.

"Can I help you, gentleman?" Merrick asked.

Everyone shook their heads, keeping their gazes respectfully lowered. Merrick swiveled my chair and gently pressed me back against the bar. The people around us had started noticing something was going on and they were looking from the corners of their eyes.

"Fuck, you look so good, baby girl," Merrick said, voice husky.

It hit me then. He was tipsy too. That shook me a little, but not enough to scare me away.

No, I wanted to see how far he would take this.

How dirty was the Welsh king willing to get?

"Two shots, salt, and a lime," Merrick said, tapping the bar.

The bartender handed them over and stood back, watching with interest. I glanced to the other side. Everyone nearby was blatantly staring now, including Vincent Galt who had paused at the far side of the bar. There was a disapproving twist to his brows that sent a twinge of shame through me.

Merrick leaned over me and fitted the shot glass between my breasts. My nipples tightened. That glass was cold. Heat curled, heavy and slow, down between my thighs. Deep inside, I shivered.

He bent over me. "Open for me."

I obeyed and he fitted a thin slice of lime between my teeth. The tart juice dripped down my chin and spread across my tongue. He licked his thumb and dragged it over the rise of my left breast and stuck the salt to the saliva he left.

There was a ripple of murmuring around us, but Merrick's eyes stayed locked on mine. He lifted me, sitting with his knees spread on the stool. My thighs wrapped around his waist, my dress riding up to my hips.

He bent, and in a fluid movement, he licked the salt from my breast and took the shot from between them and tilted his head back.

With his free hand, he set the glass aside and then his mouth was inches from mine.

Biting the lime and spitting it aside.

Then he kissed me. In front of everyone.

The lights and the music and the roaring disappeared and there was nothing but his mouth and the sharp taste of citrus and tequila. Kissing me, consuming me. Burning me alive.

"Goddamn," Liam muttered from the corner. "You were right, he is fucking her. Guess I owe you four grand."

If Merrick had heard, he didn't care. He reached behind me and the bartender handed him the second shot. He took it like the first, licking the salt off my breast and taking the shot from between them.

Then right there, in front of God and everyone, he spat the tequila into my mouth and chased it with a lime. Crushed in his lean fingers over my tongue until the juice dripped between my lips.

"Holy shit," I heard from somewhere behind us.

I swallowed.

Merrick bent, kissing my neck. "That's my good girl," he whispered.

The spell broke and reality hit me like a cannonball. Everyone was looking. Everyone would know and now, the minute Osian returned from Europe, he would know too.

"Merrick," I whispered. "Take me outside."

He obeyed, lifting me down and pulling me across the room. Ignoring all the eyes on us. There was a hallway in the corner lit by strips of light across the floor and he ushered me down it. Not speaking until we were through the exit and standing behind the compound.

He was on me, hand on the back of my neck.

"Merrick," I said. "What are you doing? Osian is going to find out when he gets back."

"I'll fucking deal with it," he said shortly.

His eyes flicked to my mouth and back up. Fear tingled up my spine. The dark, burning jealousy was back, stronger than ever. His hot mouth dragged over mine, across my jaw, to my neck.

"Open your legs, baby. Take me," he breathed.

The desperation in his voice shot to my core. My nails dug into his ribs and my spine arced, my body pleading for him.

"I didn't know you were like this," I whispered.

"What do you mean?"

I drew back, just an inch. "It's just a different world than back home. The drinks, the dancers, the people here. I thought you were so laid back, but this...this is your world."

His lids flickered. "I'm a businessman and I'll fly off this island with a lot of cash."

"How much?"

His hand slid down my stomach and pushed up beneath my skirt. Pulling my panties aside and parting me so he could slide his middle finger into my pussy. I whimpered, letting my head fall back as he stretched me open and stroked that sweet spot.

"Several million," he said.

"What...where does that go?"

"I reinvest it."

He was trying to distract me with his talented fingers and his piercing gaze. But I was determined to resist him.

"Merrick...what do you do?"

"That question has a broad answer."

"Alright. What is the main reason you're here on this island?"

"You."

"Please be truthful."

His fingers stilled, but stayed inside me. I clenched my inner muscles and he hissed under his breath.

"Tell me," I coaxed.

"You pretty, little slut," he breathed. His throat flexed as he swallowed. "I'm auctioning off some goods."

My hips moved gently, riding his fingers the way I would his cock. His forearm tensed and fire surged in his eyes.

"What goods?"

His mouth parted.

"I'm move weaponry," he said, his voice cooling slightly. "Is that what you wanted to hear?"

My hips stuttered and went still. I was too drunk to really understand what he was saying, but I had an idea what it meant. He sold guns, the kind I hated, the kind my father had kept in his office.

"That's illegal," I whispered.

"I know," he said, amused.

"You could get arrested."

"I won't. I have a deal with the feds. I help them catch the really bad guys by tracking the guns I sell to them and they turn a blind eye to the rest."

"What...kind of people?"

"Traffickers and the like," he said, pulling his fingers from my pussy. He took a cigarette from his pocket and lit it without cleaning his hand. "I have a particular loathing for men who do shit like that, so it's a win-win."

I stared up at him, mind whirling.

"I'm very selective about who I sell to," he said. "Predominantly we arm private, international security forces for very rich men."

My mouth was dry. "Do you have a gun on you right now?"

His brow arced and he nodded.

"Show me."

He opened his jacket, revealing shoulder holsters with pistols beneath each arm. My heart thumped oddly in my ears and my nails cut into my palms.

My chest was a whirlwind of emotions, drenched in liquor, and somehow still tinged with desire.

"You bought me this dress," I whispered. "With your dirty money."

"I did."

"And my bra and panties underneath."

He dipped his head.

"My diamonds." I lifted my hand and turned it to watch my rings and bracelet glitter. "My nails."

His lids were heavy. "You like being a mafia princess, *cariad*?"

"Does it matter?"

319

"It matters to me."

I had no answer for him. Instead, I took my zipper and pulled it all the way down until my dress fell in a heap. He was transfixed, unable to tear his eyes from me.

Worshiping me with his gaze.

My panties came next and then my bra, until I was fully naked in the moonlight. In the background, I could still hear the music inside the compound. But out here, it was quiet.

I flipped my wrist and made to undo my bracelet.

"No," he said. "Keep the diamonds on."

I looked up at him through my lashes and began backing up slowly. Lifting my hand and beckoning him to follow me.

He went, chasing me as I broke into a run. Tearing through the dark, leaving the compound behind us. Breaking out onto the beach.

I splashed into the water up to my knees, letting the salt sting my naked body. Behind me, I saw him stripping down to his boxer briefs. Then he was in the water with me, so sexy with the moonlight glinting off his body.

He reached for me, but I plunged below the surface and reappeared a few yards away. There was a glitter in his eyes I'd never seen there before. Soft, consuming. Like he was seeing something so beautiful it took his breath away.

We swam in the places where the water was still warm. Salt collected in my hair and dried on my diamonds.

He caught me. His mouth found mine in the dark. His arms cradled me, holding me to his chest.

I let him bring me to the shore. We were both tipsy and euphoric as he carried me to the compound, taking the back stairs to the bedroom.

He spilled me onto my back. The ocean rushed in the distance and the moon glowed blue, falling across the bed. Across our bodies tangled in the linen sheets.

He kissed my mouth slowly, his tongue tasting like heaven. When he pulled away, his eyes were naked.

"Do you hate me now that you know what I'm doing here?"

I swallowed, my brain foggy from drink and moonlight.

"No, but don't hate me when I have a bad reaction to it once I'm sober."

He laughed softly. "Hate me all you like when morning comes, baby, but I'll still adore you."

There was a long silence. His eyes widened as the words left his mouth and I felt my mouth drop open. A part of me had known, very deep down.

But hearing it in his words...in his voice.

"Merrick," I whispered.

He swallowed with difficulty.

"*Cariad.*"

I was about to say I didn't want to marry Osian. I was about to beg him to give the bracelet back to him and refuse the rest of the jewelry. To throw away his deal with the Cardiffs.

Instead, I jerked from his arms, rolled onto my side, and threw up all the alcohol roiling in my stomach.

CHAPTER FORTY-ONE

MERRICK

It ended up being good that Clara was extremely hungover the next morning. After she'd evacuated about fifteen shots of liquor onto the floor, I put her in the shower and had housekeeping clean the room and change the linens.

Then I laid next to her all night and wondered why I had said that.

We both knew it already, but speaking it aloud made it worse.

Selfish, jealous thoughts crept in early in the morning as I dragged my body from the bed and went for a swim in the pool to clear my mind.

Why couldn't she be mine?

I dove beneath the water and resurfaced at the edge of the pool. The morning was clear and the ocean was calm. Stretching on and on into infinity. It made the reasons I'd held onto for not being with her seem so small.

So insignificant.

I laid them out now, in the clarity of the ocean air and the quiet morning.

True, I was old enough to be her father and then some. But I also looked younger than I was so we weren't visually mismatched.

There was a maturity gap. That was the part that bothered me the most. No matter what we did, we would always be at different places in our lives. I had lived half a lifetime before her and I would always have different priorities and desires.

But if we could accept that, we could overcome it.

And then there was the heavy question of children.

That was a tough one and unfortunately not something I was able to discuss with her yet.

There was the question of the loss I would take from breaking off her engagement.

It was so much fucking money, but more than that, it was all my plans for the organization for the next decade. It was the future of so many men, so many families, that depended on me.

But...Clara. She was worth all that and more.

The money wasn't what held me back.

I felt like I was robbing her of her potential and her future. Without me, she would have a husband her own age and chance to see grandchildren someday.

Those weren't small things.

If I refused her and broke things off between us...I was robbing her of the man she loved.

Because she did love me. I heard it in her voice, saw it in her eyes, felt it in her body when we fucked in the dark.

I got out of the pool and went to shower and change. My mind wasn't any more tranquil than before.

Downstairs, I found Yale and Caden having breakfast on the patio. There was a spread of fruit, eggs, and coffee on the table. I took a seat near the end, ignoring their smirks, and asked the waiter for an espresso.

"Some night," Yale drawled. "Feeling alright?"

I pushed my sunglasses down. "I'm upright."

Caden was sitting stony-faced, his eyes fixed on his book. I bent to look at the cover. *The Art of War*.

"Where's Clara?" Yale asked.

"Sleeping."

Caden flicked his gaze up and set his book aside, shifting back so he could prop his crossed legs up on the table. He folded his arms over his chest.

"So you're just openly admitting you're sleeping with her now?"

Irritation flickered through me, but I kept my face impassive.

"Who I sleep with is my business," I said crisply.

Caden's jaw worked, but he kept silent. Yale had a stupid smirk on his face. There was a long silence as I had a plate of egg whites and several espressos. Once I felt human again, I stood and put my sunglasses back on.

"Hey," Caden drawled.

"Yes?"

His jawline worked again and he turned, looking out over the water.

"For what it's worth, I think you should marry her," he said. "You think everyone will judge you for marrying her...I disagree."

I kept quiet, listening. Caden was my advisor when it came to the underground side of the organization. I respected his thoughts.

"If they're not judging us, what will they think then?" I asked.

"It's a powerful move," he said. "Edwin was easily the best soldier in the organization in decades, second to you. The men still hold him up as an example. Marrying his daughter is a good strategic move for you."

"I won't use her," I said.

"You don't have to," Caden said, rising smoothly. "Think of it as a happy, but accidental, side effect of marrying the woman you're tripping over your own feet for."

"I'm not," I said.

Yale laughed aloud, his head falling back. "She's had you by the balls for a while now."

"Watch your tone," I said, annoyed.

"Come on then," Caden said. "I see your expense reports, I know what you spend on her. Let me guess...the house was so you could take her into the mountains and fuck her without being found out."

He had me there. I cleared my throat, lifting a hand. "Enough."

Yale laughed again. "What about the car? Fucking hundred grand."

Caden nodded. "Or the renovation you did on her room."

"Do you know how much sending someone bi-weekly flowers adds up to?" Yale said. "A fucking lot, that's what. Oh, and can't forget about the diamonds either."

I picked up my jacket. "I highly recommend you both go fuck yourselves."

"Merrick," said Caden, his voice going serious. "If you want her, I will find another way to fund the expansion into Wyoming."

I gave him a hard stare. "How?"

"I don't know," he admitted. "But I'll figure it out."

That wasn't enough, I had to have a tangible solution. I turned on my heel and left them, going back to the bedroom to start packing.

I wanted to be pissed, but I'd done too much therapy with Gretchen to fool myself like that. They were both absolutely right, down to the letter. At some point during the last year, she'd gotten her pretty, manicured fingers around my neck and put me in a chokehold.

I'd passed it all off as showing her how she should be treated.

But that was a fucking lie.

No, I'd spent all that money because I wanted her to be mine.

CHAPTER FORTY-TWO

CLARA

He adored me.

The Welsh King adored me.

I turned the phrase over and over in my mind the whole plane trip back to Providence. He hadn't meant to say that out loud, but he had and now it was out and everything had changed.

He sat across from me, one ankle crossed over his knee. Laptop balanced and fingers flying over the keyboard. Every time he'd stop, he'd jiggle his foot in a way that made me anxious.

He was antsy, unable to hold still. I watched him for the next hour, counting the times he shifted position, took his reading glasses off and put them back on, and got up to get coffee. After a while, he put his laptop away and closed his eyes, turning to the window.

"Are you okay?" I asked.

He didn't open his eyes. "I'm good, just tired."

"Alcohol isn't good for your OCD and ADHD is it?" I asked. "I read up on both of those things after you told me you had them. You know...so I wouldn't do stuff that bothered you."

His eyes snapped open, fixing on me. "You never bother me, but thank you, that's very thoughtful."

There was a note of astonishment in his tone, like no one had ever made allowances for those parts of him before. I swallowed back the urge to go to him and curl up in his lap.

I wasn't really sure where we stood after his admission the other night.

Instead, I curled up in the bed and he remained in his chair for the rest of the flight. When we got home, he went upstairs to his office and I took a shower and changed into a sweatsuit, intending on going to sleep.

"Clara," he called from the stairs.

I leaned out of my room. "What is it?"

"Can you come up to my office?"

My stomach tightened and I padded up the hallway and stairs. He was going to break it off, I knew it. He was going to end this beautiful, fantastical dream and leave me with nothing.

He was at his desk, sleeves rolled to the elbow. I dragged my leaden feet into the office and shut the door, slumping in the chair opposite him.

"I apologize for doing body shots off you in front of everyone," he said.

"It's fine. I liked it," I said, my voice small.

He cleared his throat. "Osian and his father will be in Europe for the next two and a half months. If either of them hear anything and contact us, I will handle it. Right now, we are going to deny anything between us."

"Okay," I said miserably.

"For the next two and half months, you will let me love you," he said.

My whole body went hot and cold. Shock tingled down my spine and I jerked my head up, meeting his gaze. There was a flicker of softness deep in that cobalt blue.

"At the end of that time, if you decide you don't want to go through with getting engaged to Osian, I'll take the financial hit and call it off."

"How much...will it be a lot?"

"It's a lot," he said. "I'm not sugarcoating with you. But I would lose a great deal of money to ensure you have a happy future."

"If I choose to break it off with him? What happens then?"

His jaw worked and there was a long silence. Then he rose and circled the desk and knelt before me. Taking my hands in his, looking up into my eyes with such naked trust it made my stomach twist.

"Then, we'll talk," he said.

"Talk?" I breathed. "That's it? Talk?"

His jaw tightened. "Clara, I am old enough to be your father."

I glared at him, my lashes wet.

"So you love me so much you have to let me go? Is that it?"

"No," he said swiftly. "I love you enough not to set you up for heartbreak. We will never be at the same place in our lives, I'll always be twenty-one years ahead. That's clearer to me than it is to you now."

A sob rose in my throat and I caught my breath, trying to swallow it back down. His throat bobbed and I swore his eyes glittered with tears, but then he blinked and they were gone.

"That's so fucking morbid," I sniffed.

"It's realistic."

I wiped my face angrily. "Can you give me a ballpark figure that the organization would be losing if I broke it off with Osian?"

His lips thinned.

"Merrick, I'm not a child."

He sighed, a short, harsh sound. "Not as much as my net worth, but definitely a lot of it."

"So...what is your net worth?" I said.

He was quiet.

"I'll just look it up online if you don't tell me," I warned. "Clearly you have a lot because you bought me a car like it was nothing."

"Multimillions." He cleared his throat. "Maybe more like billions."

My ears rung. My heart skipped a beat.

"Wait...you're a billionaire?"

He nodded.

"How did I not know that until now?"

"Net worth is different than what you actually have in your bank account," he said. "No billionaire actually has billions in an account somewhere. Mine is tied up in businesses, real estate, some less savory operations, and investments."

My mouth felt dry, my tongue stuck to the roof of it.

"Okay, so the Cardiffs must have billions too?"

He nodded once. "They have one of the most successful hotel chains in the world."

"So...what's in it for them?" I pressed.

"You."

I laughed, short and harsh. "I'm not worth billions."

He was quiet again.

"I'm not...am I?" I faltered. "I don't have any money."

His jaw worked.

"Merrick?"

His eyes darted up. "Osian Cardiff wasn't the only person to make a bid for you. You're the Welsh Princess, *cariad*. Anyone who marries you gains my favor and a very coveted position."

My jaw hung slack. "So...how many people made a bid for me?"

"Sixty-eight."

"*Sixty-eight?* Like eight and six?"

He nodded.

I stared at him, reeling.

"What the fuck, Merrick," I said.

"The Cardiff family outbid everyone," he said. "And I thought Osian seemed like he fit the bill for what you wanted."

My stomach churned.

Shit.

"Okay," I said slowly. "Osian doesn't get home for a few months. Can I just...think about it for a bit?"

His lids flickered. "*Cariad*, I don't want you to make this choice based on money."

"How can I not?" I whispered.

329

"Because you are priceless," he said. "And if you want me, regardless of everything we've discussed, I'll find a way out of this mess."

I wanted to speak, but my mouth wouldn't move.

There was a long silence and he rose, lifting me to my feet. He cradled my face and his mouth moved over mine. Slowly, drawing that breathless, burning sensation from the deepest parts of me.

"Do you love me?" he whispered into my neck.

"Merrick," I breathed. "You know the answer to that."

"Tell me," he demanded.

The energy in the room had done a complete turnaround. My core pulsed hot, so empty, begging to have him inside me. His hands were hard on my body and his mouth was dragging up my throat, scoring me gently with his teeth.

"Tell me you love me or I'll eat it out of you," he said.

"I'll take that option."

He lifted me and laid me out on the desk, pressing me to my back. He worked my sweatpants and panties down my legs and spread me wide. In his office, surrounded by all his dark wood, leather, and brass, I felt so vulnerable.

He ran a finger up to my clit, parting me as it went.

"Love me for the next two and a half months," he said. "Make sure this is what you want before I say anything to anyone. Then, I will move heaven and earth to make you mine."

I nodded, wordless.

His mouth came down on my pussy, warm and familiar now. His tongue slid up until it lingered just below my clit and then he pulled back. My hips writhed, begging for his touch where I needed it most.

He was relentless. Building me, stroking me, nipping me with his mouth and his teeth. But never getting close enough to touch my clit.

He was evil, torturing me like this.

I wound my fingers in his hair, pushing my hips up to his mouth. Quick as a flash, he gathered my wrists in one hand and pinned them against my breasts. Never moving his head from between my legs.

"Do you have something to say to me?" he breathed.

"Fine," I burst out. "I love you."

He laughed softly and his mouth touched my clit, sending heatwaves through my hips. His hot tongue curled around that sensitive place, licking it with tiny, circular strokes. My spine arced as an orgasm sparked and began building deep inside.

He teased me slowly for what felt like forever. I was panting, dripping onto his desk. My thighs were tight from straining up to his mouth and my orgasm burned, ready to explode through me.

"I fucking adore you," he whispered.

He pulled my clit into his mouth and sucked it in slow, rhythmic pulses, licking it with the tip of his tongue at the same time.

Fuck, that was my sweet spot.

I cried out and came hard, breaking my hands free so I could push his face into my sex. He groaned and I was dimly aware of him undoing his belt while I rode his mouth.

He pushed my hands off, stood, and was inside me faster than I realized what was happening. Stretching and filling me as I pulsed hard. Sparks danced in my vision and pleasure washed over my body in waves that just kept coming.

And coming. And coming.

He pinned my hands above my head, slamming into me. "That's a good girl. Come on my cock the way you'll never fucking come on his."

I was still raw and shaking when he finally let me leave his office. My gait was off, my sex a little sore, and I saw the satisfaction in his eyes as he watched me go.

Back in my room, I picked up my phone. I'd texted Candice earlier to ask her to hang out, but she hadn't texted back.

Which meant one thing.

Yale had told her, that asshole. That meant they must be on speaking terms again. But what would I know? I'd been the world's shittiest friend since I'd started sleeping with Merrick.

I went to her house and knocked on the door. It took several minutes, but she finally pulled open the door.

"Hi," she snapped.

"Candice," I said. "Can we talk?"

Her brow arced. "About the fact you've been fucking Merrick and you never thought to tell me? Yeah, no."

I winced. "Please, let me in and I can explain."

She shook her head. "You had months to explain. I'm your best friend, I tell you everything. You've been lying to me. Not only that, you haven't been ditching me so you can do engagement stuff, you ditched me so you could get laid."

My eyes stung. "Candice, I didn't mean for it to happen like this. You're not being reasonable."

"Reasonable?" she yelled. "You've been fucking your forty-five-year-old guardian. What's reasonable about that?"

"Lower your voice!"

"My parents aren't home."

I wrapped my arms around my body, my stomach like ice. "I'm sorry I kept it from you."

Her face went stone cold. "Me too."

"Candice, can you just let me in and we can talk about it?"

Her eyes narrowed and she stepped back into the hallway. My heart sank and tears gathered, one slipping down my cheek.

"No," said Candice. "I'm fucking angry and I need time to cool off."

"Okay," I hiccuped. "I understand. I'm really sorry."

She just nodded and closed the door. The sound echoed through my head as I trudged back to my car and got in.

The fantasy was crumbling and the real world was showing through. I'd known this would happen eventually. I just hadn't expected it to hurt so much when it did.

That night, Merrick held me while I cried. He didn't offer to intervene, which I was grateful for, he just stroked my hair and rubbed my back until I fell asleep.

CHAPTER FORTY-THREE

MERRICK

I'd fucked up a lot in my life, but this wasn't one of those times.

No, this...this was paradise.

It got warm quickly that spring. On my days off, she opened all the windows in the house and turned her music all the way up. I taught her how to cook a few more dishes and she did a horrible job. I kept having to take the smoke detectors from the ceiling and scrub charred substances off the stove.

She could make brownies though so I put her in charge of dessert. I even caved and tasted them, although I wasn't sure I liked it very much.

I told her I loved it.

We ate outside on the patio most nights. She wore little dresses without panties underneath and teased me until my resolve broke. Then she made me chase her around the lawn and carry her up to the bedroom.

We fucked. A lot. Our mornings started out with a quickie that always made me late for work. At night, I took my time with her, keeping her up past midnight. On weekends, she was all over me, barely giving me time to reload.

I kept getting this feeling that we needed to stop. But I couldn't keep my hands off her, couldn't keep my pants buckled, couldn't keep her off my dick.

She was my new drug and I couldn't stop taking her.

Morning, noon, and night.

In my bed, in her bed, in my car, on my desk, and surprisingly, once on the front porch. The security footage of that incident found a permanent place on my phone.

We drove with the Audi's top down, her bare feet hanging out the window. Along the shore and down the country roads. We went into the city and she pointed at what she wanted and I swiped my card and made it happen.

Her pretty hands found their way into my wallet and my pants on the daily. I was powerless, completely smitten.

We ate out some nights along the coast and watched the sun sink into the ocean. I got us a private room more often than not and she perched on my lap and we ate from the same plate. I tipped oysters and lemon down her throat and fed her caviar off a golden spoon.

The world moved slow and we moved fast, trying to fit everything in before...before what?

That was the question that tugged at the back of my mind at night. After we'd spent all day together, after I'd fucked her senseless.

We were in so deep I didn't know how or when this would end.

I didn't think she saw it, but she was changing.

Slowly, day by day.

One day, I noticed that she was dressing differently. Not drastically, but just enough that I could tell. Slowly, the girlish things in her wardrobe phased out. The pink and black colors stayed, but there was a kind of breezy elegance to her new clothing I liked.

She appeared one night in a silk robe and lounged in the doorway of my bathroom. She'd cut her hair to her shoulders and it fell around her face in soft waves. Highlighting her neck and collarbones.

I set aside my book and beckoned her, but she shook her head. A little smile broke over her face, tinged with shyness.

"What?" I asked, rising to go to her.

"I have something for you," she whispered.

"Really?"

Her hands came up and untied her robe, letting it slip onto the floor. My dick went rock hard before the silk even left her skin.

Underneath, she wore a lace lingerie set in deep, peacock blue. The top cupped her breasts, giving her the prettiest overflow. The garter belt cinched around her waist just above her navel and her thong came up just below it.

Usually, I had all the smooth words to tell her how beautiful she was, but for the first time, I was speechless.

I was glad that night that my house was miles from anyone. I didn't need anyone else hearing the way she called me daddy while I fucked her over the edge of the bed.

Especially not at the pitch she screamed it.

She was getting more and more comfortable living in my space. Every morning when I got in the shower, the white walls were decorated with swirls of dark hair and conditioner made the floor slick.

Her makeup bag appeared on my sink. Then makeup started stacking up behind the faucet. I gathered it all up and gave her a designated drawer to use.

"Are you serious?" she asked, frowning. "I literally left...maybe one lipstick out."

We both looked down at the makeup stains on the sink and the scrunchie covered with bits of dark hair. There was a clear print where her bottles had laid.

"You can have the bottom, largest drawer," I said firmly.

"Maybe I'll just bring it all back to my bathroom."

"No. Bottom drawer."

She pushed her lower lip out, but I could see she was pleased that I'd insisted on it staying. I pulled my shirt off and turned on the shower and she loitered by the sink.

The look on her face reminded me of the first time she'd sat on my lap. Wary, unsure if she would be accepted.

I frowned. "Would you like to shower with me?"

She chewed that spot in her mouth and shook her head. "I can't right now."

"Okay...why not?"

She shifted and her face flushed and whispered something under her breath.

"What?"

She cleared her throat. "I'm on my period."

I stared at her, still confused. Up until now, she'd been incredibly secretive about her cycle, probably from having grown up without a mother. I wasn't an idiot though, I'd noticed last month when she suddenly refused sex for five days, saying her stomach hurt.

I hadn't pressed her to tell me. If she wanted to, she would.

"I don't mind," I said. "Why would I mind?"

"It's just not the most sexy thing," she mumbled.

I stepped beneath the showerhead, running a hand over my face to slick back my wet hair. "I think it's sexy."

Her jaw dropped. "You do."

"I mean, I think it's sexy because you're sexy. And it makes me feel good that you're willing to share the vulnerable parts of your life with me."

She shook her head slightly, the corners of her mouth turning up.

"Sometimes you're so mentally healthy it makes me jealous."

I laughed aloud, but sobered quickly as I turned over her words. She watched me for a moment before slipping off her dressing gown. She must have been wearing a pad because she hid her panties under her clothes before crossing the room to get into the shower with me.

I bent and kissed her wet mouth. "I know I use a lot of lingo I picked up in behavioral therapy, but...I wasn't always this way."

Her eyes grew concerned.

"You sound serious," she murmured.

"I just...I was in a really bad place after the arena," I admitted. "It fucks up your head. I drank a lot, did a lot of drugs, fucked up my relationships. I was essentially a very functional addict for about ten years before I met your father."

There was a painful silence.

"Oh," she said. "I didn't know that."

"The amount of tears Daphne and Ophelia cried for me over that decade still haunts me," I admitted. "You knew your father was sober, right?"

She frowned and shook her head. "No, I guess I didn't. I thought he did drink, but...I never really thought to pay attention."

"He got sober about five years before we met. There were some things that happened around that time that made me realize I needed to clean up or forfeit my place as *Brenin*. And I couldn't fucking stand to listen to Ophelia cry into the phone anymore."

"Did he help you get sober?" There was a cool note to her voice.

"Yes and no," I admitted. "He was pretty tough love, he left the getting sober to me, but he supported me through it."

"So how did you do it?"

"I stopped. It was the hardest thing I've ever done."

"Oh. But you still drink."

"It wasn't the alcohol that was doing it, it was all the undiagnosed shit I had going on. All the PTSD I had from the arena."

She nibbled at her lower lip, her brow creased.

"I had a friend who was sleeping with a woman casually and he recommended I see her at her clinical practice. That's how I met Gretchen Hughes."

"She fixed you?"

"She gave me what I needed," I said. "But I had to fix myself when it really got down to it. She just turned on the lights so I could see what was going on inside my head."

She made an odd face.

"Are you...jealous?" I asked.

Her brows darted up. "No, of course not," she said. "I'm not a child, Merrick. I'm grateful to Gretchen for everything she did for you and I hope you keep seeing her."

It was my turn to be caught off guard. I stroked through her wet hair, running my thumb over her jaw.

"You're very well adjusted," I said. "It doesn't make sense considering how you grew up."

Her lashes flickered and she shrugged, clearly uncomfortable. "Some fucked up things happened in my childhood and I'm still working through that. But Candice and her family gave me a stable experience. I wasn't really raised by my father, I was raised by her parents."

She was deflecting again, but I could tell now wasn't the time to push back.

"I'm glad," I said.

"And of course I'm not jealous," she said, smirking. "I know I'm the best you've ever had."

"Without a doubt."

I was done reliving my darkest moments. We still had a little over a month left before Osian returned, forty-five days of pure bliss. I was going to fucking enjoy every minute that she was mine.

She gasped as I lifted her, wrapping her legs around my waist. Her gasp turned to a shriek of protest as I pushed her against the cool wall. My erection brushed the inside of her thigh.

She swatted my shoulder. "Merrick, not now."

"Why the fuck not?" I murmured into her neck.

"Because...you know why."

"No, no, I really don't," I teased. "Enlighten me."

She moaned as I shifted my hips, the head of my cock slipping over her clit.

"I'm bleeding," she whispered.

My mouth met hers, parting her lips. Her tongue tasted so sweet against mine. When I pulled back, her eyes were glazed and her nipples pressed hard against my chest.

"So you don't want me inside you, *cariad*?"

I kept eye contact and she shivered, her hips working against mine.

"Do you know what I like the most about you?" I asked.

"No," she gasped. "What?"

I bent, barely kissing her mouth. "The parts of you I love the most are imperfect and vulnerable. I find the most beautiful things when you let your guard down."

"Oh," she breathed.

"So let your guard down for me, my love."

I saw her hesitation melt, her throat bob, and her eyes flutter closed. Her head fell back as she nodded and her hips relaxed. I was so hard I barely had to guide myself as I pushed my cock into her pussy.

Her inner muscles drew me in and held me there, floored by just how extraordinary she felt. Tight, soaked, and so fucking familiar.

Like I'd always been here in an echo playing again and again at the edge of my mind. Like I would be here for the rest of my life, my body so deep inside hers.

A pale stream of crimson slipped down the inside of her thigh and disappeared down the drain. She didn't notice. She just let me fuck her, head back and fingernails digging into my shoulders.

CHAPTER FORTY-FOUR

CLARA

I made the choice without Merrick. Not because I thought he wouldn't support it, but because I didn't want him to have to take the blame. I didn't want his peers to look at him with distrust. To call him dishonorable.

I couldn't protect him from the financial fallout breaking off my engagement would cause, but I could take on some of the blame.

After all, I was the one who had asked Merrick to sleep with me in the first place. I had set this all into motion.

I was a big girl, I could take the consequences too.

The day Osian was due back in the States, I sat in the kitchen, every other light in the house turned down low. I wanted to call Candice, but she still wasn't speaking to me. Earlier I'd gotten a text from her with an extremely Candice-like message:

I love you, but you're such a dick for keeping this from me. I need time to cool off.

I told her I loved her too and that I was sorry. The whole incident made me feel like a jerk so I went and poured myself a glass of pity wine. That glass became another.

And another.

I wasn't drunk, but it impaired me enough I couldn't drive. At some point in the evening, I decided I needed to see Osian, even though he'd just gotten back that morning.

I knew because he'd texted me he wanted to see me and I'd ignored it.

It was past time to break this off. I was going to be a grown up instead of relying on Merrick to convey the message. Osian deserved to hear it from me.

He picked up on the first ring.

"Hello," he said crisply. "You never returned my text."

He sounded like he was in a horrible mood. My mouth was dry. He had to know, it was probably the first thing he'd heard when he stepped off the plane.

"Sorry, I was busy. Could you come over so we can talk?" I squeaked.

"Right now?"

"Yeah," I said. "It's just me at the house. We can have some wine and talk."

There was a short silence and he cleared his throat. "Okay. I'll be over in thirty minutes."

He hung up the phone without saying goodbye. I pulled myself off the kitchen stool and padded down to my bedroom. Breaking off our future engagement was going to be a horrible experience so I might as well pull myself together so he didn't see me crying in my sweatpants.

I did my hair and makeup and put on a lacy tank top and jeans. By the time I was done, I could see his headlights coming up the drive.

I let him in, shrinking under his gaze. He flipped his keys once over his hand and caught them.

"You smell like a fucking winery," he said.

I stared after him as he walked down the hall toward the kitchen, completely shocked. It took me almost thirty seconds to gather myself and shut the door, locking it. I hurried down the hall and found him standing by the table.

"What do you want to talk about?" he said.

"I...um...do you want some wine?"

"Sure."

I poured him a glass, but he didn't touch it. He was just standing there, looking at me like I was something he'd scraped off his shoe. My chest tightened and ice formed in the pit of my stomach.

He had to know.

"How was your trip?" I asked, my voice brittle.

He rolled his eyes. "Fine."

"Okay," I said, taking a deep breath. "I think we should just go ahead and talk then."

He narrowed his gaze on me, his lip curling a little. "You know my father has a lot invested in our engagement, right?"

"Yes, I know," I said.

"So if you're going to tell me you're getting cold feet, don't bother. I'm not breaking it off."

I gaped at him.

"You want this?" I stammered.

"I want Clara Prothero, the ward of Merrick Llwyd and Edwin Prothero's daughter, as my wife," he said. "You, I could do without."

I frowned, confused. "So you only ever wanted this for the status?"

"It's an arranged marriage. Of course."

"But...you kept asking me for sex and things...I thought you at least were attracted to me."

"I want to fuck you," he said, shrugging.

My body felt strange, like it was slowly icing over. My limbs tingled as I stared up at him. Had he always looked so angry? So big and intimidating?

My breathing came faster and my vision began tunneling.

A memory was resurfacing slowly. Unwelcome and dark, a horrible nightmare I'd kept locked deep in my mind.

***

I was sixteen, sitting at the dining room table. There was a faint scar across the wood and I kept my eyes on it. My father was walking down the hall, his footsteps heavy and loud.

For the first time in my life, I'd talked back to him.

He'd told me to sit in the chair while he got something. I'd sunk down, my stomach roiling, nausea pushing up my throat. My fingers dug into the edge of the chair, pain etching up my knuckles.

He appeared in the doorway. I glanced up and my body went ice cold.

There was a gun in his hand.

My body was shutting down, shivering uncontrollably. There was nothing in my brain but fear, killing my ability to think or move.

He crossed the room and knelt before me, never touching me. He never touched me, ever.

"Clara," he said.

Tears seeped from between my lashes, dripping down my jaw. I didn't move to wipe them, or even acknowledge their presence.

He lifted his hand and fear seared through my body anew as he put the gun to my temple.

"I can kill you," he said softly.

I whimpered through clenched teeth. He'd never done anything like this to me before. Up until now, he'd just been distant and neglectful.

"Say you understand me," he ordered.

I pried my jaws apart, mouth shaking.

"I...I understand, sir," I sobbed.

He rose and laid aside the gun, sinking back down to his heels. A tinge of relief filled my chest, but it was quickly replaced by growing horror as he spread his hand out, palm up.

His eyes locked with mine.

"I don't need a gun to kill you, Clara," he said. "You are barely over five feet, you're weak, you're small. I could hit you as hard as I can and it would kill you instantly."

My throat was so dry I could barely breathe. The heartbeat in my ears felt raw and my mouth ached from being bitten.

There was a scar in my mouth, inside my lower lip, from when I'd fallen as a child. I focused on that, trying to block out the panic. Maybe if I chewed it, I could feel only that pain.

I bit it hard enough to bleed. Copper filled my mouth as I bit it again, chewing on the tender skin. Ripping it open with my teeth like an animal chewing its leg free of a trap.

Something slipped from the corner of my mouth and trickled down my chin. But I didn't stop gnawing at that spot.

"You will respect me from now on because in the back of your mind, you'll always remember how easily I could kill you. Now tell me you understand."

I swallowed the mucus and blood pooling in my mouth. My lips stung as I licked them.

"I do," I gasped.

"No, say it. Say you know that you're weak, that I could kill you if I wanted to."

My jaw shivered as a sob worked its way up.

"I'm weak," I whispered. "You could kill me if you wanted to."

He didn't say anything, he just got up and left with the gun in his hand. After almost three hours, I heard him leave the house and I peeled myself from the chair and made it to my bathroom.

I threw up everything inside me. My father never brought up the incident again and I sometimes wondered if I dreamed it.

But I knew I hadn't because there was a scar inside my mouth.

And I couldn't stop chewing on it.

**

I'd never told anyone what had happened that day. Not Candice, not Merrick. I'd dissociated from it and blocked it from my mind. But now, standing in the kitchen with Osian, that memory was creeping back into my body.

He was tall and anger simmered in his eyes. I was five feet and two inches, barely reaching his shoulder.

"What the fuck is wrong with you?" he asked, frowning.

It took everything I had, but I managed to pull myself together. Breathing deeply, I squared my shoulders and looked him in the eyes.

"You don't want to marry me, Osian, and I don't want to marry you either," I said. "We just don't have any chemistry. Let's call this off before it gets ugly."

His jaw tensed.

"Who says I don't want to marry you?"

"You clearly don't," I said. "You've been fucking as many other women as you can before our engagement. Clearly you don't want to be tied to me."

"Who said I wasn't going to fuck other women while being tied to you?"

There was a short, shocked silence.

"Are you serious?" I spat.

"Yeah, I'm fucking serious."

"Okay, we are done," I snapped, grabbing both wine glasses and dumping them in the sink. "I'm not marrying you."

His hand shot out and gripped my upper arm. My stomach turned over and I froze, keeping my eyes on my reflection in the dark window.

"Are you still a virgin?" he asked softly.

No, I couldn't tell him that. His grip tightened and pain shot up my arm. I gasped, dipping my head.

"Are you?"

"Osian, let me go," I whispered.

He shook me, just a tiny bit, but it was enough to snap me out of it. I pulled my arm hard, twisting to face him, and he let go.

His eyes blazed and his chest heaved. I needed to get out of this room and get somewhere that had a lock on the door.

He could kill me. Would he? Probably not. But he could.

"He fucks you," Osian spat.

"Go away. Get out."

"Just fucking tell me," he roared.

I stumbled back, catching onto the countertop. There was nothing I hated more than when men raised their voices. It stirred a panic in me that made me want to run, to curl up on the floor.

"Tell me," he repeated.

"Fine," I breathed. "He fucks me. Please, just don't...just go."

"Do you know how fucking humiliating it is to be engaged to you? Everyone knows and they're just pretending not to. They fucking laugh at me."

"Osian, I'm sorry—"

"You dirty cunt," he snapped. "When did he do it?"

"No, I'm not talking about this," I gasped.

"Yes, the fuck you are. Merrick Llwyd set me up to look like a pussy in front of everyone who matters. He's done nothing but undermine and humiliate me every chance he's gotten. When did he fuck you?"

"In the late fall," I said, keeping my eyes down. "I said I was with Daphne and Ophelia, but I was with Merrick."

His nostrils went white, flaring. His mouth was a rigid line in his jaw.

"Did you bleed?"

My stomach churned. "What the fuck? What is wrong with you?"

"Answer me," he roared, his hand coming down on the countertop.

"Yes, I did," I said, a sob finally escaping my lips. "Why the fuck does that matter to you?"

"Everyone knows," he shouted. "Everyone fucking knows that Merrick Llwyd is fucking my future wife right under my nose. You dirty, little bitch, you fucking whore."

My body had been telling me to keep away from him for a long time. Something in my brain clicked and my instincts rose to protect me.

I was going to listen this time.

Throwing up my hand, I sent him a death glare. "Get out," I hissed. "Don't you dare try to touch or fucking speak to me. Get out of my house."

Something about seeing me stand up to him made him lose the last shreds of his control. His scarred brows drew together and a look that made my blood go cold flashed in his eyes. His body blurred and it took me a moment to realize he was coming at me.

Arm raised.

In the last second before he hit me, I found myself wondering why. He didn't love me.

What had I done to warrant this rage?

The pain was so intense I didn't feel it both times. I just hit the wall and slid down, stunned. Breathless.

CHAPTER FORTY-FIVE

MERRICK

I was on my way home that night when I decided it was time I followed Gretchen's suggestion and talked to my aunts about Edwin. It wasn't a conversation I wanted to have, but there was something that had been bothering me for a while and it just wouldn't go away.

Clara had said she thought her father drank. But I'd spent my entire life thinking he was sober. It was time I got some answers.

The lights were on in the farmhouse as I pulled up the drive. I stepped out, breathing the clear air in, and lit a cigarette.

Overhead, the stars burned bright, unhampered by city lights. An owl hooted softly in the dark treeline and the wind picked up just enough that I could smell the damp, mushroom scent of the forest.

I'd grown up here and every time I was back, a familiar sense of peace settled in my chest.

Finishing my cigarette, I walked up the drive and knocked. There was a rattle and Daphne pulled the door ajar, her face splitting in a grin.

"Merrick!" she said. "Ophelia, guess who's here."

They were all over me, dragging me into the kitchen. I complimented their kitchen renovation and they asked me the usual series of invasive questions. Was I drinking too much? Eating enough? Seeing anyone?

Ten minutes later, I was sitting at the table with a cup of tea that smelled like flowers. It probably was. Ophelia gathered herbs and plants from the fields and made use of them in her kitchen.

"How's Clara?" Daphne asked, sitting down across the table.

"She's really good," I said.

"Is she engaged yet?"

"No, not yet," I said. "Soon maybe."

Ophelia shot her wife a look that wasn't lost on me. A pointed stare like she knew something she wasn't saying. Then she put a hand on her hip and started rummaging through the breadbox.

"Do you want something to eat?"

"No, thanks," I said. "I'll have dinner when I get home."

There was a short silence as Ophelia ignored me and made up a plate of bread with butter and jam. Then she took a seat beside Daphne, staring at me until I took a bite.

"So were you just passing by?" Daphne asked.

I leaned back, wiping the jam from my fingers.

"Actually, I was hoping to talk to you both about something," I said. "Especially you, Ophelia."

"Everything okay?" Daphne asked.

I nodded. "I was just hoping to ask you about Efa."

There was dead silence in the kitchen. My aunts looked at each other and their brows creased in tandem. Ophelia bit her lip and took a deep breath.

"Efa Prothero?"

"Yes, of course."

"Okay...what did you want to ask?"

I hated how uncomfortable they were. It was making a hollow form in my stomach, but now that I'd opened the door to this conversation, I would see it through.

"Do you know why she left Edwin?"

"Did...Edwin ever tell you why?"

I shrugged. "He said their marriage wasn't going well and she just walked out."

There was that worried glance again.

349

"What is going on?" I asked, frustrated.

Ophelia rubbed her hands together, working her wedding band. There was another long silence that seemed to stretch into eternity.

The owl in the forest hooted softly again.

"Efa came to us the night she left," Daphne said finally. "She left because she was afraid of him."

My stomach twisted and there was a soft roaring in my ears.

"Afraid of what?"

Ophelia stood up, pacing to the stove. When she turned around, she had a determined look on her face.

"Edwin hurt her," she said.

Sickness seeped into my veins. "Sexual violence?"

"Some," Ophelia whispered. "But usually just mental and emotional abuse. Gaslighting, isolation, some physical abuse."

"Jesus Christ," I breathed. "Why did you never tell me this?"

"Efa didn't want anyone to know," Daphne said. "She asked us not to tell."

I stood up so fast the chair fell back and I had to catch it, pushing it back in.

"Jesus fucking Christ," I said. "Don't you think I deserved the truth? I was friends with him for fifteen years."

Ophelia's eyes glistened. "Please don't say such ugly things."

"Ugly things?" I said, staring at her. "Are you really correcting my language right now?"

"Edwin Merrick Llwyd," Daphne snapped. "Sit down and don't speak to Ophelia like that."

I sat.

"But...she left Clara?" I said. "How could she leave her daughter with an abuser?"

They both shifted and looked at each other for a brief moment. Ophelia cocked her head and Daphne nodded. They both faced me.

"When Efa left, she gave us a tape where Edwin confessed to everything," Daphne said. "I sent a copy of it with a letter telling Edwin that if he laid a hand on Clara, I would release it. He would lose you and his life. You know what the organization does to abusers."

"I do," I breathed. "I would have hunted and killed him. According to our laws."

"So he never laid a hand on her," Ophelia said.

I was spinning through cold space. Watching as my entire world broke into pieces around me. I could almost hear the sound of it shattering in a slow implosion.

"You both blackmailed Edwin for years behind my back," I said.

"We did," Daphne admitted.

"What...where's the tape?"

"I destroyed it when Edwin died," Ophelia said. "Burnt it in the fireplace after his funeral. I never wanted Clara hearing that."

"But...she deserves to know the truth," I said.

"And when she comes looking for answers, we'll tell her the truth," Daphne said. "But the truth is ugly, Merrick."

"Is Efa still alive?"

Daphne shrugged. "We don't have any reason to think she's not."

There was a third long, painful silence. I stood again, this time slowly, and began pacing around the table. My whole body felt numb, but through it was breaking a horrible realization.

"I let this happen," I said, halting. "I should have known what he was doing at home. I should have paid more attention. I'm responsible for this."

"No, darling—" Ophelia began.

"No, don't," I said. "I know this is my fault. I failed Efa as her *Brenin*, I let her be hurt by my closest friend. And I let Clara grow up with a monster for a father. And I've been defending him to her all this time."

Ophelia wiped her eyes and Daphne stood, going to put an arm around her waist.

"You didn't know," Ophelia said.

"I'm a hypocrite," I said slowly.

"Merrick, you're not—that doesn't even make sense."

"Yes, it does. I've been talking such a big fucking game about women's rights in the organization, about protecting them. And I was sharing my life for fifteen years with a fucking abuser. Maybe a rapist, I don't know. I don't fucking know anything."

"We don't know he went that far," Daphne interrupted.

I whirled. "I need to go."

I took a step towards the door, but Daphne stepped in front of me. "Where are you going?"

"I'm going home," I said, anger making me reckless. "I'm going to beg forgiveness on my knees before Clara."

"Merrick, stop," Ophelia cried out.

We both turned, shocked. Ophelia was crying, tears etching down her lightly lined face.

"You can't do that," she said. "This is Clara's pain too and you're making it about what you feel."

Shame washed over me and I nodded, stumbling back to the table and sinking down.

"Jesus, you're right. I'm sorry."

Ophelia sat down beside me and her familiar hands curled in mine, holding me for a moment of silence. Then she sniffed and gave me a broken look.

"Edwin had some deep, deep issues," she said. "He loved manipulation, the more complex the better. He liked power, I think he enjoyed the sway he had over you. He liked hurting his wife and making her too ashamed to reveal her abuse because it gave him control."

The sickness in my stomach grew as I adjusted to this information.

"After Efa left, I tracked down his elderly mother," said Daphne softly. "She'd gone no-contact when he turned eighteen because he was so toxic and abusive towards her."

"What was wrong with him?" I breathed.

"I don't think there was anything wrong with him exactly," she said. "He was just an evil, manipulative, seductive person. He hated authority and the desire for power just corrupted him. So he did what had to be done to make himself untouchable."

"So...we were never really close," I murmured. "All of it was just...bullshit."

"You are a powerful man," she said. "Edwin was intelligent, he knew what to say to gain your trust."

There was a long silence and I cleared my throat.

"Was...was Edwin sober?" I asked.

"I would say not, considering Efa said he used to get drunk and verbally abuse her," said Daphne.

"But...but he was sober when I met him," I said. "It was one of the things we bonded over while I was recovering."

My voice cracked. We were all quiet for a long time, just staring down at the table.

"I didn't know him," I said finally.

Daphne cleared her throat. "He had everyone else fooled, it wasn't just you."

"This feels fucking worse than when he died."

No one had an answer to that so I stood up and gathered up my jacket. Ophelia was quiet as I hugged her and Daphne followed me out to the porch. Under the porch light, the hollows under her eyes were apparent.

"I'm sorry, darling," she said. "I wanted to tell you after he died, but I always felt so guilty because Efa asked me not to."

I swallowed. That part, I understood. I had my own secrets that, if revealed, would be just as earth shattering. Secrets that weren't mine to share, but were mine to keep.

"I just feel so stupid," I said.

She shook her head. "Opening yourself up to another person isn't stupid. And it's not your fault he took advantage of your vulnerability and used you."

I nodded once.

"It'll take time to process," she said. "We love you, Merrick. So much, no matter what."

I hugged her and when I drew back, her eyes were wet. She ran a hand over her face and pulled the Audi door open.

"Go on, go home," she said. "I'm sure Clara is waiting for you."

She said it like she knew something. And she probably did. But now wasn't the time to get into the chaos that was my love life.

Not when the rest of it was such a fucking mess.

CHAPTER FORTY-SIX

CLARA

No one had ever hit me before in my life, but that changed in a second when his hand contacted my face hard. Twice. I cried out and he stood there shocked as I hit the wall and slid down to the floor.

My face burned like fire. My eye throbbed.

It was going to bruise badly.

He backed up slowly, holding his hand by the wrist. Gazing down at me like a fucking coward, horrified by what he'd done.

"God, I didn't mean to," he breathed. "I didn't mean that."

I knew it now. That this had never been about anything more than owning me, getting to brag that Merrick Llwyd's ward belonged to him. He'd wanted to own me. Nothing more.

As soon as I wasn't able to be controlled, his pleasant mask had slipped.

Rage flooded me like I'd never felt before. Like someone had pulled the supports from a dam and let the river burst forth like a storm.

Hands shaking, I pushed myself to my knees and crawled upright. Gripping the counter for support. His eyes were wide as he stumbled back towards the doorway. Shaking his head back and forth.

"You've done that before," I whispered.

"What—what did you say?"

I turned on him, eyes dry, face tingling, rage calming to a pillar of ice inside my chest.

"I'm not the first woman you've hurt," I said. "Tell me the truth."

He hesitated and in that split second of silence, I found my answer.

The world went quiet and my father's face swam into my vision. He'd trapped me for so long in the ice cold prison of my childhood home. He'd put a gun to my head and shot down every hope I had of truly trusting anyone.

I was a child then. Unable to fight back.

But I wasn't a child anymore and I had all the power of the Welsh King behind me. I was going to make sure that Osian Cardiff came face-to-face with my rage.

That he felt the full fury of it.

My fingers curled around the drawer, pulling it open, wrapping my hand around the knife handle inside.

It was a large blade, sharp and lethal.

His eyes widened, big and afraid.

"You're insane," he breathed.

"Not insane," I said flatly. "Just fucking tired of taking whatever you give me."

He ducked as the knife flew past him and stuck in the wall. Luckily for me, there was a full set of knives in the drawer.

They littered the kitchen and the hallway as I pursued him into the dark. He ran from me, his fingernails scraping at the lock as he ripped it open. When I ran out of knives, I tore the books from the shelves and rained them down on him.

There were no words, I had no desire to speak with him. That part was over with and all I had was the bitter taste at the end.

Just a dry mouth, no tears, and the anger in my chest.

There was a brass statue in the hallway—it had been there for as long as I could remember. Osian ripped open the front door and stumbled back. I picked up the figure of a man and an angel wrestling. It was solid brass and cold in my hands as I scrambled down the porch to where he'd parked his car.

His brand new sports car with shiny red paint.

The engine revved and I threw it as hard as I could, watching it shatter his back light and smash in the metal around it. Bits of paint and plastic littered the ground as he peeled out of the drive and disappeared into the dark.

"Fuck you," I screamed. "I hope you fucking die."

The world went quiet as I stood there in the rubble. The air smelled sweet, like spring, and I could faintly hear frogs from the pond at the corner of Merrick's garden.

Oh no...Merrick would be home soon. There was no hiding this from him, he would have to know. And when he knew, he would kill Osian.

He might have shielded me from the less savory parts of the organization, but I knew what would happen next. As my male guardian, Merrick now had the right to Osian's life if he chose to take it.

There was a blood debt that had to be paid.

My hands shook as I looked down at my palms. Tracing every line, wondering if I had what it took to sign Osian's death warrant.

But...it didn't really matter if I did or not because as soon as Merrick found out what had happened, he would hunt down Osian. He would kill him tonight, I was sure of it.

Upstairs, my hands shook as I filled the tub and sank into the steamy water. I couldn't find an ice pack, so I wrapped a frozen pack of mixed vegetables in a washcloth and pressed it to my swollen face.

Downstairs, the door banged open. I squeezed my eyes shut as Merrick's steps faltered. Pausing as he took in the mess down the hallway. Then his footfalls continued, but they were soft and steady. Like he was stalking as quietly as a cat down the hall.

My bathroom light was the only one I'd left on, knowing he would come looking for me.

His footfalls came down the hall and my bedroom door creaked open. There was a long, long silence and I wondered if he had left. My scalp prickled and I pushed myself back against the opposite wall of the tub. The pulse in my face quickened, making the bruise throb.

Quick as a flash, Merrick pushed open the door and entered, his gun out. A shriek burst from my lips. We gazed at each other in shock.

"Clara," he said huskily. "Is there anyone else in the house?"

I shook my head.

His whole demeanor changed as he shoved the gun under his belt at the small of his back. He leaned over the tub, wrapping my wet body with a towel, lifting me to sit on the sink.

His eyes fell to the bruise spreading slowly over my face. Heat radiated from my eye, making me squint. His hand came up and almost touched it, but then he stopped himself.

"What happened?" he said.

He was so professional, so controlled. I was infinitely grateful for it. I needed stability right now, not panic and concern.

The hands on my face were so gentle, so tender. Cradling my chin and keeping my eyes on his, locking me into the safety of his gaze.

"Osian came here and I tried to break it off with him. He found out we were sleeping together and things escalated really badly, really fast. He hit me twice with the back of his hand," I said in a rush.

I didn't want to cry. Now that the rage had worn off, emotion reared its head. My eyes stung and I blinked hard, trying to keep the tears at bay.

"Okay," he said calmly. "Did he throw the knives at you?"

"No, no, that was me," I said. "I threw the things. And I'm sorry about your statue, I hope it wasn't worth much."

His fingers raked through my hair, guiding my head to his chest. The front of his shirt was soaked from my wet body, but he didn't seem to care. He just cradled me to his chest.

"My brave girl," he whispered. "I am so sorry this happened."

A hiccup escaped me, followed by a little sob.

"I'm going to call my doctor and have her come here and look at you," he said. "Who would you like to stay with tonight?"

"What?"

"Candice? Let me call her," he said.

"Why not you?"

He lifted me in his arms and picked up a towel, carrying me out and setting me on the bed. I sat there numbly while he dried me off and dressed me in a soft, pink sweatsuit. Then he sank to his knees and there was a grave hardness to his face that chilled me.

"There is a debt that needs paid," he said.

Sobs shook through me, rattling in my chest. He leaned forward and his big, strong arms wrapped around my waist. His head buried in my lap.

"When you cry like this, darling, it brings me to my knees," he said, his voice fragile.

"I'm sorry," I mumbled.

"Don't apologize." He brought my hands to his mouth and kissed my palms. "I have to go now."

"Where are you going?" I asked, although I already knew the answer.

He straightened. "Osian will leave the country if I don't go after him tonight. I won't let him get away with what he did to you."

"What...you're just going to kill him?" I whispered.

"I'll gather Caden and Yale and we'll go and negotiate the terms," he said. "But it'll end the way it always ends for men who put their hands on our women."

The silence between us was deafening. My throat went dry. He was so powerful, so deadly, but he hid it so well behind his unruffled exterior.

"You're so calm," I said. "I thought you would flip out, that you'd be furious."

He blinked and lifted his eyes to mine. My stomach went cold as a shiver moved down my spine.

There it was, that rage I'd expected to see. Rising in him like a tsunami, ready to come crashing down at any moment. Destroying everything in his path.

All the warmth was gone and his eyes went from blue to black. In them, I saw the hell he was capable of unleashing.

I caught a glimpse of the man who had fought in the arena.

"It is not your responsibility to deal with my anger as well as your trauma," he said. "You were hurt. It's my job to make sure you're safe. Then, I'll indulge myself in his blood somewhere else where you never have to see it."

Another shiver split down my spine. My throat felt like it was swelling, knotting up and choking me until tears started falling again.

"Wait, Merrick," I whispered. "Please don't destroy everything you've built."

"Unleash me, Clara," he whispered, eyes glittering. "Let me kill him."

"You'll do it without my blessing," I breathed. "So why ask for it at all."

He took my wrist in his hand and brought it up to his lips. Kissing it softly before wrapping my fingers around his throat.

"I want his blood," he said. "But that debt must be paid of your behalf. Let me go into the night, let me be your monster, because that's the man you love, the man you lie with every night. Taste me, *cariad*, I taste like retribution. I'm a king sitting on a throne of the bodies of murdered men. My soul is dead already...take it and use it to kill Osian Cardiff. You deserve his blood."

I had nothing to say. What were my sputtering words after that speech?

"Unleash me," he whispered, holding my hand tighter. Choking himself with my fingers.

"Merrick," I managed, my tears streaming. "Do what you need to do."

I pulled my hand away and he gave a little gasp, catching his breath.

"Just come back to me," I begged.

He rose and paced across the room. He paused and ran a hand over his face. When he blinked up at me, some of the rage had been put away.

"You are my priority," he said. "I'll always come back to you."

My body tingled, weightless, as I got to my feet and went to him. He pulled me against him and I wrapped my arms around his warm, naked torso and laid my head on his chest. I closed my eyes, listening to his steady heartbeat.

"Where were you?" I whispered.

"I'm so sorry I wasn't here."

"No, it's not your fault," I said quickly. "I didn't mean that. I just wondered where you went."

"I just went to see my aunts."

I nodded and his fingers stroked through my hair for a long time. His breathing evened and I felt mine follow suit as calm settled over me for the first time since Osian had arrived.

Everything would be okay, he was here, he was handling it.

He lifted me and put me in bed, pulling the covers up over my lap. "I'm going to call Candice, alright? I'll have her and her father stay with you."

I nodded. "She's still mad at me."

"Candice will be here right away when she hears what happened," he said. "If there's anyone who might be more angry with Osian, it's her."

He stepped out into the hall and I slid onto my back, staring up at the ceiling. My face still throbbed, but nothing felt more tender and shocked than my heart.

Let me be your monster.

I squeezed my eyes shut, rolling into a fetal position.

If there was a God, I hoped he took mercy on us both.

CHAPTER FORTY-SEVEN

MERRICK

I was still reeling from the revelations about Edwin when I found her, but somehow I managed to keep it together.

She needed stability, comfort, and safety.

The news of Edwin's betrayal had filled me with hurt and confusion. The news that Osian had put his hands on Clara had killed that. Inside, there was nothing but ice and a deadly calm.

And the focused need for blood.

Candice led her down the hall and I heard her bedroom door shut. Owen stood on the opposite side of the table. The kitchen was deathly quiet.

"Are you doing it tonight?" he asked.

I nodded once.

He hesitated, his jaw working. "You know what you're doing, Merrick?"

I glanced over, pulling my jacket off. My fingers were steady as I rolled my sleeves up to my elbow. My clothes were already soaked so what did it matter if I wore them tonight.

"What would you do in my stead, Owen?" I asked harshly.

"The same," he said. "I helped raise Clara, she's like a daughter to me."

"Stay here," I said, taking my gun from the small of my back and passing it to him. "Lock the doors, don't let anyone in. I'll send a handful of soldiers out to stand guard outside the house."

He nodded, checking the magazine and safety before pushing the pistol under his jacket. Then he held out his hand and I shook it, his grip firm.

"Good luck," he said.

"I don't need luck," I said flatly. "I'm the fucking Welsh King and this is my goddamn city."

He must have seen the fire, the sweeping rage, inside because he balked. I spun on my heel and left the house, striding down the steps to the Audi.

On the highway, I called Caden. He picked up on the first ring.

"Yeah? You good?" he said.

I cleared my throat. My knuckles were white on the steering wheel. The road blurred before me, streetlights streaming past.

"Osian put his hands on her," I said.

I heard the bed springs creak.

"Is she okay?"

"She's bruised, but she's not hurt."

"So what are you going to do about it."

"I'm going to kill him," I said coolly. "What did you think I was going to do? Let that fucker put his hands on Clara so I can keep a fucking business deal?"

I heard him set his phone down and then cold metal clinked heavy against a countertop. He was loading his gun.

"Meet me at the warehouse in ten minutes," I said. "And call Yale."

"Fuck, it's been a while since I went hunting," said Caden with psychotic relish.

"No hunting tonight. He'll be easy to find. I'll bet anything he went straight to his father's house to beg for sanctuary."

I hung up the phone. The rage in my chest kept building slowly to a terrifying crescendo. Never in my life had I felt more enraged and ready to burn the world down.

Ten minutes later, I strode into the locker rooms at the warehouse to change. In my office I pulled on a set of black military style pants and a t-shirt. Usually I wore my shoulder holsters because they concealed my weapons, but tonight I didn't need to.

Osian Cardiff knew exactly what I intended to do to him.

The door to the locker room swung open and I stepped out to check who it was. Caden strolled in and pulled his shirt off, revealing his network of tattoos. His hair, normally slicked back, was tousled.

His cobalt eyes were alight.

"Where's Yale?"

The door banged open and Yale walked in, already dressed casually in black pants and a shirt. He had both guns strapped to his waist and a semi automatic over his shoulder.

"I'm not hunting him," I said.

Both their eyes narrowed. Oblivious as always to the indoor smoking policy, Caden dragged a cigarette from his pocket and lit it. He blew two streams through his nose and passed me the cigarette.

"You look like you're about to tear him apart with your bare hands," he said. "Have a smoke, calm down."

Yale's brow jerked up. "You do look like that."

Caden's heavy lidded eyes flickered. They exchanged a glance.

"That's what you intend on doing to him, huh?" Yale said.

I put the cigarette between my teeth, checked the magazine of my pistol, and pushed it into my thigh holster. My head spun slightly as I took a slow drag and passed it back to Caden.

"We're a traditional people," I said. "I'd hate to break with that."

Without waiting for their answer, I walked past them and out into the main room.

"Jesus," said Yale under his breath.

The warehouse doors screeched closed as we left the building and I took the wheel of one our work vehicles, a black jeep. The Cardiff's lived less than fifteen minutes away and we drove in silence the whole way there.

The gates were shut, locked with a heavy bar. I pulled up and took out my phone, dialing Rhys Cardiff.

He picked up right away.

"Merrick, give us a chance to sit down and—"

"Open the gates or I will burn your house to the fucking ground."

I hung up, tossing my phone into the console. There was a moment of silence before the bar slid back slowly and the gates parted. We drove up the dark driveway to the mansion at the end and I stepped out onto the gravel.

Caden joined me with another cigarette hanging from his lips. He needed to quit, but it wasn't my place. Nor was it the time to bring that up. Yale appeared at my other side and paused, his large body looking relaxed, but beneath it all I knew he was tensed up like an arrow waiting to be released.

The lights were on and I thought I saw a flicker of movement, but the door remained firmly closed.

"What a pussy," said Caden. "Hiding behind his daddy."

"I might too if my daddy was as powerful as Rhys Cardiff," said Yale reflectively, eyes passing over the enormous modern house.

"I wouldn't," said Caden flatly.

I glanced at him sharply, but he was staring up at the house with a distant expression. Pulling my attention back to the front door, I took out my gun and unloaded two shots into the soft earth of the garden by the step.

Someone screamed inside and something fell, maybe a chair.

"Come out, Cardiff," I called. "I'll make it quick."

The front door pushed open and Rhys appeared, his pistol up by his shoulder. His eyes were wild, the whites glinting, and he was bathed in sweat, his t-shirt plastered to his body.

I took a step closer and he raised his gun. In one perfectly trained movement, Yale and Caden turned their guns on him and waited.

Waiting for my word like a pair of dogs ready to attack.

"You know what happens now," I called. "There is a debt that must be paid to my household."

"I won't just hand over my son to you, please let's negotiate. I'll give you anything."

"I want retribution for Clara," I said coolly. "I will get it if I have to shoot you dead, burn your house to the ground, and drag your son out. That boy belongs to me, his life is mine to do with as I please."

From behind him, Osian appeared. Shaking like the fucking coward he was, drenched in sweat. His eyes were wide like a panicked deer and his hair hung wet over his forehead.

It took everything I had not to lift my gun and shoot him on the spot.

He had hit her, he had struck her so hard she bruised. Never in my life had I even imagined a scenario where I put my hands on a woman. It was unconscionable. And I was the worst fucking person I knew so there had to be something so dark, so rotted, in this man that he would strike Clara.

I was the Welsh King, the defender of the weak, the scales of justice.

But I was also Merrick Llwyd, trained to kill, to take a life with nothing but my hands.

It was the path Daphne had put me on so many years ago when she told me I was meant for greatness.

This was greatness—twisted, dark greatness.

I lifted my hands to look at my scarred knuckles and my whole body went quiet. My mind pulled me back to the arena when I'd finally pushed myself to my feet. The sand drenched red with blood, some of it mine.

I'd turned my palms over, shocked to see how pure white the bones of my knuckles were through the mangled flesh.

"Please," Osian whimpered.

I jerked back to reality and a slow, cold poison seeped through my body. Everything stilled until there was nothing but the two of us, looking each other in the face.

"Please, God," he begged under his breath.

"There's no God here tonight, no heaven, no hell. I'm not a forgiving man when it comes to Clara," I said softly. "I have no mercy to offer you."

His mouth parted, shaking. Speechless.

I took a slow step towards him, not tearing my eyes away.

"How could you?" I whispered.

He gasped, sweat pouring down his forehead.

"Answer me. How could you do that to her?"

"It was an accident," he panted.

I shook my head, unperturbed. "I've been angry many times, but I've never struck a woman in the face. It was no accident, you've done it before."

The expression on his face confirmed my words. I faltered, the world shifting around me.

Was that what it had been for Edwin too? Just a sick habit? Or had he calculated, carried it out, and reveled in it, all while lying to my face about what kind of man he was?

How had I never looked at either of them and saw what they were capable of?

I'd been deceived by them, made to believe they were both good men.

And in both cases, Clara had borne the consequences.

Without warning, rage erupted behind my eyes like a migraine flashing through my skull. My hand went up, training on Rhys. He drew back against the door, every fiber of his body taut.

"Give me your son. I'm owed his blood," I spat. "Or I'll kill you, I'll kill your father, your brothers, their sons. And I'll burn your bodies right here where you stand."

Osian turned to flee back into the house, but Rhys's arm shot out and he gripped his forearm. His gun came up, pressing to his son's temple. Pure panic and fear rippled behind their eyes.

My work here was done. I knew Rhys had gotten my message loud and clear. I let my gun sink down to my side.

"I'll return his body," I said.

The look on Rhys's face was haunted, trapped like an animal looking down the barrel of a rifle. I turned on my heel, heading for the car. As I passed Yale and Caden, I jerked my head back.

"Take him," I said. "Put him in the back seat."

Caden seized my elbow and I swung around, adrenaline pumping. I could smell the cigarettes on his breath, inches from my face. He put his hand on my shoulder to steady me.

"Let me just shoot him here, Merrick," he said.

"I love her," I breathed. "She deserves revenge."

"I won't have you hate yourself in the morning."

I reached up and gripped his wrist, tearing it from my shoulders. There must have been something truly evil in my eyes because he shrank back like I'd burned him.

"I am your *Brenin*," I said, my voice hoarse.

"Jesus, fuck," he swore under his breath.

"Take him," I said, pivoting and striding across the gravel. "Now."

I didn't look back, but I heard them dragging him across the driveway. My hand shook slightly as I found a cigarette in the console and lit it. My head fell back. Head buzzing, I pulled in the smoke and held it.

The world was quiet save for the soft pleading in the back seat, muffled by the hood.

The stars glinted in the velvety darkness overhead.

In that moment, I wished I could turn back time and pick a different path. I wished I could rage at Daphne, to beg her for answers, plead with her to tell me why she'd put me on this path.

Why had she told a young boy he was destined for greatness?

Because this...this wasn't greatness.

This was just fucking pain.

Back at the warehouse, I stripped off my shirt as Caden and Yale hauled Osian into the basement and strapped him to a chair. Securing his hands behind his back. He was soaked in sweat, shivering. The whites of his eyes bloodshot.

I knelt on one knee before him and he dragged his gaze to mine. His lips cracked open.

"Please," he whispered.

"Have you ever fucked any organization women?" I asked.

His chest heaved, stuck to his shirt. He nodded once.

"How many?"

368

"Three," he croaked.

I reached up and tilted his chin, making him look me full in the face. "And did you put your hands on them too?"

He shuddered and his jaw gritted.

"Silence is a yes, so pick your words," I warned.

"Not all," he snapped. He spat at me, catching me in the jaw.

I wiped it off.

"There is one thing I can't fucking stand," I said evenly. "And it's a wolf in sheep's clothing."

His head lolled to the side. "Like your hands are so fucking clean," he panted. "You fucking murdered twelve people just to be *Brenin*, you sick fuck. Scales of justice, protector of the weak, my ass."

"Twelve is alright," I said. "But thirteen is my lucky number."

I beat him to death with my bare hands. I needed to feel the life slip from him. Yale and Caden stood there in the shadows, eyes down, until it was done. My knuckles split and blood spattered over my naked torso. Pain blurred and rushed up my spine, making my skull buzz.

I swore that in the middle of it, he looked at me out of Edwin's eyes.

But that couldn't be.

I drove home, my split knuckles on the steering wheel leaking blood. I'd found answers in the echo of Rhys Cardiff's scream out into the night as I pushed his son's body onto the dirt at his feet. I found them in the blood that covered my forearms and the ravaged flesh on my knuckles.

Daphne hadn't put me on this path to destroy me, she'd done it to contain the man I would become.

She was a kingmaker and she'd made me king to protect the world from my darkness. Because she trusted my ability to control my anger and my bloodlust, because she knew I could take on the burden of standing between the darkness and the people I loved. Because punishment was the devil's work.

Because she knew this world was no place for weak men.

CHAPTER FORTY-EIGHT

CLARA

I woke with a start, less than an hour after I'd fallen asleep. Candice was fast asleep with just a bit of blonde hair showing under the pink comforter. I lay still for a second before picking up the faint sound of conversation in the kitchen.

Slipping down the hall, I peered around the corner.

My stomach roiled.

Caden stood in the back door, smoking. He was bare chested and flecked with blood, a crimson handprint on his neck. Yale was at the table, his body blocking my view, but I knew Merrick sat on the other side.

I stepped into the kitchen, forgetting I wore only a cami and a pair of panties. Caden glanced over and averted his eyes quickly.

"Merrick," I whispered.

Yale turned sharply, revealing Merrick sitting at the counter with his palms flat. His hair was tousled, falling over his forehead. He was soaked with blood, staining up past his elbows, flecking over his throat and jaw. I took a step closer and my eyes fell, my head spinning.

His knuckles were split open, leaking blood onto the counter. His right hand was halfway sewn up, the black stitches stark against his skin.

The back door slammed. Caden was gone, clearly not interested in sticking around. Yale took another step back and set the needle and thread down.

"You may go," Merrick said softly. "Wait in the living room."

Yale walked past me without a word.

Silence fell. Merrick's eyes met mine and the look in them cut me to the core of my being.

This wasn't my Merrick who had taken me to bed and been so gentle with me when he'd slid down between my thighs. It wasn't the same man who kissed me softly and told me he adored me.

This was the man who had fought in the arena and I didn't know him.

He was frozen, blood leaking down his hands and pooling on the table. I stared at his knuckles as it sunk in what he'd done.

It was thirteen now, thirteen men dead by his bare hands.

"I—are you hurt?" I whispered, backing up.

"Clara," he said. "Go back to bed."

My heart broke when he said that. His voice was cold and it sat low in his chest. Like he didn't know me at all.

Heart aching, I turned and fled into the hall and locked my bedroom door. There was only one thought left in my head.

What happens now?

My heart wasn't just aching, it was tight and getting tighter. I could barely breathe and my heart was beating at an odd, hysterical rhythm. My lips tingled and I couldn't feel my legs.

Panic set in. I needed out. I needed space to think. To recover.

I squeezed my eyes shut and into my mind swam the image of the pine forest in New Hampshire. Spread out below the window, silent beneath the starlit sky. Witness to the first time I'd loved him.

They went upstairs. I heard their footfalls and then his office door shut. I shoved some clothes and my phone in my bag and crept through the house and out to the attached garage.

The door slid up soundlessly, revealing a hot, muggy night. My hands shook as I stowed my bag in the back and slipped into the front seat.

Merrick tracked my car, I knew that. But where was it?

I slid my hands beneath the wheel and by some stroke of luck, I felt it. A little disk with a blinking red light. It came away easily and I threw it into the back of the garage.

Then I put my car in reverse and drove out into the night. Knowing he would be alerted when I opened the gate.

Knowing that the Welsh King would come for me.

CHAPTER FORTY-NINE

CLARA

I stopped once at a gas station on the other side of the New Hampshire border. The woman behind the counter stared at me as she rang up my coffee, cheese danish, and ice pack. I offered her a tight smile and she tore her eyes away, clearly not interested in getting involved.

It was pretty clear that I'd been hit and now I was on the run. Only, the story was a lot more complex than that.

By the time I arrived at the house, the sun was just coming up over the horizon. The temperature had dropped. It was chilly and the sky was clear, stars fading into the distance as it grew lighter.

I grabbed my bag and stepped out of the car, acutely aware of being completely alone. It was healing, this stark silence. The air smelled so good, so pure and fresh. In the distance, spring birds twittered and I could hear a stream bubbling. It must have been frozen last time we were here.

I climbed the steep stairs to the front porch. The same place I'd stripped my clothes and made him want me so badly he took my virginity right there. On the living room rug.

I punched in the code and the door flashed green and I pushed it ajar. Someone had clearly been here since we left because the frame he'd knocked from the wall was fixed. Everything smelled clean and the stain on the carpet was gone.

The silence was loud and getting louder, but I welcomed it.

I needed this time before he arrived to think. To sort through everything I was feeling so I could speak honestly with him.

My future depended on it.

His future depended on it.

I couldn't bring myself to open the door to our shared room, much less sleep in the bed, so I put my bag in the guest bedroom. Then I showered, cleaned myself thoroughly, and put on a clean pair of sweatpants and a white t-shirt.

There were non perishable foods in the cupboards. I made myself a cup of espresso and took a pack of salmon and a bag of asparagus out of the freezer to thaw.

I stood there listening to the milk frother whir, feeling like I was living in another person's body. My hands looked alien as I poured the milk over my espresso and stirred it.

Merrick was on the road, I didn't doubt that. He would be here before the day ended.

I would see his wounds, his stitches, up close.

My hands were steady as I took two Ibuprofen for my face. It had stopped swelling and the puffiness had gone down a lot over the night. As I'd driven, I kept the cold pack in the passenger seat and applied it every fifteen miles for a few minutes. It had worked wonders.

When I was a little girl, Candice's cat had hurt its back leg. We'd spent hours pulling it from under the house so we could take it to the vet and the cat had put up a fight. It didn't want to be inspected and bandaged, it wanted to crawl somewhere where it could be alone and lick its wounds in peace.

I understood that now.

I was doing the same thing. Crawling away to be alone so I could work through the shock quietly.

My feet carried me to the porch. Outside, it was slowly getting warmer and the breeze felt pleasant on my face. I leaned on the railing and sipped my latte and soaked in the view over the pine forest.

Years ago, my father had put that gun to my head and told me he could kill me if he wanted.

He'd told me my life was fragile.

I'd felt the full force of that sentiment in Osian's hand.

Life was so delicate, full of good people and terrible people, full of darkness and light. The world was a confusing, lethal, but sometimes heartrendingly beautiful place.

My lids closed and the wind tickled my hair.

Every moment in the last six years when I'd been truly happy involved Merrick. He'd taken me out of darkness and into light. He existed as his own kind of ecosystem of safety and happiness. In his arms, I was safe to be who I was, to heal, to thrive.

He adored me.

The first time he'd told me he felt something for me, he'd said he *adored* me, not loved me.

That word meant so much more.

I'd wept for him, for the ugly stitches over his knuckles, for the realization that he wasn't gentle with everyone. It was hard to wrap my mind around the knowledge that under the right circumstances Merrick could be far crueler than my father.

"Don't cry for me, cariad. Your tears bring me to my knees."

I hadn't fled from his arms because he scared me. I'd fled because I hadn't understood the depths of what he felt until I saw him deny his anger to put me first. Before anyone and anything.

Until I saw him split his hands open for me.

I should have listened to him when he told me what he felt. He hadn't said he loved me.

He'd said he adored me.

The sun came out and I finished my coffee on the porch. Then I padded upstairs to lay down and read on my phone for a while to clear my mind. In the hallway, I paused outside our shared bedroom.

Housekeeping would have washed the sheets, but I would do anything for just a hint of his scent.

I pushed open the door and my stomach clenched at the familiar sight of the big bed covered in white sheets and a comforter. This was our place, our secret corner of the world. Where he'd made love to me, where he'd called me *cariad*, beneath the stars.

I'd been so innocent then.

I hadn't understood that there were so many things to be and that it would stretch me thin to choose between them.

Was I his ward? His best friend's daughter? His lover? His friend? His future wife?

Because if I didn't choose, I was afraid I'd be nothing at all.

CHAPTER FIFTY

MERRICK

I'd never driven so fast in my life. She'd taken the main tracker out of her car, but she'd kept her phone. It didn't make sense, but I knew she'd been distraught.

My hands gripped the steering wheel. The stitches on my knuckles were dark, surrounded by oozing blood and water. My forearms ached.

The darkness slipped by until my headlights blurred in my vision. I stopped once for coffee and to relieve myself and kept going. She was going to the house and she would be safe, but that didn't stop me from pursuing her as fast as possible.

Clara was not getting away from me now.

I adored her. I was ready to give her my body, my soul. I had been for a long time.

But I wouldn't accept anything less from her. I wouldn't have her wake up years down the road and wish she'd chosen a different path.

She had to come willingly so I never second guessed if she was in my bed by choice. She had to choose me free of the pressure of my violence, my wealth, and my age.

Otherwise, it was bullshit.

Her car was parked in the driveway and the lights were on in the house when I pulled up. I hadn't packed anything, I'd just put my clothes on and left. The only thing I had was my phone so I could track her as I drove.

She hadn't changed the security code. I punched it in and the door swung open. The hallway was empty and the house was quiet as I moved inside and locked the door behind me.

The back door was open. I strode through the kitchen and stepped out onto the deck and stopped short.

The hot tub was uncovered, bubbling hot and smelling of chlorine. She stood in the corner, leaning on the railing. There was a glass of red wine in her left hand, her black fingernails stark against it, and one of my cigarettes in the other.

She was completely naked.

Almost naked— she had on a full face of makeup. Raspberry purple lips, heavily lined eyes, thick, dark lashes. Her hair was done, falling around her shoulders in dark waves.

She was a siren, rising from the water. Beautiful like the inky dark shadows of the forest surrounding us.

"Hey, Merrick," she said.

"Hello," I said, scanning her body. "Clara."

She put the cigarette to her mouth and inhaled deeply, letting her head fall back. Smoke streamed from her glossed lips.

"Took you a long time to get here."

"I came as quickly as I could."

"Stop along the way?"

"Once."

"Why?" Her lashes flickered.

I shrugged, stepping closer. "Needed to take a piss."

She tilted her head, staring at me hard. There was something different in her eyes, a wariness that hadn't been there before.

"He's dead. Isn't he?"

I nodded.

She moved through the water to the edge and beckoned me. I went and she took my hands and turned them over to look at my knuckles. They were scabbed over, swollen, and ugly beside her pretty fingers.

"Clara."

Her eyes jerked up.

"Did you run from me because I frighten you?"

Her brow arced and her shoulders went back. "Do I look afraid?"

"Why then?"

She was silent for a long moment. Then she lifted her eyes to mine and they were calm.

"Adele said you were a good man who does bad things. It didn't make sense to me then, but it makes sense now."

I took the cigarette from her fingers and pulled from it. Releasing the smoke and handing it back.

"I ran because it's time for me to make my choice," she whispered. "And that part scares me a little."

"It doesn't scare me," I said. "The first night you slept in my bed, I got up and went out to look at engagement jewelry. Then I started thinking how stupid that was when you could still choose Osian."

"I don't think I was ever going to choose Osian."

"Neither did I," I said. "But just in case, I fucking killed him."

Her jaw dropped and the stunned silence was loud.

She turned as she put the cigarette back to her mouth. I was completely distracted and hard in my pants. Entranced by her naked, wet body and that lipstick stained cigarette balanced in her fingers.

Fuck, I'd do anything to be that cigarette.

"I shouldn't have given you the choice between Osian and I. Sometimes I wish I'd been more selfish and cared less."

Her jaw dropped.

"If I had been more selfish, I'd have gotten rid of Osian a lot sooner. And he never would have put his hands on you."

"Merrick," she said, her voice thick. "What Osian did was Osian's fault. No one else is to blame."

"I understand that in here," I said, tapping my temple.

"But you don't really believe it."

"That's not your problem to deal with," I said quickly. "Right now, in this moment, all I want to know is how do I get you to say yes to me."

Her eyes widened and she dropped the cigarette in her wine and set it aside. The water sloshed around her thighs as she moved to the edge of the tub. Stopping just inches from me.

Steam rose in a thick cloud between us. My heart quickened.

"Say yes to what?" she whispered.

'Being my wife," I said. "You said it was time to make your choice." The words tasted so sweet, so overdue.

"You love me that much?"

"Darling, I love you so much more than that," I said, taking hold of her waist and pulling her wet body against mine. Our breath mingled and her mouth tasted of wine and chlorine as I kissed it.

"You adore me?" she breathed.

"I adore you the way I have never adored anyone before. When I kissed you for the first time, I realized that everything up until then was just wasting time. You kissed me back and I've been tripping over myself ever since, trying to figure out ways to adore you more deeply every day. You make me a love drunk fuck-up and I don't mind. I never want to get up in the morning or sleep at night because I don't want to miss a moment of you."

I hadn't planned the speech, but it rolled out of me all at once. I half expected her to laugh, but she didn't. Her lip trembled, her eyes big and vulnerable. Then she grabbed the front of my shirt and kissed me hard.

I felt her yes, her enthusiastic yes that defied all barriers.

Her yes that made the world stop just for us, that made the stars and planets step aside just to make room for her to adore me back.

I pulled away, panting.

"Be my wife," I demanded.

Her lip trembled. "But what about...what about the deal with the Cardiffs?"

"I'd say that ship has sailed, don't you think?"

"But...how will you get the money you need if you marry me instead of arranging my marriage to someone else?" she asked, her voice small.

I had no fucking clue, but it didn't matter anymore. "Caden said he had some ideas," I said recklessly. "Now, say you'll marry me."

"Fine, alright," she said, kissing me through her smile. "Fine, I'll marry you, I guess."

I pulled her naked and soaked into my arms and she wrapped her legs around my waist.

"That's my girl," I breathed. "Now, I'm fucking you upstairs and then we'll talk."

It took far too long to get her up the stairs and into the bed we'd shared all those weeks ago. Her fingers tore at my clothes, ripping them to the ground. Then our bodies slid beneath the covers together and her thighs parted.

Her spine arced and she gasped, her eyes going soft, as I pushed inside her. Heat enveloped me, so hot and familiar, like finally coming home. Like all the broken, open ended bits of my life had finally come to some perfect conclusion.

"Oh my God," she breathed, clenching around me.

"Fuck, I know," I said, kissing her forehead.

We didn't speak, we didn't have to. The warm afternoon sunlight spilled in through the window as I rocked inside her, keeping us both on the edge for a long time.

My knuckles split and blood stained the white pillowcase behind her head. But it didn't matter because it didn't matter what had happened yesterday or the day before, or what was in store tomorrow. All that mattered was the woman beneath me, the woman who had accepted me completely.

Without reservation.

I plied her clit until she came and my orgasm followed soon after. Then we lay in a haze, murmuring the sweetest things into the space between the sheets where only we could hear them.

Euphoria. Perfection.

All those words were too weak to describe this feeling.

This was the beginning of the rest of my life.

I rolled onto her and we made love again, this time quickly and breathlessly. When we were done, we lay together and I slid my hand down between her thighs and touched her clit.

"Do you want me to have you pierced here, *cariad*?"

"Yes, please," she said without hesitation. "When we get back."

I shook my head. "Let's wait."

She frowned as I rose. "Why?"

"Because you have to abstain for a bit after being pierced," I said. "And I don't want to abstain, I want to fuck my fiancée as often as possible for the next month or so. After that, we can get it done."

It was getting late and the outside world faded away with the sunset. We had dinner and went out on the back patio. She was beautiful in the hot tub, her soft curves glittering with water and her diamonds gleaming on her naked body.

I got on my knees and made her count orgasms until her knees gave out.

CHAPTER FIFTY-ONE

CLARA

When I woke the next morning, he was gone. I pulled on his shirt and padded downstairs to find him in the kitchen with a cup of coffee before him. He didn't have his laptop, he was just staring into space. His phone sat a foot away, facedown.

"Hey," I said softly.

He started, blinking.

"Good morning," he said, his voice hoarse.

Feeling okay?" I said, leaning over the counter to kiss him.

His kiss was all wrong. A bit rushed and his energy was strange. Almost agitated. My stomach dropped.

"Yeah," he said, rising to pour me some coffee. "But I think we should talk about the future. Now. I want to get some things out of the way."

My heart sank as I sat down. My fingers were cold, tangled in my lap.

"What happened?" I whispered.

"Nothing," he said, handing me a mug. "But if we're getting married, I have to be completely truthful with you and, up until now, I didn't have permission."

"You're scaring me," I whispered.

His arms slid around me, pulling me to his chest. His chin rested on my hair.

"I'm not leaving you, *cariad*," he said. "Ever. This is about the future you had planned before you went to college. We need to talk about children."

I pulled back so I could look him in the eye. He'd gathered himself and his hands felt steady on my waist.

"Do you want kids?" I asked, sniffing.

His lips parted and he looked like he wanted to say something, but it was getting stuck. There was a short silence and I was beginning to think I knew the answer to his question.

"Have a seat," he said, guiding me to the stool. "Before I answer that, I need to discuss something else."

I sat, gripping the countertop until my knuckles went white. He circled the table and leaned over it opposite me. His eyes were deadly serious and they scared me to my core.

What was it? Had he had a vasectomy and he'd been hiding it?

"Merrick," I said. "Tell me what the fuck is going on."

His lean fingers rubbed together. His eyes were a deep blue, almost black. The way they always were when he got reflective.

"There were some things that happened a while ago that made me change my mind about what I wanted for my future," he said.

"Is this something about my father?" I whispered, tears brimming.

"No, no," he said swiftly.

"Merrick," I begged. "Just tell me."

He looked like he was about to throw up.

"I have a son," he said in a rush.

My entire body went numb as shock moved through it in a ripple. My jaw went slack and a slow roaring sound began in my ears.

I peeled my mouth open, my dry tongue tingling.

"What?"

His eyes were wide and vulnerable. Pleading with me.

"I have a son," he said, his voice hoarse.

"And...and you never told me this before," I whispered. "You lied to me, Merrick."

"No," he said. "I'm not the only one involved in this. I was always fine with telling everyone, but he doesn't want anyone to know I'm his father. I didn't raise him, I didn't even know he existed until about a decade ago."

"You could have told me," I said.

Why did this hurt so badly?

Because it felt like he didn't trust me?

"I was a failure as a father," he said. "Not on purpose, I just didn't know I even was one. His mother didn't want him involved with the organization so she concealed him from me. I met him around the time I met your father."

My body felt like it was floating and my stomach felt sick.

"Who is his mother?" I asked. "Do you have contact with her?"

He shook his head once. "She passed away and I didn't know her well."

"She was an outsider?"

He nodded.

"What happened to him?" I asked flatly. "Your son."

Merrick took a deep breath and released it. He leaned on the counter and turned those gorgeous, heartbreaking eyes on me.

"Nothing, he's fine," he said.

"So you just...let him go on living his life alone after his mother died?"

"No," he said. "I'm not that much of a fuck up. No, I finished raising him insofar as I could...he was basically an adult when I met him. But he is very determined that no one know he's my son."

I was sputtering, unable to fully wrap my brain around this news.

"So...so who knows?"

"You, me," he said. "And him."

"So Ophelia and Daphne don't even know?"

He shook his head. "That kills me sometimes because they always wanted grandchildren, but I'm his father and my duty is to respect his wishes and protect his identity."

There was a short silence as we stared at each other. He'd wiped my brain clean and there were too many roiling emotions in my chest for me to even realize what I was feeling.

"Who is he?" I whispered. "Where does he live? How old is he?"

His jaw worked. "I spoke with him and he gave permission for me to tell you so long as you signed an NDA afterwards."

I gaped at him. "Merrick, I'm going to be your wife."

His eyes flashed.

"And he's my son, Clara," he said. "It's my duty to protect him. I signed an NDA too."

I took a beat and breathed in deep, releasing it slowly. When I opened my eyes, he was pacing back and forth, his hands on his hips.

"I understand," I said evenly. "I'll sign the NDA."

His shoulder relaxed. "Thank you, *cariad*."

"So where is he now?"

He stopped pacing and returned to the table. His energy was all over the place, still jittery and unfocused. His eyes were pleading as he laid out his palms and I placed my hands in them. Praying this wouldn't change anything.

"He's here in Providence," Merrick said softly. "It's Caden."

I shot to my feet.

"What?"

"I don't know how no one has figured it out," Merrick said. "We both have the same hair and eye color and we're around the same height. I got a paternity test when he showed up and he's definitely mine."

I just stood there like an idiot, wringing my hands and running over every interaction I'd had with Caden in my mind.

"That makes sense," I whispered.

"What does?"

I jerked my head up. "At the auction, Caden pulled me aside and he told me not to hurt you. I remember thinking he was so protective of you and I thought it was weird because he's such an...asshole most of the time."

Merrick's brow rose. "He can be."

My feet ached as I paced back and forth, my knuckles raw from rubbing them with my thumb.

"Baby," Merrick said softly.

I paused, looking up.

"Don't chew your mouth."

I hadn't realized I was, or that blood had blossomed on my tongue.

"It's fine," I whispered.

"Was that all he said?"

I shook my head, resuming my pacing. "He wanted us to get together, he said it was the happiest he'd ever seen you."

A ghost of a smile moved over Merrick's face. "He's always been very supportive of us being together."

"Does he blame you?"

"Blame me?"

"For not being there."

A flicker of pain moved through his eyes. "No, thank God. It was his mother who deliberately kept us apart, not me. And as soon as I learned about him, I brought him here and he started training to join the organization."

"So...so he's not a magician?"

Merrick laughed. "No, he's just a very talented asshole with a massive chip on his shoulder about being my son."

"But if he doesn't blame you...why does he care?"

"He wants to be his own man," said Merrick.

Some of the shock was wearing off and I was left feeling numb, but relieved. This wasn't that bad, we could work with it. Of course, it would definitely be an adjustment.

"That feels weird," I said. "Caden is older than me."

"I had him very young," Merrick said. "My pull out game was a lot weaker then."

"Did you know his mother well at the time?"

"She was a friend of a friend," he said. "We hooked up a handful of times and then she disappeared and I never thought anything of it."

He was less jittery, but now he was looking at me like a lost puppy. Like he'd do anything for me to assure him that everything was fine.

I swallowed back the whirlwind of emotions still raging in me and went to him, sliding my arms around his waist.

"I'm sure it's very hard for you to keep this a secret," I said.

"I have to," he said, fingers ghosting through my hair. "He deserves privacy if that's what he really wants. But the main reason I told you is because...well, I don't think I want anymore children."

There was a short silence and, to my surprise, a wave of the most intense relief washed over my body.

"I don't know if I want to have children anymore," I said quietly.

His eyes darted to mine. "Why?"

I chewed my mouth and he touched my jaw, stopping me.

"Because you are all I've ever wanted, Merrick," I said. "I don't think having children together is part of our story."

He bent, brushing his lips against my forehead.

"I don't think so either," he said, his voice thick with emotion. "But I'm still going to give it a few years before I do anything permanent."

"Permanent?"

"Like getting snipped."

"Oh," I said softly. "Okay, I think that's a good idea. Waiting for a bit, just to be sure."

I met his gaze and it hit me that Merrick wasn't alright. He was doing everything he could to stay calm and in control, but when I gazed into his eyes, I saw a flicker of something haunting.

Pain. Grief. Shock.

My jaw jerked and I bit down hard on that spot. Too hard. Blood filled my mouth and I felt it slip down my chin.

"Fuck," Merrick said, shooting to his feet and grabbing a towel. He cradled my head, pressing the towel to my mouth. "Jesus, baby, why do you do that to yourself?"

I couldn't speak. He pulled me close and gently pried my mouth apart, revealing the mangled scar inside my lower lip.

"*Cariad*," he whispered.

I told him how my father had put a gun to my head and he was quiet, eyes fastened to me. When I was done, he picked me up and carried me to the upstairs bathroom and set me on the sink.

I winced as he dabbed my mouth with a cold washcloth.

"Are you just...not going to say anything?" I whispered.

He glanced up and I saw that deadly violence in his eyes. This time it didn't scare me.

"I wish I had killed him," he said flatly.

My whole body went still. It was the first time I'd ever heard him speak badly of my father.

"Do you actually?"

He nodded once. "But we're not talking about this right now."

True to his word, he shut up and refused to speak of it. It was a little strange for him and I could tell there was something he wasn't telling me. But I was spent, completely worn out.

He ran a hot bath and slid into it with me, pulling me onto his lap. Wrapping my legs around his waist and laying my head on his shoulder.

"I adore you," he said.

His words didn't heal us, but they were the first step there.

"I adore you too," I whispered.

CHAPTER FIFTY-TWO

MERRICK

I told her about her father in the car on the drive back. It took everything I had not to let the bitterness creep into my voice. Not to reveal how fucking betrayed and disoriented I felt knowing a friendship I valued so deeply was fake.

Knowing I'd been so eager to trust that I'd let myself be used for years.

She sat curled in the seat and stared through the dark windshield. When I'd told her everything, I let her sit silently for several minutes and process.

She took a shaky breath.

"I'm sorry," she said.

"I'm fine," I said quickly. "I'm just sorry you had to grow up the way you did. I'm sorry I never saw who Edwin was and I'm fucking sorry I ever defended him to you when he put a fucking gun to your head. I never saw myself as particularly gullible, but I guess I was wrong."

"This isn't you fault."

"It is—"

She shifted, turned to face me. Her eyes simmered, dark and full of unexpected energy.

"No, don't fucking say that," she said. "I lived with him and I never imagined he was that manipulative. I thought he was just cold and fucked up. It's not either of our faults that he was an evil person."

"Clara—"

She brushed her fingertips over my arm, silencing me.

"I don't want to dwell on this, Merrick," she said hoarsely. "This spring has been so good, the best few months of my life. Even with everything that happened with Osian. It felt like a dream and I keep waking up at night wondering when it's going to have to end. But...when you said you wanted to marry me, it hit me."

Her fists were clenched in her lap. I waited for a beat. It was so hard to get her to open herself up to me and I didn't want to scare her off.

"What hit you?"

"That it's not a dream. That if I just choose this life I get to be happy and I get to be your wife."

She started crying, hiccuping, trying to keep it in. I put my hand on her thigh and gripped her gently.

"I want to look back in thirty years and realize I really lived. Without all the coldness and guilt I grew up in. I want to take pictures of us outside our stupid white picket fence house and in our topless car. I want to realize that I have something good and not waste a single second of it."

There was a long silence and I cleared my throat.

"I'll give you that," I said. "I'll give you everything."

"Do you think it's stupid?"

I threaded my fingers through hers and brought her knuckles to my lips. Her mouth curved in a watery smile.

"Never. I think you are a woman who knows exactly what she wants," I said. "And that's why I love you, *cariad*."

There was a long silence as we drove through the darkness. Her fingers twisted tightly in mine, almost painfully.

"Make me a deal," I said.

"Okay," she said hesitantly.

"Start seeing Gretchen once a week for at least six months," I said firmly. "I don't want all this...shit to just sit in your head and get worse and then erupt later. You need to deal with it now, but you can do it at your pace with a therapist."

I expected her to balk at the prospect, but she nodded.

"I think that would be good. I...I think I'm ready to start talking about it."

"Thank you," I said. "That means a lot to me. There's one more thing."

She gave a little sigh. "What is it?"

"Do you want me to look for your mother?"

I glanced at her, watching as her profile went as still as a statue. Then her throat bobbed and her fingers twisted in her lap.

"No," she said, her voice as fragile as a snowflake. "If she'd wanted to come back, she would have. All it would have taken was a quick online search to find out my father was dead."

There was a lot of pain behind her words, but there was also resignation. She'd thought it over before, I could tell.

"I want to move forward, Merrick," she whispered. "I don't want to look back."

I glanced down, my eyes catching on the tattoo above my wrist. Fuck...I'd forgotten about that. Distracted, I kept glancing up and down, trying to keep my eyes on the road. The ink beneath my skin felt like it was crawling.

"Are you okay?" she asked.

"The tattoo on my wrist," I said. "Edwin had one just like it. It's Welsh, it means 'brothers in arms.'"

Her eyes drifted down and I saw her throat bob. Her lips compressed and she took a quick breath. "It's okay," she said.

"No," I said. "I'm getting it covered up."

"It's your body," she said firmly. "If that's what you want to do, do it. But do it for you, not for me."

She was so fucking strong. I reached over the console and took her hand in mine, threading my fingers through it. Holding her tightly as we drove on through the night.

We returned to an empty house and I brought her luggage upstairs to the bedroom. She got ready for bed while I showered and then I pulled her close between the sheets.

"You are the best thing that's ever happened to me, Clara Prothero," I said. "I'm so fucking sorry that my life is messy, I'm sorry I had to keep secrets from you. And I'm sorry I was ever friends with Edwin."

"I'm not," she whispered. "If you hadn't been, we never would have met."

"That's some good from a shitty situation."

She wound her hands around my neck, pressing my head to her breasts. I loved feeling her like this, her hands in my hair, her heart beating under my ear.

"Make love to me," she whispered.

It started out slow, our bodies entangled. The window was open and cool air wafted through as I slid down between her legs. She kept her thighs spread for me, her eyes sleepy while I ate her out.

It felt like we'd passed some kind of test.

She didn't come, but I didn't mind. I was doing this for comfort more than pleasure. I fucked her gently with my hand on her throat, holding her in my arms. Keeping her close to me.

"Are you mine now that all your secrets have been spilled?" she breathed. "Or will there always be space between us?"

I kissed her forehead.

"I'm done with that. No secrets, no spaces," I whispered. "I'm yours forever."

CHAPTER FIFTY-THREE

MERRICK

The morning after we returned, I rose early and left Clara sleeping and went to Daphne and Ophelia's house. My body and mind were raw from the last few days. Raw, but euphoric because the Welsh Princess was mine.

I knocked on the door and it took almost ten minutes for Daphne to put her head out, her pistol held down by her side. Old habits died hard.

When she saw me, she swung open the door. It was barely seven and she still wore her bathrobe, tied at her waist. Ophelia stood at the far end of the hall in her nightgown.

"Merrick," Daphne said. "Oh no...God, what's wrong?"

"Nothing," I said. "Everything is fine. Can I have some coffee?"

They exchanged a look of concern, but Daphne stepped aside and let me in. Ophelia made coffee in the kitchen and brought it out to the porch so we could sit in the pale light of the rising sun.

"Alright," said Ophelia, narrowing her eyes at me. "Why are you here so early?"

I looked between them and soft warmth blossomed in my chest. God, I was so lucky to have them. Despite how Ophelia worried about me and despite how hard Daphne had been on me, I wouldn't have wanted to be raised by anyone else.

I owed so much to them. Daphne had made me strong, she'd let me embrace my dark side. Ophelia had kept me gentle enough so someday I could be worthy of a woman like Clara.

"I'm getting married," I said.

Their jaws fell open in unison. Ophelia groped blindly for her wife's hand, gripping it until her knuckles paled.

"To who?" she squeaked.

"Clara," I said.

The porch was mayhem for a good five minutes. Ophelia shot to her feet, wrapping her arms around my neck, crying into my chest. Daphne sat back with a smug expression on her face and sipped her coffee.

"I thought you might eventually," she said.

Ophelia untangled herself from my arms and kissed my jaw. "I'm so happy, darling," she said, wiping her face.

"There's something else," I said.

Last night, before I joined Clara in our bedroom, I'd called Caden again. He was reluctant to grant my second request, but after a solid thirty minutes of convincing, he'd agreed. I could finally tell my aunts about him, so long as they signed the NDA too. I knew they would so I agreed.

Daphne's face sobered as she caught the look on my face. She leaned in, eyes narrowed.

"What is it?"

I shifted back and crossed one leg over the other. I had to clear my throat twice before I could speak.

"I have a son," I said.

Ophelia gasped. "You mean...Clara's pregnant?"

I shook my head. "No, I have an adult son. I met him over a decade ago."

Their expressions changed as this information sank in, both sobering. Ophelia shifted in the bench beside me and sent me a long, calculating stare.

"And you hid this from us?" she whispered.

"You have no room to judge me for that," I said firmly.

Her lips parted and then she shut them. There was a long, painful silence and Ophelia returned to sit beside her wife. They exchanged a quick glance.

"Who is your son?" Daphne asked gently.

"Caden," I said, my ears starting to burn. The last thing I wanted was to discuss the fact that I'd gotten a girl pregnant when I was seventeen because I was too stupid to wear a condom.

"How...how old were you?" Daphne asked.

"Seventeen," I said.

"Oh my," Ophelia whispered. "Well...that's disappointing."

Daphne elbowed her in the ribs and she scowled.

"What?" she snapped. "He got someone pregnant when he was a teenager. Of course I'm disappointed."

Before they could start arguing, I lifted a hand.

"I think we can all agree that I've made a lot of mistakes," I said. "And I'm sorry for them. I'm sorry I drank, sorry I did drugs, sorry I knocked someone up and had to keep it from you for years. I'm sorry for all the pain and the heartache I caused you both."

To my surprise, they both got up and sat on either side of me. Ophelia wrapped her arm around my waist and rested her head on my shoulder and Daphne rubbed my upper back.

"Hush," she said. "You're our son. We love you, no matter what."

My throat felt like it was closing up as I looked up into the rising sun. This was the line that had held me back from becoming a true monster. This was the only reason I was capable of loving Clara as deeply and an unconditionally as I did.

"Now, tell us the details," said Ophelia, after a while. "I want to hear about your son and then I want to hear all about Clara."

We talked for another hour and Ophelia made me a cup of coffee to-go. They stood on the porch and waved as I drove down to the road. As I got on the highway, my body was lighter and my head clearer.

Now, I just had to deal with the catastrophic fallout of killing Osian Cardiff and losing my deal with his family.

Instead of heading home to Clara, I made a detour and parked at my office in the city. Caden lived a few blocks down in a lofted apartment several stories up. I stopped at a bakery on the way and picked up two black coffees and rode the elevator up to the sixth floor.

I knocked on the door and there was a long silence.

Maybe I should have called first.

The door cracked and Caden's eye appeared. He blinked and it swung open to reveal the rest of him. Wearing only a pair of sweatpants and the tattoos that covered half his body and his throat, up to his jaw. His hair was tousled.

He stared at me for a long moment.

"Not a good time," he said.

"We need to talk," I said.

"I talked to you last night."

"No, we need to talk about the Cardiffs."

He blinked and stepped back. "Okay, come in at your own risk."

I usually avoided Caden's apartment because it was fucking weird. He had a large collection of weapons that he kept locked in a glass case on the wall. In the center of the room was a huge table made of a slab of marble and overhead hung a chandelier of steel and the bones of what I assumed were animals.

What I *hoped* were animals.

The sun cut through the floor-to-ceiling windows, shedding light over the Turkish rugs and the low couches in the living space. The bedroom door was shut.

"Is that my coffee?" he asked.

I passed a cup to him. "You said that you would figure out how to get the funding we need for Wyoming. Can you actually do it?"

Caden shrugged. "Sure."

"Do you mean that?" I frowned.

"Yeah, sure, I can get it," he said. "Just get someone to cover my organization work and I can get you another patron."

I leaned on the table, the cold marble radiating through my sleeves. "How can you be so sure?"

Caden took a cigarette from the pack over the sink and lit it, breathing in the smoke. He tilted his head back, gazing up at the ceiling.

"I'm very good at getting what I want," he said.

"Do you have a plan?"

"No, not yet," he said. "But give me a week and I'll have one."

I gazed at him for a moment and shook my head. "For whatever reason, I believe you."

"Because I'm fucking good at what I do," he said.

"Watch that ego," I said. "It'll trip you up someday."

There was a scuffing sound from the bedroom and the door pushed open. A blonde woman and a slender, shirtless man, both in their mid-thirties, walked out and stopped short.

I turned. "I didn't know you had guests."

"Yeah," Caden said. "I do."

Another woman, older than the others, appeared behind them and froze. I stared at her for a moment until I realized that I recognized her. It had been over ten years, but I had definitely hooked up with her at some point even though I couldn't remember her name.

"Oh," I said. "No, you're right. Bad time. I'm leaving."

I grabbed my coffee and ducked out. He followed me into the hall and shut the door.

"Hey, when are you sending me out to Wyoming?" he said.

I paused on the stairs. "After you get the funding."

He put his cigarette to his lips and expelled the smoke. His dark blue eyes were distant as he fixed them on me. "Good," he said. "I'm going fucking crazy in this city. I need some space, something to work on. There's only so many orgies I can attend before it gets boring."

"Please don't," I said, wincing. "And wear a condom."

He laughed, shaking his head. "Learned that the hard way, huh?"

I sobered. "I got lucky," I said. "I'm proud of my son."

He rarely wanted me to treat him like he was my son and I knew I'd make him uncomfortable with that statement, but I needed him to hear it. He nodded once and went back into the apartment, shutting the door.

I sighed, a bolt of fear shivering down my spine. I'd tried to be patient with him for years, I'd done everything his way. It was the least I could do after he'd grown up without a father.

But deep down, I was so fucking scared that we would go on like this forever.

CHAPTER FIFTY-FOUR

CLARA

I sat cross-legged on the floor. Gretchen was in her chair, twirling her pen. We'd just started our first session and I could already tell why Merrick liked her. She was nice and she hadn't blinked when I asked her for a cup of hot chocolate with whipped cream.

"I probably need a lot of therapy," I admitted.

She took a sip of her herbal tea.

"That's alright," she said. "Let's get started with me asking you some questions. I find that can be more helpful with clients who've never had therapy."

"Okay," I said, settling back. I'd worn my favorite pink sweatshirt and shorts. My feet were bare, my sandals laying by the door.

"How's your sex life going?"

I felt my brows shoot up.

"My methods can be unorthodox," she said. "I want this session to be about the things you love, the things that give you joy."

"And next week?"

"Next week, we'll cover the things that are holding you back."

"Okay," I said slowly. "Sorry, this is really weird for me."

Gretchen settled back, crossing one leg over the other. "I've heard it all, Clara. Nothing you say can shock me."

I put my finger in my whipped cream and licked it off. My nails were dark pink, the same color as my shirt, and covered with rhinestones.

"We have good sex," I said. "Great sex. Like...better sex than I ever thought I would have with anyone."

"What word would you use to describe your partner in bed?"

"Giving."

"And that's good for you?"

I nodded. "Of course. He likes just giving...and giving...sometimes giving a little too much, but that's okay."

Her mouth twitched. "And what does that do for you emotionally?"

I sobered, fixing my eyes above her head.

"It makes me feel...like my needs matter," I said. "Like, he loves me so much that fulfilling my needs fulfills his...and that feels really good."

"What else does he do that makes you feel that way?" she asked. "Outside the bedroom."

I didn't have to think about it.

"Everything," I said.

Her lips pressed together. "Hmm. Now, do you think Merrick has faults?"

"He tries to fix everything," I said. "And he...he gets so wrapped up in trying to be everything for everyone that sometimes he makes mistakes. He's made some big mistakes that way. Ones that really hurt people."

"How does that affect you?" she said. "Also, I like how perceptive you are. It's making my job easier."

"Thanks," I said. "I don't know how it will affect us moving forward, but it's definitely caused problems in the past."

"But you are aware of it," she said. "And that's good. Now, what are your biggest faults?"

I started to chew my mouth and stopped, taking a deep breath.

"I'm selfish," I said. "And closed off."

Her brow arced. "Selfish?"

I swallowed, my throat dry. "I like being pretty, being taken care of, being spoiled. I like all the attention Merrick gives me, I like that he spends so much time making me feel good in bed."

"So you want him to make you feel like a princess?"

I nodded, dropping my eyes.

"Why is that bad?" she asked.

Wait...what?

"Um...because it's selfish," I said. "All I want out of my life is to be happy and taken care of. I don't want to do anything grandiose."

Gretchen shifted in her chair and closed her notepad. She folded her hands in her lap, a slight smile on her mouth.

"Those aren't bad things to want," she said. "You've been through a lot. There is nothing wrong with wanting to be happy. Just make sure that you're holding up your side of your relationship."

"How do I do that?"

"Merrick takes care of you," she said. "Just make sure you're taking care of him too."

We talked for a while after that and then I left, feeling oddly hollow. Like I'd unzipped my brain and emptied everything onto the floor of Gretchen's office.

That night, we had dinner at the restaurant on the east side. The first place we'd ever gone together.

"How was your session?" he asked.

"Good," I said, looking at him through the candlelight. "She asked about my sex life and I said you were horrible in bed."

His brow shot up.

"Kidding," I said quickly.

"You're a menace," he said. "I don't care anyway. You're going, that's all I care about."

I slipped my foot out of my heel and slid it up his leg under the table. His eyes narrowed and he shifted, parting his legs further. Letting me stroke up his thigh and find the hard ridge beneath his zipper.

"When are you going to marry me?" I asked.

He reached into his pocket and took out a black velvet box and slid it over the table. I froze, my heart thumping.

"Open it," he ordered.

I obeyed, revealing a full set of engagement jewelry. Yellow gold and fine diamonds. So delicate it took my breath away. I glanced up at him and his lids were heavy, his eyes hungry.

"I made an appointment for you," he said.

I swallowed, heart thumping. "To get pierced?"

He nodded once.

"Can you go with me?" I whispered.

"Traditionally the man doesn't. Usually only women go, so I would ask Candice to accompany you."

"When is it?"

"August," he said. "If you'd like, I think September would be a good month to have the wedding."

"Okay," I said slowly. "That sounds perfect."

He cocked his head. "Is this what you want, *cariad*?"

"Yes," I said, without hesitating. "This is what I want."

CHAPTER FIFTY-FIVE

MERRICK

Clara and Candice went out together a few weeks after we returned from New Hampshire. They had a lot of catching up to do so I had Yale and Caden take them out to the club. Before she left, Clara promised not to drink and I believed her. She'd stopped except for the weekends and a glass of wine at dinner.

Work was beating my ass. Cleaning up the mess from breaking the deal with the Cardiffs and losing the deal kept me up until well past midnight. I'd lost a handful of deals with some of Rhys Cardiff's friends and there was a general distrust that was going to take time to undo.

All work in Wyoming was put on hold. For the last few weeks, I had no idea where we'd get the funding for the expansion, but Caden made it his top priority. Yale took over his organization duties and Caden put himself on a plane a day for the next week, meeting with top billionaires all over the world.

He'd returned with several promising opportunities. I'd spent most of the day in a meeting with a potential investor and left encouraged, but exhausted. It looked like we might get our funding after all.

After everyone had left for the club, I went upstairs to my study and poured a drink and lit a cigarette.

On the opposite wall, the curtain covering Edwin's portrait stared me down. Holding me in its grasp.

I downed the whiskey and crossed the room and jerked it ajar. Edwin's tall, angular face looked down at me. Eyes stern, shoulders back. Looking every bit the perfect Welsh soldier.

Before Clara, this painting had always made me feel safe, watched over. But now that I knew what he'd done to both of us, it felt like mockery.

Poison crept into my veins, coupled with desperate rage.

"Fuck you," I breathed.

My feet carried me to the bedroom closet down the hall and I gathered up his knives and returned to the study. Leaving all the doors open because...fuck it, Clara wouldn't be back till midnight.

This was my secret. My opportunity to let my pain show.

I lit a cigarette and sank into the chair, propping my feet up on the desk. Edwin gazed at me blankly. Gone for six years and yet so alive in this room tonight.

The knives lay in a pile in the drawer at my side. I'd moved them a few weeks ago. My fingers closed around the one Clara had found that day. The one she'd said belonged to her. I leaned back, cigarette burning on the ashtray, and balanced it between my two index fingers.

"I hope that wherever you are...I hope it hurts," I said, my voice husky.

It felt unnatural, talking to a ghost.

But it also felt good.

"She trusts me," I said aloud, keeping my eyes on the blade. "She sleeps in my arms."

Silence.

"You never fixed me, Edwin," I said.

Did I believe that? My chest tightened, but I forced myself to keep talking.

"I fixed myself. Not for you, but for Caden," I said. "You were just there, manipulating me into thinking it was all you. When you died, I didn't fall apart because it was never you."

Anger surged in my chest and my shoes hit the floor. The blade was cold in my palm.

"It was never you," I said, louder this time. "I saved myself for my son and now I'm doing it all over again for your daughter. You were nothing to me when it came down to it, nothing but slow poison. A weak man who put a gun to an innocent girl's head because you were too broken to love her."

My feet took me across the floor, back and forth.

"I did what you never could," I whispered. "I love her."

My lashes were wet as I paused, several steps back from the painting. My eyes connected with Edwin's.

"If you could see her now...she's so fucking happy," I managed. "But you wouldn't care because...because you weren't a good man. And you were a goddamn awful excuse for a father and a friend."

That felt good. It hurt, but it hurt like pulling a splinter out.

"You weren't my friend. That was a lie," I said. "And it's time for me to let you go."

Impulsively, I lifted the knife and flicked it. Sending it across the room and into the painting, right into Edwin's heart. The sound ignited a dull roar in my chest and I strode forward and yanked the painting to the ground.

It fell at my feet with a huge crash. Not hesitating, I dragged it down the hall and out the back door. Throwing it into the firepit and stepping into the center to break it in two.

That felt so fucking good, so freeing.

From the house I dragged the rest of his knives. From the attic, I pulled a box of odds and ends I'd cleaned from his desk when he died and tossed it into the firepit. One of his shirts hung in my closet, in the back. I seized it and threw it on top of the pile.

Then I doused it in gasoline from the garage and tossed a match.

The flames roared and I stumbled back. Shocked by the intensity of them.

Overhead, the sky was clear. Stars dappled the darkness overhead and the dewy ground soaked through my shoes. My fingers were steady as I lit a cigarette and stood there, smoking and watching the flame burn out.

I wasn't fixed, but I felt better.

I'd learned that from years of therapy, from living with the damage of PTSD. Healing didn't always feel positive. Sometimes it felt raw, like I'd ripped off a bandage and taken all the infected flesh along with it.

Upstairs in my room, I cleared all the weapons from the closet and put them in my office. Then I moved the contents of Clara's dressers and closet into the spaces that had previously held Edwin's things.

Then I cleaned.

I was fully aware of what I was doing, of what was happening, but I needed it right now. So I let myself do it.

Instead of washing the sheets and towels, I bagged them and threw them in the trash. All the surfaces in the room were scrubbed with disinfectant. The curtains were ripped down and replaced with fresh ones.

The floor was steamed and mopped, scrubbed until it gleamed.

Everything I didn't need, everything I no longer wanted, everything that reminded me of the past, was bagged and thrown into the dumpster in the garage. The things I couldn't replace were put into the washer twice with hot water and soap.

It was almost midnight when I stepped into the shower, breathing hard.

I was purified.

Once I was clean, I put on a pair of boxer briefs and went down to the kitchen for a glass of water. The whiskey had worn off, leaving my head buzzing and my lids heavy.

The front door opened. Her heels moved down the hall and I felt a twitch at the sound.

She appeared in the kitchen door in a tiny, glittering black velvet dress. The sides were ruched so it clung to her body. The hem sat barely more than an inch or two below her ass. Her cleavage swelled over the neckline, dusky with body glitter.

"Merrick...what is happening?" she said, her nose wrinkling. "It smells like bleach and smoke."

I shook my head. "Nothing."

My voice was so hoarse, but not from the cigarettes or the fire.

A crease appeared between her brows. "Okay...I'm going to go shower."

Shaking her head, she turned and strode down the hall. I set aside my glass, blood thumping and pooling in my groin, and pursued her up the stairs.

She was almost to the bedroom, ass swaying. Lean legs pumping in her high heels.

"Clara," I said, my voice echoing down the hall.

She stopping, whirling.

My darkness was coming through the cracks. Our eyes met and I knew she saw it because a little shiver moved up her spine.

She backed up against our bedroom door as I closed the space between us. Sweat had made her body glitter clump in the delta between her breasts.

"Get down on your knees, *cariad*," I whispered.

"Merrick, are you sure you're okay?"

I cradled her head, stroking her cheek with my thumb. We stood there in silence, our breaths coming fast in the space between us. Then I stepped back and unfastened the front of my pants. Baring my erection.

Her eyes fell and she swallowed.

"You want me to suck you off?" she said, her voice wavering.

"I'm going to fuck your mouth," I said. "So get on your knees, open that pretty mouth, and take my cock like a good girl."

Clang. Her purse hit the ground, the chain strap loud on the hardwood. A blush crept up her throat and broke over her cheeks. In the dark, her eyes were like starlight.

Dreamy and flushed with arousal.

She drew near and stood on her toes to kiss my mouth. Then, eyes locked on mine, she sank to her knees before me.

Her mouth wrapped around my length. Burning hot, making my vision blur in the dark hallway. Her grip tightened around the base and I gritted my teeth as her nails scraped me.

I cradled her hair, stroking the silken strands. Brushing it back and gathering it in one fist. Then I pushed in a little further and she gagged, eyes locking on mine, her throat fighting me.

Her fingers gripped my thighs as I pushed in a little further and felt her resistance against the head of my cock. Her throat convulsed around me, but she didn't pull away.

Tears spilled over and streamed down her face, dragging her mascara with them.

"Relax for me, sweet girl," I said, my voice hushed.

I felt her shudder and I pushed, forcing my cock past the final bit of resistance. Her eyes widened, holding to mine like I was a lifeline. Tears streaming, nose dripping, lips swollen and wet. Fingers piercing my skin through my pants.

"See, I knew you could do it," I praised. "Breathe through your nose when I pull back."

She whimpered around me, the vibrations making pleasure surge along my spine. I cradled her head with both hands and pulled back, thrusting in gently.

I fucked her mouth, holding her steady. Her gaze never left mine as she took it until the end. Until I put my palm on the back of her head and pushed into her all the way. Holding her into my groin as I came hard.

She gasped explosively when I pulled out and I lifted her in my arms, carrying her into the bedroom and laying her on her back in our bed. Her dark ocean eyes glazed as she struggled to catch her breath, tears still streaming down her cheeks.

I pushed her skirt up, not bothering to take her heels off. She was too weak to even speak as I pulled her panties down and buried my face between her legs.

My churning mind went quiet as my mouth touched her sex.

Tasting her night out. Sweat, body glitter, and pussy on my tongue.

Her hand came up and I gripped her wrist. Feeling the bracelet and ring I'd put there under my palm.

"Daddy," she moaned.

Zing. Lightning struck the base of my skull and splintered down my spine, down my fingertips, down my legs, right to my cock. I was rock hard again, grinding my hips on the bed.

"Oh, fuck, baby," I breathed, licking up to her clit.

Her lower back lifted as I sucked on it. Her fingers buried in my hair, holding me against her sex.

"You're all I could think about all night, daddy," she whispered. "You're all I ever want anymore."

I needed to see her, to look her in the face when she came. I pulled my head free and rose to my knees. She gasped as I dragged her hips closer, spreading them. Lifting her and sinking her down onto my cock.

Fuck, she was tight.

Her clit was swollen and it pulsed as I circled it with my thumb and began rocking my hips. Taking her with shallow thrusts against her G-spot.

Her fingers skimmed up and tugged down the top of her dress. Baring her breasts, streaked in glitter. Nipples erect.

Her nails were pointed and dark, glossy red. They dragged over her breasts, gathering the soft flesh. Teasing her nipples.

"Come on my cock, princess," I urged, riding her hips.

Her lip quivered and her fingers kneaded her breasts. Playing with her nipples, pinching them between her index and thumb. Tugging on those delicate peaks.

I gripped her hips, feeling her tighten. She'd come such a long way from the first time I'd made her orgasm. Now she was relaxed, she trusted me completely.

Her eyes widened and her slick muscles pumped around my cock. Her stomach trembled and her fingers stopped working her breasts and slid above her head. Gripping the pillows.

"That's right, baby," I breathed, transfixed. "You come for your daddy like a good girl."

Her eyes rolled back and her spine locked, her legs clamping down on me. She was right on the edge, frozen in that space before her pleasure tore her to pieces.

I drew out and slammed back in.

Her body exploded and she screamed. Usually she whimpered, begged, cried out. But this time she screamed and her hips twisted as a little gush of wetness hit my groin.

I fell over her, pounding hard. My hand closed over her throat and her eyes flew open. Delirious with pleasure, riding it out like a wave. Reveling in her total loss of control.

"Don't come," she gasped.

My hips stuttered. "What?"

She writhed, still throbbing. "Don't come inside my pussy, come on my face. Please...it's all I could think about tonight."

If I wasn't so close, I'd have teased her, called her a dirty girl. But all I had time for was to pull from her and get to my feet. She rolled over, falling onto her hands and knees on the floor.

She'd have bruises tomorrow.

"Come all over my face, daddy," she begged.

I gathered her hair in one fist and gripped my erection, jerking it. Pleasuring myself with the slickness she'd left all over me.

She squeezed her eyes shut and bit her lower lip. Pleasure spiked and I felt it rush down my spine and gather in my groin. Culminating in an orgasm that made stars dance in my eyes.

Cum shot over her lovely face. Painting her with my desire, with my love. White mingled with her ruined mascara and her streaks of glitter.

Dripping down her cheek, sliding down her neck to her bare tits.

I stepped back, satisfaction flooding my chest as I tucked my dick back in my pants.

Clara on her knees, dress hiked down so her bare tits were out and pushed up so I could see her pussy. Makeup a mess, mouth swollen. My cum dripping from her face.

She took a quick breath, eyes still shut, and I grabbed a handful of tissues and sank to my knees. I wiped her face gently until she could open her eyes.

Her lips curved and her lashes fluttered.

She was feeling shy, she needed aftercare so she didn't regret it.

I brushed her hair back and kissed her mouth.

"You are such a good girl," I said simply. "You did everything perfectly tonight and you should be proud of yourself."

"Really?" she whispered, melting a little.

"Yes, really," I assured her. "Now, you let me clean you up in the shower and then I'll tuck you in bed and get you some water and a snack. How does that sound?"

Her arms slid around my shoulders, pulling me near. Kissing my neck.

"I love you so much, Merrick," she whispered.

We showered together and I used her favorite body wash, the kind that smelled like creamy jasmine. Then I dried her, rubbed lotion into her skin, and slipped one of my t-shirts over her head.

I left her in bed, propped on the headboard with the blankets tucked around her lap, and went to the kitchen.

Outside, the fire had died down to a thin column of smoke.

It was gone. It was all gone.

And yet, here in the ashes of it, a phoenix had risen.

I made myself a vodka soda and her a bowl of chocolate ice cream and went back up to our room.

"Can we get a TV for the bedroom?" she said the minute I'd sat down.

"Uh...no," I said, handing her the ice cream.

"Merrick, why not? I'm tired of having to watch movies on my tablet."

I sank down beside her, propping myself up on my pillow.

"They're distracting," I said. "When I'm in our bedroom, I want us to focus on each other."

"I do too, but I also want to watch movies with you. In bed."

412

"Clara," I said firmly. "I'm not comfortable with it. Let's redo the lounge and you can put a more comfortable couch and a larger TV in there. But having a TV in my bedroom is a hard limit for me."

My room and my office were my sacred space. I didn't want a portal to the outside world hanging on the wall.

She shoved a spoonful of ice cream in her mouth and swallowed. "You can be so particular sometimes."

"TV doesn't mix well with my brain," I said. "It's very distracting for me."

"Oh," she said, realizing what I was saying. "Sorry, I didn't know it was like that. I thought it was just a preference. The lounge is fine for me."

I held out my arm, setting aside my drink. She climbed into my lap and I stroked her hair until she'd finished her ice cream. Then I kissed her head.

"Thank you for being understanding with me," I whispered. "Now, let's get you into bed."

CHAPTER FIFTY-SIX

CLARA

Three months before the wedding, I found myself crying in the kitchen.

It was all too much. Too many traditions, too many things I wasn't allowed to choose on my own, too many eyes watching my every move.

The wedding had to be in a church, which I didn't want. I had to wear baby blue and a crown of myrtle leaves, which I also didn't want. I didn't have anyone to walk me up the aisle, but I was required to be escorted up to Merrick.

Candice and Ophelia were so excited and it was brimming over and suffocating me. The entire organization buzzed with the anticipation of the Welsh King's wedding. It was the event of the season, even outside the organization. Apparently there were several notable politicians and an actor coming.

I just wanted to scream.

Here I was, the bride, and it felt like I was the last person anyone cared about. It was all a buzz of gossip and the high pressure of hundreds of years of tradition.

The clock above the sink struck five and I knew Merrick would be home soon. He couldn't find me like this, my eyes puffy and my hands wrinkled from washing dishes.

I never washed dishes or cleaned, but lately I was doing it for a distraction. My nervous energy was killing me.

The door banged open and someone strode down the hall. Not Merrick, he walked with an even, soft tread. This was a bit of a swagger—a familiar one at that.

I turned and Caden appeared in the kitchen doorway. He wore a black t-shirt and fatigues, his boots a little scuffed. His motorcycle helmet hung from his fingers and an unlit cigarette was stuck in the corner of his mouth.

He reached up slowly and pushed his sunglasses down just enough to look over them.

"How's it going, mum?" he drawled, smirking.

Oh no, fuck that. It hadn't even occurred to me that marrying Merrick would technically make me Caden's stepmother. Horror flooded my chest and I whirled around, grabbing the dish towel.

"Don't you dare," I hissed.

He laughed softly and strode past me, kicking open the back door and pushing the doorstop in place. He fumbled in his pocket for a moment and came up with a lighter, flicking it. His heavy lids flickered as he breathed in.

"I'm just pushing your buttons," he said. "Merrick let me know he told you."

I joined him on the porch. It was hot and the sprinklers were on in the yard. Whirring softly around us.

"Want a cigarette?" he asked.

I shook my head.

"Is this weird for you?"

He shook his head, smoke drifting from his lips. "Not really. But we're not a usual kind of father and son. Maybe if I was living with him it would bother me. And no one knows."

"Why is that?"

He put a hand on his hip, staring down at me. Knowing that he was Merrick's son now, I wondered how I'd never seen it before. They were about the same height, but Caden had a lankier build. The tousled, wavy hair was the same.

Maybe the neck tattoos and the massive attitude had thrown me off.

"I'm my own man," Caden said. "I don't want to be *Brenin*."

"It's not passed down from father to son."

"I know, but there'll be pressure for me to step up and fight in the arena when Merrick retires. I'm too fucking good of a soldier to waste my time running things anyway. I just want to be left in fucking peace to do what I do best."

"Which is...killing people?"

He shrugged. "Yeah."

I crossed my arms over my chest, fixing him with a pointed stare. "You're a pretty honest person."

A crease appeared between his brows. "I have no reason to lie to anyone. Either you like me or you don't."

My heart fluttered. "What happened that night?"

Caden froze, the cigarette halfway to his lips. "Do you mean the night when Merrick killed Osian?"

I nodded, my mouth dry. "I just...I want to know."

He took a deep breath and released it slowly, a thin stream of smoke coming from his nose. Absently, he dug the heel of his motorcycle boot into the deck.

"I've never seen him like that," he said quietly, eyes down. "I put my hand on his arm at one point to stop him and he turned on me...it was intense."

"He hurt you?"

"No, no, he just had this look in his fucking eyes. I knew right then there was no stopping him. So we just took Osian and brought him to the warehouse basement."

My stomach flipped uneasily. "And then?"

"You don't need to hear the details."

My shoulders went back, spine straightening. "I'm marrying him."

"Jesus," Caden muttered. "Alright, Merrick tied him to a chair and he beat him to death with his fists. It wasn't my fucking business so I just stayed back, but I've never seen him like that."

"Was he...out of control?"

"No, he was ice cold. Completely in control," Caden said. "Everything he did, every hit, was fully intentional. Merrick doesn't lose control...at least I've never seen it. He means what he does."

My mind went back to last night, which was like any other night with Merrick. We'd had dinner, had a glass of wine, and had a little sex before falling asleep in his bed. I'd woken up early and kissed him awake, tracing my fingers over the sensitive parts of him.

Over his pulse points. Dragged my nail down the V on his lower abdomen. Skimmed my fingertips along his inner thigh.

He'd been so gentle and vulnerable, like he always was with me.

Caden cleared his throat, jerking me from my reverie.

"Just because he shows a different side to you doesn't make it any less real. Merrick is a good man. Sometimes he does bad things. But, at his core, he's a good *Brenin* and, insofar as I've let him, he's been a good father. He'll be a good husband."

I knew it took a lot for him to say that. Before I could speak, I caught a quiet step behind me and I turned to find Merrick.

In the doorway, arms crossed.

"What are you two doing?" he asked. "I hope you're not giving her cigarettes, Caden."

"She smoked a whole pack," he drawled.

"Get the fuck out of here," Merrick said, joining me on the deck. His arm slipped around my waist and he pulled me back against his body.

"I'm about to," Caden said. "Before this gets too close for comfort."

He and Merrick spoke briefly in the kitchen. They were talking about Wyoming—I could hear fragments of sentences. I no longer cared to know what was going on in the organization. Their world of fighting and dying, of blood and power, wasn't mine.

Caden drove off on his motorcycle and I went back into the kitchen and started drying the dishes. Merrick appeared behind me, wincing slightly as I slammed the porcelain bowls into the cupboard.

"Something wrong, *cariad*?" he asked.

I shook my head and slammed the cupboard door. His big hands wrapped around my waist and he picked me up and lifted me onto

417

the edge of the counter. Pinning me in place with his grip on my wrists.

"What's wrong?"

I sighed, chewing that spot.

"Hey," he said softly. "Don't bite yourself, just talk to me."

I swallowed, trying to speak without tearing up.

"This is all...just...a lot," I managed.

His face cleared slowly and he nodded. "I see...you're starting to realize why Caden doesn't want anyone to know he's my son. I understand. It's hard to be associated with me."

"Merrick, it's not that," I said in a rush. "I'm not ashamed, that's ridiculous."

"I never said you were. But you are overwhelmed by it."

Disputing that would be a lie. I released a sigh and nodded and he winced slightly, turning to look over my head. His gaze was a pale blue in the waning light.

My fingers twisted into a knot in my lap.

"It's just...I wish this was just about us," I whispered. "I've barely been able to choose anything for my wedding. All the colors, the location, the vows—it all has to be done by the book. I just want you, Merrick, I don't want this huge wedding. It's just...too much for me."

"I know," he said, kissing my forehead. "I wish I could change that, but I can't."

I took a deep breath, knowing he felt horrible about it. "It's fine, I can make it through to the honeymoon."

His lids flickered and his hands slid up my waist, his palm grazing my breast for a second. A quick tingle shot down my spine.

"God, I can't wait," he murmured.

We had dinner and I went upstairs to get ready for bed. He stayed in his office to finish his work for a few hours and I watched a movie on my tablet. It was almost midnight when he finally came up to bed and began undressing in the bathroom.

I popped my retainer in and put my tablet away, snuggling up under the blankets.

He heard me stir and appeared in the bathroom door, toothbrush in hand. He was shirtless, his sweatpants hanging deliciously off his hips.

"Do you want to fuck before bed?" he asked.

I smiled sleepily. "You're so romantic now that you have me nailed down."

He laughed. "So that's a no?"

"No, let's have a quickie," I said, stretching out on my back. "But I'm too tired to come, you can take care of that tomorrow night."

He turned to go back in the bathroom and paused. There was a moment of silence and then he pivoted slowly and leaned in the doorway. His face was contemplative, his jaw working slightly.

"Listen, *cariad*, I can't get you out of the wedding. It's the event of the season. But...what if you and I eloped and got officially married before that?"

Wait...really? I pushed myself up and popped my retainer out so I could talk properly.

"You would do that for me?" I whispered.

"I'd do anything for you," he said. "Let's run away together, get married in a courthouse somewhere in secret. Spend a few days fucking each other senseless. No one will ever know."

"Where?"

"Anywhere you want."

"When?"

He ran a hand over his face, slicking his hair back.

"Well, tomorrow is Thursday," he said. "Let's leave after I get off work."

My whole body went still, my heart thumping like a drum.

"What...what?"

He shrugged. "Let's run away and get married, Clara. We'll leave tomorrow night and we can get married Friday morning and honeymoon until Sunday night."

I just sat there and stared at him, completely taken aback.

"You want to marry me this Friday?"

"I would marry you last Friday if I'd thought of it then."

He looked so pleased with himself that I couldn't keep back my laughter. My ears roared as I searched for the right words to describe what I was feeling. Euphoria? Relief? Breathless anticipation?

He crossed the room, laying aside his toothbrush, and climbed atop me. I let my body slide back until I was fully on my back, my palms curled on either side of my head.

"Mrs. Llwyd," he murmured.

"Who says I'm taking your name?"

His brow rose. "Do you need me to spank your ass?"

I gasped. "I thought you were a feminist."

"I am, but I'll still spank your ass," he said, kissing down my stomach. "And I don't want you keeping your fucking father's name."

He had a point.

"*Cariad*," he murmured, nipping my inner thigh. "Run away with me, marry me on a Friday morning, take my name. Be my wife, love me until I die."

"Oh, if that's all you want, then sure," I said.

"That's all I want."

"Then it's yours," I murmured, closing my eyes.

CHAPTER FIFTY-SEVEN

CLARA

I pulled the bathroom door shut behind me and paused before the mirror. Fingers twisting together. My stomach fluttered as I met my eyes in the mirror.

Merrick Llwyd was my husband.

It was Friday night. We'd gone to the courthouse in Concord, not far from where we'd slept together for the first time. We'd signed papers, shared a kiss, and walked back out into the sunlight.

Married.

Now, the Welsh King lay on the other side of the door waiting for his wife.

My pulse hadn't let up pounding since I'd opened my eyes that morning. I bit my lip, forgetting all about that spot inside my mouth. This wasn't that kind of nerves.

This was the good kind, the sweet anticipation kind that knew whatever happened, it would be alright because he was mine.

I slid my rings off and laid them by the sink before getting in the shower. The warm water relaxed my muscles. When I got out, there was a glass of white wine on the sink. Warmth blossomed in my chest and lower belly. It felt so good to be thought of, to be cared for.

I sipped the wine, taking my time, as I dried my hair and moisturized my skin until it was pure silk. The white lace lingerie set slid over my hips and breasts and settled against my skin. Fitting me to perfection.

He liked the lipstick I wore so I didn't change it tonight. I knew the berry pink made his pulse move faster when I left it on his neck, on the inside of his wrists.

My wine was empty by the time I put my wedding rings back on. I'd never felt so relaxed.

So at peace.

So free.

He was naked when I stepped out of the bathroom. I saw the rise of his cock between his legs, hidden from me by the sheet. His head cocked and his mouth parted, showing a sliver of his lower teeth.

He was transfixed.

"Come here, *cariad*," he murmured.

I hesitated, lifting the empty glass. "Thank you for the wine, it was lovely."

"It's a vintage," he said, rising. "I was saving it for a special occasion."

His naked, warm body pressed over me, pushing me gently against the wall. Lifting me in his arms and guiding my legs to wrap around his waist. His stubble tickled my neck as he pressed hot kisses down to my collarbones.

"How long were you saving it?" I whispered.

"I took it from the cellar at the compound."

"For our wedding night?"

I felt him smile against my throat. "I hoped so, I always hoped we would end up like this."

His head ducked and he nipped my breast through my bra.

"Like what?" I pressed.

He pivoted, taking the glass from my hand and setting it aside, and fell onto the bed. I wriggled beneath him and he pushed his knee between my thighs. Applying gentle pressure to my sex.

"I hoped you'd be my wife," he murmured. "I hoped you'd let me adore you forever."

Oh, when he said things like that, I melted into a puddle like that hard candy I'd left in his Audi. I felt my lids flutter as his mouth began undressing me. Tugging my garter belt open with his teeth, dragging my panties down, flipping me over and using his tongue to unhook my bra.

He kissed down my spine and bit my ass gently.

"How many times do you want to come?"

I wriggled my hips, his breath burning the curve of my ass, right where it met my thigh.

"Just start and don't stop until you can't take it anymore," I whispered.

That was a mistake. We'd slept together enough times at this point that he knew how to build me up and draw an endless stream of pleasure from between my thighs without even trying.

An hour later, I was on my back, regretting all my choices. So blissed out I could barely move my limbs. My skin was drenched, the remnants of my lingerie stuck to my hips and waist.

His fingers were deep in me, so wet I could hear the sounds of him stroking my G-spot. His mouth moved leisurely over my overstimulated clit. Sucking so gently I barely felt it until pleasure started building and licking over my sex when I begged him for a break.

My fingers dug into his rumpled hair, tugging his head back. His eyes fixed on mine, glazed and burning with a darkness that no longer frightened me.

"I'm not done," he murmured.

"Don't you want some satisfaction?" I panted. "It's your wedding night too."

"This is how I want to spend my wedding night."

His tongue flattened and slid soft and wet over my sex. Flicking my clit and making my back arch.

"Merrick, this is torture," I begged.

"Good," he said. "So beg me for mercy."

His face disappeared between my thighs and his grip tightened on my hips. Holding me in place, holding me still.

His demeanor changed and his mouth moved over me with one goal. He'd been gentle, he'd coaxed my orgasms out, he'd praised me when I came again and again.

Now, he was demanding them.

Forcing them out of me. Bending my pleasure to his will until it submitted to him.

My hips bucked, struggling against him. Eyes rolled back, fingers twisted in the sheets, mouth sore from being pinned between my teeth. Tears started in the corners of my eyes and slid hot into my hair.

But I never asked him to stop.

It had to be over an hour later when he finally pulled his mouth from me and moved up my body. I swallowed back the little sob caught in my throat and found his eyes in the dark.

"Merrick," I whispered.

His gentle, lean fingers slid up and cradled my head. The pad of his thumb ran over my cheek.

"You're alright, *cariad*," he said, his voice a hoarse whisper.

His cock brushed the entrance of my sex. My hips spasmed, a deep shudder moving through me. God, no, there was no way I could take him now.

"Merrick," I begged.

His cobalt eyes were black in the shadows, but I saw every bit of his emotion in them. Fully vulnerable, wide, fixed on me like I was the most precious thing he'd ever touched.

"You're such a good girl," he soothed, dragging himself over my tingling pussy. He applied light pressure, working the very tip into me.

"Oh fuck," I gasped.

"That's my girl. Just breathe through it."

Could I?

He didn't give me time to think it over because the thick head of his cock pushed past my tight entrance and slid into me. My inner muscles spasmed and twitched, gripping the pure, silky heat filling every inch of me.

424

My nails pierced his back and a whimper slipped out.

"Look at me," he whispered.

Our eyes locked again, less than an inch apart.

"Trust me?"

I nodded, throat dry.

"I'm yours, *cariad*," he said, sliding the rest of the way into me. "You were made for me. Made to take me, made to love me."

He didn't just fuck me, he melded with me until the lean warmth of his body fused with mine. He thrust slow and deep and whispered the dirtiest, sweetest things into my neck. When he couldn't hold out any longer, he bent me over the edge of the bed and finished deep inside my hips.

When I woke the next morning, he was facedown and there were deep red nail marks I barely remembered making down his back.

I shifted, wincing slightly at the little ache between my thighs, and pushed myself up. My body was sticky, wrapped in the tangled sheet. The bottle of lube had fallen to the floor and was seeping into the carpet.

I jumped up and scooped it up, grimacing. Merrick wouldn't be happy with the mess.

He rustled and I spun, lube slipping down my wrist.

His eye cracked open and he rolled onto his side.

"Uh oh," I whispered. "I don't know which one of us did this, but it spilled all over the floor."

A smile flickered over his face.

"Come here," he said huskily. "Fuck it, who cares."

My heart pattered as I dumped the lube into the sink and washed my hands. As I dried them, I noticed there was a little bag on the sink with a bit of chain poking out. Frowning, I unzipped it and gasped as a pair of metal handcuffs slipped out.

Oh, I hadn't known Merrick was into that sort of thing. Feeling guilty and flustered, I pushed them back into the bag and pulled the zipper shut. Then I put a towel over it, like I hadn't noticed anything.

When I returned, he had propped himself up against the headboard. The sheet trailed over his lap, barely covering his cock.

"Come sit in my lap," he said, holding out his hand.

I obeyed, climbing up to sit on his upper thighs. He stroked up my stomach absently and cupped my left breast. Squeezing it once and gently flicking my nipple to make it harden.

My clit tingled as he played with me lazily. Teasing my other breast until my nipple went hard and flushed under his fingertips.

"So fucking pretty," he murmured.

"Merrick," I managed. "Why are there handcuffs in the bathroom?"

I'd expected him to be taken off guard, but he wasn't. His eyes lit up, glittering just inches from mine.

"I thought you might like using them," he said. "Then I forgot all about it last night."

I chewed my lip. "I don't know if I'd like being restrained with handcuffs, I haven't thought about it."

A devilish smirk slid over his face. "Oh, no, those are for me, *cariad.*"

Wait...what? My whole body froze and my jaw went slack. A bolt of heat moved down my spine and blossomed between my thighs, making me pulse once in his lap.

"Wh...what?"

"I teased you last night," he said, still grinning. "I can take a little payback."

For a second, my mind was blank and whirling. Then my eyes fell on his chest, broad and well muscled, and slid down to his slender abdomen. A rush of heat surged through me. When I shifted off him, there was a sudden slipperiness between my legs, sticky down my thighs as I padded back into the bathroom and grabbed the bag.

He slid onto his back, kicking all the blankets off the end of the bed. Stretching out fully naked and already beautifully hard.

My God, this was my husband.

I unzipped the bag and shook it onto the bed. Two sets of silver handcuffs fell out, rattling as they did.

"Two? Why two?"

He opened his mouth to answer just as it hit me and I couldn't bite back a giggle. Never in my life had I imagined I'd want to do this, but suddenly I was aching to see him like that.

Arms spread, wrists fastened to each bedpost.

The Welsh King, helpless between my thighs.

I hooked them on my finger, climbing up and straddling his hard, lower stomach. "Are these going to fit you? You have big arms."

"They fit, I tried them before we left."

He shifted and put his hands out, baring his inner wrists to me. Shaking a little, chest fluttering, I locked them around his wrists. He spread his arms up, biceps looking so damn good while he was at it, and gave me an encouraging nod.

"Attach the free end to each bedpost, *cariad*," he murmured. "You can do it."

I obeyed quickly and slid back to settle myself on his hips. Between my thighs, his cock was hard and pressed urgently against my pussy. The little pulse running through it tickled, sending jolts of pleasure through me.

He took my breath away. My love, my Welsh King. I ran my fingertips over the sensitive skin of his inner bicep. Up and around his elbow. His chest heaved as my touch trailed all the way up to his wrists, to where the silver metal of the handcuffs bound him to the bed.

He looked beautiful, so sexy and dark and vulnerable.

My mind went back to that day in the New Hampshire house when I'd spread chocolate sauce and whipped cream all over his abs and licked it off. And right away, I knew what I wanted.

"Where are you going?" he asked as I jumped down and disappeared into the kitchen.

"Just relax," I called, flushed from the rapid pulse between my legs.

I wrenched open the fridge and found the chocolate sauce where I'd put it after our earlier shopping trip. I grabbed the cold bottle in my fist and padded back to the bedroom.

His brows shot up, eyes falling.

"I hope that's going on my cock, *cariad*," he said. "I'd love to see you lick it off."

"We'll see," I murmured, straddling him with the bottle of syrup in hand.

The first drizzle hit him between the pecs and he flinched, his stomach muscles contracting.

"Fuck, that's cold," he breathed.

I shifted down and brushed the bottle over the underside of his rock hard cock. Watching him closely. His pupils dilated and his hips jerked beneath me at the contact of cold plastic.

"Is that good?" I murmured.

He swore softly in response and I leaned forward, propping myself up on the bed. He was breathing hard and his eyes were glued to me, taking in my every move.

I drizzled it between his pecs again and his lids flickered, his jaw going tense. The syrup continued down...down...down to his tightened abs. Pooling lightly in the little indents. Making a circle around his shallow navel.

The cap made a sharp pop as I snapped it closed and set it aside. Then, eyes locked to his, entranced by the blue flame beneath his heavy lids, I bent and tongued his navel.

"Oh—Jesus—fuck," he gasped.

"Did you know that you have nerves in your navel that go all the way down to your penis," I teased softly.

"I did know, actually," he said through gritted teeth.

Pushing the tip of my tongue into it, I circled it slowly. Tonguing it the way he did to my pussy. My right hand slid down between us and found his cock, wrapping around his thick, warm length.

"Do you want me so badly?" I whispered.

"So fucking much." His eyes were heavy with desire, glued to me with animal watchfulness.

Gazes locked, both breathing hard, I shifted up and began lapping up the chocolate over his chest. His hips twitched with every touch of my tongue, desperate for some contact.

428

His cock was leaking pre-cum, the tip glittering in the early morning light spilling from the window.

Slowly, just as cruelly as he done to me last night, I drew it out until he was visibly panting. Licking up every bit of chocolate with slow, small flicks of my tongue. His fists gripped the handcuff chains, his knuckles white. Sweat etched down his neck and soaked into the pillow.

His pupils were blown, his jaw taut.

"Fuck, put me out of my misery," he begged.

"But I'm not done."

"You have me for the rest of our lives," he managed. "Just let me come in you, I promise you can do whatever you want to me later."

I took pity on him and shifted over his hips, gripping his cock by the base. Our eyes locked, his lips parting, and I guided him into my soaked pussy. Sinking onto him, taking his heavy length until it sparked pain deep inside.

"Oh God, you're so hard," I whispered.

He made a sound, a half growl, half whimper.

"That's what you do to me," he said. "That's what you fucking do to me, darling."

I rode him hard and fast and he came in seconds. Eyes rolling back, stomach tensing, hips shuddering. Lips spilling my name beneath his breath.

He gave one last twitch in me and his eyes snapped open.

"Goddamn," he murmured.

Flushed with pride, I ran my nails gently over his stomach. Still a little sticky.

"Good boy," I said, before I could lose my nerve.

He made the most delicious sound, like a satisfied purr, deep in his chest.

"You're a bad girl," he said. "Now release me so I can make you come."

CHAPTER FIFTY-EIGHT

CLARA

We never told anyone that we got married.

With how overwhelming the wedding planning was and how many people were in my business, I wanted just one thing that belonged to only us.

It also made everything more fun.

We kept our rings in his bedside table. At night when we were alone, we could slip them on before we got in bed. He called me Mrs. Llwyd and I loved it.

"You know, it's not pronounced 'loyd,'" he said one night.

I turned over to face him. "How's it pronounced then?"

"The Welsh double L makes a breathy sound," he said. "But it's very difficult for English speakers so my grandfather changed the pronunciation."

"Say it," I ordered.

He complied.

"Wait...seriously? I don't think I can do that with my mouth," I said.

His eyes lit up and I knew he couldn't resist. "I've got something you can do with your mouth," he said.

"My appointment is tomorrow," I said. "If you want anything, better pick sex because it's blowjobs until I'm healed."

The next morning, I took a shower and Candice picked me up and drove me to the piercing shop. It was clearly incredibly expensive because the floors were marble and the private room was decorated with life sized Greek statues. Even the faint scent of gardenia wafting through the air smelled like a million dollars.

"Can I hold your hand?" I asked Candice.

"Duh, that's why I'm here," she said, sinking down beside me.

My heart was pounding and I kept telling myself it was just like going to the gynecologist. I'd done that once and I could do it again.

The door swung open and a woman with dark hair and neck tattoos entered. She wore shorts and a tank top, revealing the curling ink over her arms and legs.

"Hey," she said in a soft, southern accent. "You must be Clara Prothero? I'm Jan."

I nodded.

"Alright, let's get this done," she said, sitting down on a rolling stool. "Don't worry, it's actually not a bad piercing. My nipples and my cartilage piercings hurt like a motherfucker, but I didn't flinch when I got my VCH."

I felt instantly better. She had me slip my panties off and lie back with my feet in stirrups. It wasn't too bad—not very different from going to the doctor. She disappeared between my legs and I sent Candice a worried glance.

She squeezed my hand.

"You're Merrick's girl, huh?" Jan said, popping her gum.

"Yeah," I said hesitantly. "So, how do you like your VCH?"

"Love it," she said. "I had it done about eight years ago and I don't regret a thing."

"How about nipple piercings?" Candice asked.

"You thinking of getting them done?" Jan glanced up.

To my surprise, Candice nodded. Before I could open my mouth and ask her when she'd decided to do that, Jan said something I didn't catch and a little shock of pain rippled through me.

"Ouch," I whispered.

"You did great," Jan said. "Took it like it was nothing."

"Thanks," I said, blushing.

Jan stood up and stripped off her gloves and turned to face Candice. "So, did you want pierced, sweetheart? I can fit you in real quick."

Candice's jaw worked and then she stood, shaking her hair back. "Let's do it."

I was shocked, but also proud. I knew her breasts were a huge insecurity and this felt positive, like a step towards accepting her body. I reached out and took her hand, winding our fingers together.

"Hey, I think you should," I said. "And I think you should send in your application for law school too."

"I just might," she said.

I could tell Candice's piercings hurt a lot more than mine, but she kept a straight face. We cleaned up afterwards and put our clothes back on. Candice winced as she put her bra on and slid the pads to catch any bleeding beneath the cups. There was a faint ache between my legs and it felt like there was something there, rubbing against my clit in a way that wasn't unpleasant.

We drove home and Candice dropped me off outside the house.

"I'm really proud of you," I said.

She smiled, looking a little tired. "I'm really proud of you too. And I'm happy you two are getting married. I mean it. Merrick is good for you."

We hugged and I ran inside before I started crying and watched her disappear down the driveway. Everything felt more emotional with my wedding coming up in the next month.

That night, I heard Merrick come home and go into his office. I was in bed, but as soon as I heard his door close, I changed into a silk slip and padded down the hall.

I knocked and he called for me to come in.

He sat at his desk, his laptop open. Warmth rose in my chest as he lifted his eyes. They lit up and he held out his arm, beckoning me close.

Our mouths met and I still tasted a sky full of stars. Fireworks still went off and meteorites streaked across the galaxy. His scarred hand came up and cradled my head. So gentle it made me want to cry, to kiss the marks where his stitches had been.

I pulled back, breathless.

"Do you want to see it?" I whispered.

"Fuck yes, I do."

He picked me up and set me gently on the desk, rising to lower me on my back. My heart skipped a beat as the warmth of his palms skimmed up my thighs and lifted my slip. Baring my sex and the little diamond between my thighs.

"My God," he said.

There was a long, long silence. Then his mouth contacted my inner thigh as he kissed me.

"No touching," I breathed.

He kissed my knee and the underside of my calf. A shiver of pleasure moved up my leg and settled deep inside.

"I know," he said, his voice thick with arousal. "This is going to be hell."

"It's just until I heal," I said.

He pulled me upright and brushed my slip down. His lids were heavy and his lips were parted, showing a sliver of bottom teeth. His stare was so intense it was making me feel naked.

"What is it?" I asked, fighting the urge to chew my mouth.

He blinked.

"Nothing," he said softly. "I just got everything I ever wanted. I really believed I would never fall in love and get married. But it happened."

I slid my arms around him and rested my head over his heart.

"It happened," I whispered. "And now I get to annoy you for the rest of your life."

He laughed and I wriggled out of his arms and darted out into the hall.

"Do you want a whiskey?" I asked. "I'm going to the kitchen for some ice cream."

"That sounds perfect," he said. "I'll be down in a moment, *cariad.*"

EPILOGUE

MERRICK

TWO YEARS LATER

Clara was still out when I got home that night. It was the two-year anniversary of our legal marriage. Unfortunately, I'd had to work during the day so she'd taken herself out to the salon for a massage and to have her nails and hair done.

Which meant, of course, that I was getting laid tonight.

I went into the house through the back door. Tonight was one of those nights where Yale and I came back after a long day of more traditional mafia work and had to figure out how to get the blood off before anyone saw.

In the basement, I removed my clothes and put them directly into the washer and set it to the most powerful setting. Then I turned on the hall shower and began the slow ritual of scrubbing every inch of my body until it was purified.

Until there was no trace of violence on me.

My skin felt raw. Perhaps she would notice, but she wouldn't say anything. She'd just put her arms around my neck and kiss me and tell me how much she loved me. She'd perfected the art of willful ignorance over the last few years.

I kept a few changes of clothes in the cabinet. Up above, I heard the front door shut and her heels sounded on the floor. I pulled on a pair of sweatpants and a t-shirt and climbed the basement stairs into the kitchen.

She appeared in the doorway, holding a bag of take-out. Her eyes lit up just as I knew they would and she crossed the room and leaned in to kiss my mouth.

So sweet, so calming.

I brushed her hair back. "What's for dinner?"

She lifted the bag onto the table and began taking cardboard boxes out and stacking them. "I went to the Italian place because they know how you like your steak. I got lasagna and chocolate cake for myself. And I had them wrap up a bottle of our favorite wine."

I slid my arm around her from behind and gently kissed the top of her head.

"Thank you, *cariad*," I whispered.

I felt her little shiver of pleasure at my touch. She never stopped having those reactions when I touched her, when I kissed her, when I fucked her in the dark.

It still felt like the world breaking apart, like the universe shifted on its axis just to make room for her, at the center of it.

We ate at the table and she went upstairs to shower and put on her silk robe. Then I opened the bottle of wine and we went out to the back porch to watch the stars come out.

I leaned back in my chair and she curled up in my lap. Her wine balanced in her slender fingers, draped with the jewelry I'd put there. My eyes slid lower and I set aside my glass and ran my palm up her inner thigh.

Beneath her silk robe, she was naked. I licked my fingers and eased them between her legs. Her eyes flicked up to mine, her pupils already blown and her cheeks stained with pink.

My fingers found the gold and diamond between her thighs and I stroked over it. Playing with it so gently it made her body arc and her hips began moving in my lap.

"My Welsh Princess," I murmured, kissing the side of her neck.

She set aside her wine and her soft palm skimmed up my chest, down my bicep, and rested above my wrist. I'd covered up that tattoo a few months after our wedding. There was no trace of it, the words concealed by a black ink Welsh dragon.

"I've been thinking," I mused. "It might be time for you to get off birth control and I'll go in and do my part."

She sobered. "Are you still sure you don't want children?"

I nodded. "How do you honestly feel?"

Her fingers moved back up my forearm and wove through my hair. Brushing it back.

"I'm positive," she said firmly.

She kissed me and the warmth sank to the core of my being. When I drew back, her eyes were hazy with contentment.

"Alright, I'll make an appointment," I said. "Speaking of children, I saw Caden this morning before he went out to Wyoming. He's so fucking eager to get out there, the last two years have been killing him."

"Did he end up having to have someone shadow him?" she asked, clearly not very interested. She tried to keep out of organization business.

I nodded. "It was part of the deal. We only got the money if they could send one of their agents in to supervise him."

"Well, hopefully he won't cause a problem."

"It's a woman," I said.

Clara's brows rose. "Caden is very good at a lot of things, but he's not good at keeping it in his pants. You'll want to keep a close eye on what he's doing out there."

"Believe me, I gave him a fucking lecture," said Merrick. "I'm hoping how hard it was for him to secure this funding will make him think twice before he sticks his dick into the enemy."

"The enemy?"

I worked my jaw, not wanting to give too many details. "Let's not think about it anymore tonight, darling. Caden will pull it off, I believe in him. And all you need to do is be happy and let me handle the rest."

She snuggled closer to me, laying her head on my collarbone. "I know Caden doesn't tell you this, but you're a really good father. You're doing a great job with a shitty situation."

My chest ached. I didn't get told that and...well, I needed to hear it sometimes. It was hard to learn how to be a father to an adult child. It was even harder because I would always carry around the guilt of being unknowingly absent.

Tonight wasn't about the scars we carried. Tonight was for rest, for peace. Tomorrow there would be the usual responsibilities, the usual struggles. But at the end of the day, I got to come home to Clara.

That was the deepest kind of happiness I'd ever known.

THE END

If you'd like to read Caden's story, Prince of Ink & Scars is now available on Amazon KU & paperback

CONNECT WITH RAYA

Connect with Raya on Instagram, TikTok, and Pinterest for updates on upcoming books.

BOOKS BY RAYA MORRIS EDWARDS

The Welsh Kings Trilogy
Paradise Descent
Prince of Ink & Scars

The Sovereign Mountain Series
Sovereign
Redbird - novella
Westin - September 2024

The King of Ice & Steel Trilogy
Captured Light
Devil I Need
Ice & Steel

Additional books in the Ice & Steel World
Captured Desire
Captured Solace
Captured Ecstasy

Made in United States
Troutdale, OR
06/26/2024

20823000R00275